I have enjoyed all of
Grace to Save may be
~ **Katy C.**

MW00618099

Reading a new book by Carol Moncado is like getting together again with a bunch of old friends to find out what's new in their lives. Her newest release, *Grace to Save*, fits right in there…Get ready for a good read as you find out more about old friends. Now I need to get back to the housework I neglected to finish reading, Travis, Cassie, & Abi's story!
~ **Margaret N.**

I love a good romance and this one is good with a whole lot more…I loved the story and how the author weaves Serenity Landing into all her stories. Her characters are old friends who pop in for a visit now and then. We see God's redemption and love throughout the book.
~ **Linda R.**

What a read! Moncado brought a lot of emotions into *Grace to Save*…trauma of 9/11, bad decisions, inability to forgive, abandonment, romance, and then soooo many consequences. I sooooo love the way that this author is so great at weaving Serenity Landing and the people that we know and love from other stories into each of her books!
~ **R. H.**

Grace to Save

Serenity Landing Tuesdays of Grace

Carol Moncado

USA Today Bestselling Author

This is a work of fiction set in a fictionalized southwest
Missouri and a redrawn, fictionalized Europe. Any
resemblance to real events or to actual persons, living or
dead, is coincidental. Any reference to historical figures,
places, or events, whether fictional or actual, is a
fictional representation.

Scripture taken from the Holy Bible, King James Version.
Cover photos:
Couple: photography33/depositphotos.com
House: onepony/depositphotos.com
Girl: CANDID Publications, 2016
Author photo: Captivating by Keli, 2010

First edition, CANDID Publications 2016
ISBN: 1-944408-93-2
978-1-944408-93-0

For Brittany S. and the kids...
I'm so very happy to see God make something beautiful
out of where you found yourselves.
Thank you for letting me witness it from a distance.

Travis S.
My favorite Panera manager
Thank you for always being so kind to this author who
sat at the table in the back
and for inspiring Travis Harders.

Rest in Peace, Travis.
1989-2012

Chapter One

September 11, 2001

A ringing jolted Travis Harders from a deep sleep. He cursed as the phone knocked to the floor with a clatter. "This better be good," he snapped when he got the handset in place.

A glance at the clock nearly made him groan.

4:07.

"You'll be hearing from the police soon."

He rubbed the sleep out of his eyes with the heel of one hand and tried to process the statement. The words didn't really register as the guy, whoever he was, kept talking until Travis interrupted. "What? Who is this?"

"Mark's dad." Right. Travis's best friend. "You remember us? The ones who treated you like family? Let you live with us?"

Travis's stomach sank. Mark's family had practically adopted him when he moved from southwest Missouri to the Big Apple. They had filled the gap in his life left by parents who disapproved of Travis's choice to move to New York. Mark's parents let him spend holidays and birthdays with them, with Travis making only the obligatory phone calls back home.

But none of that explained why Mark's dad would be calling the police.

"Who is it?" a sleepy Jennifer asked.

Travis covered the mouthpiece and whispered to his girlfriend, "No one." His feet hit the cool floor, and he headed for the other room. At least he had a place to escape to. Being an out-of-work-actor-turned-barista didn't pay much, but he'd lucked into a fabulous apartment. Closing the French door behind him, he tried to focus on the voice yelling from the other end of the line.

But he only caught "my daughter" and "spring break" and "drugged."

If possible, Travis's stomach clenched further as that night flooded back to him. Memories of bringing her back to this very apartment when she was in no condition to go home without risking the wrath of her parents. But after what happened between them...it was only right for him to be on the receiving end of her dad's anger. "I don't know what she told you sir, but..."

"I know all I need to know," he bellowed.

Even though he was in the other room, Travis lowered the volume on the handset. "I take full responsibility for..."

"You're right, you do!" He let loose a string of obscenities. "You'll spend years in prison! Drugging a girl! Sleeping with her!"

"What?" His whole world spun. Travis regretted every minute of that night after they got back to the apartment, but he hadn't drugged her. He didn't even know where to get those kinds of drugs. They weren't in love, never had been, but to place the blame solely on him? The next morning, they'd talked about it enough to know she hadn't blamed him.

What changed? Feeling sucker punched, Travis hung up on the man. What he said didn't matter. Travis would find out when he was on trial for something he didn't do. On autopilot, he dressed for his five a.m. shift. Coffees of the World wasn't the best job, but it had flexible hours and had led to finding this sublet. There was no shortage of interesting characters to populate his imagination. Like the skinny brunette with the shoulder length bob who worked for Morgan Stanley and always ordered a short nonfat mocha, decaf, no foam, no sugar, no whip. She could be the heroine in one of his screenplays even if he never knew her name.

He kissed Jennifer's hair and told her he'd call after work. Five flights of stairs later, the sounds of the city waking up greeted him as he walked toward the train that would take him to the Trade Center. Standing at the top of the subway steps, he changed his mind. Travis headed for his car parked a couple streets over and called in.

Two hours later, he stopped in McLean for gas about seven thirty, filling up the tank of his Toyota Corolla hatchback. Three hours after that, he could still drive for a while longer before he'd need to stop again. He contemplated leaving the state, but decided not to, instead turning northward before leaving Allegany County.

He'd gone through more emotions than he knew he had, none of them good. Anger. Fear. Frustration. Blame. Worry. Intimidation. In western New York, things were more peaceful than they ever were in downtown Manhattan, but his insides were in utter turmoil at the thought of an arrest and trial.

_____

His favorite heavy metal CD blared from the speakers. During the lull between songs, Travis could hear his cell phone vibrating on the passenger seat where he'd tossed it. After an hour and a half of the stupid thing ringing nearly nonstop, he finally snatched it up.

"What?" Travis growled.

"Are you okay?" Though he only talked to her twice a year, there was no mistaking his mother's voice.

Or the panic in it.

The tremor set him on edge. "Yeah. Why?"

"Thank you, Jesus," she whispered, though Travis couldn't figure out what she was thanking Him for. "Where are you? You got out okay? Were you working? There was no answer at your apartment."

Why was Mom calling just to ask if he was okay? Why was she frantic? "I'm in western New York State. Out for a drive. Get out of where?" Could Mark's dad have called already?

"You don't know?" Frenzy changed to disbelief.

"Know what?" Travis held the phone against his shoulder as he downshifted into a turn.

He could hear the tears over the static-filled line. "Two planes, Trav. They hit the Towers. Both of the buildings are on fire."

His heart thudded to a stop. "What?" Hadn't a bomber hit the Empire State Building in WWII? But two planes? On a brilliantly clear day? No weather in sight. "How bad is it?" he croaked.

"They're saying it's a terror attack. The Pentagon is on fire. There's another plane out there somewhere. Big jets, Travis. I saw the second one hit. The explosion. Papers flying everywhere. The people..." Her voice broke. "You really weren't there?" she confirmed.

"No, Mom. I'm not anywhere near there." But he

needed to find a place to stop. A television. He had to see for himself. Tens of thousands of people would be dead and dying. Did he know any of them?

"There are people jumping, falling, out of the upper stories. I can't imagine." He could almost see her pacing around the kitchen alternately running her hands through her hair and wringing them together. "They're jumping from a hundred stories up. What could be so bad to make that the better option?" Her voice caught. "I don't know how I can watch this, Trav, but I can't turn away. All I can do is pray."

Pray. Right. A face flashed before Travis. The uptight former-football-player-turned-businessman from the 102nd floor of the North Tower with his caramel macchiato and corny joke of the day. Was he one of those jumping?

She gasped then whispered. "Dear God, no. No!" Her scream made him move the phone even as his stomach sank.

He pulled into a café parking lot near Danville. "What?"

"The tower. It's gone. Just gone. The south one, I think." Her voice trailed off in prayer.

The shock he'd felt after the phone call from Mark's dad paled compared to what he felt now. "Mom, I gotta go." Jen. His friends. His coworkers. He needed to make calls of his own. Find out if they were okay. And Mark. His best friend had been a firefighter for a year. He'd be down there. Inside one of the Towers. Travis hadn't talked to him since that night, the March before, but part of him, the part that still believed there was a God in heaven, whispered a prayer that Mark was somewhere safe as faces of customers and friends flashed through Travis's mind.

The blonde. The cute, petite one who ordered a crunchy, cinnamon pastry and half caf, double tall, easy hazelnut, non-fat, no foam with whip extra hot latte on

Tuesdays. She flirted shamelessly, though he knew she was recently and happily engaged to some guy in Tower Seven. Her family lived near his in Serenity Landing, Missouri, and she worked at the Marriot World Trade Center in the shadow of the Towers. Could it have survived the collapse? Was Joanna now buried underneath the rubble?

"Be safe, Travis. Do you have somewhere you can go? They're evacuating Manhattan."

"I'll be okay." He hesitated. "I love you, Mom. You, Dad, Jay. I love all of you. I'll call when I can, but I have to try to find out about my friends, about my girlfriend. I'll talk to you soon."

His mom's "I love you," came through the line as he clicked his phone off.

He started his first call as he walked into the café. Call after call failed as he stood with others, watching the screen in horror as the second tower crashed down. His problems. Mark's dad. Mark's sister. All of it fled as the enormity of what was happening sunk in.

The whole world had changed.

December 18, 2001

"It's a girl."

Abi Connealy collapsed back onto the bed, tears streaming down her cheeks as a newborn squawk filled the delivery room.

A girl.

A million thoughts flew through her mind, few of them happy, as a nurse laid the baby on her chest. So small. So scrunched up and red. Dark hair. Abi couldn't see her eyes as she wrapped her arms around the tiny bundle. "Hi, baby," she whispered. "I'm so glad you're here."

"How are you?"

Abi looked up at Brenda Wardman. Her brother's girlfriend had been a rock the last few months. She didn't need to clarify, because Abi knew what she meant. "I don't know." The voice mail she'd left her parents on the way to the hospital remained unanswered unless Brenda knew something she didn't.

Her fingers brushed over the cheek of the tiny girl. "She's perfect, Bren." Another tear fell, this one landing on her new daughter's face as Abi closed her eyes.

The nurse took the baby to the warmer and did whatever it was nurses did, but Abi didn't see any of it. Her eyes remained closed, and she clasped Brenda's hand as more hot tears streaked into her ears. Just under twenty-four hours of labor meant she didn't have the energy to wipe them away. She knew she didn't have the will to do so even if she could have.

"Do you know what you're going to do?"

Abi wanted to yell at her friend for bringing up the most difficult decision of her life just moments after the birth of her daughter. But since Abi hadn't made up her mind beforehand, Brenda needed to know to help make the arrangements.

Except Abi didn't know.

Not for sure. She knew what the smart decision was, though her head and her heart didn't agree. But she had to put her baby first. "I'll have them call."

"It's going to be fine," Brenda tried to reassure her, but Abi heard the doubt in her friend's voice.

Right.

Fine.

Once the social worker arrived, she'd never be fine again.

Somehow, Abi managed to doze for several hours

during the afternoon, but after listening to the message from her parents, the one that told her all she needed to know without really saying anything, her eyes refused to close. Instead, she stared at the bracelet encircling her wrist, rotating it around time and time again.

A knock sounded half a second before the door pushed open. "Hi, there, Abi. Someone's looking for her mama." The nurse compared the baby's bracelet to Abi's before lifting the blanketed bundle out of the clear bassinet. "The card says you're giving her formula?"

There was no judgment in the woman's voice, but Abi felt her own condemnation eating away at her. All she could do was nod.

After a few minutes of helping them get situated, the nurse started to leave, but stopped before walking out the door. "The emotions are normal, honey. They get everyone at one point or another."

Abi nodded but didn't take her eyes off the little cheeks sucking in and out. She memorized the sounds, the smells, the essence of the tiny bundle in her arms. Or tried to. Even as she did, she knew it would never work. In the morning, a social worker would come and Abi would sign the papers put in front of her.

And she'd never see her daughter again.

But when the social worker sat in the chair by the window, asking the questions, one tripped Abi up.

"Do you know who her father is?"

The night was burned in Abi's memory banks. Part of it anyway. When she hesitated too long, the worker prompted her again. Abi nodded. "Yes. I know who the father is."

"Then we'll need his signature, too."

"He doesn't know," she whispered. "I haven't talked to him since. I was going to, but then 9/11..." Her voice trailed off.

"Was he in the Towers?" the social worker asked as gently as she could.

Abi shook her head. "I don't he was. I mean, I know he wasn't one of the three thousand, but I don't know if he was there or not." She'd called his apartment from a pay phone a few weeks later. When he answered, she hung up.

"If you know who he is, we have to have him sign away his parental rights, sweetie."

Something she hadn't considered when she made this plan.

The nurse walked in, once again pushing the bassinet. Her face fell when she saw the social worker. "I'm sorry. I didn't realize you were..."

With a swipe of the overused Kleenex, Abi wiped her face. "I wasn't sure, but now I can't anyway."

The social worker left a couple of fliers and walked out with a sympathetic smile. The nurse awkwardly helped Abi get situated to feed her daughter one more time.

"Do you have a name you like?" The woman sat on the edge of the bed holding Abi's empty water bottle.

"Cassandra."

"That's beautiful."

"It was my grandmother's name. She died this past summer." The grandmother who would have adored meeting her great-granddaughter, who would have taken Abi and the baby in when she needed somewhere to turn. Had given Abi hope she'd do just that before succumbing to a sudden, massive stroke.

Abi didn't have anyone else like that in her life. Brenda would if she could, but there was no way. Abi had no other family. No one else in her life who would support her no matter what.

Darkness descended, but Abi refused to send little Cassie back to the nursery. She didn't know what she planned to do about adoption, but she wouldn't give up another minute with her baby.

Yet another round of tears leaked down her face as Abi cuddled the tiny bundle against her chest. With all but one light turned out, the desperate whisper ripped from her throat. "God? Are you there?" She'd never prayed before, but this seemed like the time to start if there ever was one. "I don't know what to do."

Baby Cassandra yawned and blinked her eyes open, staring up at her mother. The light caught them just right and struck Abi with the bright blue.

Then it hit her.

The one place she could take her daughter where she'd be safe. And loved.

December 23, 2001

Two days before Christmas, Abi sat in a coffee shop on Long Island and waited. Calling him had taken every ounce of courage she had. Leaving the voicemail took more.

Sitting there, Abi didn't know if she could go through with it. The stroller with her little girl sat to her right. On the other side of it, Brenda sat with her back to the door. Diners nearby sipped on gourmet coffee, but Abi focused on the stationary in front of her. She arrived early so she could write the note, but the paper remained nearly blank.

When she'd arrived at her parents' Long Island home after leaving the hospital, a note reiterated her father's threat. Since then, Abi had planned what to say, but realized she'd never make it through even the shortest speech. She'd planned the words to write, but now the time had come to put pen to paper, and she only managed his name. A glance at her watch told her she didn't have much time. If she didn't write it now, she'd have to make the speech. No way could she do that.

She picked up the Mont Blanc knock-off she'd received for graduation from her grandmother and scribbled a few lines. Her heart squeezed as she reread the note. She couldn't be a student and a mom. But this? Abi had her suitcase packed. She wouldn't return to her parents' home but would crash at Brenda's for a few days while her friend went out of town. Brenda knew most of what happened, but not everything. Abi's fingers furrowed through her hair, and she turned to stare out the window. There he stood. His six-foot frame seemed shorter with his shoulders slumped and hands shoved deep in the pockets of his coat. He looked at his watch and trudged across the street.

The bell over the door jangled. Abi crossed through the unfinished sentence, scribbled a last sentiment and her name, and shoved the note in her purse as he sat down across from her.

"Hi." At the sound of his voice, the knots in her gut tightened.

Abi looked up, knowing he'd see the remnants of her tears. She twisted the napkin in her hands and tried not to think about the weight she'd gained. And if he'd notice.

"Thanks for coming. I wanted to try to explain, but..." Abi shrugged. "After 9/11, after Mark..." The thoughts of her brother nearly overwhelmed her already overwrought emotions. "Daddy isn't going to pursue anything. I tried to tell him you weren't guilty, but he didn't believe me at first. He found your name in my journal on 9/11-before it was '9/11.' I'd left it lying out by accident." This time the shrug was a mere halfhearted lift of one shoulder.

"Mark?" he interrupted. "I read the list of firefighters a bunch of times to make sure he wasn't there."

"He wasn't on the lists. He was killed at a fire on 9/11.

11

Not at the Trade Center. Another fire where they didn't have enough manpower because of everything else. They think he died right around the time the first tower fell."

Were those tears in his eyes? He and Mark hadn't spoken in months. "I'm so sorry."

Cassandra let out a cry. The disguised Brenda made a shushing sound, but Abi didn't look. She couldn't. It was too much. She had to get out. "Can you excuse me for a minute?"

She didn't wait for a reply but motioned toward the back, leaving before he had a chance to stop her. Brenda went out the front door. Abi dug the paper out and waved the barista over. "Can you give this to that guy?"

The woman nodded. Abi fled to the other side of the street and collapsed in Brenda's arms.

Travis read the note three times before it began to sink in.

Dear Travis,

She had to have written it earlier. There hadn't been time since she excused herself.

I hate doing this to you, especially like this. I tried to handle it on my own. I thought I could, but this semester was so hard. Even more than just everything on 9/11 and Mark. I can't do it. I can't be a college student and a mom.

It took several minutes for that to really register.

A mom?

He read on, his disbelief growing with each word.

The baby in the stroller is yours. From that night. I hate that I haven't told you sooner, but I didn't know how. I couldn't tell my parents what happened, not all of it. They would blame you, and it wasn't your fault. I know this is the coward's way out, but I can't tell you to your face. Everything you need for a couple of days is in the diaper bag and the duffel on the bottom of the stroller. So is her birth certificate.

Her name is Cassandra. She's only a few days old. Please take good care of her for me. I won't be home for a while so you can't reach me. My parents left for vacation out of the country, so they wouldn't be here when she was born.

I wish things had worked out the way we planned. The way we talked about all those times. I wish

Whatever she wished, she didn't finish the thought before scribbling through it. About like their relationship had been. A wish that was never finished. He went back to the letter.

Tell Cassandra I love her.

I'm sorry.

Abi

He read it two more times, starting to come to grips with what it meant.

And then the baby began to fuss.

Taking a deep, steadying breath to fortify himself, he turned to the blanket tented over the handle of the car seat. Lifting up one corner, he saw pink. Fuzzy bunnies on the toes of a sleeper. A tiny foot kicking those bunnies in the air. He looked further and saw the bluest eyes he'd ever seen staring back at him, almost as though she knew who he was.

Her father.

Her daddy.

The one responsible for her from here on out.

And in that moment, he fell helplessly in love.

December 25, 2001

Christmas night, the little gray Toyota turned off I-44, south towards Serenity Landing, as the wailing in the backseat reached a new level.

"I'm sorry, Cassandra. We're almost there. I'll get you something to eat in a ten minutes, I promise." Jennifer kicked him out the moment he tried to explain his arrival at the apartment with a baby. Instead, he'd boxed up all his worldly belongings along with the things Abi had left for the baby and packed it in his car. They headed for the only place he knew he could get the help he needed until he had a better handle on things.

Over twelve hundred miles. Stopping every two or three hours to feed his daughter or change her diaper. Sometimes more often than that. Always taking much longer than it should. Failing to take into account how many things would be closed on Christmas Day, he ran out of the bottled water when he needed to make one more meal for his daughter. He pressed the pedal a little closer to the floor in an effort to reach Serenity Landing a little faster.

The newborn squalling had quieted a bit when Travis finally pulled to a stop in front of the house where he'd grown up. In the front window, a Christmas tree stood, multi-colored lights twinkling. In the window next to it, he could see Mom and Dad sitting at the dining room table, though he knew they wouldn't be able to see him. His brother walked in with a platter, piled high with a turkey way too big for the three of them. They'd be eating leftovers for a month.

Another squeak came from the back. "Okay, baby. We're here."

Somehow, Travis managed to get the diaper bag and the baby seat out of the car and headed toward the door, snow crunching under his boots with each step. The smell of oak burning in the fireplace both comforted him and heightened his anxiety. What if they turned him away? Then what?

Should he knock?

He hadn't been home in two and a half years. Did he just walk in?

Even with his hands full, Travis managed to press the doorbell. He took a deep breath and blew it out slowly, finishing as the door opened.

Mom stood there, her jaw hanging down for a second before her hands covered her mouth. "Travis!"

He tried to smile but failed miserably. "Hi, Mom." In the space of a heartbeat, he saw what he needed to in her eyes. Forgiveness. Acceptance. Love. Grace. With a prayer tossed heavenward, he tried again to smile, this time successfully. "There's someone I want you to meet."

Chapter Two

April 2017

"Cassie!" Travis hollered toward the back of the house. "The bus will be here in two minutes. Unless you want to ride with me..." He let the threat trail off. She was fifteen. Driving to school with her teacher-dad was her least favorite thing ever.

She shouted something he couldn't quite make out.

"Cassandra Julianne Connealy-Harders, you better get moving!" In quiet moments, Travis thanked God Abi had listed him on the birth certificate and had given Cassie his last name, as well as her own.

Travis hadn't heard from Abi since that day, two days before Christmas when Cassie was five-days-new. She didn't ask about her mom very often or about the circumstances surrounding her conception or birth. He didn't know what to tell her if she did, so he just kept thanking God she didn't. And Travis constantly thanked Him for family who took him back like the prodigal son instead of treating him like a leper. Mom had already contemplated quitting her job. She'd done just that and became a full-time babysitter while he went back to college. By the time he landed a job as the drama teacher/theater coach at Serenity Landing High School, Cassie was almost five.

She started kindergarten. Travis started work. Most of the year, he was home when she was, except when they were getting close to one of the school productions. Then he worked longer hours. Summers he spent with the little girl who'd stolen his heart that day in the coffee shop.

His ears picked up the sound of the bus turning on the next street. She had sixty, maybe ninety, seconds before the bus pulled up in front of the house. "Cassie!" He yelled one more time. "Last call!"

She rushed out of the hall, jacket on, backpack slung over one shoulder, dark brown curls streaming behind her as she headed for the door. "Love you, Dad!"

It was the only acknowledgment he'd get as her father until near dinner time. She refused to say anything family related to him while at school. Even though she was only a freshman, Cassie was one of the best actresses he had. He now had someone help him cast the girls' parts so he couldn't be accused of bias.

"Don't I get a hug?"

She turned with a roll of her eyes, gave him a quick squeeze, and a peck on the cheek. "Bye!" Bolting out the door, she didn't stop to close it behind her because the bus was already turning off Arizona Avenue, the street that came to a T at the house. By the time it reached a complete stop along the yard, she was nearly there.

With a sad shake of his head at how grown up she was, and how much Abi had missed out on, Travis locked the door and headed for the garage. He'd beat her to school by a full fifteen minutes or more, but at least she wouldn't suffer the humiliation of arriving with Dad. That would be the ultimate in high school embarrassment, mortifying her until the day she graduated.

The garage closed with the push of a button. His beat-up hatchback had been ditched not long after he returned home. His parents let Travis buy their older car, financing it themselves. He'd since traded it in for a Camry that was now "older" itself. Cassie was already bugging him to give it to her when she turned sixteen. He hadn't said yes yet, but they both knew he probably would.

The day went well - easy compared to what the rest of the week would bring with final rehearsals.

"See you guys tomorrow!" Travis called as his last class of the day filed out of the room.

"Mr. H?" He looked up to see one of his most promising students standing there.

"What's up, Zach?"

He set his bag on a desk. "I wanted to talk to you about what I should do after high school."

Travis hopped up onto the table at the front of the room. "You've got a year so you don't have to decide right now, but what options are you looking at?"

"College, obviously. One with a strong drama department. I don't know that I want to teach. I want to act, but I think having a degree would be a good idea, too."

Travis nodded. Zach was better than Travis had ever been. Better than any of his students, really. Except maybe Cassie. "Good plan. We can research some of the best colleges for drama and see which ones you like. I've got a list that can get you started." He'd have to find it first. He tried to be prepared, but not many of his students actually wanted to pursue drama or acting as a career.

Zach leaned back against the desk. "My other thought was moving to New York. Start auditioning and taking classes on the side at a school there. I'm not good enough for Julliard. I know that, but I think I could get some small parts and work my way up."

This time Travis's nod was slower. "I think you probably could."

"But?"

Travis sighed. "I tried that. It's not easy. And I wasn't trying to go to college at the same time. I was working at a coffee shop around my auditions and the few parts I got."

"You were only there a couple years, though, right?"

Some of his story floated around school. It was another source of irritation for his daughter. Everyone knew Travis had only come home because he didn't know what to do with a baby. Her.

"I was there about two and a half years. I had a few really good auditions and was the understudy for one of the medium sized parts in an off-Broadway play once."

"Was it a good experience for you?"

A loaded question if there ever was one. "Like most things, it had good moments and bad. I got some great experience that helped me land this job. New York is a different world and everyone has a different experience. Mine might not be the best to judge by. I met some amazing people, but I was also working downtown on 9/11. I hadn't gone into work that morning and was actually in another part of the state, but some of the people I served coffee to every day never made it home."

Travis didn't talk about his somewhat removed 9/11 experience often. What he'd experienced paled in comparison to so many others. His story would never be on a Dateline special on the anniversary, but he still bore some of the scars of that day. His scars came more from the accusations his daughter's grandfather made, but it was all intertwined.

19

"You knew people who died?"

Travis nodded. "A few. One blonde lady had only been engaged for about a week." A sad smile crossed his face. "Her name was Joanna. Her family was from this area, but I don't remember her last name. She worked in the Marriott World Trade Center and ordered something different every day. Mondays she got the most complicated thing possible. A..." He struggled to remember. "Venti, one pump caramel, one pump white mocha, two scoops vanilla bean powder, extra ice Frappuccino with two shots poured over the top apagotto style with caramel drizzle under and on top of the whipped cream, double cupped and two cinnamon sticks on the side."

Zach's jaw had dropped. "You remember all that?"

"You make it often enough, and yeah, you do. I remember looking through the posters put up all over the place and seeing her on there. I saw several others I knew but for some reason, probably her connection to Serenity Landing, she always stuck with me." It's why he wrote the one act play in her honor.

The teen nodded. "But you got Cassie, though, right? Out of your time in New York City?"

Deep breath in. Breathe out slowly. "I did. She's the best thing to come out of my time in New York, but I didn't do things the easy way. A baby at twenty? Without stable income? Not something I recommend." And something he'd lectured Cassie about ad nauseum. He had a feeling Zach would be getting one of those lectures from him in the future, too. Travis knew Zach had gotten at least one from his parents, but if the looks he'd seen passing between Cassie and Zach were any indication, Zach would get one from Travis sooner rather than later.

"Uh, there's something else."

Travis looked up to see Zach looking anywhere but at

his teacher. "What's that?"

"Can I ask Cassie to prom?"

Travis's eyes nearly popped out of his head. Prom? She was only a freshman! She shouldn't be going to prom for at least another year. It shouldn't have surprised him but still, somehow, it did.

"Mr. H?"

Travis hesitated for another minute. "Um, I don't know. She's not allowed to date until she's sixteen." If he had to choose someone to take her this year, Zach would be the guy. But did he have to?

"I know, but I was hoping you'd make an exception. Just this once. I'll have her home as soon as prom's over. Dinner. Prom. Home immediately after." Zach crossed his heart. "Promise."

Travis stared into Zach's eyes before answering. "Maybe. I'll think about it."

"That's all I ask. But I do have to get tickets by next week."

"Duly noted."

They talked for a minute longer about Zach's post-high school plans and he left. Two minutes later, Cassie bounded in. "Hi, Daddy!"

Travis's eyes narrowed. She wanted something. There was no other reason she'd use a name of any kind for him. She didn't call him anything at school. Not Dad. Not Mr. Harders. And certainly not Mr. H like most of the other students. "What do you want? And why aren't you on the bus?"

She wiggled onto the bar stool at the front of the room. "I thought I'd ride home with you today. Isn't Kristy coming over tonight?"

"That's Ms. Tomlinson to you, young lady."

She made a pffft noise. "She told me I could call her

Kristy when we're not at school. Besides she's going to be my step-mom soon enough."

"I haven't asked her to marry me, kiddo."

"But you like her a lot, and she likes you. And I like her, too. And she likes me. What more do you need?"

Travis crossed his arms over his chest. "There's a lot more to relationships than that."

She shrugged. "Us liking each other is a good start, isn't it? Way better than the Lisa floozy."

"Cassandra!" His sharp rebuke barely fazed her.

"What? She was."

Cassie was right, though most people didn't use the word "floozy" for Lisa. Regardless... "I don't care. You don't talk like that."

"Everyone else does. And she was. She was only after one thing and you know it. She was going to ship me to some girl's school as soon as she got you hitched."

"Doesn't matter what everyone else says. You don't talk like that." He picked up some papers and watched her out of the corner of his eye. "Now, what do you want?"

Her most winsome smile crossed her face. "I can't spend a little extra time with my dad without having some ulterior motive?"

"No."

She smirked. "I see how you think."

Travis stashed the last of the papers to grade in his bag. "Spill it."

"Can't I go with Zach? Please?" A bit of pout entered her voice.

He should have known. The timing was too coincidental. "I told him I'd think about it. That's what I'm telling you, too." Travis pointed sternly at her. "No wheedling. No going to Grandma. No trying to get Kristy on your side, understand? This is my decision and trying to undermine me is just going to get you a 'no,' capiche?"

She rolled her eyes and headed for the door. "Whatever."

With a groan and a silent prayer for strength, Travis followed her, locking up behind him as he did.

Twenty minutes later, he'd changed into a pair of jeans and one of his favorite Serenity Landing Patriots T-shirts. Cassie didn't help him make dinner, something he'd gotten much better at over the years, but she did sit on the island in the middle of the kitchen and kept up a running commentary on the gossip at SLHS. Nothing too salacious, thank goodness, but there had been a time or two where things Cassie knew had helped him prevent something bad from happening.

Nothing too bad, of course, this was semi-small town USA after all, but Travis thanked God for his little girl's conscience. At least one kegger had been prevented. There was no way to know for sure if stopping it had also stopped something else. Like a drunk driving accident or another girl roofied who would then find herself pregnant way too young with little memory of being drugged or how she'd ended up that way.

A few minutes after five, the doorbell rang, and Cassie was off to answer it before he could ask her to. Kristy – tall, blonde, and gorgeous – walked into the kitchen with her arm around his daughter's shoulders.

"Prom, huh?" she asked. "I knew Zach was going ask you."

Travis didn't have to look at her to know Cassie winced. "The answer's no, Cassie. What did I tell you?"

"I didn't bring it up!" she protested. "Kristy asked me what happened today, and Zach asked me to prom. I didn't try to get her on my side! Honest."

Oh the drama.

The irony wasn't lost on him.

Kristy dropped her arm from Cassie's shoulders and slid it around his waist, lifting her face for the kiss she knew was coming. Travis obliged, quickly, but wasn't going to give in that easily.

"She's telling the truth, Trav. I asked about her day. She didn't ask me to convince you."

"Fine." Travis took in his daughter's big doe-eyes and bottom lip caught between her teeth. The look she always used when she was trying to get her way. The same look he'd seen Abi use a time or two in the years he'd known her. "But you've been warned. And it's Ms. Tomlinson to you."

Kristy rolled her eyes at him. "We've been over this."

"Still."

They spent the rest of the evening imitating a happy family, though Kristy wouldn't stay the night. She never stayed the night. He wasn't that guy anymore, the one who'd lived with two of his girlfriends and slept with more. Cassie curled by his side while they watched The Voice, just like she had when she was little and they'd watched episode after episode of Blue's Clues together because it was her favorite. The show changed, but the peace that came from having his arm around his favorite female in the world hadn't.

Cassie gave him a kiss on the cheek about eight-thirty, and headed for her room to read until lights out an hour later. Kristy took the spot Cassie had vacated. He missed this. Being so close to a woman. The only thing missing was a couple of wedding bands and her clothes in his closet.

Travis had been thinking about it for a couple of months. He and Kristy had been dating the whole school year. It was her first year in Serenity Landing and she'd volunteered to help with some of the ancillary stuff that goes along with putting on a play, like ticket sales. They'd hit it off and sparks flew.

But was he ready to marry her? To make her a permanent part of his life? Of Cassie's?

The peace that had come over him with Cassie at his side remained with Kristy as they shared a few soft, short, sweet kisses and talked about their days.

"There's something I want to talk about," Travis said before he could change his mind.

"What's that?" She looked up at him, luminous green eyes threatening to pull him in and never let go.

"The future."

Kristy moved away, just a bit, her face guarded. "Like what? The summer? Retirement? The future is a pretty broad topic."

Travis took her hand in his and laced their fingers together. "We haven't talked about marriage yet, but I think maybe we should. We've been dating for months. We're in our thirties. Cassie said we have her approval. I'm not proposing, but I wanted to see what you think."

She settled back in next to him. "I've thought about it. If you asked, I know what my answer would be."

Travis rested his head against hers and nodded. "Good to know."

The next morning was a repeat of so many mornings before that.

"Cassie! The bus will be here in two minutes. Unless you want to ride with me..."

"Chill out, Dad!" This time Travis could understand what she was saying as he kept an ear tuned in for the bus.

Instead the doorbell rang. That was odd. A glance at his watch showed 6:19. Awfully early for company. Travis answered the door, taking a sip of his coffee as he did. Kristy stood there, looking frantic.

"Is my phone here? I can't find it anywhere."

Grinning, Travis pulled it out of his pants' pocket. "This it?"

She closed her eyes and let out a sigh of relief. "Thank you, God."

"Battery's dead, though. And I don't have the right kind of charger for it."

"No problem. I brought mine." She walked in and Travis shut the door behind her. "I have that training in Springfield today. It doesn't start until ten, but I wanted to make sure I caught you."

Travis grinned at her and pulled her into his arms. "As long as I get a good morning kiss, it's all good." One thing they'd been very strict about was a no PDA policy at school. Good morning kisses rarely happened.

She smiled at him in a way that made Travis want to drop to one knee and pop the question right then and there. "Of course," she whispered, her lips meeting his in a kiss beyond anything they'd shared the night before. But his mind wouldn't let him forget the impressionable teen banging around in her bathroom.

"You guys should just get married," the teen in question said, storming through the entry on her way to the kitchen. "I can't find my notebook."

"Check the counter," Travis called, his eyes still on Kristy's lips. "Good morning."

"Morning."

"This is why I keep a home phone still, by the way." He gave her another kiss. "Much easier to find a phone attached to the wall."

She started to say something, but was interrupted by another ring of the doorbell.

"Grand Central station around here this morning." Travis let her go and turned toward the door.

"You have some lipstick," she whispered, pulling on his arm until he turned and she could wipe his mouth with her thumb before she headed to the kitchen to help Cassie find her notebook.

"Thanks." Travis opened the door with a smile splitting his face, but when he saw who was standing there, his stomach, jaw and pretty much everything fell to the floor, and he felt the blood drain from his face.

Bathed in the light of the coming dawn, a ghost from the past stood there, flesh and blood, staring at him.

"Abi?"

Chapter Three

There, in front of Abi, was the face that had haunted her dreams for sixteen years.

But then he turned white as a sheet, like he'd seen a ghost.

Which he kind of had.

"Abi?" he whispered. His vivid blue eyes, just as she remembered them, filled with pain and confusion.

"Who is it, honey?" A blonde woman appeared at his side, her hand coming to rest on his shoulder.

His wife?

Abi wasn't proud of it, but she'd been stalking him for a week trying to summon her courage and knock on the door. So what if early on a Tuesday morning wasn't the best time for it? She'd let the weekend slip by and if she waited any longer, she'd run away.

Again.

Like she had more than once.

Starting two days before Christmas all those years ago.

"I shouldn't have come." Abi's voice cracked as she turned and fled.

"Abi! Wait!" He caught up with her before she finished crossing the yard. His hand on her arm spun her around until she faced him. He was blurry as tears obscured her view. "What are you doing here?"

Abi shook her head. "I don't know. I just thought... I wanted..."

"I found it, Dad!"

Whatever compassion had been on his face fled.

Dad.

Could it be?

The stinging liquid in her eyes overflowed.

"Leave," he growled. "Come back in an hour. We'll talk then."

"I'm sorry," Abi whispered as her heart tore in two again. She tried to pull her arm away but his grip was too strong. "I shouldn't have come. I'll leave, but I won't come back. I'll leave you alone."

"Dad?" This time the voice was closer and nearly drowned out by the sound of a school bus pulling up behind them.

Travis moved, trying to block the girl from seeing Abi. "Get on the bus, Cassie. We'll talk later."

Cassie.

He'd kept her name.

And then Abi saw her.

The face she'd seen every time she looked in the mirror as a teenager. Except for the brilliant blue eyes the teen had gotten from her father.

There was no question.

She was Abi's daughter. The one Abi had given up just days after she was born.

The one she had no right to see again.

The color of her daughter's face matched that of her father before he'd gone livid.

A horn sounded from the school bus, but Travis waved it on with the hand that wasn't still gripping Abi's arm.

"Everything okay, Mr. H?" a voice called from the bus. A teenager. Not the driver.

"Go to school, Zach," he yelled back. "Everything's fine."

And the whole time, he'd never taken his eyes off her.

Neither had Cassie.

"You're my... mom?" she squeaked out.

Travis didn't say anything but just stared at her. Abi caught movement out of the corner of her eye as Cassie turned and ran back into the house. The front door slammed behind her. The blonde still stood on the sidewalk.

"What do you want, Abi? Why are you here?"

Abi shook her head. "I don't know." She did know what she needed. She didn't know if she had the guts.

His eyes swung to where his hand still held her arm. As though just realizing he was touching her, he dropped it like a hot potato. "I have to go take care of my daughter." He turned and stalked off, stopping to talk to the blonde as tears slipped down Abi's cheeks faster than ever. The blonde hadn't taken her eyes off Abi. She accepted a kiss on the cheek before resting her hand on the side of his face. She said something that looked like "call me", but Abi couldn't be sure.

She headed for the car parked in the driveway. The same one that had been there the last several nights.

As the blonde drove off, Travis called to Abi.

"Are you making a mess and running away again? Or are you going to stick around long enough to pick up the pieces this time?" He didn't wait for her to respond but went inside, leaving the door ajar.

Abi stood rooted to her spot in the front yard, eyes

glued first to the door and then to the window with the bright pink and purple flowers on it. Was that Cassie's room? What did it look like?

One of her other questions had been answered already. She looked like Abi, with Travis's eyes, and maybe a little bit of Mark.

Another question had been answered too.

Cassie hated Abi.

She had every right to.

Abi hated herself.

What she'd done.

Not Cassie.

Abi'd never hated her.

But she'd always hated how she handled everything. Her only excuse was youth and selfishness and fear.

With a deep breath, Abi put one foot in front of the other. *You can do this. You have to.* She ran her tongue over dry lips, hoping she'd have the strength to voice the question she'd waited fifteen years to ask.

Can you forgive me? One hand pushed against the slightly open door and she walked in. *Can you forgive me for missing years of dance recitals and piano practice? For running off minutes before telling you we had a daughter and leaving you alone with dirty diapers and sleepless nights?*

And even though Abi doubted they could forgive her, she had to ask something else.

Abi had to ask her daughter to take a test.

Abi sat on the edge of the couch for nearly an hour before Travis finally came into the room. She'd spent the time studying the pictures sitting around. Cassie growing up. Travis always by her side. The smiles on their faces told her how much they meant to each other. Abi tracked her through the years. Her first Christmas with her other grandparents. Travis must have headed straight to Serenity Landing after Abi left Cassie with him. Then there was Cassie's first day of preschool, her father kneeling next to her, big grins on both their faces. Her first day of kindergarten. A dance recital of some kind. Easter egg hunt. More Christmases. Eighth grade graduation. Her first day of high school. A few pictures of her with others in what appeared to be a school play.

That made sense. Travis had been a decent actor, if not fabulous. It was only right his daughter would want to act, too.

His heavy steps let her know of his arrival before his voice did.

"You're still here?" Well-deserved sarcasm laced every word.

"How is she?" Abi twisted a Kleenex in her hands.

"How do you think she is? The mother she never asks about shows up out of nowhere then tries to run off again? She's just peachy."

"She never asks about me?" It wasn't what Abi meant to say, but it's what came out.

Travis stared at her before he started pacing. "It's not about you, Abigail Connealy. It never has been, no matter what you thought years ago. It's always been about Cassie. Or it should have been. Did you even think about her once? What you were putting her through? Did she *ever* cross your mind?"

Tears filled Abi's eyes as she nodded. By the time her parents returned from their European vacation a week into the New Year, the only things Abi had left of Cassie were a couple of pictures she kept carefully hidden and her bracelet from the hospital. Every year, on her birthday and again on the day she'd left her with Travis, Abi took them out, cried over them, and called out to a God she didn't believe existed and asked Him to take care of her little girl.

Abi's parents had never mentioned her. Never asked if she knew if the baby was a boy or a girl. Never asked what happened to her. For all they knew, Abi left her in a trash can somewhere in Brooklyn.

Over fifteen years later and they never mentioned their grandchild.

But it was different for Abi and she told Travis the honest truth. "Every day. Every hour. Every minute. I've wondered about her, prayed for her, for you, that you were okay. I even went by your apartment a week later to talk to you and see if we could figure something out together, but the woman there said she'd never heard of you."

"What woman?"

Abi shrugged. "Redhead. About twenty. Twenty-one, maybe."

He snorted. "Jennifer. She kicked me and Cassie out when I got home. I had nowhere to go. A baby to take care of. Do you know I had to ask the lady at the coffee shop how to make a bottle? How to change a diaper? How to take care of the umbilical cord? Scared the living daylights out of me when it came off in Ohio. I knew *nothing* about babies. Leaving her with me wasn't much better than leaving her with a perfect stranger."

His eyes flashed her direction. "What were you thinking, Abi? That you didn't want to ruin your life? Your scholarships? Still mourning Mark? What?"

Abi shook her head. The twin tragedies of 9/11 and the death of her brother hadn't helped any, but her parents had threatened to stop paying tuition and essentially disown her if she didn't give the baby up for adoption. If only Mark had lived, things would have been different. But that didn't matter. The only things that mattered were her choices. "Nothing that seemed like a valid reason back then still holds water today. I know that. I know it was stupid to leave her with you, but I knew you'd love her and take care of her even if you did have to figure it out."

"I had to drive cross-country with a week-old-baby. Used the last money I had for formula, diapers, and gas. We pulled up to my parents' house on fumes, praying they wouldn't turn me and a baby out in the cold."

"Did they?" Abi couldn't bear the thought of his parents turning their backs on him and her baby. The things he'd told her about them were one reason she'd been convinced he was the best choice. Because they were the kind of people who would take their son and grandbaby in and help, no questions asked.

He ran his hands through his hair. "No. They took us in. Why you couldn't depend on your parents, though, instead of foisting her off on me, I don't think I could ever understand that."

"They were going to disow..."

"Foisting?" Another voice entered the conversation. "Is that what you thought, Dad? That I was foisted on you? You didn't want me?" Cassie's blue eyes sparkled with unshed tears and her face showed remnants of a crying jag that probably wasn't over.

Abi winced under Travis's glare as he walked toward Cassie. As mad as she was, whatever questions she had, Cassie let him wrap his arms around her as she broke down.

"At the time, at first, I sort of felt like that, sweetie. I didn't even know you existed until the day she left you with me. I didn't know she was pregnant. I had absolutely no idea I was about to become a full-time dad. So yeah, at first, that's how I felt." He tipped her chin up until he could see her eyes and kissed her nose. "But then you cried. I looked in the stroller and there you were, so tiny, so perfect with your nose all scrunched up, and you stole my heart right then and there. From that moment on, I knew it was you and me. I knew Grammy and Grandpop would help me, so we came back here. But you have never, *ever* been a burden of any kind to me. From the first moment I saw you, I wanted you." He held up one hand, little finger out like he was drinking high tea. "Pinkie promise."

Cassie stared at his finger for a moment before linking one of hers with it. "I believe you." She let him hold her until her tears stopped. Then she looked at Abi. "You? I never want to see you again." Cassie turned on one heel and fled to the back of the house.

Travis's shoulders slumped as he stuck his hands deep in the pockets of his khaki pants. "What do you want, Abi?" He sounded old. Defeated. And Abi was the cause of all of it.

But she couldn't not answer him. Not now. She had to tell him. If she wasn't honest, if she made a false overture, he'd know. He'd never let her back in Cassie's life. Not until it was too late.

It was time to go for broke.

"I want to find out if she's a bone marrow match for my father."

Chapter Four

How many times could one tiny woman sucker punch a guy before he fought back?

"You want to find out if my daughter, the one your dad wanted *nothing* to do with, is a bone marrow match for him? No." Travis shook his head. "I'm not letting anyone from your family anywhere near my little girl."

"She's fifteen, Trav." Abi's voice was soft. "Can't you let her make up her own mind?"

"You don't get to call me Trav," he snapped. "You gave that right up a long time ago."

"Because of what happened that night? No one was at fault. We agreed to that."

"That's not what your dad thought." And the reason Travis hadn't seen the fireball blow out the elevators in the Mall at the World Trade Center when the first tower was hit. He would have been right there, living through the nightmare of 9/11, instead of oblivious for another hour and fifteen minutes.

Abi sank back into the couch, looking, for the moment, like the eighteen-year-old girl he remembered. If he closed his eyes, he could see her. Sitting across from him in the coffee shop. Tear stained cheeks. She'd put on weight since he'd seen her last, but somehow she still looked gaunt. Like she hadn't been eating. Dark circles under her eyes. A sadness he didn't understand until later. Her voice brought him back to the present.

"Dad wouldn't listen to me. He snuck into my room early that morning, saw my journal, and read it. He read me the riot act for not telling him sooner you'd drugged me."

She let him believe that? "I didn't..."

"I know!" she interrupted. "He didn't read the whole thing. I tried to tell him what really happened but he wouldn't listen. I hadn't even told them who the father was, because I knew he'd go ballistic. Mark thought it was you. Mom and Dad suspected. I told them it wasn't, but I know Mark didn't believe me. He didn't go after you since I wouldn't tell him for sure, but he wanted to." She wiped her nose with her Kleenex. "Mark missed you. He asked about you the night before, if I ever heard anything from you, if you were the father. If I'd told you."

That had bothered Travis for years. "Why didn't you? Even if you didn't want your dad or brother to know, why didn't you tell me? I would have been there for you. At the doctor. When she was born." Tears he didn't know he still had filled his eyes. "You took that from me. You didn't let me see my baby be born. You left. *That's* why you don't get to call me Trav anymore."

What Abi called him didn't matter. He'd given anything to erase the heartache his daughter had found in the last hour. She was the only thing that mattered. The reason he'd sent Kristy to school with instructions for his classes, to cover for him for half an hour or so until the vice-principal,

Shawn, could get a substitute and shuffle people so someone could supervise while the kids rehearsed as best they could in his absence.

Travis flopped into the recliner and ran his hands over his face until his fingers furrowed rows in his faux-hawk. The one that made the kids think he was way cooler than he really was.

God, are you there? I thought You and I repaired our relationship years ago. Keeping Abi and her family out of our lives was part of the deal, wasn't it? And now You're asking my daughter to see if she's a match for a man who never even wanted to meet his grandchild? Really?

He'd never heard God's voice, audibly or in his head. Never the still small voice or the fire in a burning bush, but in that moment, he heard words in his mind in a voice he'd never heard before.

Be still and know that I am God.

Really? That's what He was going with?

My thoughts are not your thoughts, neither are your ways my ways.

Travis blew out a long breath. This was really what God wanted? He argued with that little voice for a few more minutes before giving in.

Fine, he shot heavenward. *But I'm not going to tell her she has to. If she's going to do this, she has to make the decision on her own. I'll make sure she knows the potential risks and rewards, but I won't make her decision for her.*

For now, he had to get this woman out of his house.

"You need to go," Travis told her. "I'll talk to her, but not with you here."

Abi nodded and stood. She dug through her purse until she found a card and held it out. "My cell phone number's on there. Call me?"

"I'll let you know something." It could be that he'd let her know he and Cassie wanted nothing to do with her. He could do that with a text.

If he never saw or talked to her again, it would be too soon.

Abi headed toward the entry, but stopped in front of a framed photo collage Cassie put up a couple months earlier. "Who is she, Trav?"

The picture in the middle of Cassie, Kristy, and him. "What does it matter?"

"Is she your wife? You don't wear a ring, but I know lots of men who don't."

"What does it matter?" he asked again. "You want to apply for the job? Don't want to know I'm already taken?" There had been a time when he'd thought it could be a possibility, but not any time in the last decade and a half.

This time when she shook her head, sadness filled the action. "No. When we first met, I thought maybe, someday, after high school, maybe you could look at me like that. But since that night, and especially since that day in the coffee shop, I knew there was no chance you'd ever be more than my first."

With her head hanging down and shoulders slumped, she trudged out the door, and maybe, just maybe, out of his life for good.

Again.

Travis spent over an hour on the phone with his vice principal, working on stuff for the play. At least Shawn had a background in high school theatre so Travis *could* take the day off. But, even as he worked, nothing kept his mind off what Cassie must be going through.

He knocked on the wall by her open door. "You ready to talk, punkin?" He leaned against the door frame and watched her breathe. She was curled around her favorite teddy bear. One Abi had left in the duffel bag under the stroller. Cassie had no idea. It had never seemed right to tell her the bear's origins.

After a moment, she shook her head.

"Do you want me to go for a while longer?"

Another pause. And another shake of the back of her head.

"Do you want me to sit with you for a bit?"

This time there was no delay before the nod. A barely perceptible movement of her head.

He went into her room. Even with the lights off and the curtains drawn, it was fairly bright. One benefit to having windows that faced east. Her double bed with the walnut four-poster frame and tulle canopy had been a birthday gift from his parents. He leaned against the headboard as Cassie sat up and curled in next to him, her head resting on his shoulder. He held her as tight as he could, wishing she still believed he could chase away the monsters.

"I want to know," she whispered. "I want to know everything. About you and her. Me."

"Are you sure? Because once I tell you everything, I can't untell you. And I don't want you to believe I never wanted you, because that is categorically untrue. For about three minutes after I found out you existed, I was in shock, but after that... You mean everything to me, punkin. I hope you know that."

She nodded against him. "I know. I've always known how much you love me. But I want to know the whole story."

Travis took a deep breath and brushed his fingers against her hair like he had when she was little. Gentle stroking at her temple. Hoping to comfort her.

"I left Serenity Landing when I was eighteen. The

summer after high school, I was convinced I was going to be the next big thing on Broadway. I went to New York and lived with my old camp friend's family for a couple months until I found an apartment in Manhattan." There was more to it, but he wouldn't tell his daughter that. Not yet. Not when he could still see himself leaning toward Abi with every intention of kissing her. "Even after I moved to the city, Mark's family practically adopted me. Grammy and Grandpop didn't approve of what I was trying to do. We didn't talk much, and I missed them."

He stopped as he remembered the heartache he must have caused his parents. "Anyway, on spring break almost two years later, Abi, Mark's little sister, was at a party. She'd just turned eighteen and there was alcohol. She'd been drinking, but swore to me she'd only had two beers. She felt funny and called me to come get her. She knew if her brother or parents found out, she'd be in trouble until the end of time. She was supposed to spend the night with a friend, but instead I took her back to my place. I had this little apartment in The Village, and she was going to sleep it off. I'd take her home the next morning. When I picked her up from the party, she had a cup of coffee in her hand. I'd been up since five that morning, and it was after midnight. She was trying to sober up. She shared her coffee with me to keep me from falling asleep. Once we got to my apartment, she collapsed on the couch."

"What does the coffee have to do with it?" Cassie asked through her sniffles.

"I'm getting there. I hadn't had anything to drink, but I didn't feel right either. I didn't think I could move Abi, so I covered her up on the couch and went to bed. I woke up a while later, and she was there with me, in my bed. Kissing me." He closed his eyes and prayed for strength. How was he supposed to tell his baby girl she was the result of spiked coffee? "The next morning, we talked about it a little bit. She told me more about how she felt when she called me, and I had enough experience to know it sounded pretty normal, especially for someone who'd never had a drink before. But we split that big cup of coffee, me because I was tired and Abi because she was trying to sober up, and we both felt weird after that. The only conclusion we could come to was that someone had drugged her coffee. We checked and there was some powder residue in the mug, so it seemed like a logical conclusion."

"So I'm the result of some sleaze ball drugging a girl's coffee, and you sharing it with her?"

Travis kissed the top of her head. "See why I've never told you before? I never wanted you to feel like that. It may have been where you came from, but, sweetie, you're the best thing that's happened in my whole life, no matter how you started."

She shrugged but didn't say anything.

"Do you want to know any more, or is that enough?" He prayed it would be enough.

"I want to know everything."

Of course she did. "I took her home the next morning and didn't return any of Mark's phone calls, basically cutting myself out of their lives. I knew Mark would never forgive me. I had a hard time forgiving myself even though I knew it wasn't completely my fault. We were both drugged, somewhat, but I'd betrayed Mark's trust. And Abi's. I moved on with my life. I worked at a coffee shop, met a girl who eventually moved in with me. She'd been living with me about a week when Abi's dad called early one morning, yelling at me for drugging his daughter."

He took a deep breath in and blew it out slowly. "It was a day the whole world changed."

Cassie moved back and gave him a skeptical look only

she had mastered. "The whole world changed because the dad of some girl you slept with got mad about it?"

Travis gave a quick shake of his head. "After I hung up on him, I started for work but called in sick and went for a drive instead. Grammy called me a few hours later. She'd been calling for a long time before I finally answered. It was 9/11. I worked at the mall under the Twin Towers and she'd been afraid I was hurt or dead, especially when I didn't answer. They were saying on the news that cell phone coverage was spotty in Manhattan, but she was still so worried. I don't know if Abi's dad said anything or was going to say something about her being pregnant with you. I didn't hear him if he did because I was in shock and hung up on him."

She nestled back in next to him. "I'm glad you weren't there."

"Me, too. As far as I ever heard, everyone in the mall got out okay, but I'm still really glad I wasn't there. Anyway, the next few months went by. I kept checking the fire fighter names to make sure Mark's name wasn't on the list and it wasn't."

"I have an uncle who was a fire fighter on 9/11?" She sat up, a light in her eyes for a moment. "Maybe it's not too late to change my paper topic to him. That would be awesome! I could interview someone who was there. That would get me an A for sure!"

Travis shook his head. "No. He was a fire fighter on 9/11 but on Long Island. He was called to a fire in upper Manhattan because they didn't have enough manpower because of everything in lower Manhattan. I never saw his name because he wasn't one of the 343 killed in the Towers. Anyway, a few days before Christmas, I got a voice mail from Abi telling me to meet her the next day. I showed up. We talked for about two minutes, and she told me about Mark's death. She excused herself to go to the bathroom. A minute later, an employee gave me a note saying the baby in the stroller next to me was you. I thought the stroller belonged whoever was at the table on the other side of it, but she was gone by then. I never got a good look but she must have been a friend of Abi's. I told you the rest earlier. A few minutes later, you started crying. I got a good look at you, and I was a goner. I fell in love at first sight."

"What about your girlfriend?"

He didn't get straight to Jennifer. "Some lady at the coffee shop took pity on me. She said I should turn Abi in to the police, but I didn't see the point. You weren't abandoned. You were left with your father. The lady helped me figure out formula and diapers and swaddling. I managed to get back to the apartment, and Jennifer said she wanted nothing to do with either one of us. Either I send you back to your mother or we both leave. Kind of ironic since it was my apartment, but I didn't see much choice. We drove for three days straight, stopping every couple of hours so I could feed or change you. The only way I could afford to get all the way back here was to sleep in fleabag motels. You slept in my arms because I didn't trust the neighbors or the beds. We pulled up in front of Grammy and Grandpop's house on Christmas night, just as they were sitting down for dinner with Uncle Jay."

Travis kissed the side of her head. "They welcomed us with open arms. Mom sent me up to bed since I was obviously exhausted. I hadn't slept more than ninety minutes at a time since I left the café because you had your days and nights mixed up. She took care of both of us even after I told them everything. They helped me get on my feet until I could take care of you myself."

He crooked a finger under her chin until she looked up

at him. "No matter what, I wanted you. As soon as I knew about you. I've said that about eighty-two times already but I need you to know that."

She nodded. "I believe you."

They sat there for a few more minutes before she asked another question. "So what does she want now? Why is she here?"

CASSIE

CALL ME AS SOON AS YOU CAN. I texted the message to Zach, knowing it would be hours before he could. Unless he snuck off somewhere and risked getting in trouble. I glanced at the clock. Drama was starting. With Dad at home, Lindy would be in charge. A sub wouldn't know the difference if she let him sneak off for a few. Except Zach was the male lead in the play.

My phone buzzed a minute later. "Hey." It was all I could muster.

"What's going on, Cass? Who was that woman? Is everything okay?" Zach's words came out in a rush.

"She's my mom."

Stunned silence met my words. "Your...mom...? Like your birth mother? The one you've never met?"

"I've met her. Before she abandoned me when I was five days old." I used snark to cover the hurt. I knew that. Zach knew that. I thought I'd come to terms with my mom's abandonment years earlier, but now that she'd been in my house, maybe I hadn't.

"Wow. What's she want?"

"Her dad needs a bone marrow transplant and they want me to get tested. Me! She said he's the reason she gave me up, but now they want me to save his life? Really?"

"Cassie." The gentle reproach in his voice matched the still, small one inside.

"I know. I know. What would Jesus do?" I mimicked.

"What does your dad say?"

"He says he'll support me no matter what decision I make." I sighed and stared at the popcorn ceiling. "But he didn't say what he wants me to do. There's no guarantee I'm even a match."

"No, but if you were tested and found out you were a match, would you really say no?"

I sighed again. "No. If I were a match, I don't think I could get their hopes up then say no."

"So you need to decide soon before you get tested?"

"Yeah." Swirls of emotions churned through my stomach. I was going to be sick. I'd probably do it, but I'd be sick first.

"Do you have to meet them? Do you want to?"

I turned that over in my head. "I don't want to meet them. Maybe that's what I'll tell Dad. I'll do it, but I don't want anything to do with Abi or her parents."

"I think that sounds good, but you should talk to your dad."

"I will." I heard something in the background. "Is that Lindy?"

"Yeah. I gotta go. Hey - I was gonna tell you this morning, but SLAC called the lifeguards last night. I bet they'll be calling the desk staff soon."

Another minute and we said good-bye. He was going to be a Serenity Landing Aquatic Center lifeguard again. He loved his summer job, and the girls loved him doing it. How many girls had I seen flirting with him last year? This year would be worse, and the swimsuits would be smaller. He'd promised me he had no interest in dating anyone but me - once I was old enough. Seven more months.

Or three weeks.

If Dad let me go to prom with Zach.

The thought took my mind off my long-lost mother and sent a smile spreading cross my face. Would he kiss me? How many times would we dance together? Would he dance with any other girls? Except maybe Mai. I'd be okay if he danced once or twice with my BFF. I didn't worry about Maile taking the guy I loved. My eyes closed as I hugged my favorite teddy bear, and the enormity of it overwhelmed me.

"Daddy, why don't I have a mommy?" I stared at my shoes where they scuffed the ground underneath the swing.

Daddy sat in the next swing over. He was thinking like he does when he doesn't know what to say.

"Is that why we live with Grammy and Grandpop instead of our own house?"

"We're getting our own house in a few weeks, punkin." We'd looked at it together. I liked it. It had a big backyard.

Daddy never talked about my mama. Did she die when I was born like Maile's mama did with her little brother?

He wrapped my hand in his big one. "You do have a mama, Cassie. When you were a baby, something happened, and she couldn't take care of you anymore. She wanted to more than anything, but she just couldn't. So she gave you to me, your daddy, and we came back here. To Serenity Landing. To Grammy and Grandpop. Because I didn't even know how to change a diaper."

That was silly. Even I knew how to change a diaper. At least on my dolls.

His voice sounded like he might cry. "Your mama loved you though, Cassie. I know she did. She does."

"Then where is she?" Didn't she care that everyone made fun of me because I didn't have a mama?

Daddy seemed to think for a minute. "I don't know where she is.

I tried to find her a while ago and couldn't. I guess whatever made it so she couldn't take care of you isn't over yet."

If it wasn't over yet, *then did that mean... I didn't ask Daddy if it meant she might be coming back for me someday. Not to take me away but to make us a real family.*

Maybe...

My phone buzzed at me pulling me out of my doze. The time surprised me. Had I nodded off longer than I thought? School was over and had been for a while, but the caller wasn't one of my friends.

"Hello?"

"Is this Cassie?"

"Yes."

"This is Alivia from SLAC."

A smile snuck out. "Hey, Livs. What's up?" My heart quickened at the thought of what this could mean.

"We're calling the front desk and concession stand people today. Are you still interested?"

I laughed. "Not so much concessions, but yeah. Definitely."

"I can't promise you'll never need to work in the concession stand, but we have you down primarily as front desk. You'll need to learn both before we open." I could almost see her shrug. "They're easy, though. You'll be fine."

"Thanks, Alivia. I need some good news today."

"Is everything okay, kiddo?" She wasn't that much older than me. Normally, it bugged me when someone my dad had in class called me kiddo but with Alivia, it was kind of sweet. Just like her.

"A lot of stuff going on today," I told her after weighing my options. "I'll tell you about it some other time. Long story."

She made a "hm" sound and seemed to be thinking.

"What if we go out for lunch this weekend? I make a great shoulder to cry on."

"I know, but the spring play is this weekend." At that moment, I'd rather have lunch with her.

"That's right. I'll be there Friday night with CJ and his sisters." Her lifeguard fiancé was also guardian for his sisters. I'd gotten to know them both a little bit over the last year.

"Find me afterwards?"

"Of course. Maybe next weekend."

"I'm hoping Dad's going to let me go to prom so I may be shopping, but I would like to sometime soon."

Her voice took on the sing-song tone it always did when she picked on me. "With Za-ach?"

I blushed, even though she couldn't see me. "Yeah." A knock on my door kept me from saying anymore. "I gotta go. Dad wants to talk." The door opened, and he leaned against the frame. "Thanks for the call. I'm looking forward to working at SLAC this summer."

A smile crossed Dad's face.

"Oh wait!" I had one more question before she hung up. "Can I still do swim team?"

"You think I'd hire you if you couldn't?"

We laughed and hung up. Time to tell Dad my decision.

Chapter Five

Abi sank to the bed in her hotel room and cried like she hadn't cried in years. She hadn't expected Travis to welcome her with open arms and she *really* hadn't thought Cassie would, but the hostility surprised her. It probably shouldn't have, but it did.

And she'd failed. There was no way Cassie would even get tested to see if she was a match. Travis wouldn't let her.

Her phone buzzed and she answered without thinking. "Hello?"

"Hi, honey. Where are you?"

Mom. Great. Just who she wanted to talk to.

"I had a trip to take. I told you I wouldn't be home when you got back."

"You did?"

"Yes, I did."

Dad might need a bone marrow transplant but that didn't stop them from vacationing while he was still able. This time it was a cruise to Mexico.

"Where are you?" she asked again.

Abi thought for a moment, trying to decide what to say.

"Grasping at straws," she finally told her mom.

"What are you talking about?" Confusion colored Mom's voice.

They'd never talked about Cassie openly, but Mom had known intuitively the days that were hard. Like Cassie's birthday. Mom always made Abi's favorites or called just to chat, while never mentioning the elephant in the room.

"I saw her," Abi whispered.

"Who?" Mom was truly puzzled.

"The one person who might be a match for Dad."

She could almost see the wheels turning in her mom's head and then came the gasp. "You found..." Her voice trailed off as she tried to figure out how to word her revelation.

"Yes." That Mom heard the whisper amazed even Abi. "And I saw her."

"A girl?" Mom's voice cracked with emotion.

"A beautiful teenager. She looks just like I did when I was fifteen, except she has the bluest eyes." There was no point in trying to wipe the tears away. Abi was long past that point.

"How'd you find her? The adoption agency?"

It was so hard to tell her the truth. There was no way but to just do it. "She was never adopted. I left her with Travis. They're living in his hometown."

"You left her with the man who drugged you to and took advantage of you?" Mom's words betrayed her barely concealed fury

"You wouldn't listen to me then, but you will now." Abi could be forceful when she needed to and this was one of those times. "Travis didn't drug me. We shared some coffee I'd gotten at the party. It had a lid on it. He couldn't have done it. We were both drugged. Not a full dose since we shared, but enough. He's been a wonderful father to my baby girl. A much better father than I was a mother. So don't even bring all that nonsense up again. Understand me?"

The silence on the other end of the line lasted long enough that Abi checked to make sure her mother hadn't hung up.

"Okay," she finally said quietly. "If you still insist that's what happened, I have no choice but to believe you."

Abi's voice softened. "It is."

Cautious hope filled her mom's voice. "Is she going to get tested? Did you talk to them?"

"I don't know if she is or not. I talked to Travis. I talked to her for about three seconds before she ran off. Travis knows Dad needs the transplant and promised to talk to her about it. He has my card. I don't know what else I can do to convince them."

Another long silence. "How is he?"

"I don't know. I think he's a teacher at the high school. He's either dating or married. I couldn't really get a good read, and he didn't answer my question about it. He's still furious about how I left her with him."

"I think maybe it's time I heard the whole story."

Abi winced. She wouldn't be happy. Abi wasn't happy, but she *had* waited to make sure he took Cassie with him, hiding across the street with Brenda until they'd left about an hour later. With a deep breath, she launched into the story.

Mom was furious.

And sympathetic at the same time. For the first time, she acknowledged the impossible situation they'd put Abi in.

"Do you want me to come stay with you until you know something?" she asked, love filling her voice.

"No. You need to stay with Dad and I don't want him to know anything about this. You remember how he was that morning. The whole time really. The only reason he didn't try to put Travis in prison was 9/11. I don't want to drag all of this out again if they're not willing to get Cassie tested or if she's not a match."

Abi's phone vibrated in her hand. She held it away from her ear. She didn't recognize the number but the message was clear enough. *TONIGHT. 9PM. MY HOUSE. DON'T EXPECT MUCH.*

She told her mom and extracted a promise that her dad wouldn't find out until she said it was okay. After hanging up, Abi decided to try to take a nap.

It was going to be a very long night.

The nicest black slacks she'd brought along seemed woefully inadequate. The cobalt blue silk shirt clung to her skin. Normally, this was her "feel good" outfit, but somehow she doubted anything would serve that purpose on a day like this.

Abi sat in her car, in Travis's driveway, next to the car driven by the blonde, and tried to work up her courage to get out, walk up to the door, and face her daughter and her daughter's father.

The courage wasn't coming. Just a stomach full of butterflies feasting on MiracleGro.

Travis standing there glaring didn't help. He must have come around the corner of the walkway to the front door when she wasn't looking. He wore the same clothes he had earlier - khaki pants with lots of pockets and a black collared shirt with a logo from the local high school on one side.

With his arms crossed, his biceps were much more pronounced than they had been all those years ago in New

York. Abi stared at him, avoiding the firm set of his jaw and barely concealed fury on his face. Instead, she focused on his broad shoulders, the chest that had soaked up the tears of his daughter earlier. Where he had to have cradled her as a little baby, held her when she needed burping, snuggled with her as he rocked her to sleep.

He had been the devoted father Abi knew, deep in her soul, he would be. The male counterpart to the mother she'd always wished she had been, hoped she would be someday. But she'd never even come close to having a family. Never dated a guy seriously enough to contemplate babies with him.

Because in the back of her mind, none of them ever measured up to the man in front of her car. Or to the daughter she figured was hiding in the house.

"Are you gonna sit there all night?" he called without moving. "If so, don't bother coming back."

She had to get out of the car. "Baby steps," she whispered to herself. "One thing at a time."

And the first thing Abi had to do was get out of the car. Before she could talk herself out of it, she did just that. Travis didn't say a word but waited for her to walk past him, arms still crossed, stern look on his face, then followed her through the front door.

Cassie sat on the couch, her back to Abi. She didn't turn around. The blonde sat close to her, though they weren't touching. She looked back at Travis, willing her arms to stay at her sides so she couldn't wring her hands.

He walked past and took a seat next to Cassie. He motioned toward the recliner. "Have a seat."

Abi did, clutching her purse with one hand. Perched nervously on the edge of the chair, she stared at the bag, too scared to look up at her daughter.

Travis introduced them. Sort of. "Cassie, this is Abi. The

woman who left you with me."

That was her cue. Abi looked up to see Cassie staring at her hands where they were folded in her lap. "Hi, Cassie." What else was there to say?

Cassie didn't say anything right away. In fact, if Abi had to guess, nearly four minutes passed before she said anything. An eternity. "I'll get tested. If I'm a match, I'll donate, but I don't want to meet my grandparents, and I don't want to see you again either."

"I understand." A tear slid down Abi's cheek. It wasn't what she hoped for, but it was what she expected. "Thank you."

Her daughter gave a slight shrug. "I'm not doing it for you or for him. I'm doing it because it's the right thing to do. If Grandpop needed a transplant and Uncle Jay had a kid no one knew about, I'd want that kid to be willing to help him. It's what Jesus would do. But I don't want to have anything to do with any of you outside of the medical stuff."

Travis rested his hand on Cassie's back, running it up and down, comforting her.

"I understand, but thank you. It means the world to me." Abi told her again. "If you ever change your mind, I hope you'll contact me. But if you never do, I hope you know I did what I thought was right, and I'm glad you and your dad are doing so well." She swiped at her cheeks and turned to Travis. "I'll let you know what she needs to do to get tested."

He nodded and stood. "Thank you for coming."

And that was it. Somehow, her legs straightened until she stood, too. With a nod, she headed for the door. She heard solid footsteps behind her and knew Travis followed. He didn't say a word until she was out the door.

"Thank you for giving me Cassie, Abi."

Abi turned to face him. No emotion showed on his face at all. "I'm glad she has you, Travis." She brushed more tears away. "She has a much better life here than I ever could have given her."

He nodded. "We have a good life we love. Don't expect her to call you anytime soon."

"I don't. I just wanted her to know that she could, if she ever changes her mind."

"Goodbye, Abi."

One side of her mouth quirked up, just a bit. "Bye, Travis. I'll call you with the information."

"A text is fine. Or an email. You can find mine on the Serenity Landing High School website."

Of course. He wouldn't want to talk to her if he didn't have to. She nodded again. "Okay." His bright blue eyes held her gaze for an eternity before tears blurred her vision once more. Before they could fall, she turned and headed to the car. She couldn't hope for more.

Except that she did.

There was no future for her and Travis. There never had been.

But maybe, just maybe, her daughter would decide she wanted to get to know her mother after all.

Even a little bit.

Abi would take anything.

She just prayed she wouldn't be left with nothing at all.

Chapter Six

Travis didn't round the corner to see Abi getting in the car, but he did watch until she drove away, nearly ten minutes later.

After listening to her earlier in the day, he understood a little better why she had done what she'd done, but that didn't mean he wanted her back in his life - or his daughter's life.

He was proud of Cassie for making the decision she had. So proud he was going to let her go to prom, though he hadn't told her that yet. Truth be told, Travis probably would have let her go anyway, but being so mature about everything solidified the decision.

For a while after he sat on the bed and told her the whole story, she'd sat next to him, just sitting there, thinking. Then she'd asked for some time, which he'd given her. He'd used the time to work on play stuff and conference called with the vice principal and Lindy, his student director. A couple hours later, Cassie came out and told him what she'd decided. Get tested and donate if she's a match, but nothing to do with the maternal side of her family. He couldn't say that he blamed her.

Kristy had been a God-send as well. Spending time with Cassie during the afternoon and evening when he had some work he *had* to get done - including rehearsal for the play later in the week. Being there for moral support for both of them when Abi showed up and, at the same time, lending an air of family to them that could, at least in theory, discourage Abi from thinking she had a place in their lives.

After the car turned up Arizona Avenue and the taillights disappeared from view, Travis went back inside to see his daughter still sitting stoically on the couch. He sat next to her and she leaned into him before he could get his arm around her.

"I'm proud of you, punkin." Travis kissed the top of her head. "As much as neither one of us like it, it's the right thing to do."

She sniffled. "I know."

Kristy reached over and squeezed Cassie's hand. "Now that that's over, why don't I dish up some ice cream?"

Cassie shook her head against him. "No, thanks. I think I'm going to go to bed in a few minutes. It's been a long day and I'm exhausted."

"I think I am, too," he told them. Possibly with the help of a couple Tylenol PM. Sure to knock him out. "Do you want to go to school tomorrow?"

"Not really. Can I take tomorrow off, too?"

"Yeah." Travis tilted her head up with a finger under her chin. "But that's it. You need to be at rehearsal tomorrow night. Thursday, it's back to normal."

"I know."

Kristy gave her another squeeze and stood. "I'll get out of your hair then." She ran a hand over the back of Cassie's head then kissed her fingertips and pressed them against his cheek. "Call me later, or I'll see you in the morning."

"Probably just see you at the meeting."

Her nose wrinkled in the cute little way he adored. "I forgot about that. You just had to remind me, didn't you?"

Travis grinned at her. "Don't want to stay for the late meeting after school, do you?"

"No." Her fingers brushed through what was left of his faux-hawk. "I'll see you there."

They talked about the mundane for another minute before she let herself out.

Cassie and Travis just sat there, each lost in their own thoughts for longer than he cared to admit. "You want some good news, punkin?"

"Sure."

"You can go to prom with Zach."

He expected schoolgirl squeals and a big hug, but instead he got a slightly enthusiastic, "Awesome."

"You don't want to call him and let him know?"

She shrugged. "I'll text him later."

"We'll have some ground rules and curfew and all that, but I know how much you want to go, and I like Zach a lot."

"Thanks, Daddy."

"I love you, Cassie. Do you know how much I love you?" A smile crossed his face as he thought of the game they'd played all the time when she was little.

"A lot a lot a lot a lot," she replied. "More than all the stars in the sky or the grass on the ground or the sand by the sea or the trees standing tall. More than the bugs in summer, the snow in winter, the flowers in spring or the leaves in fall. You love me more, much more, than anything."

"You got that right."

Her other arm flung around his middle and squeezed. "Thank you, Daddy." Her voice was husky with emotion.

"For what?"

"For loving me. For not dropping me off in a trash can somewhere when she left me."

His other arm came around her, holding her tight. "I might not have known about you, but I could never do that. Not ever."

"Will you keep me forever?" she asked, her voice small and reminiscent of another game they used to play.

"Forever and always, dear one," he told her, not adding theother lines they'd made up over the years. About her leaving him for some boy one day when she wanted to get married. For now, she needed to know she would always have a home with him.

And she always would.

Forever and always. Until the stars didn't shine and there were no more diamonds to mine.

She was his world.

"Okay! One last time, everyone! Just the finale!"

The orchestra had already left, so Travis motioned to the sound guys in the back of the theater and music piped through the speakers. He did his best to watch everything and pointed out a slight misstep to one of the secondary characters. The kid nodded but continued on. Cassie, as always, was amazing. He tried not to be biased, but she really came into her own on stage.

Too bad Abi would never see it.

It had been thirty-six hours, and he hadn't heard anything, but he couldn't worry about her. They had their spring production in just a couple hours and his focus had to be on it. By the time they dismissed a bit later, they were as ready as they'd ever be. Zach was going to do a great job as the male lead and Cassie had overcome her stress levels to put on a great performance as the second biggest female role.

"Everyone take it easy for a while and I'll see you back here at five-thirty!" As they started to disperse, he hollered one more time. "Don't forget to eat dinner!"

Cassie descended the steps and came to sit next to him in the fourth row. She didn't say anything as he made a few more notes on his clipboard. He finished about the time everyone cleared out of the theater.

"How's your day been?" he asked, one arm looping around her seat.

She gave a half-shrug. "Okay. Tried not to think about any of it. Do you think she's left yet?"

"I have no idea. I haven't heard from her at all. I'm not sure where she's staying." He massaged the back of her neck for a minute. "Are you changing your mind about seeing her?"

Cassie shook her head. "I don't want anything to do with any of them. They didn't want me. Now I don't want them."

Travis nodded. "I understand. Do you want some of my pizza? It'll be here in about half an hour."

"No thanks. Some of us are going to the Serenity Landing Chick-fil-A. We'll be back before five-thirty."

"Who's driving?"

"Zach."

"Does he have his mom's van or his dad's truck?"

She smiled. "Neither. He got his car a couple weeks ago, but it needed new tires. He finally got them yesterday."

"How many seatbelts?"

"Five."

"How many people with you?" Yeah. He was over-protective. But he remembered too many close calls with over-full cars in high school.

"Zach is driving. I get shotgun and three people in the back."

Travis kissed the side of her head. "Good."

She pulled her cell phone out of her pocket when it buzzed. "Zach just pulled up outside." Before she left, Cassie gave him a quick kiss on the cheek. "Love you, Daddy."

He grinned. Not only did he get a "love you", but a "Daddy", too. Even if there was no one else around. "Love you, too, punkin."

She bounded up the aisle, dark hair flying behind her, stopping to talk to Kristy for a minute before she left.

"You guys ready for tonight?" Kristy collapsed into the seat next to him.

"I think so. They've worked hard and they're a good group of kids. Talented group."

She rested her head against his shoulder. "They'll be fine. How about you?"

"Busy weekend, but I'm used to it."

"I mean with everything else. With Cassie's mom showing up. Old feelings resurfacing?"

He shrugged and took a swig of water out of the bottle. "It's not like Abi's an ex-girlfriend or ex-wife. Her brother was my best friend, and I hung out with her family. I understand a little better why she left Cassie with me, but that doesn't mean there's some relationship to salvage. If anything, I feel sorry for her missing out on Cassie's life, but there was never anything between me and Abi. I almost kissed her. Once. I knew her for almost two and a half years after that and nothing *ever* happened." He had to keep telling himself that.

"But you liked her and you loved Mark. He was your best friend. And you liked her parents, right?" *Cassie. She exists. There must have been* something *with Abi.*

Travis hadn't told Kristy everything about how Cassie had been conceived. She knew he'd been with several girlfriends and that "Cassie's biological mother" was his only one-night stand. She knew it had been years earlier and, since Cassie's birth, the move home and his recommitment to Christ, he'd been living a Christian life. He'd kissed a few women but nothing more.

He'd never told anyone everything about his relationship with Abi. Not his mom. Not Cassie earlier in the week. And he wasn't ready to tell Kristy either.

Finally, he propped a foot up on the arm of the seat in front of him and told her a version of the truth. "I liked Abi a lot, and I thought about asking her out after she graduated from high school, but after that night... I talked to her dad once and her once. That's it."

"So you did have some feelings for her, even if they never developed into more."

"True." He contemplated each word. "But there's no relationship to remember. No residual affection or anything."

"If it didn't affect you, it wouldn't be normal."

He ran a hand through his hair. He'd have to fix his faux-hawk before show time. "Okay. It's affected me. I don't want her here." He gave voice to the fear he barely let himself recognize. "What if she tries to take Cassie from me?"

Kristy's hand rested on the back of his neck as she gently massaged. "Do you really think a judge is going to give her custody?"

"Technically, a judge never gave me custody. Abi bolted, and that was it. My name was on the birth certificate. I never tried to get child support from her. There's never been any legal action of any kind. For all I know, she still has legal custody of Cassie. Never had a DNA test done. Nothing." The thought hadn't bothered him since Cassie had turned six-months-old, and it seemed obvious Abi wasn't coming back.

Her fingers expertly kneaded the space between the tendons of his neck. "Do you have any reason to believe she might not be your daughter?"

Travis shook his head. "No. Abi wasn't promiscuous." In fact, he'd always thought the opposite. That it had been her first experience, and her words earlier in the week had confirmed it.

"I can't imagine a judge ignoring the last fifteen years, but maybe you should call a lawyer."

That was something he needed to put on his to-do list, just to cover all the bases. And he would. On Monday. After the musical was over, and he could breathe again. A glance at his watch told him it was time to get his pizza from the driver who would be pulling up any minute.

The rest of the night went both fast and slow. By the time he made it home, Cassie was already fast asleep, tired after her big performance. She'd done wonderfully.

He stood in her doorway, watching her sleep, moonlight filtering through the blinds and the sheer curtains. A small smile crossed his face as he thanked God once more for the gift He'd give him in the form of the daughter he didn't know how to live without.

After a quick shower, he pulled on his favorite pajama pants, the ones he wore every night during a performance, and was asleep almost before his head hit the pillow.

Travis's feet hit the floor on the side of the bed, and he ran his hand through his hair, jaw creaking as he yawned.

Fledgling bits of memory came back to him. A warm body cradled next to his in the dark. Kissing. More. Much more. The images sent heat flooding his cheeks. He couldn't remember the last time he'd woken up wishing his bed wasn't so cold and lonely.

"Morning, handsome." A very feminine voice purred in his ear as slender arms wrapped around him from behind.

His heart stopped, and he willed his breathing to slow down. Had he married Kristy? Why didn't he remember? A glance at his left hand, and hers, showed rings. That was a plus. Not remembering was not.

A slim thigh, encased in some kind of light, shiny purple pants came to dangle over the side of the bed next to his leg. "I wish you were on summer break already," the voice said. "I don't have to be at work for a while, and you wouldn't have to get up so early."

Travis had to figure out who this was. What was going on? But there, on the side table was a picture of him. With Cassie. And...

His eyes went wide and he turned. The woman flopped backward on the bed, smiling up at him as he took in the sight of her.

"Abi?"Travis sat straight up in bed, drenched in sweat as a bit of street or moonlight wormed its way in around the heavy, dark brown curtains in the room. His heart raced, and he didn't think he'd be able to catch his breath anytime this century.

Knees shaking, he made his way to the bathroom, stumbling against the wall before using the counter to prop himself up. It was a good thing he kept a real cup in there because the grip he used to keep it from spilling everywhere would have crushed a paper one. He guzzled about six ounces of water before refilling the cup and downing it again.

He sank down, back to the wall, staring at the doors of the vanity. His elbows rested on his knees as he buried his face in his hands.

When was the last time he'd dreamt of a woman in his bed?

When Cassie was a baby? Years. Longer than years. Over a decade. He couldn't remember the last dream he'd had - both that vivid and of that nature.

And to realize he wasn't dreaming about his girlfriend, the woman he was considering spending the rest of his life with. No. He dreamt of a woman who abandoned her baby. His baby. Because she'd been too much of a coward to talk to him, to let him help her figure out a way to hold things together so she could finish school, and they could raise their baby girl together. Here. In New York. Wherever. That didn't matter. That she'd run out on them did.

In the deep recesses of his mind, he remembered dreaming about Abi once or twice before that night. But it had never been anything like that. They'd gone on a dream-date or two. Dream-kissed. But they hadn't shared a bed or a daughter.

"Daddy?"

The knock on his bedroom door caught him off-guard. Trembling, he hoisted himself up, flipping the light back off as he went into his room. "What is it, sweetheart?"

"Are you okay? I thought I heard you fall." Her hair was tousled and sleep-filled eyes looked at him with concern.

"I'm fine. Just needed a drink and wasn't paying attention." He rested his hands on her shoulders. "Go back to bed." He kissed her forehead. "I didn't see you but for a minute earlier. You did great. You were made for that part."

A twinkle appeared in her eyes. "No. That part was made for me."

They laughed together, before he turned her around and lightly swatted her rear. "Bed, young lady. You have another performance tomorrow night and your director can be a real bear if he doesn't get enough sleep."

She shuddered as she walked away. "He's awful enough when he's rested."

He laughed again, grateful she'd driven the dreams so far away so quickly. "Cassie?"

She turned at the doorway to her room and waited for her to speak.

"I love you. I'm so glad God gave you to me."

Another smile lit her face. "I love you, too, Dad. And I'm so glad *she* walked off that day and left me with you. I can't imagine a better life somewhere else with *her*."

"You don't know that, but I'm glad it's you and me, kiddo. Now, get some sleep."

Her back turned to him as she nodded, and he headed to his own bed. This time sleep didn't come so easily as he turned the dream over and over in his mind. If Abi had come with him, instead of just leaving Cassie. If she'd told him weeks after that night that she was pregnant. She had to have known before he started dating Jennifer. Would he and Abi have made it work? Would they have dated? Gotten married? Moved back to Serenity Landing together and prayed his parents would help them through the tough times when hers bailed?

He found no answers in the swirls on the ceiling. Finally, heart still heavy, he prayed to the God who created the stars on the other side of the swirls. The One who held the whole universe in the palm of His hand.

When sleep found him a few minutes later, peace filled his heart and in his mind that passed all human understanding. Despite all of the turmoil of the last few days, he slept.

Chapter Seven

Abi looked in the mirror, triple checking to make sure the wig cap was in place. Once certain, she took the red hair and slipped it on. Much shorter than her normal length. Heavy bangs over her forehead would drive her nuts, but it would all be worth it. The usual pantsuit or nice jeans and blouse were still in the closet. Instead, Abi had donned a denim jumper dress that came to mid-calf with a bright yellow t-shirt underneath. Knock-off Birkenstocks and bright purple and green knee-high socks completed the strange look.

After double checking the directions with the desk clerk, she hopped in the car, coming to a stop ten minutes later in front of the high school. Abi didn't know where to go once there – and the desk clerk hadn't either – but the steady stream of people headed through the doors pointed the way. She stood in line with cash clutched in one hand.

"Anyone with reserved tickets, please head for the theater." A loud, female voice caught Abi's attention.

It took everything in her not to stare as Cassie stood

near the sign for the play, smiling brightly at the patrons who headed her way. She directed them around the corner, hugging one young girl who came through. Abi shuffled forward, watching out of the corner of her eye and listening intently to everything her daughter said. Cassie's ability to be outgoing and gregarious definitely came from her father. Generally, Abi was much happier in the back of the room observing than she was in front of people. Over the years, she'd forced herself to learn, but would never be truly comfortable with it.

Abi did her best to hide her surprise, and fear, when the woman sitting at the table looked up.

"How many tickets?" the blonde from Travis's house asked.

She held up one finger and didn't say a word, avoiding the woman's eyes all together. Abi gave a teenager the money, took the offered ticket, and the blonde woman pointed out the general admission seats.

Purely by accident, Abi bumped into Cassie as she headed for the auditorium. The teen apologized but showed no indication she recognized her birth mother. Abi followed the stream of people into the foyer area and was directed by another cast member, this one dressed as a townsperson, to the best seats left in the general admission section.

"Is there any way to find out if there's just one better seat available?" she asked quietly. "I wouldn't normally, and I'm happy back here, but I'm a relative of one of the cast members. She doesn't know I'm here yet, but I'd love to be able to see a bit better."

A grin crossed the girl's face. "You're going to surprise her later?"

Abi just gave a "what do you think?" look and shrug rather than confirming or denying.

The townswoman thought for a minute before responding. "Mr. H always gets four tickets for every show. His parents are coming every night since his daughter is in the program, but her aunt and uncle are coming tomorrow, so I doubt the other seats will be used. I'll find out and if they're empty, I'll let you know. And if not, I can probably find another spot for you, okay?"

"Thank you."

"Sit here for now, and I'll be back in a bit."

Abi nodded and sat, flipping through the program, running her fingers over Cassie's name. Tears filled her eyes as it sunk in. Her daughter's name was listed a couple of places in the program, but on the official cast list she was "Cassandra Connealy-Harders." The rest listed her as "Cassie Harders" but knowing that, at least sometimes, she used the full name Abi had given her, brought both unspeakable joy and unbearable pain.

In the back was a section for ads, and there was a small one from Travis's parents to Cassie – telling her how proud they were of her. Abi was, too. About ten minutes before the curtain was to go up, the young lady caught Abi's eye from the far side of the theater and motioned to her.

"Mr. H's family did use all of their seats," she whispered when Abi got to her side. "My brother didn't come though, so you can sit with my family if that's okay with you."

"Thank you, so much."

The girl led Abi to the third row from the front, right in the middle. The end seat was open and waiting. She smiled politely at the people sitting next to her and turned her attention back to the program. The lights dimmed briefly and went back up for a few minutes before dimming completely. A voice called out from onstage, capturing her attention completely for the next ninety minutes until intermission.

One actress in particular kept Abi enthralled. Cassie was good. Very good. After the lights came up, most of the people in the seats left for the sodas and cupcakes available to purchase to support the theater department. The people in front of her stayed put. Two of them anyway. Abi couldn't help but overhear their conversation, though they were obviously trying to be quiet.

"Cassie's doing great," the woman told the man in a stage whisper. "She did last night, too, but I was afraid opening night euphoria was carrying her through and that, after everything else this week, she'd be off her game tonight."

"Me, too," the man whispered back. "But she's great. As always. She is her father's daughter."

The woman ran an affectionate hand through his hair. "And he's his father's son."

The man threw back his head and laughed out loud. "I couldn't get up there and do that if my life was on the line."

A feeling of dread had been growing as they spoke. These were Travis's parents. Cassie's grandparents. People who had every reason in the world to hate her and probably did. She wondered what they thought about her showing up, about Cassie's decision, about Abi in general.

Abi's stomach continued to churn as the cast took the stage again. Nearly an hour later, they came to the final dance number with a couple dozen people on stage at once. Her eyes remained glued to Cassie as she sang and danced on the balcony of a castle.

But then everything went in slow motion.

The male actor up there with her tripped over something. Cassie did her best to try to help him maintain his balance, but with everything slowed down so time nearly stood still, they both crashed through the railing designed more for aesthetics than protection.

Cassie's scream echoed throughout the room as her partner grabbed for her and the side of the balcony. He managed to grab hold of the edge so he was dangling with his feet about thirty-six inches above the floor.

The floor where Cassie landed with a thud.

No one on the ground had been hit, but everything came to a screeching halt. Travis ran onto the stage, waving the rest of the actors to the side. His parents stood, watching as their granddaughter lay motionless on the stage. Travis knelt next to Cassie, along with another adult and two of the other students.

Travis had his phone out, talking to someone on the other end, probably 911.

A voice came over the loudspeakers. "Ladies and gentlemen, we apologize for the delay but at this time, we're going to ask for you to leave the auditorium in an orderly fashion. We ask that you remain in the building, in the designated area until the ambulance has arrived. We will be evaluating the situation over the next few minutes and will make an announcement regarding the rest of the production when the decision has been made. Thank you for your patience and cooperation."

All around Abi, people gathered their things and headed for the doors. She heard whispered prayers and concerns from all around. Before the room was empty, sirens could be heard speeding their way toward the high school.

By the time the paramedics knelt next to Cassie on the stage, she was moving, and Abi could hear her moans through the sound system. Abi hung back, just a bit while Cassie's grandparents made their way up the side stairs. Staying in the shadows, she heard Cassie answering questions from one of the paramedics.

They rolled her carefully and put a back board on her. Abi thought she heard the word "precaution" from someone, as they wrestled Cassie's big costume into place. It had to concern Travis. Some of the costumes, Cassie's included, had to be on loan or rented from somewhere. They were too nice, too Broadway, for most high schools to have on hand.

Most of the cast had disappeared backstage, but the boy playing the male lead hung behind, holding her hand. Was he her boyfriend?

Travis's voice drifted over. "Shoot. Let me grab my bag out of the sound booth, and I'll meet you outside." They snapped the gurney up as Travis ran toward the stairs. He didn't pay any attention as he trotted down them. Abi tried to sink back into the wall, but there wasn't time to move anywhere. He knocked against her, turning and the first half of a "Sorry" came out before he realized who she was. Abi had known all along the disguise wouldn't hold up to close scrutiny.

He grabbed her arm and pulled her up the aisle. "What are you doing here, Abi?"

She winced and tried to keep up with his near run. "I just wanted to see her in the play. That's all. But I couldn't leave when she got hurt."

He let go long enough to grab a soft sided briefcase before dragging her out of the building.

Abi's wrist ached just a bit from his grip, but she knew he wasn't trying to hurt her. "I just wanted to watch her in the play, Travis. That's it. I never planned to see either one of you."

A glare almost made her stop talking.

"And now I just want to know if she's okay. Will you at least text me, and let me know?" She wouldn't follow them to the hospital, wouldn't try to see her. Abi just wanted to know her daughter would be all right.

"You mean you want to know if she's still a potential

donor for your dad."

"No!" Abi couldn't believe he'd accuse her of that. Except he was right. Sort of. She hated that he was right. Hated how shallow it made her sound. But she'd promised herself she'd be honest with him, no matter what he asked. "Well, yeah. Maybe for a second, but mostly I just want her to be okay. That's the most important thing. Honest."

They reached the front of the ambulance as Cassie was loaded into the back.

Travis's shoulders slumped as he let go. "Fine. My parents will tell you how to get to the hospital. Stay in the waiting room. I'll come find you when we know something, but don't expect to see her."

Abi shook her head. "I don't."

He looked past her, over her shoulder. "Mom, help her get to the hospital?" he asked, nodding at Abi. Without waiting for a response, he climbed into the cab of the ambulance, shutting the door behind him, and turning to look at Cassie in the back of the vehicle.

They took off, no sirens, which made Abi feel a bit better.

"Honey, they're going to Cox South." Travis's mom, put her hand on Abi's arm. "Do you know how to get there?"

Abi shook her head.

"Are you a friend of Travis's? Or Cassie's?"

She tried to say something, but had to clear her throat a couple of times first. "Something like that."

"Why don't you follow us?" she offered after giving brief directions. "It's not too far. If we get separated, head east until you get to National. It's a big red brick building just north of James River Freeway. Anyone should be able to tell you where it is if you get lost."

Abi managed a weak nod. "Thank you."

Mrs. Harders pointed out their car and, a minute later,

Abi pulled up behind them on the drive leading out of the school.

Fifteen minutes later, she walked into the emergency room waiting area. Travis's parents were already seated, his dad's arm wrapped around his mom's shoulders.

Abi sat near but not with them. They nodded her direction, acknowledging her, but not saying anything. The big skirt on the jumper made it easier to pull her knees into her chest, giving her a place to rest her forehead.

They'd been sitting there a while when someone sat next to her and a gentle hand rested on her back.

"Are you okay, Abi?"

Abi looked up through tear-filled eyes to see Travis's mom sitting there. "How'd you know my name?"

His mom held out a box of generic hospital tissue. "It's pretty obvious, though the wig is a nice touch. You and Travis didn't tell us who you were and why you'd be coming to the hospital with us, but you're obviously very upset. Cassie's birth mother has been in town. It makes sense."

Abi sniffled and took the offered Kleenex. "Do you hate me?"

Mrs. Harders shook her head. "No. Fifteen years ago we might have, and we didn't at first. It took us a long time, but we figured you must have had a good reason for what you did. Watching Travis struggle to be a single dad took a toll on us. We helped but didn't enable, and it took him a while to find his stride. He's a fabulous father and a better man, but he wouldn't be the person he is now if things had been different. I don't know that Travis or Cassie have made it to this point, but a few years ago we decided instead of hating you, we'd be thankful you left Cassie with Travis and that he came home. We'd been praying he would since he left and by giving him Cassie, you sent him our direction."

"I always hoped that's how all of you would see it."

"Do you want to talk about it?

Haltingly, Abi told her the story. Not quite all of it, because she didn't know if they knew about the roofied coffee. Or the truth about her history with Travis.

When Abi finished, the older woman nodded her head. "Once Keith and I talked about it, we figured it was probably something along those lines."

Abi rested her head on Mrs. Harders's shoulder. "Thank you for being so understanding."

Keith stood up as someone walked into the seating area. Abi looked up and there he stood.

Travis.

And he looked furious.

Chapter Eight

W hat was Mom doing?

Her arm was around Abi's shoulder and Abi's head rested against her. Were they bonding? Travis didn't like that idea one little bit.

And what was with the red wig and everything?

"How is she?" Mom asked.

Travis decided to talk to her later about her apparent acceptance of the woman who abandoned her granddaughter. "She's shaken up. They're going to keep her here overnight for observation and she'll be sore for a few days but overall, she's fine."

"Can we see her?" That came from Dad.

Abi didn't even look at him.

Good.

Because she wasn't going to see Cassie anytime soon.

"They're moving her upstairs in a few minutes. I'll go with her, and you guys can see her up there. Technically, visiting hours are over, but since she's just getting here they'll let you in for a few minutes."

"Good." Also Dad.

Abi stood, wiping her eyes. What had she and Mom been talking about? "Thanks for letting me stay for a bit. For letting me know how she is."

Travis shrugged. He didn't really like Abi, but she was there, knew Cassie had been hurt, and she *was* Cassie's mother. His phone buzzed and pulled it out of his pocket. "Cassie says it's going to be about half an hour before they move her," he told his parents. "She wants to know if you guys would come back to see her."

Abi's eyes looked up at him, guarded hopefulness shining in them, but the look he gave her quickly squelched that. Cassie didn't even know she was here. And she wouldn't know unless his parents told her before he had a chance to tell them not to.

"I'm surprised her friends aren't here," Dad said, oblivious to the visual by-play going on between them.

"Kristy told them to keep an eye on Cassie's Facebook page rather than all rush over here. I posted on there earlier for them not to come." It was the easiest way to communicate with all of them at once.

"Not even Zach?" Mom's eyes twinkled, making Travis wonder just what Cassie had told her.

"He and Maile may be by later," he acknowledged. "But no one else." Seeing her two best friends would be good for her and for them. Travis knew they were worried. Zach actually texted to ask about her. He had Travis's cell phone number for emergencies related to the plays, but he'd never used it before. Travis nodded toward the desk. "If you ask them, they'll tell you where she is. Tell her I'll be back in a few minutes."

Mom nodded before giving him a big hug. "She's going to be fine." Before letting go of him, his mom whispered, "Don't be too hard on Abi, Trav. She's been through a lot.

She did what she thought was best for everyone, even if she didn't handle it quite right at the time."

Travis hugged her back. "It's under control, Mom."

She gave him another pat on the back before walking off with his dad.

"I'll leave now," Abi said, slinging her purse over her shoulder.

"Why are you still in town?" Travis asked, shoving his hands deep in his pockets.

"When I waited for you in your living room, I noticed the pictures of Cassie in a play so I got online and looked up the theater department at the high school. Plus, I wanted to get your email address. I saw the play was this weekend, and Cassie had a major role. I wanted to see, that's all. I didn't want either of you to know I was here. Didn't want to bother you at all."

Tears flowed freely down Abi's cheeks as she pulled off first the wig and then the wig cap holding her hair in place. "She's amazing, Travis. And you're a wonderful dad. I knew you would be. Thank you for taking care of my baby."

With a sigh, he did the right thing. For the first time in over sixteen years, he gave Abi a hug. Travis pulled her into his arms and wrapped them around her, letting her cry into his black Serenity Landing Theater T-shirt.

Holding her close, one arm around her shoulders. The other hand running up and down her back, something stirred deep within him. Something he hadn't felt in a very long time. Something that scared him.

Not the feeling per se, but who was evoking it in him.

Abi.

Travis tried to forget the last time he'd felt it, really felt it, was with her, too.

The woman who'd abandoned her daughter.

His daughter.

The one woman he could go his whole life without seeing again, while, at the same time, seeing her every day in his daughter who was her spitting image.

Travis didn't know how long they stood there before her sobs slowed and she moved away.

"Than..." She stopped mid-word as she saw something past his shoulder.

Travis turned to see Kristy standing there, her face an unreadable mask. "I'll text you later," he told Abi, taking a big step back. "And I'll see if they can test Cassie while she's here anyway."

Abi nodded. "Thank you." She snatched her purse from the floor where it had fallen and practically ran out of the emergency room.

"How's Cassie?" Kristy asked, tossing her purse onto a chair and sitting in another one.

"It wasn't what it looked like," he told her. "Abi was crying. I couldn't just..."

She still didn't look at him. "I know. But how's Cassie?"

Travis sank into another seat and told her what the doctors had said. "There's nothing going on with her, Kris." Would Kristy believe him? He'd seen the doubt written in her eyes.

"I believe you." Her words said one thing, her body language another.

Travis moved to sit next to her, taking her right hand in his as his left arm wrapped around her shoulders. "Have you thought any more about what we talked about the other day?"

"What's that?" At least she relaxed into his side.

That there weren't the tingles he'd felt while holding Abi didn't matter. "Getting married."

"Now's not the time to be thinking about that, Trav.

Not with Cassie's birth mom back in the picture and her grandfather so ill. And being hurt?" She shook her head. "We can talk about it again after everything calms down."

Travis kissed the top of her head next to where his cheek had rested. "Thank you." He wouldn't stop thinking about it. Kristy needed to know where she fit in his life. He needed to know where she fit in his life.

"For what?"

"For being there for Cassie this week. She needed someone besides me to talk to."

"She's a good kid. She made the decision on her own before I even got there."

"I know, but you reaffirmed her decision. If you hadn't, she might have changed her mind. I may not be happy with how Abi's dad handled everything and what he accused me of, but I don't want him dead when there's a way to save his life. Just like Cassie."

Her other hand reached over and drew random patterns on his. "You never have told me what happened with you and Abi. Obviously, you slept together, but..." She took a deep, shaky breath. "Were you involved?"

Travis flashed back to Abi, at seventeen, sitting next to him on the back deck of her parents' house while her dad grilled burgers. Her shoulder rubbing against his. The stars and... He shook his head to break out of it.

"Not really. Friends. Her older brother was my best friend at the time. You know I've slept with several women, though none since I got Cassie. That was when I got back into church and started down the straight and narrow again. I'm not proud of that part of my past, but I can't regret Cassie. Never could I do that." He gave her an abbreviated version of events, mentioning that somehow, they'd both been drugged and how her dad had accused him of being the culprit. "I didn't talk to her from the time I dropped her off the next morning until the day she left Cassie with me. To this day, I don't know why our lack of birth control never occurred to me. I should have checked with her a few weeks later, just to be sure, but the thought that she could be pregnant never entered my mind."

"So you really were shocked?"

"Shocked would have been the understatement of the year. I was way beyond shocked. But there was never anything between me and Abi except friendship because she was my best friend's little sister."

"Did you want there to be? Would you have married her if you'd known she was pregnant?"

That question was harder to answer. So he didn't. He thought about it long enough that his cell phone buzzed. "They're getting ready to take her upstairs." He kissed her hair again. "Are you coming?"

She nodded and they stood.

Travis pulled her into his arms, and tipped her chin with a crooked forefinger. "There is no me and Abi, Kris. There never was. Today, it's you and me." He leaned down enough to brush his lips against hers before coming back for a longer, more searching kiss. One intended to convince her of his feelings.

If only it didn't feel like he was also trying to convince himself.

"You don't have to spend the night, Dad." Cassie looked frustrated enough to be in the horrid hospital gown. Having Travis stay the night wasn't improving her mood. Not even Zach and Maile popping in for a few minutes was enough to cheer her up.

"Wanna tell me what's really bugging you, kiddo?"

The room was dim with most of the lights off and the curtains closed as tightly as it were going to get. She fiddled with the blanket, but he couldn't see her well enough to know what she was thinking.

"Who were you talking to right before we left the school?"

Travis blew a prayer heavenward. So much for not telling her. "Abi."

"It didn't look like her."

"She wore a wig because she didn't want us to recognize her. Said she looked at the theater website and wanted to see you in the play."

"She saw me all right," Cassie muttered.

"It wasn't your fault. It was an accident."

"I know, but still." The silence stretched to several minutes. "What did she want at the ambulance?"

"She wanted me to let her know if you were okay."

"Was she here?"

Travis nodded. "For a little bit. She left when I went to get Mom and Dad."

"So they've met her?"

"She and Mom were thick as thieves when I got out there."

"Great."

"What?"

"If Grandma likes her and wants her to hang around more, even without me, she will, and I'll hear about it all the time until I finally give in and at least pretend to be all happy with my new-found birth mother. Because otherwise Grandma will go all matchmakery on us. At least you've already got Kristy, or she'd be trying to get you and *her* together, and you know it."

She had a point and it was one of many reasons he was glad Mom hadn't seen him hugging Abi. Because of his relationship with Kristy, Mom would have been more subtle about it, but her matchmaking side would certainly come out.

"There's nothing for you or Kristy to worry about. I have no intention of a relationship of any kind with Abi. Just whatever we need to do for her dad and all that. If you decide to have a relationship with her, I'll see or talk to her about you, but that's it."

Deep inside, in the place Travis didn't like to go, the one where the still small voice seemed to live, he wondered if that was really true. If he wasn't dating Kristy, would he be wondering if there could be a future with Abi? Especially if Cassie decided to have a relationship with her?

He squelched those thoughts deep down and pulled the blanket up to his chin as he tried to get comfortable on the fold out plastic chair that wasn't comfortable as a chair, much less a bed.

A long, miserable night later, Travis sat in the rocking chair, leaving the fold out chair unfolded as his parents, Zach, Maile and Kristy joined them.

"Are you going to be able to perform tonight?" Maile asked Cassie. "I mean they're letting you go home soon, but what about the play."

Cassie picked at the blanket. "The doctor said it was up to me, but he'd advise taking tonight off, and maybe I can go tomorrow."

"What about Tina's part? If she's got yours, could you do hers? She's not in much, and she's not essential to any of the big dance numbers so you don't even need to know them."

"She's got a point, punkin." Cassie hated it when he called her that in front of others. "You could take Tina's part tonight." There was no love lost between the two girls. Tina was a junior, a young junior, with a crush on Zach and an ego commiserate with a much better actress.

"Maybe. When do I have to decide?"

Travis shrugged. "By cast call. Gotta know which make up and costumes to put on who. I'm sure she knows it's a possibility."

"Could we do halvsies? She does half, I do half?" He'd bet good money Cassie really wanted to do her part, but didn't want to admit she might not be able to.

And so he shook his head. "I don't think so. If someone got hurt or sick in the middle maybe, but not from the get-go."

"What if I start and decide I can't finish?" She still wouldn't look at him.

"If you're not sure you can do the whole thing, then you need to let Tina, honey. You can either take her part, or sit with your grandparents or stay home if you want to. It's your call, but if you're not sure, the responsible, adult thing to do is bow out."

"I've done enough adult stuff this week," she muttered. "I'm willing to try to save my nearly non-existent grandpa's life, aren't I?"

"And I'm very proud of you for that. And it's one of many reasons why I'm letting you go to prom if you still want to." Her head shot up at that, and her face flushed. He was embarrassing her. Part of his job as her dad. She looked first at Travis while he tried to conceal his grin and then Zach, who didn't do nearly as well.

His daughter bit her bottom lip before replying. "Of course I want to!"

Travis chuckled. "I figured. We still need to talk about ground rules, but you can go. With Zach," he clarified. He couldn't imagine either of them changing their minds, but wanted to be clear that Zach was the only option. She couldn't change her mind and go with someone else without clearance.

Cassie caught Maile's eye, and they squealed together. "Shopping trip!"

Great. There went more of his hard-earned cash. Maybe he hadn't thought this through.

"I'll take you next weekend," Kristy volunteered, her fingers linked through Travis's.

His phone buzzed and he took it out of his pocket.

DAD'S TAKEN A TURN. ANY WORD ON TESTING? HE'S OKAY FOR NOW, BUT WANTED TO GIVE YOU A HEAD'S UP.

No signature, but he knew who it was from even though he hadn't put her info in his phone. Plus she'd already texted several times to check on Cassie.

THEY DID A CHEEK SWAB. THAT'S ALL I KNOW. I'LL FIND OUT WHERE THEY SENT IT AND WHAT ELSE NEEDS TO BE DONE. Travis slid it under his leg but didn't tell anyone what it was about.

Travis knew it was the right thing to do, but that didn't mean he liked the idea that Cassie could save the man's life.

Not when he'd been so willing to throw Travis under the bus.

They would help.

But Travis wouldn't like it.

Chapter Nine

Abi texted the information for Dad's doctor to Travis. There was probably a more formal way to go about all of it, but she had no idea what it was. She just knew that if Cassie wasn't a match... As awful as Dad had been the whole time she was pregnant, he'd redeemed himself, somewhat, in the years since. Sort of. Mostly.

As she lay on the bed in her hotel room, wondering if Cassie was really okay, her phone rang.

"Hello?"

"Hi, Abi. Where are you exactly?"

Kevin. Her boss. Always a bit brusque, getting straight to the point, but with a heart of gold. "Just outside Springfield, Missouri until tomorrow. Why?"

"We've got a client there who needs a face-to-face meeting and proposal before hiring us. You have work clothes with you? I think you'd be perfect to work with them anyway. He sounds fairly clueless. You're the best with those types."

"I have enough for a couple days. You sure you want me to handle it?" She already dreaded telling Travis she'd be in town for a while longer, but at the same time, maybe she'd have the chance to see Cassie a bit more.

And Travis.

Abi couldn't deny the flutter she'd felt as Travis held her in his arms, letting her cry at the hospital. Her junior and senior year of high school flashed before her eyes. When she'd tried to be cool around Mark's incredibly cute friend. The one who barely knew the little sister was alive most of the time. Except that day at Chelsea Piers or when Mark and Brenda took off. Until near the end. The same one who'd taken such good care of her until she took advantage of him, even though they were both drugged.

Even all these years later, she could still see it in her mind's eye.

Abi's eyes fluttered open, and all she knew for sure was that she wasn't at home.

On a couch. Facing a refrigerator with a television sitting on a small table between her and the kitchen. She sat up and looked around, puzzled at the splitting headache. It took everything in her to stand, but she managed. When she turned, the smell of stale cigarettes caught her off-guard. What had happened?

There was rustling in the room to her right. Turning, she caught a glimpse of a bed and a bare back through open French doors. But whose? A wallet sat on the side table, and she picked it up. Some strange man's apartment in the middle of the night? This couldn't be good, but maybe she could get out before something worse happened. At least she was on the couch and fully clothed.

The face smiling off the driver's license sent a wave of relief through her. Travis. She was safe with Travis. But the couch was out of the question.

Not thinking about what she was doing or the potential

implications, Abi stripped off her jeans and went to slide under the covers on the other side of the bed. She had no intention of touching him. They were both adults. Surely they could share a bed, platonically.

But when he turned onto his side, facing her, all her fuzzy head wanted to do was kiss him. Just once when he wouldn't remember it. He'd be annoyed when he found her in his bed, but as long as the kiss stayed just with her, it would be okay.

Abi's forefinger brushed against his soft lower lip before she slid closer and covered his lips with her own. That was all it was supposed to be, but when he responded, just enough for the kiss to linger, she decided to try again.

And when his arm came around her and pulled her to him, deepening the kiss, bringing to the surface feelings Abi had no experience with...

His eyes fluttered open, and she could see a bit of shock register behind the sleepiness.

"Abi?"

All she could do was nod.

"Are you real?"

Abi nodded again then kissed him, stilling slightly when his hand first slid over her hip and onto the skin of her back, but throwing caution to the wind, she kissed him all the more.

Now, lying in her hotel bed, Abi shook her head to clear the last semi-coherent memory she had from that night. None of it was very clear, but once he started kissing her, it really went fuzzy.

With a sigh, she pulled her phone out and texted him. MY BOSS ASKED ME TO MEET WITH A LOCAL CLIENT. I'LL BE IN TOWN ALL WEEK. I WON'T BOTHER YOU BUT WANTED YOU TO KNOW.

She had enough time to pick up the remote and flip through the channels before he replied.

THANKS FOR TELLING ME.

Nothing else. Not that she'd expected much.

Abi grabbed her laptop bag and sat on the couch. No time like the present to review the information Kevin would have sent, certain she would accept the assignment to stay here a bit longer. He didn't know why she was here, but knew her well enough to know she wouldn't turn down his request.

The email was waiting in her inbox, just as she'd expected. The floor plan showed up as an attached jpeg. The questionnaire from the potential client was a PDF file. No way to make notes on it, but she could see about printing it if this hotel had a business center. A phone call to the front desk confirmed her fears. They had a business center but no printing capability for guests. They didn't cater to the business traveler the way some hotels did. A glance at the clock told her the library across the street would already be closed.

That left her with only one option she could think of.

Another text.

Abi bit her lip waiting for the response from Travis. It was an address and a time with instructions that she'd need to be done by 6:30 so she'd better hurry.

She punched the information into the GPS on her phone. Just under four miles away. Snapping her laptop shut as she unplugged it, Abi wondered where he was sending her. Not his house. His parents'? Kristy's? Was Abi even sure the blonde wasn't his wife?

Ten minutes later, she pulled up in front of the nice brick home and knew instinctively this was where Travis had grown up. What could it have been like? Driving up to this place with a newborn baby in the back seat, unsure how his family would react. It couldn't have been easy. It had to have been much harder than her dropping Cassie off with him. She'd taken the coward's way out. But not Travis.

Travis's mom, Julie, stood in the driveway, talking with a woman with long, dark hair, perhaps a bit younger than Abi. Noting the time, Abi gathered her things and hurried up the walk.

Julie introduced them. "Abi, this is a writer friend of mine. Anise, this is Abi." No mention of her relationship to the family.

Abi shook the other woman's hand. "Nice to meet you."

"You, too." There was an accent, but Abi couldn't place where it was from. "I have to run. Thank you for your help, Julie." The two women hugged as Abi watched. Would she ever have a close relationship with someone else? Close enough to hug on a regular basis? When *was* the last time someone had just given her a good hug? Except for Travis at the hospital.

She and Julie took a step back so Anise could drive off, but before they went inside, Julie turned to her. Before Abi realized what was happening, she was wrapped in the arms of Travis's mother. Her eyes closed as warmth washed over her, but the hug didn't last long enough for her to truly sink into it like she had with Travis the day before.

As they went up the walk, Julie kept her arm around Abi's shoulder. "Travis didn't really say what it is you needed, honey. But if we can help…"

"I need to print a couple files out for work," she explained. "Maybe twenty pages total, tops, but there's no place to print at the hotel."

She motioned her further in. "Come on upstairs. That's where my office and the good laser printer are."

"Your office? I thought I heard Travis say you were retired?" Of course, that had been fifteen years earlier. A lot could change in that time, especially with a grandbaby to help raise.

"Oh, I am, but I'm finally trying to write my version of

the great American novel."

"Really?" *Color me impressed.* "How's it going?"

She gave a half shrug as they reached the second floor. "I'm on my sixth manuscript. I'm winning some contests and stuff, but no big bites from editors or agents yet."

"Well, good luck." Abi looked around Julie's office. Eclectic. Not how she would have pegged Julie Harders. She would have thought Travis's mom was more refined taste. It worked, just not what she expected.

And when Abi turned around, she was shocked by the sheer number of books in the bookcases. She tilted her head and read through the titles as the computer booted up.

"See anything you've read?" she asked.

"No, not yet." One full shelf was full of books she'd seen at her local Wal-Mart. The Cambridge Family by... the name on the spine was Linscott so that had to be right.

"Those are good ones if you like historical romance." She nodded toward the left end. "Grab the first one if you want. Borrow anything you like, especially if you're going to be here for a while, you might need something to do." Her eyes were soft as she looked up. "I'd love to see you some while you're here, get to know you better, but I also don't want to alienate my son and granddaughter."

Abi pulled the first book off the shelf and stared at the cover. A pretty brunette and a handsome blond man from sometime around the American Revolution if she wasn't mistaken.

"Computer's online. Print away."

Sitting in her chair, Abi logged into her email on the desktop and downloaded the files.

"What do you like to read?" Julie asked, scanning her shelves.

"Pretty much anything. Mostly romance though, I

guess."

"Contemporary or historical? Romantic comedy? More serious? Suspense?" She fired a bunch of questions, pulling random books off shelves as she did so. Did Abi like Jane Austen? What about Regencies? Or Victorian era England?

She stammered no to the Regency question, unwilling to admit she wasn't sure what a Regency was. The Jane Austen she'd suffered through her freshman year in college held bitter memories, but that probably had more to do with the fact it was the fall semester of 2001 than Jane Austen herself.

As soon as the printer stopped working, Abi logged out of her email and closed the files. A stack of books nearly a foot and a half high sat on top of the Cambridge Family book.

"Wow, Mrs. Harders. I can't read that many books in the next week."

Julie waved Abi off. "Take them. Read what you want. Don't read what doesn't interest you." Her neatly manicured finger pointed to one about halfway down the stack. "This one is by a local author. Travis had her in class his first year at the high school. Great historical romantic comedy."

"Good to know." She slid the papers into the folder.

"And I'm not Mrs. Harders, sweetheart." Her arm settled on Abi's shoulders. "You're my granddaughter's mother. Julie is fine."

Abi swallowed hard. What would Travis and Cassie think about that? "Okay then, Julie. Thank you very much for your hospitality."

Julie pulled a canvas tote out of a drawer and started putting the books in. "How long will you be in town?"

"At least until Friday. It depends on how this meeting goes. Sometimes, we meet once. Sometimes, we meet several times. Since the first meeting isn't until Thursday, I'll work from the hotel until then and if it's three or four meetings, they'll bleed into next week."

"What is it you do, anyway? I don't think Travis ever mentioned what your interests were."

"He never knew, I don't think. I didn't really know until my sophomore year of college, but I'm an interior designer. Usually, my company works with fairly high end clients. I don't know anything about this one yet."

"If you need anything else, feel free to call." She tucked a card in the bag. "My numbers and email are on there."

"Thank you."

"My pleasure."

By the time Abi climbed back in her car, she felt more than accepted by part of Travis's family. Julie and Keith waited in their car in the driveway until she drove off. Julie hadn't told her if Cassie was going to be in the musical that night, and Abi hadn't asked. She had the impression they'd be going either way though.

Back at the hotel she flipped through the information. Josh Wilson and the Serenity Landing Comedy Club. It had been given a facelift a few years earlier, but they'd recently expanded into the space next door, doubling their capacity, and they needed to unify the whole thing. The construction was already done, but it could be a pretty big project, depending on exactly what they wanted to do.

After pouring over it all for a couple of hours, Abi took a stretch break, ordered pizza, and settled in with the first Mya Elizabeth Linscott book. Page after page, she pulled Abi in, sucking her into the world created in the pre-American Revolution South. The religious aspect of the book caught her off-guard, and she pulled up Google on her phone. Who knew there were whole bookstores, a whole side of the publishing industry even, dedicated to religious, or Christian, fiction? Were all of the books Julie sent religious romances?

It didn't bother her, per se, like Abi knew it would her mother, but the sometimes casual way the characters talked to and about God, like He was right there, like He cared about them, was a bit unnerving at times. Were there really people out there who believed that way? Abi could believe it two hundred and some odd years ago, but now? That was harder.

Abi finished the book a few minutes before eleven. As tired as she felt, the bed didn't call her name just yet. She picked up another book, thankful she'd always been a fast reader. This one was by Pepper Basham. Her picture was on the back cover and she looked fun. The first few pages of *Twist of Faith* hooked her, though the story of a single father struck a bit too close to home. She wondered if Julie had picked it out on purpose.

It was after two by the time she closed the book, turned off the lights and slid under the covers. It would be so easy to slip back into the dark place Abi found herself from time to time, but she couldn't go there. And really, she had good reason not to. Travis and Cassie might be ostracizing her, but with them came hope for her dad and Travis's parents seemed much more accepting. Julie's newly forming friendship alone made the whole trip worthwhile, even if nothing more came from it.

Abi slid into a sleep she prayed would be dreamless.

Because if she had any more dreams about Travis, like the ones she'd had the week before setting out to find him, she'd go crazy.

CASSIE

"Zach's coming over for lunch." I lay on the couch with my feet propped up on the arm.

Dad finished tucking in his polo shirt as he walked into view. "I won't be here. I thought I was picking you up to take you to Grammy's?"

I shrugged. "I'm sore all over, and I really don't want to move. Grandma said she understood."

I could see Dad turning it over in his mind as a frown crossed his face. "I'm not sure I like it."

"It's *Zach*, Dad. Nothing's going to happen."

He sat on the coffee table. "Exactly. It's Zach. Your prom date. The guy you've been half in love with for years."

I felt the blood rush to my cheeks. "So?"

"He's been half in love with you, too," Dad reminded me gently. "I'm not sure it's a good idea."

It took the better part of ten minutes for me to wear him down. I think with everything else going on with Abi and her dad and my fall, he just didn't want to tell me no. If he could see us when Zach was here, he'd know he had no reason to be concerned. It would surprise me if Zach even danced with me at prom. Not really, but he did go out of his way to make sure nothing happened between us that could be misinterpreted. I already knew he wouldn't kiss me, probably wouldn't even hold my hand, but a girl could dream.

He would be a perfect gentleman. Always had been. Always would be. It was one of the things I lov... liked so much about him.

Zach texted me when church let out, right after Dad called to make sure I was okay with him going to Grandma and Grandpa's and leaving me home by myself. With Zach. I told him I was fine.

Zach showed up with a milkshake from Steak N Shake, an Arby's melt, and some seasoned fries. The boy knew what I loved.

He sat in the recliner. "How're you feeling?" I watched him take a monstrous bite of his loaded BBQ pork sub. How many places had he stopped?

"Better. Still sore. Wish I was going to be there with you guys later." The final performance was in about five hours. I wouldn't be in it - not even as a member of the chorus. I'd been okay on Saturday, but this morning I could barely move. The jury was still out on whether I'd be in the audience.

Zach swallowed and shook his head. "That's not what I mean. Have you talked to your mom?"

Right. That. I refused to give her that title even in my mind. She was a pronoun. Possibly a first name. Not... that title. "Not since she left here the other night. Dad and Grandma talked to her at the hospital. I guess Kristy saw Dad hugging her when she was crying."

"Why was she crying?"

I rolled my eyes and took a big swig of my milkshake. "Who knows? Something about how upset she was..." I fluttered my eyelashes and used my baby voice. "...that her little girl was hurt and just wanted to make sure she was okay and would her baby ever not hate her?"

"You're being pretty snarky about her." He didn't look at me. Good call. He knew how I felt about the woman who'd abandoned me.

"So?"

Before Zach could say anything, I went on.

"I know. I know. What would Jesus do?" I mimicked. "I know all that but Jesus was never abandoned at birth by His mother."

Zach's gaze held mine and I knew what he'd say before

he said it. "No. But at the worst moment of His life, of anyone's life, what did He cry out?"

I took another drink of that shake. "'My God, My God, why have you forsaken me?'"

He didn't say anything as I turned it over in my mind.

"Okay. So God turned His back on Jesus during the crucifixion because God can't look on sin. I get that. But ultimately, didn't Jesus *choose* that path? Couldn't He have called the angels to His side to rescue Him? Or rescued Himself?"

Zach still didn't speak but ate his very un-kosher sandwich.

"Fine. If He had, He wouldn't have fulfilled His purpose in this world. Absolving us of our sins by becoming sin for us. So even though He had a choice, He didn't really have a choice."

One of his eyebrows hitched up.

I sighed. "And He became Abi's sins for her. So He died for her, too. And if He could die for her, I can at least not be snarky." Shooting a glare at Zach, I turned my back as I lay down. "You're worse than my dad." Getting me to admit to myself why I was wrong. Dad had it down to a science. I wasn't sure what I thought about Zach doing it.

"You know it's the right thing to do."

No. The right thing to do would be to at least attempt a relationship with Abi. Small steps, careful steps, but steps toward a friendship if not ever toward a mother-daughter thing. "I'll think about it." I couldn't promise more.

We finished our meal in silence. Zach came to sit next to the couch, facing me as he situated himself on the floor. He didn't take my hand like I wished he would. Instead, he brushed a bit of hair off my face. "I hope you give her a chance. I don't know what she's really like, but I think you'll regret it someday if you don't at least try. You want..." He hesitated, his eyes twinkling. "...*your* kids to know their grandmother if she's anything like yours. Remember, they were still in the aftermath of 9/11 and the death of your uncle, too. Your dad even still remembers some of the orders from the people he served coffee to who didn't make it out. That's not something you can underestimate."

Dad hadn't ever told me that. "Who does he remember?"

"Some lady with the same name as my mom. Joanna something from the Marriott World Trade Center. She was blonde and newly engaged. Almost sixteen years later and he still remembers that about someone he hardly knew. Imagine how much worse it was three months later with your son or brother dead and your city, your country, in chaos."

Something niggled in the back of my mind about the special I'd seen. *Hotel Ground Zero* maybe. Hadn't most people in the hotel survived?

"Remember *your* grandkids." He winked at me.

I understood his implication. He'd never come right out and said it, but I knew he saw us getting married someday. Maybe after college. The thought made me blush and Zach grin.

"I need to get going. Come see me if you make it tonight." He did squeeze my hand. As close as I was going to get. "I'm praying for you."

I knew he wasn't just praying for me to feel better, but also that I'd make the right choices about Abi. Not sure how I felt about that. With another squeeze, he stood, rested his palm on my forehead so I knew he was whispering a prayer then headed for the door. "I'll call you later."

I rested my forearm against my forehead and let out a

dramatic groan. "I'll be waiting with bated breath."

Zach laughed. I loved his laugh. "I'm sure you will."

Once he let himself out the front door, I rolled to face the back of the couch. Was I willing to risk getting hurt? Let Abi in my life?

Zach made me think about it, but for now, my answer was still no.

Chapter Ten

Travis hated that Abi was still in town. Always looking over his shoulder, hoping he wouldn't see her around. And he knew she'd been at Mom's house at least twice during the day while they were at school, and it was only Thursday.

At least the spring musical was over, and Travis could concentrate solely on making sure his daughter was okay with everything going on in her life. He whistled as he walked through the store, picking up a loaf of French bread. He had everything else needed for dinner with his two favorite women while they planned their prom dress shopping trip for Saturday. He needed to make sure Kristy understood exactly what Cassie would *not* be wearing to the event. Nothing too short or cut too low or too high or any of a bunch of other "toos", including too expensive.

A sigh of relief escaped as he headed for the front door of the store. Another excursion without an Abi in sight. His phone buzzed. He knew he should pay more attention to where he walked, but he didn't, then collided with someone he hadn't seen.

"Sorry, I wasn't pay..." Travis cut the apology off when he realized who it was.

"I wasn't watching either." Abi didn't look at him but at something over his left shoulder.

He glanced back at his phone, trying to hide a frown.

"What's wrong?"

"Nothing." Kristy wasn't feeling well. That put a damper on the night. He'd still get to spend the evening with Cassie but after she went to bed for the night, there would be no sitting on the couch with a beautiful woman curled up next to him, kissing a bit, maybe talking about the whole marriage thing.

And avoiding anything that remotely resembled the woman standing in front of him.

But then Travis got a good look at her. She looked taller than normal. He glanced down to see she wore heels with black dress pants that made her legs look much longer than they really were. A bright blue shirt of some sort with a tailored black suit jacket over the top of it and her brown hair in riotous curls hanging over her shoulders completed the look.

And the look was...very nice.

If she'd been anyone else, he would have said she looked almost stunning.

Very professional.

She must have had her business meeting Mom told him about.

"So when do you go home?" The sooner the better.

"I met with the clients today. I'll be here at least through the middle of next week to meet with them a couple of more times, and we may have another client in the area so it could be longer. Plus I'll need to come back to make sure everything's going right."

Great. Extra days of trying to avoid her.

She glanced down and took a step. "Guess I'll see you around."

Not if I see you first, Travis replied in his head, choosing to say nothing as she walked off.

Seeing her put him in funk. He had to snap out of it before he got home. If Cassie saw him like this, she'd want to know why and discussing her mother with her was not on his agenda.

And when had he started thinking about Abi as Cassie's mother rather than the woman who abandoned both of them?

He pulled into the garage and shut off the engine, staring at the wall in front of him for several minutes. Travis didn't like that Abi was in town. He didn't like that part of him felt Cassie should at least talk to her a little bit because, after all, Abi was her mother. And, given what Abi had said about her original decision, he could at least sort of understand it. Didn't agree with it, wish she'd handled it differently, but understood it a bit better.

Over the years, he'd prayed about it more times than he could count, asking God to take away any residual bitterness and anger toward Abi. Until the week before, he thought He had. Now, he wasn't so sure.

And he didn't know what to do about that.

"I understand, honey." Travis sighed deeply. "If you're sick, you shouldn't be running around anyway. I'll get Mom to take the girls. It's fine." His voice lowered. "Mostly, I miss you."

Kristy's sniffle and sneeze came through the line loud

and clear but her voice was raspy. "I miss you, too. I was really looking forward to going shopping with Cassie and Maile."

Cassie walked in, sticking something in her purse. "When's she going to be here?" She must have recognized the ringtone to be so ready to go.

Kristy's raspy voice turned to a cough before she spoke again. "I'll talk to you soon. I'm going back to bed."

"Feel better. Miss you."

"You wouldn't if you could see me now." Another coughing spell. "Talk to you later." And she hung up.

Cassie's face had fallen. "She's sick still?"

Travis nodded. "She sounds horrible. I'll call Grandma." By the time he finished saying it, the phone was ringing.

"Hello?"

Quickly, he told Mom what was going on.

"I'm sorry, Trav, but I can't. I'm on my way to a writer's workshop in Lebanon. I'm almost there already, and I won't be home until tonight."

Travis ran a hand over his face, feeling his head start to throb behind his eyes. He was going to end up in some shop. He could see it now and had to avoid it at all costs. "Any other suggestions?"

"Not really." There was silence on the other end, but he could almost see the wheels turning. "Well, I have one." The hesitance told Travis all he needed to know.

"No." He knew the answer before she made the suggestion.

"Why not?"

"No. I'm not asking Abi to take them."

Cassie's head snapped up, her eyes wide as she mouthed at him, "Grandma can't?"

Travis shook his head while he listened to Mom go through several reasons why it would be a good idea before she ended with, "It would be good for her and Cassie to get to know each other, Trav."

"I knew it wasn't a good idea," he muttered, knowing she'd hear him but saying it anyway.

"What?"

"Her over at your house three times this week."

"She's not evil, Trav. She was young, scared, and didn't trust you enough, and now she's hurting, scared, and doesn't trust herself or God enough to see that she can be forgiven and loved. And you're not helping."

He didn't say anything.

"What would Jesus do?"

Travis rolled his eyes. How many times had he heard that growing up? How many times had Cassie? "He wouldn't be in this situation," he pointed out.

"True enough. But what would He want you to do?"

He ran a hand through still messy hair. "I know."

"Think about it and float it as an option to Cassie."

"Maybe."

"Love you, but we're pulling in the parking lot. I'll talk to you later."

"Thanks anyway. Love you, too."

Cassie stared at him. "Did she suggest what I think she did?"

"Probably. She suggested Abi." Travis gave a half-shrug. "It's up to you. I can go with you if you want or you can ask her. Can you think of anyone else?"

She shook her head. "Maile's aunt has to work, and I don't want to wait until next weekend. If we don't find anything today, we'd have to go again anyway." Her eyes stared into Travis's. "What do you think?"

He tried to remember Mom's words. What would Jesus tell him to do if He was sitting here? Deep in his heart, Travis knew the answer, but saying the words took effort.

"I think Abi would really like it if you asked her, but it's up to you. If you don't want to or if she can't, I'll take you and do my best to be cool."

"Grandma asked you what you thought Jesus would do, didn't she?"

He nodded.

"What do you think He'd say?"

His head flopped against the couch. "I think He hung on a cross and asked His Father to forgive the very men who were killing him. If He can do that, I think He'd probably expect us to forgive Abi and be willing to let her try again to be a part of your life at least. Give her another shot. Be careful. Don't run headlong into anything, but that you should probably try to have some sort of relationship with her."

"Is that what you think I should do?"

Her question made him hesitate. "I think you should pray about it. If you're not ready yet, if you're *never* ready, I think God would understand, but I think He'd probably prefer it if you and your mother were able to bury the metaphorical hatchet."

"What about you and her?"

Another shrug. "We never had a relationship." While true, the truth was so much more complicated. "I've forgiven her, I think, for abandoning you with me, but I don't know that she and I need to have a relationship of any kind, except through you. Be civil to each other at family occasions, graduations, wedding, that kind of thing, but a real relationship? I don't know that it's necessary."

Cassie's eyes closed for a long time, but when she opened them, peace was written on her face. "Will you call her for me? I'll call Maile and let her know we're running late."

Travis hesitated but agreed. A minute later, the phone

was ringing.

"Hello?" The voice was so groggy, he had to have woken her up.

"Abi?"

"Yeah."

"It's Travis."

"Travis? Is Cassie okay?"

He could feel his brows pull together. "Yeah. Why wouldn't she be?"

"I have no idea, but I didn't think of any other reason you'd be calling me."

"Did I wake you up?"

Her yawn confirmed it before her words did. "Yeah. The book your mom loaned me kept me up way too late."

A smirk crossed his face. "Which book? She's got a million of them."

"One of the Cambridge Family Saga books. I forget what number I'm on. Four maybe?"

"One of her favorites."

"I can see why."

Maybe she wouldn't go. Even as he thought it, Travis knew she would. "Listen, something's come up. Kristy's sick and my mom's out of town. Cassie and Maile were supposed to go prom dress shopping, and they really don't want me to take them. Would you be willing to go with them?"

The silence hung heavy on the line. "What does Cassie say? Does she want me to, or is this your way or your mom's way of trying to get us to spend time together?"

"It was Mom's idea, but I told Cassie it was her choice."

"And she agreed?"

He didn't feel the need to tell her the whole God side to the conversation. "She thought about it for a bit, but yes."

"When are they going?"

"They were supposed to leave in about fifteen minutes, but there's no real rush except trying to avoid the mall when it's insanely busy."

"I can be there in about thirty minutes, maybe forty-five. Is that okay?"

"That's fine. I'll let her know."

More silence hung, though not so heavily this time. "Travis?"

"Yeah?"

"Thank you."

Travis shook his head though she couldn't see it. "Don't thank me. It was Mom's idea and Cassie's decision. I had nothing to do with it."

"But if you really thought it was a horrible idea, you would have told her no. I'm very grateful you didn't."

Travis didn't want her gratitude, but it was nice to hear. "I'll tell her you'll be here in a bit."

They said good-bye and hung up.

It was the right thing to do. To encourage Cassie to have a relationship with her mother – at least unless Abi made it clear she still couldn't be trusted.

"Is she coming?" The hopeful note in Cassie's voice couldn't be missed.

He nodded in confirmation as she sat next to him, her head resting on him as he wrapped an arm around her.

A few minutes later, she spoke. "Thanks, Dad."

"For what?"

"For helping me make the right decision even if it was hard for you."

Travis kissed her head. "I'm proud of you for making it, kiddo. Call me if you need anything today. I can't imagine anything would go horribly wrong, but you know you can call anytime, right?"

"I will." A minute later she spoke. "I'm going to read

until Abi gets here and we go pick up Maile." She pulled her Kindle out of her purse and turned it on, not leaving his side.

He rested his cheek on her hair and told himself over and over that they were doing the right thing.

As long as he didn't have to be anything other than civil to Abi, it was fine.

Because that was almost asking too much of him.

But he'd do it.

For Cassie's sake.

And that was the extent of it. Period.

Chapter Eleven

Abi took a deep breath and tried to steady herself. With one hand, she knocked on the door. With the other she pinched her leg to make sure she wasn't dreaming.

Cassie flung the door open. "Hi. You ready?"

She didn't hug Abi, didn't say she was glad to see her, but she was obviously excited about the outing, though it may have dimmed somewhat with her biological mother as the shopping companion. "Let me talk to your dad first." She needed to get some ground rules from him, about what Cassie would be allowed to wear or not wear and what the budget was, though Abi had already decided to cover at least half the expenses.

Cassie's face dropped just a bit, but she moved aside. "Come on in."

Travis walked out of the hallway, a coffee mug in his hand. He nodded Abi's direction. Not overly friendly, but not openly hostile either. She took it as a good sign.

"Morning." Abi tried that greeting on for size.

"Thanks for taking them."

"No problem."

He gave Cassie a look. "If they give you any trouble, call me."

"I'm sure we'll be fine."

"I'm sure you will be, too, but if there's any trouble or back talk or anything, I want to know about it."

Abi nodded. "I'm sure we'll be fine," she reiterated. A glance over her shoulder showed they were far enough away they wouldn't be overheard. "Thank you for letting her call me, Travis."

He took a sip from his mug. "I told you it was her call."

"But you didn't say no and I appreciate that."

"Don't read too much into it. Not yet," he warned.

"I'm not."

They talked for a few more minutes about the dress before Abi turned. Price was a little lower than she'd expected it to be but his restrictions on design fit the picture in her mind.

"We'll be back later," Cassie called as she bounded down the steps and ran up the sidewalk. "Bye, Dad!"

He called her back, gave her a hug and whispered something in her ear. She nodded and turned around, still smiling brightly. "You ready?"

Ten minutes later, her friend Maile was in the back seat, with a list she and her aunt had made when they'd gone dress shopping several weeks earlier. The first couple of stops were resale shops. Cassie seemed fine with that idea. Buying something second-hand. Abi wondered why that was. Because Travis couldn't afford anything else so she was used to it? Because she was frugal? Because she liked that her purchase would go to help a worthy cause?

Abi didn't ask, and Cassie didn't offer.

The prom dresses had been picked over by the time they

got to those stores. Not surprising as proms had already started happening for some local schools. Most girls had already finished shopping. Next stop? The mall and its million stores that might have something appropriate.

After a quick, food-court lunch, Cassie tried on several dresses at a number of places, but none that screamed "buy me" to any of them. Before they knew it, the dinner hour had rolled around.

"I need to get home," Maile said, looking at a text on her phone. "My aunt and uncle are coming over for dinner. Dad says I need to be there by six."

Cassie looked like she might cry. Abi hesitated then slipped her arm around her daughter's shoulders. "It's okay. We'll keep looking. I can go with you again next week, or I bet Kristy or your grandma will be able to go. They probably know better places than I do anyway."

They walked toward the outer door of the mall while they talked. "I know. I just wanted to get it today. The longer it takes, the more likely it is I'll have to settle for something I don't really want."

Over the course of the day, Abi had gotten a pretty good idea of what Cassie liked and what she didn't, but Abi had to ask. "What's your ideal dress, Cassie?"

She shrugged, but described in great detail the dress she'd design if she could make it herself.

"Maybe we can look online, too," Abi suggested, doing her best to sound encouraging. "We have time to order something if we can find it from a reputable online store. I know it's not the same as slipping it on and turning around to see it in the mirror the first time, but..."

Cassie nodded. "That's a good idea. Will you look with me tonight?"

That made Abi hesitate as they walked toward the car. "I don't know."

"Dad'll be okay with it, I promise."

They hadn't talked about anything too serious over the course of the day. Mostly things like hairdos and nail polish colors and shoes to go with the dresses they looked at. It wasn't deep. It wasn't much. But it was a start. And Abi didn't want to ruin it by pushing Travis.

"Why don't we ask him?" Cassie asked diplomatically, pulling her phone out of her pocket. "If he says he'd rather not, that's fine, but if he says it's okay, will you stay?"

Abi thought for a minute before nodding. "Okay. As long as he knows it's okay for him to say no."

Cassie's thumbs flew over the keyboard as Abi backed the car out of the spot. Maile told her which way to go and get back on track toward Serenity Landing. About the time they got on the highway, Cassie's phone beeped at her.

"He says it's fine," she said, with a grin. "We can look online after dinner. He's making spaghetti. He makes the best sauce in the world."

"Good to know." Abi made a mental note to compliment the sauce. As long as it was remotely edible. If it was swill, she doubted she'd be able to.

They dropped Maile off at her house. When Abi pulled into Travis and Cassie's driveway, she tried to still the butterflies one more time. He knew she was coming. He'd agreed to it. Cassie was excited about it.

What was there to be nervous about?

She couldn't quite explain it, but something deep inside told Abi her entire future rested on how well this evening went.

Cassie headed for the door, not waiting for Abi.

"God, I don't know if You're there or not," she whispered. "But if You are, could You make sure this night goes well? Please?" Abi didn't expect to hear anything back and she didn't.

Instead of waiting longer, she headed for the door and determined to make it a night none of them would forget.

"What about this one?" Cassie turned her laptop so Abi could see it.

"Do you like the pink?" Abi asked from her seat next to Cassie at the kitchen table.

She shrugged. "I like the dress, and I like the pink, but I don't think this color pink would be my first choice."

"Bookmark it or put the web address somewhere, and we'll keep looking."

Travis hadn't said two words to her when they walked in. He said something to Cassie, though Abi couldn't hear what it was. Dinner smelled fantastic as she got a small glimpse of what life could have been like if she'd just talked to him all those years earlier.

They looked at dresses for another ten minutes before Travis said it was time to eat. Cassie and Abi both put their laptops away, and Cassie set the table with an ease and efficiency that told Abi she'd done it many times before. Complete with nice cloth placemats and matching napkins.

Travis was a bit more sophisticated than she'd given him credit for.

He put a bowl with spaghetti and another with orange sauce, marinara mixed with Alfredo, and meatballs on the table. A basket lined with a cheerful fabric in a color contrasting the placemats and napkins contained garlic bread. Another bowl held mixed vegetables. Did they always eat such well-balanced meals, or had Travis decided he needed to impress on Abi how well he took care of Cassie?

And which seat was Abi's? Travis would sit at the head

of the table. The places on either side of him were set, but which one was Cassie's? Either way Abi would be closer to Travis than she had been in a long time – if one discounted the hug at the hospital anyway.

Standing awkwardly had become nearly unbearable when Cassie pointed to a chair. "Why don't you sit over here?" Another thing Abi had noticed. Cassie hadn't called her anything all day. Maile called her "Ms. Connealy" until she told the girl to call her "Abi." But Cassie? Her daughter? She'd avoided calling Abi anything. Not that she expected Cassie to call her "Mom" but it had been a tad uncomfortable a time or two when she wouldn't address her directly.

Abi took the seat indicated, sitting with her hands folded on her lap until she could follow their cues. Cassie sat across the table, and Travis to her right. Abi's back was to the window that overlooked the backyard and what seemed to be a hay field beyond.

And then Travis held his hands out – one toward each of them. Cassie took it without hesitation. Confused, Abi did the same, holding it as lightly as she could when his hand curled around her fingers. Both lowered their heads and closed their eyes. She followed suit, though she peeked a bit. It took everything in her to focus on what Travis said and not on the tingling feeling running from her fingertips up her arm. Had she ever held Travis's hand before? Given birth to his child, sure, but held his hand?

Abi didn't think so.

"Dear Lord, we thank you for this day and for Your provision. Thank You for Abi's willingness to step in and shop with Cassie today. Please help Kristy to feel better quickly and for Mom and Dad to have a safe trip back from Lebanon. Thank you for this food and please bless it to our bodies. In the name of Jesus Christ..."

He and Cassie both murmured "Amen" at the same time.

So that was praying before dinner. Abi couldn't remember ever experiencing it before. Travis picked up the spaghetti, dished some up then passed it to Cassie. She did the same before handing it across the table as the sauce and meatballs followed.

Personally, Abi thought they were using a few too many dishes.

At her house, growing up, they would have left the spaghetti in the strainer over the pot it had cooked in. The sauce and meatballs would be on the stove, the burner turned to low. The bread, most likely, would have been on a cookie sheet, cut into slices to grab.

Less to clean up that way.

But there was something to be said for the way Travis and Cassie did it, too. Abi stayed quiet during the meal, instead listening to the two of them talking about the shopping trip and some of the friends Cassie had run into.

Cassie hadn't introduced Abi to any of them.

The phone rang, but no one moved to answer it. Dinner time, it seemed, was sacred.

But as soon as the machine picked up, Cassie's phone began to ring in her pocket. She shot a puzzled look toward her dad, and pulled it out of her pocket. "It's Gavin Parmiggiano."

He gave a quick nod before she stood and moved away to answer it. Abi ate in silence until Cassie returned a minute later.

"They knew I fell, but needed a babysitter tonight. I guess whoever they had canceled. I told him I needed to ask you first, but I'd text him in a minute."

Travis glanced sideways at Abi. "It's up to you. You won't be able to keep looking for your dress tonight."

"I know, but they're in a jam."

"You've had a long week, and I know you're still sore."

Cassie shrugged. "It's just the girls and..." She grinned. "...they love me. I'm their favorite, and you know it."

With that, Travis chuckled. A sound Abi hadn't heard in a very long time.

And it reminded her of why she'd had a crush on him in the first place and a plan began to form in her mind.

"Go ahead then."

Cassie texted this Gavin person. "I need to be there in about half an hour."

"I'll take you," Abi offered. She wouldn't stay alone with Travis.

"Thanks. They don't live far."

"Can Gavin bring you home?" Travis asked.

She nodded. "He said one of them would." Her eyes lit up suddenly. "Did you know Bethany's pregnant?"

Travis shook his head. "I hadn't heard, but with the spring musical, I haven't been to men's group in a while. I didn't think they were going to have any more kids." He turned to Abi. "She has twin girls, and he has a boy and a girl. They figured four was plenty."

Cassie shrugged. "I dunno. I know the girls are excited though. Micah couldn't care less at this point."

Travis winked at his daughter. "I bet they are."

The rest of the meal went quickly without much in the way of conversation. Cassie gave Travis a hug as she and Abi headed out the door. Travis gave Abi a look somewhere between a smile and a grimace, but not a blank stare.

Cassie gave directions to a house in the next neighborhood over. Kids were running all over the place when they arrived. Hadn't Cassie only mentioned one?

"Those aren't all their kids," she explained. "There's a

bunch of kids in the houses around here that all play together all the time. I babysit for all of them sometimes."

A woman with light brown hair pulled back in a low ponytail walked toward the car. As she neared, Abi knew this had to be Gavin's wife. The tiny stomach gave her away.

"Thanks for the ride," Cassie said, reaching for the handle. "I'll let you know about next weekend."

"Thanks."

The woman stopped at Abi's side of the car, prompting her to roll the window down. "Thanks for bringing her over."

Abi did her best to smile. "No problem."

"I don't think we've met. I'm Bethany Parmiggiano." She held out a hand.

Abi shook it as best she could. "Abi Connealy."

"Nice to meet you. How do you know Cassie?" Abi could see the questions in her eyes, putting two and two together.

"I used to know Travis. My brother was a good friend of his a long time ago." The truth, while still not disclosing the truth.

One of the kids in the yard yelled "Mom." Bethany turned and Abi could see a little girl, maybe four or five running toward her. Abi didn't want to get her hopes up but maybe someday, somehow, Cassie might do the same.

"I'll see you later," Cassie said, climbing out of the car. "Thanks again."

"Anytime."

As soon as the kids in the yard saw her, they swarmed her way, shouts of "Cassie" coming from children of all ages. Abi triple-checked all sides of the car before backing out of the driveway at a speed that would make a snail look fast.

Once away from the kids, Abi sped up, though the car couldn't come close to matching the speed at which her mind raced.

Cassie hadn't found the perfect dress, but maybe, just maybe, Abi had a solution.

If only Cassie would go for it.

Chapter Twelve

Travis found Cassie's new-found relationship with her mother disconcerting. It wasn't anything deep, but they had talked on the phone for a few minutes a couple evenings. And now he and his daughter were headed to the first family event where *she* was going to be there.

His whole family seemed to be accepting of Abi. And it was driving him nuts. At least Kristy was feeling better and would be at his birthday barbecue on Friday.

If Abi had said anything to Cassie regarding the tests, he hadn't heard about it.

Maybe Cassie wasn't a match. That would be the best plan, in his mind. As long there was someone else out there who matched. Travis didn't want the guy dead after all.

By the time they pulled into the driveway, Travis's brother and his family were there and so was Abi. He hoped Kristy wasn't too far behind. He needed a few minutes alone with her. It had been such a busy week that they'd talked a couple times, but it had been over a week since he'd hugged her, kissed her.

Cassie ran ahead of him, eager to see her cousins. Jay's kids, all girls, were six, eight and ten. Since she wasn't an older sister, Cassie relished being a cousin. Their families were close and saw each other at least a couple times a month, which helped.

A couple seconds after Travis walked inside, but before he reached the kitchen, a rattle sounded in the drive. He frowned. Kristy still hadn't taken her car to get looked at. He needed to make sure she did. Instead of joining the family, Travis waited for her to come in.

"Hey." She smiled up at him, her voice completely healed. "What're you doing out here?"

He wrapped an arm around her waist. "Wanted to say hi before..."

"Travis!" His mom walked into the foyer, interrupting them. "Happy birthday."

Letting go of Kristy, Travis gave his mom a big hug. "Thanks, Mom."

With an arm still looped around his mom's shoulder, they walked into the kitchen. Cassie had gone into the living room while Abi frosted a cake. His birthday cake.

She looked up and smiled. "Happy birthday."

"Thanks." What else was there to say?

Dinner, as always, was a loud affair, mitigated by being the first meal of the season on the back porch. As soon as the last plate had been cleared, Cassie jumped up. "Present time!"

Before Travis knew what was happening, the table in front of him had been filled. Laughing, he ripped into the first one, finding two drawings and a painting from his nieces. He proclaimed them his new favorites, and he'd find a spot for them in his classroom. Next, a couple of new books from his parents. He took great care opening the box from Jay. It wouldn't be the first time he'd received exploding snakes from his brother. Instead, he laughed aloud.

"A voucher good for two tickets to the fall musical at Serenity Landing High School. Thanks." Everyone else joined the laughter. The tradition of goofy, normally useless, gifts went back to their childhood. Travis still had most of them in a box at home.

He picked up the last bag. "Who's this from?"

"Me." Abi shifted in her seat, and looked decidedly uncomfortable. "It's nothing big, but I had my mom send me some stuff this week, and I thought of this and had her send it."

The first thing he pulled out was a stick of Serenity Landing Beef Jerky. Years earlier, it had been his favorite. "Wow! I can't believe you remembered. I haven't had this in years." He ripped the package open and took a big bite, savoring the taste. "Why haven't I had these? I love them,." he murmured with a half full mouth. Reaching back into the bag, he nodded his thanks to Abi who still looked ill at ease.

Travis pulled out a canvas CD case, one of the ones that held twenty-four CDs. He swallowed the last bit of jerky and looked over at her. "What's this?" He brushed dust off the cover and tried to figure out why it looked familiar. She hadn't answered as he pulled the zipper back. The instant he saw the first CD, he knew. "Rich Mullins?"

The popular musician had been Travis's favorite during the 90s, but he'd forgotten about him over the years. Oh sure, every once in a while a song would come on the radio or pop in his head, but the man had a profound impact on Travis's life for several years. "Where'd you find these? How'd you get them?" The case hadn't been in his things when he'd arrived in Serenity Landing after leaving NYC, but he'd never thought too much about it. He hadn't been listening to much Christian music by the end of his East Coast stay, anyway.

Abi looked his direction but wouldn't meet his eyes. "I found them when we cleaned out Mark's room. His CD changer was full of them with the case on top of it. I put it with a few other things of yours that never got thrown out. I had Mom send it when I realized your birthday was this week."

"Thanks, Abs." The old nickname barely registered. "I never replaced them, but I know what's going to be on my playlist for the foreseeable future." He flipped slowly through the CDs, favorite lyrics ringing in his head from each one. And Mark had been listening to them? Travis knew it was far beyond too late, but he prayed that maybe, just maybe, Mark had come to know Truth before 9/11.

After a rousing chorus of "Happy Birthday", he blew out the candles and shared cake with his family. He stood in the kitchen refilling his soda as Mom, Abi, Becky, and Cassie disappeared up the stairs. Kristy walked in, looking a bit off. Her tight-lipped smile didn't reach her eyes and her posture seemed too stiff for everything to be fine.

"What's up?"

"Just wondering what the deal is with the CDs."

Travis shrugged. "I must have left them at their house. She remembered they still had them. No biggie. I'm excited though. I'd forgotten how much I love Rich's music."

Something about it still bugged her. Travis could tell so he put his hands on her hips and pulled her to him. "I'm glad you're here. I've missed you."

"Really?" She slid her arms around his waist and lifted her face for a kiss. "I've missed you, too," she murmured against his lips.

After another kiss, her head rested on Travis's shoulder and his cheek settled against her forehead. His eyes closed as he absorbed her Kristy-ness.

"I've missed you," Travis told her. "I've missed this."

"Me, too."

They stood there for several minutes before they both moved back, and she kissed him. Travis kissed her back, much more thoroughly than he had before. Almost enough to make him propose right then and there, despite the misgivings he'd had earlier.

"Travi..."

They pulled back, both looking a bit guilty as Abi walked into the entry.

She looked from him to Kristy and back again. "Um, sorry. It can wait." She spun on one heel and walked off.

Travis closed his eyes and sighed. "Guess it's time to join the crew."

"Guess so." She kissed him, this time a mere brush of lips. "Want to go out tomorrow? I think I need a real date with you."

"Me, too, but I think it may have to be Monday. I'm helping a couple from church move his parents in up the street from them tomorrow."

"The Doziers?"

Travis nodded. "Yeah."

"Why again?"

"His mom had a stroke. There's a place for rent a few houses down so his parents are moving in so they can be closer and help out."

Travis left arm around her waist as they turned for the kitchen. "Monday it is then."

"Perfect."

They walked in but it was just his dad and brother standing there, looking annoyed. "Where is everyone?"

Dad shrugged. "Abi had something to show Cassie and somehow, Mom, Becky, and the girls ended up there with them."

"Travis!" Mom hollered from up the stairs.

"What?" he called back.

"Hang on!"

"Then why did she yell at me?" Travis muttered.

Dad just shook his head. "Don't question it, son. Just go with it."

Becky and the girls came through the kitchen toward the living room, giggling as they did. "Everyone in here," Becky instructed.

"Don't question it?" he asked Dad with a brow raised.

Jay answered. "Don't question it."

Travis's arm stayed around Kristy as they followed his sister-in-law. So what if he was feeling a bit possessive?

"Are you ready?" Mom called.

"Close your eyes," Becky instructed.

Travis glanced at Dad who shrugged and closed his eyes.

Footsteps were coming toward them, along with giggles and whispers. What were those three up to?

Mom verified eyes were closed and he heard a couple more steps taken.

"Okay," she said. "Open."

When Travis opened his eyes, Cassie was standing there. In a prom dress.

And she looked so grown up, so beautiful, tears actually came to his eyes.

She bit her bottom lip and looked at him. "What do you think, Daddy?"

Travis moved from Kristy's side and walked toward Cassie. With one finger, he made a spinning motion as he checked the dress out from all sides. Light purple on top blending to darker purple on the bottom. Not too low cut. Not strapless or the little thin strap things. Floor length and no slit up either side of the skirt.

He knew she waited for his approval before she got too excited. "You look beautiful."

"I can wear it?"

Travis nodded. "You can."

With a squeal, she threw her arms around him. "Thank you, Daddy."

"Where'd you get it?"

She moved away, holding his hand in hers. "Abi got it for me. It was hers."

Travis had no idea what he'd expected to hear, but that wasn't it. "What?"

"It was Abi's from her senior prom. She was going to ask you since you weren't dating anyone, and she had the dress but hadn't worked up the courage to ask..." Her voice went from sixty to zero in no time flat. "Um, I don't know if I was supposed to tell you that."

He looked at Abi, who was shifting uncomfortably. "What?"

She crossed her arms in front of her and stared at him, defiant. "What?"

"Is there something I should know?"

"I was going to ask you to prom before...everything. We weren't speaking by that point so I didn't. I knew I was pregnant before then and I didn't go, but I had the dress. Mom shipped it to me, along with those CDs, this week. The style may need tweaked just a bit but Cassie's about the same size I was. I thought she might like it. That's all. And *you* don't have to buy her a dress."

Part of him wanted to take her out back and strangle her. He didn't care about the money. Well, he did, but not that much. He had college to think about after all. But what was with the attitude? He took her arm and pulled her away to whisper. "What's your deal?"

"What?"

"Your deal. You come here saying your dad is dying, and we don't have to have anything to do with you besides that, but now you're trying to do what exactly?"

"Travis." The voice belonged to his mother. A tone he knew better than to ignore. Could she hear them? He took a few steps further into the foyer as Abi followed.

"No. I want to know."

Abi took a step his direction. "My boss asked me to stay in the area for work. Your parents have been kind to me. Letting me use their printer. Loaning me books to fill the hours when I'm not working. Feeding me a time or two so I don't have to eat out all the time. Your brother and sister-in-law seemed happy to meet me. They're being *nice*, Travis. You *are* familiar with that concept, aren't you?"

Travis's arms crossed across his chest as he took a step her direction, bringing them closer together. "You want my family? You can have them. I'm happy to share. You want my daughter? You gave up that right a long time ago when you left us sitting in a coffee shop. So what is you're trying to do? You've got the bone marrow if it matches. What else do you want? Custody? Is that what you're after?"

She stared up at him. Her coffee-colored eyes filled with tears.

"You want to take Cassie from me? Is that it?" He could hear Mom saying something in the background, but he didn't pay attention.

Abi stared at him for a long minute. She didn't say a word. She turned on her heel and stalked off, making him wonder if he'd gone a step too far. He didn't care. He hadn't called a lawyer yet, but it was back on the list. First thing Monday. She wasn't taking Cassie.

Red still ringed his vision as someone, in a long purple dress, pushed past toward the stairs. Travis turned to see everyone just staring at him. The girls didn't know what to make of it. Mom's glare reminded him of the looks he'd gotten in high school during his rebellious phase. He and Abi must have gotten too loud.

"Go after her." There was no arguing with that tone.

With a sigh, he headed for the staircase.

"No, Travis." Mom stopped him in his tracks. "Abi."

The front door stood open where it hadn't shut all the way after she'd fled.

A glance at Dad's face said he agreed with Mom.

"You want to fix things with your daughter?" Mom asked. "Start by making it right with her mother."

Her mother.

No one had referred to Abi quite like that before, at least not to him.

Travis wasn't sure she was right, but Mom was seldom wrong, so he headed out the door to see Abi sitting in her car. Her arms were folded on the steering wheel, and her shoulders shook.

When he reached the driver's side, Travis opened the door and held a handkerchief out to her. "Here."

She glared, but took it, wiping her cheeks. "Who still carries these anyway?"

He shrugged. "I learned it from my dad."

Her eyes closed as she held it to her eyes. "You had one back then, didn't you?"

The sudden shift in topic threw him. "What?"

"That night. You gave me one, didn't you? In the car?"

It took him a minute to walk through the events, but finally he nodded. "Yeah."

"I think I still have it. I found it in my laundry and didn't know how it got there but figured it was from that night since Dad and Mark never carried them. I wasn't sure it was yours though. I kept it anyway, to give back to you and then, once I knew I was pregnant, because..."

"Right."

He stood there. She sat in the car for several minutes before she spoke. "I don't want custody, Travis. I don't want anything but a chance to get to know my daughter for as long as she'll let me. That's it."

"Good to know." He was still calling a lawyer Monday morning.

"I know you hate me. You have every reason to hate me. I get that. And Cassie has every reason to hate me, too. But for whatever reason, she doesn't. Not right now. She's reaching out to me. If you really want me to stay away, I will, but if you'll let me, I want to be a part of her life."

"Then why did it take your dad's bone marrow to bring you here?"

She sniffled and wiped her nose on the white cloth. "Can we talk somewhere else? Away from everyone but not here?"

Travis sighed. "Yeah." One hand still rested on the top of the car door, but with the other he pulled his phone out and texted Mom they'd be back in a bit. "Come on."

Without waiting to see if she followed him, he started down the sidewalk. There was a little park, a nice one, about two blocks down the street. If she wanted a quiet place to talk, there wasn't any better place for it. The car door slammed shut, and he heard her hurry to catch up.

"Where are we going?"

"To talk."

"I got that. But where?"

"Somewhere away from *my* family." The subtle emphasis he put on the word didn't make him proud, but he did it anyway.

The rest of the walk passed in silence. It wasn't until they were seated on a wood and iron bench that he spoke. "What do you want, Abi? Why didn't you come sooner if you wanted to be a part of her life so badly?"

Abi took a deep breath. "I couldn't."

CASSIE

I reached one hand over my shoulder as the tears streaked down my face. My fingers wiggled, desperate to reach the zipper. I didn't want to wear this anymore, but was just out of reach. My other hand reached up from beneath.

Almost.

Had it.

Instead I collapsed on the bed, shoulders shaking as the sobs came. Didn't care if the dress got wrinkled. The perfect dress Abi had found for me.

It wasn't until Grammy came in and sat next to me on the bed that the gut wrenching sobs started to calm. It probably had something to do with her. More likely, it came from the prayers she whispered as her hand ran up and down my back. After a minute, I sat up and curled in next to her like I had when I was little.

"Your dad went to go talk to your mom."

My mom.

I hadn't heard the phrase much in my whole life and never applied to Abi in the last couple of weeks, even if was technically true.

"What does she want?" Even to my ears, my voice sounded small.

Grandma rubbed my arm as she thought. "I think maybe she regrets what happened that day and wishes she'd found a way to work things out so the three of you would be together. Or at least that you'd know both of your parents. I think she just wants to get to know her baby girl."

Her baby girl.

Me.

I'd never thought much about my mom regretting giving me to Dad. I figured she'd walked away and never looked back. Dad hadn't really answered my questions about my mom until a few years earlier. As a little girl, when I asked why I didn't have a mom, he said I did, but she wanted me to be raised with the best dad in the world. And he'd change the subject. Looking back, I could see...manipulation? Maybe. Dad manipulating me into not asking about Abi. Not until I was thirteen.

"Dad?"

He looked up from his book. "What's up, kiddo?"

"Where's my mom?"

A look crossed his face and he started to give his standard answer. "Well, she wanted..."

"No!" I cut him off. "Where's my mom? For real?"

He sighed and stuck a bookmark between the pages. "Come here." He held his arms open, and I cuddled next to him. "I honestly don't know where your mom is. Your mom and I..." Dad seemed to be thinking. "We weren't married. We weren't even dating. But after you were born, she asked me to take care of you because she couldn't."

"But I was born in New York, right?" I knew that much. I thought I knew that much.

"Yes. She gave me your birth certificate and stuff to take care of you, and we came here where Grammy and Grandpop could help." He kissed the top of my head like he always did.

"Why didn't she want me?" I blurted out the question before I could stop myself.

He didn't answer right away. "I don't know for sure if she didn't want to take care of a baby or not, but what I think is that she didn't feel like she could take care of you like you needed to be, and so she gave you to me. I wanted you from the moment I found out about you."

I let it go then but Dad had never said more until after Abi showed up a couple weeks ago. If I'd really begged and pleaded with him or weaseled with Grandma, I probably could have found out her name. I knew her last name, but never her first. I could have Facebook stalked her if I'd known. I had since she arrived but very little of her profile was public. Given the number of friends she had, she either wasn't on often or kept a very small social circle. Dad was friends with more former students than she had on her entire page. I hadn't sent a friend request and wasn't sure I'd accept one from her if she sent it. Not yet. Maybe soon. She'd started growing on me. Sort of. And I was grateful for the dress.

That thought gave me pause. Could it be that Abi was lonely? What was her family like? She'd lost her brother years ago, but was she close to her parents? Sure, she didn't want her dad to die or she wouldn't be here, but were they close? Did she know her parents loved her no matter what?

As much as Dad annoyed me sometimes, I knew he had my back. He'd never turn on me completely. If, and this was an if the size of the solar system, something happened between me and Zach on prom night, or any other night, and I ended up pregnant, what would his reaction be?

Disappointment, but he wouldn't turn me out on the street. He'd be supportive. Either helping me or supporting me through the adoption decision and process.

Did Abi have parents like that?

My gut told me no, but I didn't think I could bring myself to ask her.

Grandma interrupted my thoughts. "I think she just wants to be loved, honey. Like all of us."

"Is her family not like ours?"

"I don't know. I know she's been hurting for years over giving you to your dad and walking away. She just wants to get to know both of you. I don't think she has any intention of trying to take you away."

That was good. I didn't want to live with anyone but my dad. If she tried to take me away, I'd tell a judge and anyone else who would listen just what I thought about that. I liked her well enough, as a distant acquaintance. Not as my mom. Never as my mom.

But the question burning a hole in my heart stayed where it was.

Why didn't she want me then? And why doesn't she want me now?

Chapter Thirteen

You couldn't find us?"

Abi didn't blame Travis for his incredulity.

"Were you out of the country? In prison? Unconscious? What?"

She should have known that's where he'd go with it. "No, none of those."

"Then what?"

"First of all, I didn't know where you'd gone. Remember the girl at the apartment? Your girlfriend? She told me she didn't know you. I didn't know how to find you."

"You knew where I was from."

"Not really. I knew you were from a town in Missouri. Do you know how big Missouri is? How many little towns there are?"

He gave a half-shrug on that one. "You didn't hire an investigator? Or call my co-workers? Or one of the people I'd worked on a play with?"

"I didn't know any of them. And last I knew you worked at the Towers. They were gone. I had no idea where you'd gone after that, and if you weren't in the apartment, how did I even know you were still in New York?"

"I wasn't."

"Exactly. So if I had found one of those baristas you worked with, would they have known where to find you?"

She could see him concede the point though he didn't do so verbally. "I searched for you online, but I couldn't find you."

"Your mom knew."

"I couldn't ask her. They didn't know I'd given Cassie to you. And they both blamed you for everything. I think Dad still might even though I've told him over and over you weren't."

He mulled that over for a minute. "What about later?"

"Later, once I found you on Facebook, it had been too long. Eight years. I couldn't just show up. I stalked your page though. Kept up with your profile pictures and cried every time I saw a new one of my baby girl. And every year, from her birthday to Christmas, you change it to a picture of you and her when she was still a newborn." Abi didn't know why she'd grabbed her purse but she had. She pulled out her wallet and opened it. "See."

He took it from her and stared at the poor quality print of the picture.

"I know it's creepy and stalkerish, but she's my baby, too. I never *wanted* to give her up. I felt forced to. So once I found you, I knew it had been too long to just waltz back in, but I kept up the best I could."

"Your dad was the excuse to waltz?"

"Excuse? Maybe. Reason to open myself up to even more heartache if one or both of you refused to let her see me? Yes."

He sat there for a long time and didn't say anything.

"So what's with the dress?"

"We couldn't find anything last weekend, but we talked a lot about what she wanted. I thought she might like it. She loved it as soon as I pulled it out of the box. It fit. That's it."

"And the whole prom bit?"

Abi snorted. "Would you believe I was just forward enough to ask my brother's twenty-year-old friend to prom? As 'friends', of course." She made vicious air quotes. "After I woke up in your bed, though, I knew it would never happen. I already had the dress. I was going to go with a couple friends, but once I realized I was pregnant I stayed home and cried instead."

He leaned forward and rested his forearms on his knees. "I'm sorry you had to go through it all alone."

"I had my grandma until she died. I named Cassie after her, you know. Mark didn't shut me out like my parents did when I refused to tell them what happened. He asked me point blank if you were the father, but I wouldn't tell him. I'm surprised he didn't try to get in touch with you and force you to admit it."

Another silence. "He did try to call me. I never picked up when the caller ID showed a number belonging to one of your family. He left messages. They sounded strained but not mad. Brief. Usually just asking me to call him. Once he asked if I knew what was wrong with you." He shifted until his back rested next to hers, his long legs stretched out in front of him, crossed at the ankle. "He called September 10. That message sounded a bit more menacing, and I considered calling him back, but I didn't. The next morning, I didn't look at the caller ID when your dad called because I was still sound asleep."

"I spent an hour or more trying to talk Dad out of it," Abi admitted, "but somehow, I just made things worse. By the time he called, he was convinced you were evil personified, and I was lucky to be alive after the awful things you must have done."

He moved until he was leaning forward enough to turn to look at her. "Abi, you have to know I *never* would have..."

She raised a hand to stop him. "I know. I knew that then. I never thought you were the one who drugged me and then told me you'd been drugged yourself. And I *know* you're not capable of the kinds of things he was suggesting."

Relief flooded his face. "Good." He sat back again, but this time, he'd shifted somehow. His shoulder brushed against hers. "I never heard from Mark after 9/11, of course, but I thought it was because he was at Ground Zero when he wasn't working. I thought he didn't have time to harass me anymore. I was too grateful I'd never seen his name on any of the lists to be glad he didn't bother me any longer. I never imagined..."

"I know. We were all glad he wasn't down there. We knew that from the beginning. Or," she amended, "we were pretty sure he wasn't. We didn't know for sure until someone showed up the next day to tell us what happened."

They sat in silence long enough for her to notice twilight seeping in. "What now, Travis?" She felt weary. More tired than she had been in a very long time. "I want to get to know Cassie, but I don't want to fight with you all the time. If you really want me to leave her alone, I will." It would absolutely rip her heart out, but she'd do it. She'd walk away.

He took a deep breath in and blew it out slowly. "No. I don't want you to leave her alone. Not if she wants to talk to you. If she wants to get to know you, I'll let her. I'm not an ogre. But I won't tolerate you bad mouthing me or trying to go around me to get your way or to make me look like a bad guy if you disagree with a decision I make. You gave up that right a long time ago."

Abi let out the breath she hadn't realized she was holding. "I know. And I won't. If I really, truly disagree with something, I'll talk to you about it, but I won't question you in front of her, and you have final say. I'm not going to try to take her from you. I promise."

"Are we good then?"

She nodded. "I am if you are." He stood and she followed. Before he could move away, Abi rested a hand on his arm. "I'm not here to screw up your life."

He looked down at her, his eyes searching hers until he found whatever it was he looked for. "I know." His phone beeped at him and he pulled it out. He closed his eyes like he had when he'd prayed after he read the text.

"What is it?"

"Cassie wants to know if I've killed you yet, or if I'm taking you somewhere it's easier to hide the body."

Abi's eyes widened. "She doesn't really think that?"

He shook his head before she could finish. "She has a snarky streak a mile wide when she wants to."

She winced. "She comes by that honestly."

They started for the sidewalk. "Really? I don't remember you being snarky."

"Of course not. I had a crush on you." Abi made herself pretend she wasn't mortified to be having this conversation. "Mark could have told you."

"Probably."

They walked about a block in silence. "So you were going to ask me to prom?"

"Yeah." Did she dare put herself all the way out there? "What would you have said?"

His hands were shoved deep in his pockets, but he still

shrugged. "I probably would have said yes, but I can't guarantee it. I'd planned to ask you out after you graduated..." Her heart skipped a beat. "...but I don't know that I would have gone to prom. At that point, I might have thought I was too cool for a high school dance."

"I understand. Is it okay with you if she wears the dress? I have shoes and accessories and everything to go with it."

"If she wants to, she can."

They strolled up to the house to see the three little girls whose names Abi still didn't know playing outside. Lawn chairs were situated on the driveway while everyone relaxed and talked.

Everyone but Cassie.

Everyone including Kristy.

Abi put her hand on his arm again. "Travis?"

He turned. "Yeah?"

"How serious are you with Kristy?" At least she knew they weren't married.

His eyes narrowed. "Why?"

She shifted, uncomfortable under his stare. "I feel exposed enough as it is. Are you going to tell her everything? Everything we just talked about? Or everything about that night?"

He pulled one hand out of his pocket and ran it through his faux-hawk. How did that thing ever make it through a full day?

"I haven't told her everything. Enough, but not everything. I told Cassie a bit more a couple weeks ago. My parents know as much as Cassie does. And I don't know who I'll tell about this conversation, but I'm not sure I'm comfortable promising not to."

"So you are serious about her?" If he wouldn't promise, that was the only conclusion she could come to.

"Yeah. We've talked about getting married, though it's

nothing official yet." He crossed his arms again. "Why?"

"I told you. I feel exposed enough. Your family is one thing. Cassie is one thing. But someone else?" Abi couldn't really explain it, but she didn't want Kristy knowing everything.

"What if we were engaged? Or married? Would you expect me to keep everything from her then?"

Abi shook her head. "Of course not."

"I'll decide what to tell her and when." With that, he turned and stalked off.

He went inside, to look for Cassie, she supposed. Abi went straight to her car, grateful she didn't have to get too close to the family and got in, pulling away before anyone could stop her.

It wasn't until she'd thrown herself on the bed, crying, that Abi remembered she still had his handkerchief.

Again.

At least this time she wasn't pregnant.

Chapter Fourteen

Travis set his face in an unreadable mask.

He hoped.

"You wanna talk about it?" he asked the lump on the bed in his old room.

"You wanna tell me what you did with the body?" She didn't move.

"Abi's fine. She left a minute ago."

"I'll have to ask Grandma."

Time for a subject change. "Did you eat dinner?"

"You think Grandma would let me get away with crying all through a meal?" Her anger came through loud and clear.

"Cassandra." His voice was quiet, his meaning clear.

"What?" Purposely obtuse. Always fun.

"Did you eat dinner?"

"Yes." Sarcasm still laced the word, but at least she gave an actual answer.

"Where's the dress?"

"Hung up in the closet."

"Do you want to wear it?"

"Will you let me?"

Travis closed his eyes and prayed for patience. "Yes. If you want to."

"She still doesn't want me, you know."

And there it was. The crux of what bothered her so much.

He moved to sit on the edge of the bed, one hand resting on her back. "That's not entirely accurate." It pained him to say it, despite the truth in the words.

"She doesn't. Did she tell you she wanted me?"

"Would you want her to have custody? To move out of the house we've lived in since you were little and move to some other city, somewhere far away? Or even to an apartment here in Serenity Landing? Be honest." Travis already knew the answer.

"No." Sullen. Also fun.

"So you don't want to go with her if she did want you, but you still want her to want you?"

It took a minute, but a slight nod was visible.

Travis moved to sit against the headboard. "Come here, punkin." A second later, she was curled next to him. "It's not that she doesn't want you, but she knows how impossible that would be. You don't really want to live with her, and she knows she gave up any right to make decisions about you and your life a long time ago. She understands what her actions when you were a baby are costing her now."

He brushed the hair back at her temple. "She came looking for us, you know. At my apartment a week later, but I was gone and my girlfriend who was living there claimed she had no idea who I was."

Travis got an answer in the form of a sniffle. If he hadn't given his handkerchief to Abi, he would have given it to Cassie. Instead, she had to settle for the Kleenex on the side table.

She took it before dropping a bombshell. "Grandma said she's moving in here."

It took everything in him to keep from exploding. "What?"

"She can do a lot of her work from anywhere, and she has a couple new clients here. Grandma told her it's crazy for her to stay at a hotel that long, and she could move in here. Your room. Grandpop agreed."

"When?"

She shrugged. "Sometime this week, I guess."

"She didn't mention it," he murmured.

"What did you talk about?"

"You. Mark. Prom." Travis kissed the side of her head. "I'm sorry you saw that, punkin."

She turned words he'd often said around on him. "Are you sorry it happened, or sorry it happened where I could see it?"

"A little of both. I think the conversation was inevitable. I'm sorry we were yelling and mad at each other in front of you and the girls."

They sat there until it was dark enough outside that he heard Jay and Becky pack the girls up to leave.

"You ready to go home?"

She nodded.

"Want some Andy's?" The frozen custard was her favorite.

"Can I get a super big one?"

One corner of his mouth quirked up. "Just this once."

"Can Kristy come with us?"

"We can ask her." He thought he'd heard her car drive off a while earlier, but he wasn't sure. He'd let Cassie discover that on her own, in case he'd been wrong. "Why don't we leave the dress and everything here for now, and we'll bring it home when it's time?"

"Okay." She stood up and walked to the closet, running her hand over the purple material.

"Do you really like it that much? It's not too out of style?" Travis thought it looked fine, but what did he know?

Cassie shook her head. "No. It's timeless enough that no one will know."

"Good."

She turned and stared at him. "I've thought about a lot of stuff lately, Dad, and I'm glad you're my dad." Her footsteps carried her until she could wrap her arms around him and he could reciprocate. "I love you."

"I love you, too, Cassie-bug."

"Ugh." She shuddered. "I hate that name."

Travis laughed. "I know."

After another minute, they headed downstairs.

"I need some Advil." Cassie headed to the kitchen while Travis went into the living room to say good-bye to his parents.

"Is she okay?" His mom stood to walk out with them as he heard Cassie getting water from the tap.

"She will be." Travis put his arm around her shoulder as they headed for the front door.

"Is Kristy gone?" His daughter met them in the foyer.

Mom moved to give her a hug. "'Fraid so, kiddo." After one of the longest hugs Travis had ever seen, the two separated. "Have a great week, both of you." He could almost see the wheels turning in her head. It could be anything given the rabbit trails his mom often followed.

She gave him a hug as Cassie headed for the car. "I want Abi to be a part of our family while she's here. She's going to be around for a while, and you're going to have to get used to it."

He nodded, resigning himself to Abi's presence at family gatherings for the foreseeable future. But would Kristy be okay with it?

Travis hoped so. Or there could be trouble in paradise. Tossing a prayer heavenward, he called good-bye to his dad and headed for the car.

Travis and Kristy walked hand in hand through the park, cones from Andy's in hand.

"How's she really doing?" Kristy asked before taking the top off her ice cream swirl.

They'd avoided conversation of anything to do with Abi or Abi and Cassie during dinner, but now it was time.

"She's okay. Still a bit..." Travis searched for the right word. "Melancholy. The fight wasn't pretty for her to watch and brought out some of the feelings of abandonment she already had. Thinking Abi still didn't want her."

"Is she going to try for custody? Shared or visitations?"

Travis shook his head. "No." He shared a bit of the conversation with Abi, but not all of it. He didn't totally agree with her "exposed" feeling, but did his best to respect it. "Maybe they'll have a chance to talk on the drama trip. I'm going to rearrange the room assignments to put them together."

Kristy didn't say anything but continued eating her frozen custard until she finally changed the subject a bit. "So she really was going to ask you to prom?"

"Yep."

She bumped her hip into his. "Good thing I've already got you all sewn up for this one then, isn't it?"

Travis threw his head back and laughed. "Kris, you have *nothing* to worry about from Abi. Not just at prom but any other time. As much as I hate that my daughter isn't the product of a loving relationship, I'm so glad I have her but without the baggage that comes from a broken relationship, too."

Turning, he pulled her to him with his free arm, careful to keep his cone out of her hair. No one liked frozen custard in their hair. "I have *you* now, Kristy. Not Abi. Never Abi."

Travis lowered his lips to hers. Lost himself in the smell of her perfume, her shampoo or whatever smelled so good. She tasted a bit like chocolate custard.

He loved chocolate.

By the time the kiss ended, his custard was nearly melted. He tossed it on the grass for an animal to get. Probably not the best thing for them, but he did it anyway.

It took everything in him not to kiss her again. To keep his eyes on hers rather than focusing on her lips. "What would you say if I asked you that question? The one we talked about the night before she showed up."

She flashed a coy smile. "I think you know the answer to that, Mr. Harders." Moving away from him, she left her hand in his as they started back up the path. She finished her cone while he licked the custard off his fingers.

"I do?" he asked.

This time she looked at Travis from under lowered eyelashes. "Got that right."

His brow furrowed in confusion. It took a minute for him to get the word play.

I do.

"Good to know," he told her, coming to a stop. "But I think we should head back. It'll be dark before too long, and I don't like walking around in the woods after dark."

Another kiss, and they went back the way they came.

"We're a chaperone short." Travis leaned back in his chair and propped his feet up on the desk. Shawn, one of the vice principals, sat across from him, popping one Peanut Butter M&M after another in his mouth.

"I'll go."

"I need a woman. You won't make the cut."

The other man nodded. "Very true. What about Kristy?"

"Already thought of her. She has plans." Plus she was barely speaking to him. It might have something to do with him playing the Rich Mullins' CDs nearly non-stop, but that wasn't because of Abi. He'd realized how much he'd missed listening to those. They were classic enough the music and melodies weren't incredibly outdated. The messages were timeless. Sing praises. God's grace abounds. He is almighty. With her simple gifts, Abi had crawled under Kristy's skin. That it bothered Kristy so much bothered Travis, but what could he do?

Three more pieces of candy flew into the air then into the other man's mouth. They ran through everyone either one of them could think of, making several phone calls in the process. All requests were met with a "wish I could, but not this weekend."

"Do you think our group has a shot at winning State?" Two more M&Ms.

Travis nodded. "They're great this year. They've won almost every meet so far and this is the best play of the bunch."

"It's one you wrote, right?"

"Yep." A very fictionalized version of a woman he used to serve coffee to meeting and marrying the hero. Joanna's chance at a happy ending came to a screeching halt on 9/11, but he could give her one on the stage.

"What about Cassie's mom?"

The thought shocked Travis, though it shouldn't have. Two of his other chaperones were parents. "It's possible," he answered slowly. "Would the school let her since she's so new on the scene?"

His boss stood up and headed for the door. "Unless a court terminated her parental rights, she's a parent, and that's the only qualification we need."

With a sigh, Travis pulled his cell phone out and sent a text. Maybe he'd be lucky, and she'd have plans.

CASSIE

"You really can't go?" I gripped the phone with my shoulder and cheek, praying it wouldn't slip.

"Sorry, sweetie." Kristy sounded both distracted and annoyed.

"You know I haven't told Abi about it right? She's not coming." Maybe the only reason Kristy wasn't planning to come was the other woman in my dad's life right now. I hoped Kris would be my step-mom sooner rather than later.

Except I kinda wanted Abi to be there. She'd been so great with the prom dress thing, and she'd told me how much she liked the play. It would surprise me if she wouldn't want to come to the competition with us. What if I had to choose? If Dad married Kristy, would it always be Kristy or Abi when I had something special? Graduation? Wedding? Babies?

"I never planned to go, Cass. Last week, I thought it might work out, but it's not going to. My cousin's bridal shower is Saturday, and I'm running a workshop here at school Friday. Text me updates, okay?"

"Yeah. I will. I just hoped you'd be able to take Mrs. Gunderson's place." Kristy said a very abrupt good-bye and hung up. What was that about? Did it have anything to do with Abi?

It seemed like everything had to do with Abi these days. The beef jerky she'd given Dad irritated Kristy, even though Dad hadn't eaten it in years. And the CDs? No one knew what to make of that. I shook it off as Zach took the box out of my hands.

"Is that the last of it?" His dark eyes twinkled down at me. Would I ever get tired of looking at them?

"I think so." I slid my phone into my pocket. "Dad said he's going to be here for a while. Can you give me a ride home?"

He slung an arm around my shoulder as we walked back to the building. "Anytime."

Chills shuddered through me as I leaned against him for the four seconds or so he'd leave his arm there. Maybe one day, the half-side-hug-thing would linger.

I ran inside and poked my head in Dad's classroom. "I'm going home with Zach."

"I've got something to tell you, kiddo."

I hopped up on a desk. "What's that?"

"We found another chaperone." His resigned voice made my stomach sink.

"Who?"

"Abi. We tried everyone else we could think of, but no one could. Abi can."

I stifled a groan. "Fine. But don't expect me to hang out with her the whole time."

"I don't." He walked to where I sat and kissed my forehead. "We're leaving the house at four-thirty so you better get some rest."

"You don't have to tell me twice." I slid off. "I'll probably be asleep by the time you get home."

I gave him a hug and practically skipped out the door. It didn't excite me that Abi was coming, but it didn't disappoint me either. In twelve hours, I'd be sharing a bus seat with Zach. And if I could get away with it, using him as a pillow.

By five the next morning, I was doing just that. He leaned against the window as Miss Sandy drove out of the SLHS parking lot. Spring hadn't really made it to the Ozarks yet, but foolishly, I hadn't brought my heavier coat. A shudder ran through me until Zach, eyes shut, opened his backwards facing jacket, wordlessly inviting me to share. The cozy warmth spread through me enough to let me doze.

When I woke up, Zach's arm held me close to him. Did he know? Had he put his arm around me on purpose? Could Dad see? What about Abi? She sat near the front somewhere with another chaperone.

"Rise and shine." Zach's voice rumbled under my cheek. "Morning."

I moved away from him, enough that he moved his arm. Bummer. I liked it. "Morning." With my arms stretched over my head, I yawned my way awake. Sunshine filtered in through the trees, but dawn hadn't fully broken. "Where are we?"

"We have about an hour left." He held out his iPhone. "Your turn."

I took it from him, and swiped my finger across the letter jumble wondering how well he'd done, and if I could beat him. I rarely did. After handing it back, Dad caught my eye. Was that disapproval? We hadn't violated the rules, and I knew other actual couples who did more than just use one or the other as a pillow.

But none of them were his daughter.

I turned my best smile his way, but his look remained stern until he turned away.

About fifteen minutes and six rounds of jumble later, Dad stood at the front of the bus. He went through his usual warm-up speech, including admonitions about behavior. The warnings were probably unnecessary, but he'd been giving them for years.

The rest of the morning went fast or slow depending on what we were doing. Mostly we sat around waiting for our turn and eating snacks we brought with us. Once we finally had clearance to get ready, it didn't take long. Dad had written the play several years earlier with the goal of performing it at State one day. I *knew* he hadn't planned for me to end up kissing Zach.

Well. Almost kissing him.

The scene cut right before it would actually happen.

I hadn't seen the earlier versions of it, but it wouldn't surprise me if he'd changed it this year so there was no actual kiss. The first twenty-seven of thirty-five minutes went just fine, but when it came time to change into the "wedding" clothes, things went south.

Zach and I had fifteen, maybe thirty seconds to change before the action on the stage would start to drag too much. The clothes we wore were chosen with that in mind.

"The zipper's stuck!" I whispered to him. We always changed with our backs to each other. I wore a long strapless slip safety pinned to the more secure bra so there would be no potential wardrobe malfunctions. Short running shorts under it. But I couldn't wear a tank top or camisole with either dress. I yanked on the zipper a couple more times, but it was hopeless.

I turned to see Zach buttoning the top two buttons of his dress shirt before tucking it into his black pants. How did he do that so fast? He always beat me.

"Here. Arms up."

For a second, I felt three again but did as he said. He grabbed the hem and pulled it over my head. When it cleared my face, I noticed his eyes were clenched tightly shut as he spun around.

The white knee length dress had been designed to pull quickly over my head. No sooner had it settled in place around my waist than Zach grabbed my hand and ran toward the stage. I couldn't see his face, but I'd seen the tapes. He wore a giant smile. Mine plastered on right before I cleared the curtain as he announced to the room, "I want to marry this girl. Now. Where's the JP?"

Chapter Fifteen

Sure. Zach saying he wanted to marry her daughter was acting, but Abi's stomach tightened at the thought of Cassie marrying Zach. Even on stage. She'd seen both of them during the play, before Cassie fell to the stage, but the two of them hadn't said anything to each other - not that Abi could recall. She also hadn't known Zach's place in Cassie's life at that point.

The chemistry between them rivaled Ricky and Lucy.

The kid playing the Justice of the Peace pretend married them. Their friends whooped around the stage as he told Zach's character he could kiss his bride.

Abi felt her heart skip a bit. Zach looked at Cassie the same way Travis had looked at her that day at the subway. When he leaned in to kiss her. Cassie's eyes fluttered shut much the way Abi's had. Surely they had practiced this a million times. Did Cassie still feel the butterflies?

And, with the two of them frozen in an almost-kiss, the lights went out and the curtain fell.

The feeling roiling around inside her bordered on

disappointment. Maybe she'd been reading too many of Julie's books recently. Happily Ever Afters weren't all that common in the real world, and it broke Abi's heart that Cassie would likely get hers broken more than once.

Abi shook her head as she applauded with the others sitting there. Though she was no expert, they seemed to be the best group that had gone so far.

Cassie and Zach were beyond fantastic. The whispers from those around made Abi believe she wasn't alone in her thoughts. As the next group got ready to start, Cassie dropped into the seat next to her. "You were great," she whispered to her daughter.

"Thanks."

Something seemed off. "Everything okay with Zach?"

Cassie shrugged. "Yeah. My zipper stuck when we were changing, and he had to help take the dress off. I think he feels a bit awkward even though I had shorts and a slip on. Dad doesn't know though." Her daughter turned her blue eyes toward Abi. "Don't tell him?"

The thought of keeping something from Travis made Abi uncomfortable, but she promised to let Cassie be the one to tell him.

Two groups and a bus ride later, they walked into the hotel. Travis talked with the front desk while the students and chaperones milled about the foyer. Abi leaned against a pillar and watched the students. And Travis. The awkwardness seemed gone between Cassie and Zach as they sat next to each other on the couch, laughing with a couple of the kids she didn't know.

A whistle split the air, and everyone turned to look at Travis. "All right. I've got keys and room assignments, so listen up. When I call your name, come get them and take your stuff to your rooms. Meet back down here in twenty, and we'll leave for dinner." In groups of three and four, he called them up. It looked like one chaperone to five or six kids. The third group started with names Abi didn't recognize, but then, "Cassie and Abi."

A breath of relief left Abi's lips as she headed for him. Someone she knew. She'd been afraid she'd be with a group of girls she didn't know at all. A few minutes later, she was in the room she'd share with Cassie and one of her friends. A door connected it to four other girls.

After everyone took a turn in the bathroom, they went back downstairs. As the bus filled to about half its usual capacity, Abi found herself sitting across from Travis. He made a few notes on his clipboard, then stood to take a head count. Turning to the driver he told Miss Sandy she could go.

He sat and looked over at her. "What?"

Abi shrugged. "Sorry. I just haven't seen this side of you yet. You're great at this."

Another notation on the paper. "I wasn't always. It's taken years to get to the point where I've got the respect of the kids because of my reputation. I still have to earn it daily, but I get the benefit of the doubt from most of them these days. Plus this is a great group of kids."

She tended to agree. In her high school, there would have been at least one incident already. Probably more. Maybe it had to do with being from NYC versus semi-small town America? East Coast versus Midwest?

Abi found herself sitting basically alone as the kids ate the buffet bare. She didn't feel particularly lonely, something she found fairly odd. Loneliness was a long-time companion of hers, even in a crowd. As she ate, she enjoyed watching the interactions among the kids, especially Cassie, and the other chaperones who knew all of them. The kids she'd met had been polite, asked a couple of questions, but none had pushed for information about her relationship with Cassie and Travis. They probably knew as much as they needed to.

Once everyone had finished, the tables were pushed to the side. Abi and the other chaperones sat out of the way as Travis worked with the teens on their play. He had them run through it once, pointing out a few things, including a spot where he thought Cassie and Zach were a bit *too* cozy for the moment. They went back over a few specific spots including the very end where Zach *almost* kissed Cassie. Did Cassie wish he really would? Had Travis written it knowing it would be the two of them acting it out?

The kids begged to go to the park across the street. Dark had nearly overtaken the town, but the temperatures remained nice enough. Travis groaned at the "Please, Mr. Harders?" coming from all of them. "Okay. For half an hour, then it's back to the hotel to get some rest. You need to be sharp tomorrow."

That was how Abi found herself sitting on top of a picnic table in the middle of a field of grass watching her daughter run around a playground, before her almost-boyfriend pushed her on the swing. They took off playing tag with a few others.

Tears filled her eyes. Had she ever cried as much as she had in the last few weeks?

"Here."

She looked up to see Travis holding out a handkerchief. "Thanks."

"Want to talk about it?" he asked taking a seat a foot away from her.

"Just thinking about everything I missed." She wiped tears and probably all of the mascara off her cheeks. "I never thought I'd get to see her run around a playground with her friends."

"Not quite how you imagined?"

"No. In my mind's eye, she was a lot younger." She stared at the white cloth twisting between her fingers. "I regret it, you know."

"I know." He leaned forward and rested his forearms on his knees. "There's something I need to say to you. I know you haven't really asked for it, and my guess is you wanted to that first day here, but..." Travis looked up, and she could see his eyes following their daughter as she ducked under a slide to get away from another girl. "I forgive you. For not telling me, for leaving her with me and taking off. For making me a single dad all these years. I thought I'd forgiven you a long time ago, but when you arrived, I realized I really hadn't. I've been praying about it a lot, and I think I can honestly say that I have."

"Thank you. I doubt you can imagine what that means to me."

They sat in silence for several minutes, until Travis pointed to the sky. "Make a wish."

Abi caught the last seconds of a shooting star, but didn't dare give voice to her heart's desire, even in silence to herself. "It's beautiful out here."

"'The heavens declare the glory of God; the skies proclaim the work of His hands.'"

Travis's belief in God wasn't something they'd talked about much those nights spent on the porch, but she remembered that. "You said that to me once before."

He seemed to think about it. "Probably. On the porch?"

She nodded. "After you moved to the city. The first time you came back for a barbecue. Mom and Dad went to a late movie. Mark and Brenda disappeared. The moon was brilliant that night."

"I remember."

Time to jump in with both feet. "What's it mean?"

He looked over at her. "The verse?" She nodded. "It's

from the Psalms. Chapter nineteen, I think." One hand extended and swept across the sky. "He placed all of the stars in the sky, created the universe, and the very existence of that creation testifies to the fact that there is a Creator. Order can't come out of chaos, but God is a God of order." He moved closer until he was right next to her. "See there?"

She followed his outstretched finger until she saw what he pointed at. "The North Star?"

"Yep. For all intents and purposes, it never moves. It's unchanging. That's not strictly accurate, of course, but close enough. If you're ever lost, it's there. God hung it there, hung all the stars, named one for each of us."

She turned toward him, suddenly very aware of how close he was to her. "I'm sorry?"

"Did you ever listen to any of those CDs in that book?" He put some distance between them.

"No. I put them in a box when we packed up Mark's room before we moved. Some of them were in his CD player, but I just put them in the book and put it with the few other things of yours I found."

"The artist was a guy named Rich Mullins. He was killed about a year before I moved to New York, but in one of his songs, there are a couple of lines that always stuck with me. Lots of them actually, but this one is so simple and so profound at the same time." Travis leaned back on his hands and stared upward. Abi did the same. "Rich says something about how sometimes he looks at the stars and thinks about how God told Abraham his descendants would outnumber the stars in the sky and that one of those stars had Rich Mullins written on it."

The sounds of happy high schoolers provided the background music for the vast emptiness above them. "Thousands of years ago, without light pollution, how many stars could Abraham have seen? Millions? Trillions? Gazillions? Who knows, but one of those stars hung there in the sky because of *me*. Because of Travis Harders. Because of Abi Connealy. It has my name or your name or Cassie's name written on it. The God who can make all of this had *me* in mind when He hung a star. It's so simple and so mind-blowing at the same time."

Abi didn't know what to say, how to react, but before she had time to, he went on. "I know you don't believe in all of that, but it's true." When he looked at her, his blue eyes were as serious as she'd ever seen them. "God loves you, Abi. He was thinking of you when He created a star millions and millions of light years away in a spot you'd never visit. You were on his mind when He hung on the cross." Travis stood, brushing picnic table dust off the back of his jeans. "If you ever want to talk, I'm here or my mom's a great one to talk to." As he walked off, he took several backwards steps. "God loves you, Abi Connealy. He always has. He always will."

He turned, whistling loudly to draw the students back toward the bus.

God loved her? He thought about her while He created the universe?

She might be able to buy into the idea that a Creator existed, but that He cared so much about a woman who'd abandoned her baby? That didn't seem like much of a God at all.

Chapter Sixteen

"Cassandra Connealy-Harders?"

Travis and Cassie stood and walked toward the large desk near the double doors in the outpatient registration waiting room. A young man, maybe twenty, stood there with a clipboard. He checked the bracelet on Cassie's wrist then led them through the doors.

They made small talk about the weather until they reached a room with a computer and one of the chairs with padded arms. Cassie sat in it while Travis took the hard plastic chair next to the wall. The technician ran through a sequence of questions and input the information into the computer. After about five minutes, he stood. "All right. Someone will be here in just a minute to draw the blood, and then we'll get you on your way."

The door closed behind him. Travis leaned forward until his forearms rested on his knees. "You okay?"

Cassie shrugged. "I'm not crazy about needles, but I'll be all right, especially if I get a good vampire."

Travis groaned. He'd never allowed her to read the popular vampire books or to watch the movies, but they still pervaded popular culture. "Just don't watch."

"I never do."

A text from Kristy popped up on his phone, making him smile as he typed a short note back.

"Are you going to ask her to marry you?" Cassie stared at her hands rather than looking at him.

Travis wasn't sure how to answer that. "I've thought about it." He'd done more than think about it. He had a ring stashed at home.

"I saw the receipt from the jewelry store. I didn't mean to, but I did. It looked like an engagement ring receipt."

He blew a breath out slowly. "I did buy a ring. It's been on layaway for a month or so, but I picked it up the other day."

"So are you going to ask her to marry you?"

Before he could answer, a knock sounded on the door. They both turned to see a woman in scrubs walk in. "Is this Cassandra Harders?" She looked up, and right at Travis. "Mr. H! How are you?"

He searched his memory banks, but it only took a second for him to come up with the right name. "Hi, Dorrie. I'm good. How are you?"

"Good." She pulled the round, rolling chair up next to Cassie. "Working here during the day, but I joined your mom's CANDID group, too."

He could never remember what CANDID stood for. Something about Christian writers. His mom's favorite people outside her family. "That's right. You won the best student written one-act your senior year, didn't you?"

"Yep." She compared the information on Cassie's arm to the information on her clipboard. "I heard you won State this year."

Travis grinned. "First time in a decade, but yes." He nodded toward his daughter. "There's my star right there.

She and Zach did a great job as the leads."

"That's right! Zach's my cousin. Sort of. He's my dad's cousin's son, or something." Dorrie shook her head as she wrapped the rubber band around Cassie's arm. "This is going to pinch."

Cassie turned her head and closed her eyes and seemed to concentrate on her breathing. Three vials of blood later, Dorrie held a cotton ball on the inside of Cassie's elbow. "You're good to go." She looked at the information on the clipboard. "Um, I'm not sure how you'll get the results on this since it's not regular blood work. I'd guess they'll contact you, but you might want to call and find out what they're process is. I can try for you if you want me to, but this isn't an organization I'm familiar with personally." She put tape over the cotton ball. "All set."

"Thanks, Dorrie." Travis stood up when Cassie did. "Appreciate it."

"That's the best blood draw I've ever had." Cassie picked up her purse. "I'm totally asking for you next time."

Dorrie laughed. "I'm happy to do it, though I hope you don't have to come back for a really long time."

"Me, too." Cassie followed Dorrie out the door.

Once they said goodbye to his former student, Cassie went back to the prior conversation. "Are you going to ask Kristy to marry you? I mean, you have a ring, so you're planning on it, right?"

"I've been thinking about it for a while, but I'm not sure if I'm ready for that or if Kristy's ready for that. Or if you are, to be honest." He opened the door to her side of the car.

She waited for him to pull out onto National Avenue before she spoke again. "Why don't you think I'm ready for you to marry Kristy?"

He shrugged and merged with traffic on James River

Freeway. "I know you say you are, but I don't know that you really understand what it's like to have two parents. I know you like her, but it's not the same when she's your step-mom. It means she'd have some disciplinary power over you. It means that you won't be the only girl in my life anymore. I know I've dated Kristy for a while, and I've dated other women before, but it's not the same as having someone living with us as a parental figure for you."

Cassie was quiet until they turned onto Hines Street in Serenity Landing. "Maybe you're right, and I don't really know what it's like. But I'm not a little kid anymore. I'm growing up, and I know you must be lonely sometimes, and I don't want you to be all alone when I leave."

Her words reached straight to his heart. As they pulled into the garage, he reached over and took her hand. "I can't believe you've never told me you worry about me being lonely. I'm not, punkin. Really. I have you and lots of friends and family. I'll miss you when you're old enough to move out, a lot, but I don't *need* to be married just so the house isn't empty without you. I don't want to get married unless I'm certain I'm completely in love with a woman and can see her in both of our lives for the long term. I've never felt that way before."

"Do you feel that way about Kristy?"

Another head of dark hair flashed through his mind as he sighed. "I dunno, kiddo. I just don't know."

The family event at his parents' house the next weekend was a bit more sociable.

Travis and Abi smiled politely at each other. That was about it. He stayed close to Kristy's side. The question was how to get her away from everyone for a bit. Just the two of them.

Dad smoked ribs that were fall-off-the-bone barbecue goodness. Abi stayed close to his mom. Cassie stayed close to her cousins. After dinner, his nieces headed to the other living room to watch a cartoon. Travis pulled Kristy outside, to a corner of the backyard where he knew they wouldn't be seen.

Her smile told him all he needed to know. She wanted a few minutes alone as much as he did, and she couldn't know about the small box in his pocket. Or what he planned to ask her.

Twilight descended as they sat on the edge of a planter, feet stretched out in front of them as he reached for her hand, linking their fingers together. Another week had gone by with very little contact with his girlfriend. In fact, since he'd stopped by to talk to his mom a couple of times, Travis had seen Abi more times than he'd seen Kris except from a distance at work. They'd texted a bit, but hadn't even been able to make time for a late night phone call.

"How's your week been?" he asked.

"Not bad. Just incredibly busy. This time of year always is."

Except his time had been freed up with the end of drama season. He rubbed sweaty hands against his pants. "The assembly Monday is my last project for the year, and I'm ready for it to be over." Where he could see his daughter "marry" her almost-boyfriend and nearly kiss him.

"You rewrote the end, didn't you?"

"Yep." And he didn't regret it. In some ways, it really did work better than a real kiss at the end. The anticipation continued as the curtain fell rather than being fulfilled with the kiss.

"Has anyone said anything?"

"I think Cassie suspects, but we haven't done the play in

several years so none of this year's students were around the last time we did it." He let go of her hand and leaned forward, his hand brushing against the box in the lower pocket of his cargo pants. Could he get it out without her noticing? Instead, he stared up at the stars. "It's a beautiful night."

"A bit cool, but the stars will be nice."

"Sometimes, I look up, and I think about how Abraham looked at the same stars."

"No, he didn't. The stars are different in the Middle East." Kristy looked up at the sky. "Similar maybe, in that there's lots of stars, but not the same ones." She shrugged. "So what about Abraham?"

"He saw all these stars, and God told him his descendants would outnumber them one day. That means when God hung those stars in the sky, one of them had my name on it." He looked at the North Star. "Somewhere out there is a star that stands for me." So simple. So profound. Abi seemed to understand it, even if she hadn't believed it.

"I suppose that's one way to look at it. I never really thought about it."

"I hadn't really either. Not until Abi gave me those CDs the other day, and I listened to one of them. The lyrics are something along those lines. It made me think, you know?"

Kris just sat there, not answering. Travis reached for his pocket, but just as he un-Velcro'd it, Cassie called for Kristy from inside. Kristy stood and squeezed his shoulder before heading to the house.

Once she walked through the door, Travis pulled the small velvet-covered box from his pocket. He popped it open with a soft click and stared at the round solitaire there. Why hadn't he done it? For weeks, he'd been thinking about it, planning it. Ring shopping on the sly when he had a few minutes. Finding what he thought was the perfect one, then discarding it when Kris mentioned her disdain for colored stones. This one would do well in its place, but even while he talked about the stars and Abraham, he planned to ask.

He wanted to ignore the check he felt in his spirit. The one that said the time wasn't right. The door to the sun room opened as he clicked the box closed again, sticking it back in his pocket.

"Your mom is looking for you." Abi stopped a few feet from him.

"I'll be in soon." He stared up at the stars again. Once more, he felt the vastness, and he couldn't even see the Milky Way from his parents' backyard, not like he could from his own.

"I've been thinking about what you said." She sat a few feet away from him. "About God putting the stars in the sky and how there's one for each of Abraham's descendants."

He turned to look at her. "You have?"

With a nod, she went on. "Do you really believe all of that? That a God big enough to create the universe cares about human beings that must seem like ants to Him?"

"I don't just believe it, I know it."

"I guess I just don't understand that."

"I don't know who, but someone said, 'If God was small enough for us to understand, He wouldn't be large enough for us to worship.' A Baptist preacher from the 1800s named C. H. Spurgeon said, 'A God whom we could understand would be no God. If we could grasp Him, He could not be infinite. If we could understand Him, He could not be divine.' We're not supposed to understand. In Isaiah, the Bible says, 'For my thoughts are not your thoughts, neither are your ways, my ways...As the heavens are higher than the earth, so are my ways higher than your ways and my thoughts than your thoughts.' It's where faith comes in." He looked in her eyes. "When you found out you were pregnant with Cassie, could you see her, feel her moving around?"

Abi shook her head.

"At your ultrasound, could you tell she was moving?"

A solitary tear slid down her cheek. "She was sucking her thumb and kicking her legs."

Travis felt sucker punched again at what he'd missed, but couldn't get sidetracked. "Could you feel her moving the way you saw her on the screen?"

"No." She wiped her cheek, and he wished he had his handkerchief, but he'd given it to Cassie earlier during a sneezing fit.

"So, you can't feel her. You can see what they tell you is this baby inside you, but how do you know for *sure* they're not just showing you a video of some blurry snowstorm from 1950s television?"

"I don't know." He gave her a few minutes to think about it. "You're never absolutely certain, I guess."

"That's how God is. You knew that was your baby even though you couldn't feel or really see her. God is there, but we can't see or hear Him. He's bigger than all of that. On faith, you believed the pictures on the screen were the baby growing in your womb. On faith, we believe the things God's said, down to hanging a star for each and every one of us who would be the spiritual descendants of Abraham. I know you're not sure exactly what that means, and that's okay." Travis stood. He needed to find Kristy, say good night and get out of here. "Talk to Mom. She can help with any questions you have, but I'm glad you're thinking about it." As he walked away, he turned and told her again. "God loves you, Abi Connealy. He has since before He created that star just for you."

For Cassie's sake, he hoped Abi would believe that someday. He hoped Mark had come to know the same truth. Despite the accusations made that September morning, Travis even prayed her parents would one day know the love of Christ - the amazing, captivating, fathomless, bottomless love of the Savior who gave everything for them.

As he went inside, Travis began planning his next opportunity to propose. With Abi back in their lives, he feared his mom would decide she wanted him and Abi together and convince Cassie to help her.

And that wasn't going to happen.

Not in this lifetime.

Ten minutes later, Kristy sat next to him while Dad turned on the movie of the night. Abi had gone upstairs rather than watch with them. The thought of marrying Kristy made him happy. It did.

So why did he feel so unsettled at the same time?

That was a question Travis didn't think he wanted to know the answer to.

Chapter Seventeen

It didn't bother Abi that Travis wanted to marry Kristy. It didn't. Except that it did. A little bit. She hadn't dated anyone more than once or twice since that night her senior year of high school. She'd gone out with interesting men when they asked her, but didn't put herself out there, trying to find a guy. And, to be honest, she didn't work in an industry with a lot of eligible men. She'd dated a client or two a couple of times – after the work on their place was done, of course – but that was it. If she went on six dates a year, it was a big year for her.

And now she'd seen the father of her baby staring at an engagement ring.

Sixteen years after they'd slept together, but still.

And Abi had no one. No prospects. No one who'd wanted her but she'd turned down.

If she didn't watch it, she'd get downright depressed.

At least Cassie seemed to be sympathetic to her inner turmoil, though she doubted Cassie knew Travis was planning to propose. Could she want Abi and Travis together? The way Cassie seemed to love Kristy, no. But the way she sat with Abi and rested her head on Abi's shoulder, maybe she understood that the whole thing was a bit weird.

Before the movie started, she said her good nights and headed up to the room Travis had grown up in. There were still remnants of his high school days there as well as the days when he'd first arrived with Cassie in tow. They'd lived in this very room for nearly a year before they'd set up a room for Cassie, she'd learned. They lived in the house until after he graduated college and got a job, then they'd moved to the house they lived in now. Living with the ghosts of Christmas past unnerved her. And not in a good way.

Abi changed into some pajamas and slid under the covers, sitting against the headboard with a book propped on her knees. At this rate, she'd be done with the Cambridge Family Saga books, all twenty-some of them, in just a few weeks. But it gave her something to escape into. And might be changing her beliefs – that maybe, just maybe, there was a God out there who cared about her after all. Travis's words the week before had given her something to think about. But she wasn't ready to accept Julie's invitation to church the next day, either.

With a sigh, she dove back into the book, doing her best to ignore the parallels between the fictional world and her reality.

Abi sat on the side of the road, willing the tears to stay put. This was *not* what she needed.

Not knowing what else to do, she called Travis, hoping to catch him on a break.

"Hello?"

"Hey, it's Abi."

His voice cooled somewhat. She must not be in his phone yet. Still? Ever? "What can I do for you?"

"Recommend a mechanic."

That got her a bit of concern at least. "What's wrong with your car?"

"I have no idea. It just stopped, and yes, I have plenty of gas."

He sighed. "Do you have AutoHelp Roadside Assistance?"

"Yes. But I don't know where to tell them to take it." And that was really the least of Abi's worries at the moment. Well, not the least, but not her only concern.

"Have them take it to Yocum Automotive in Serenity Landing. It's across the street from McDonald's so you can always go sit over there while they work on it or see if they can give you a ride to my Mom's. They're usually pretty good about that."

Time to quote Shakespeare and "screw her courage to the sticking post." "Is there any way you can meet me, and I can borrow your car?"

"Why?" He sounded suspicious and she didn't blame him.

"I'm on my way to a meeting for work. I'm already going to be late if the tow truck takes very long." And she knew Mr. Wilson had another meeting after the theirs.

Another long-suffering sigh. "Did you call my mom?"

"She's at the pregnancy care center today."

"Right. Fine. I'll be there as soon as I can. Where are you exactly?"

Abi told him where she was – not too far from the high school actually and hung up to call the roadside assistance people. They promised to have someone out within the hour. That was too long. She called Mr. Wilson and told him she'd be there as soon as possible. He said his other meeting had been changed. Abi was relieved when he said it would be fine.

Ten minutes later, Travis pulled up behind her car.

"Pop the hood," he called as he walked by.

Abi did and followed his instructions to try and turn it on.

He came back to her window a minute later. "I think it's your alternator. Were you having problems with the air or anything?"

She nodded. "It didn't seem to be blowing cold, and my window didn't act right when I lowered it."

"That's probably what it is then. You can take it to Yocum, they can do it, and they'll do a good job. They won't over charge you. Or..." He closed his eyes and took a deep breath. "I can do it tonight."

"You would fix it for me?" Abi was understandably skeptical.

"Yeah. It'd save you a couple hundred bucks in labor, so yes. If it would help you out to do it, I would. If you can afford the labor, no problem, I wouldn't mind not doing it, but..."

Abi breathed a sigh of relief. "Thank you, Travis. I can't tell you how much I appreciate your help."

He shrugged. "Take my car. Go wherever it is you're going. I'll have the tow truck driver take yours to my house and get back to school."

"How?"

"I'll have someone come get me. I'm on my conference period, so..."

She gave him her AutoHelp card just in case he needed it, took her stuff out of the back, and put it all in Travis's car. The keys were still in it. He leaned on Abi's car, legs stretched out in front of him and crossed at the ankles as he pulled out his phone.

"Thank you, Travis."

He didn't even look up but just waved a hand and hollered, "No problem."

The man exasperated her to no end.

Sure he was helping her, but Abi felt guilty enough imposing on him at all. And now he was taking time out of whatever he usually did during his break to stand next to her car and wait for the tow truck. Living with his parents helped with her expenses. Since she didn't *have* to be in Serenity Landing most of the time for work anymore, the expenses were no longer covered. Plus the time off work and hotel and everything the first couple weeks she'd been in town. If he could fix the car, that would be a big relief.

Starting his car with a sigh, Abi headed for the meeting and tried to get the image of him in his jeans and untucked, navy blue, collared shirt out of her mind. Why did Cassie's father, Cassie's *practically engaged* father, have to be so good looking? Still? After fifteen years, he looked better than he had when they first met. It wasn't fair.

Abi turned into the driveway of the comedy club owners and tried to put Travis out of her mind.

She failed.

Miserably.

Abi turned into Travis's driveway and punched the garage button. Pulling his car in and stopping when the tennis ball hit the windshield, she wondered if anyone was actually home. She'd learned enough of their routines over the last few weeks to figure out they normally would be, but not always. No one opened the inside garage door.

Her car sat on the street, waiting for someone to fix it. She hadn't talked to Travis since leaving him on the side of the road. She'd texted him a couple times asking if everything went okay, but hadn't gotten an answer, so she figured he hadn't had time yet.

Abi knocked on the inside door, but there was no answer. She opened it. "Hello? Anyone home?"

"Hello?" a voice called from the back of the house. Cassie.

"I brought your dad's car back." Abi headed for her room.

Cassie walked out of the hallway with an ear bud in one ear and her iPod in the other hand. The other ear bud swung free. "Why do you have dad's car?"

"Mine broke down today."

"I wondered why it was here, but you weren't."

Cassie gave her a quick, very quick, hug. Abi would take what she could get. "Your dad said he'd fix it for me this evening."

Cassie raised an eyebrow. "He did?"

Abi set her purse on the counter. "Yeah. Why?"

"He was supposed to go out with Kristy tonight. Since they were with all of us Saturday night, and he was helping someone move yesterday, they didn't get to go out this weekend."

"Ah." Great. More guilt. Screwing up his day. Now screwing up his date night. "Do you know what the dinner plan was?" Maybe she could help out some.

Cassie shook her head. "No. Dad put chicken in the fridge last night, but I think it was for tomorrow since he and Kristy were going out. I was just going to heat up a frozen pizza or something."

Abi rolled her eyes and grabbed her purse. "We can do better than that. Let's hit the store and see what we can find."

Thirty minutes later, they were in the kitchen with the stuff to make Mexican Chicken. Abi grilled the chicken breasts while instructing Cassie on mixing up the rest of the ingredients. She put it in the oven while Cassie lamented the lack of desserts.

"A girl after my own heart," Abi laughed, aware of the undercurrents with the statement, but choosing to ignore them. "How about chocolate chip cookies? You've got the stuff."

"Perfect."

It had shocked her to realize Travis had a KitchenAid mixer sitting there, but he did. A few minutes later, it was spinning as they added ingredients to the bowl.

"I hope Dad and Kristy get here soon," Cassie said as she scooped the dough onto the sheet. "The chicken stuff will be done in a few minutes."

Abi pulled a pot out from under the stove. "I'll get the rice started. They'll be before long, won't they?"

She shrugged. "They should have been here twenty minutes ago."

Abi's brow furrowed, but as though they'd heard, the front door opened. In walked Kristy and Travis. Kristy smiled brightly, but not before Abi caught a glimpse of a scowl.

Was there something wrong in paradise?

Or was Kristy just annoyed she had to share Travis with Abi's car for the evening? Abi probably would have been so it wouldn't be surprising.

"What's all this?" Travis asked as Kristy headed into the living room without greeting either of them.

"Abi and I made dinner." Cassie bounded his direction to give him a hug. "And cookies. We haven't tried them yet, because they're not cooked, but the dough is better than

Grammy's."

Travis glanced Abi's direction. "Better than Grandma's? That's saying something."

At least he didn't get an attitude about letting her have cookie dough.

"What's for dinner?" He walked into the kitchen. "Is it almost ready or do I have time to run up to get a part for your car?"

"About ten minutes."

"Time to change then." He headed for the back of the house, untucking his shirt as he went. Probably school dress code made him tuck it back in. Abi didn't mean to watch him until he was lost in his room, but she did. And caught a glimpse of his back as he took the shirt off.

Stifling a sigh at what could never be, what she wasn't even sure she wanted, Abi turned back to the rice on the stove.

But Abi knew the image would stay with her for a long time.

If only there was something she could do about it.

Chapter Eighteen

It had been a long day and promised to be an even longer night.

Travis didn't mind helping Abi out. He'd do the same for just about anyone in a similar situation, but particularly a single woman far from home. At least one he knew. Maybe not a stranger. Except Kristy had turned it into a much bigger deal than it should have been. He hated postponing their date, but also had a feeling that if it had been just about anyone else, it wouldn't have mattered to her.

After changing into an old pair of shorts and a raggedy T-shirt, he headed into the garage and started pulling out the tools needed. Abi's keys were still in his pocket so he headed to her car to double check a couple of things. The alternator didn't look like it would be too hard to get to, thankfully.

Cassie opened the front door and hollered that dinner was ready. Going back inside, Travis washed his hands, sat at the table, and realized the awkwardness had set in. Abi sat in the same seat she had when she'd eaten with them before. Next to him. Kristy sat at the other end of the table. If he was at the head, then his significant other should be at the other end, right? That was the way it worked, didn't it? That was how his parents did it when they had company though Mom always sat by Dad when it was just family. But Kristy always sat by him. Was that the reason for the tension? And why did it really matter?

Because when he reached for Cassie's hand so they could pray, he also reached for Abi's? Because Abi and Kristy were then holding hands?

Travis tried to put it all out of his mind and focus solely on thanking his Maker for the things He provided them with. Including friends and family. He tried not to think about which group Abi fit in.

Abi explained how the meal worked. Tortilla chips, topped with rice, then the chicken/chili meat/red enchilada sauce mixture, followed by cheese and sour cream.

It looked wonderful.

It tasted better.

"Cassie said you both liked spicy so I went with the 'hot' enchilada sauce and less of the cream of mushroom to offset it," Abi explained.

Kristy muttered something that might, or might not, be a compliment.

Cassie tried to keep up a chattery conversation with everyone, but the tension was palpable. At least to him. Once dinner ended, Travis started to clean up, but Abi waved him off, saying she'd clean up the kitchen and promised the cookies would be done in twenty minutes or less.

Thanking her, Travis headed to the garage, followed by Kristy. Before he went to work on Abi's car, he gave Kristy a quick kiss. "You wanna help me?"

"I don't know anything about cars except how to turn one on and put gas in it. Anything else I call you or the guys at Yocum."

"That's okay. You can hand me tools and we can smooch." Travis grinned at her. She smiled slightly in return but not as warmly as he would have liked. "We can talk summer plans." Surely that would perk her up a bit.

That made her smile widen.

"Fine. I'll hand you tools and talk about fun day trips and stuff."

It took longer than he expected to get the stupid thing off Abi's car, but by then they'd talked about what she was wearing to prom and what he should. She talked about colors and kinds of tuxedos.

There's more than one kind of tux?

I hadn't planned to wear a tux.

"Okay." Travis held the alternator up triumphantly. "I'm going to get Abi so she can pay for the new one and we'll be back in twenty, okay?"

"You haven't fixed my car," she pointed out.

"I don't know what's wrong with your car. The guys at Yocum will fix it for you, you know." Kristy didn't say much of anything so he kissed her. "And then we can talk about a trip to St. Louis while I put the new one on," he promised with a wink.

That made the smile he loved appear.

"Fine. I'll see what Cassie's up to while you're gone with *her.*"

Travis frowned and tried to placate her a bit. "I'm really sorry, honey. I know we had plans and I'd love nothing more than to spend the evening with just you, you know that right?"

She nodded, but didn't answer, instead winding her hand behind his neck and pulling him down to kiss her. He couldn't hold her, but held his hands to the side and avoided getting grease on her clothes. Long moments later, they broke apart.

Travis brushed a kiss on her forehead. "Is this more than just being annoyed that we can't go out tonight?"

Her eyes focused somewhere near his chin. "Are you *sure* there's nothing going on with her?"

"Of course not. I'm dating *you*, Kris. I'm your date to prom, your date every time I go out with anyone, but I'd offer to fix anyone's car in this situation and you know that."

"I know."

"You have *nothing* to worry about, honey." He kissed her again.

"I think I'd rather you paid to fix her car than do it yourself," she muttered, walking toward the house.

Travis frowned. "Kris, what is it?"

She turned, her arms crossed in front of her. "I don't like her, Trav. At all. And it makes me wonder if she's not just out for something from you."

It took everything in him to stifle a sigh. "Like what?"

"Like you."

Travis couldn't help it. His head fell back as he laughed to the sky. "She doesn't want me, Kris. Promise."

She still looked mad. Maybe even more mad than she had been. Probably more mad, and getting more so every second.

"Do we even know her dad's sick?" Kristy demanded. "It's been a long time since that test, and we haven't heard anything."

"Why would she lie about that?" He didn't understand women.

"I would."

That got him to cock an eyebrow at her while setting

down the alternator and use his rag to wipe the worst of the grease off his hands. "What?"

"If, and this is a big if because I've never slept around, I was pregnant and gave the baby to the father and never saw them again but suddenly realized what a great thing I'd given up, in both the baby and the father, I'd make something like that up, too. Not just try to waltz in and insert myself into their lives, but come up with some emergency that's not too easily check-able and worm my way in."

Travis's eyes narrowed as she spoke. "Abi didn't sleep around."

"How do you know? Are you *sure*? Are you even sure Cassie's your daughter? How do you know there weren't a dozen other guys? That she wasn't, and maybe still is, a little..."

Travis cut her off before the derogatory word came out. "You'll stop right there, Kristy." This was a new side of her, one he didn't like. "Abi wasn't promiscuous. I have no idea about since then and it doesn't matter, but I don't need some DNA test to know Cassie's my daughter. She has been since before she was born. And, even though it's not what either one of us would have chosen, Abi's a part of our lives now. She's my daughter's mother, and we're both going to deal with her on a regular basis. I never would have believed you to be capable of saying such things, but if I find out you're saying them to Cassie, you'll answer to me, understand?"

Kristy's eyes flashed fire. "Standing up for her? Really? I thought you hated her."

"I never *hated* her. I wasn't happy with her, didn't like her decisions, and a million other things, but never hated her and never thought she'd show up on our doorstep."

She snorted. "I'm still not so sure she didn't just decide

you were the biggest sucker out of all her boyfriends, so she foisted the baby she didn't want off on you. Lord knows, you didn't want her so stick you with the baby that's not yours? Poetic justice."

A dark side Travis didn't know he had roiled around inside. "I think you better go home, Kristy. Before we both say things we'll regret." He made no move to stop her as she stomped toward her car, pulling her keys out of her pocket as she got closer.

The glare she gave as she passed him said everything.

If they weren't over, they were awfully close.

With a sigh, Travis headed toward the house. He couldn't deal with the fallout from Kristy just yet. He had alternator to put on so he could get Abi out of his house and out of his mind.

If only it was that easy.

"Kristy's not coming?" Cassie's eyes filled with tears the night before prom. "I know you guys are fighting, but she's not going to help me get ready for prom?"

Travis gathered her in close. "I'm sorry, sweetie, but no." He hadn't heard from Kris since the tire squeals Monday night, but without confirmation she'd be here, he figured it was best to let Cassie know not to count on her. "Grandma will be here though. Isn't that enough?"

Cassie shook her head. "Kristy was going to do my hair. Grammy already said she didn't think she could do it well enough." She pulled out her phone. "I need to text her and let her know we moved the time up."

"You did?"

"Yeah. Zach's mom wanted to know when we were stopping by to take pictures but he hadn't planned to so we moved it up an hour."

He nodded as another head of dark hair appeared in his mind. "What about Abi? She does some...fancy stuff to her hair." He'd never understand how she could pile it all up on her head and have curls escape everywhere. A messy mess if he ever saw one and yet it never tumbled down into an actual mess.

Cassie nodded. "If Kristy won't be here, then yeah. Abi would be great. She does cool stuff to her hair, maybe she can do it to mine." She pulled her phone out as she stood and called Abi. By the time Abi answered, Cassie was too far away for him to make out what was being said, but hopefully it would be straightened out before they arrived at school.

He heard the bus turning up the street and called to Cassie, as she headed out the door, backpack slung over one shoulder. "She's going to call you on your prep period, but she'll be here!"

Before he could answer, she was gone.

Several hours later, Travis was in the main office talking to one of the assistant principals when Abi called. They talked for a couple of minutes about when she should get there and what, if anything, was off-limits for hairstyle and he was about to hang up when Shawn made a hand motion.

"What?" Travis whispered.

"Who is that?"

"Abi."

"Things still going well with her?"

He shrugged. "Mostly."

"Would she want to chaperone? I just had three people cancel."

That left Travis speechless. "Um... I can ask. But are you sure it would be okay?"

"She's a parent, isn't she? She went on the drama trip."

He nodded and went back to the phone. "Uh, Abi, one of the assistant principals wants me to ask you if you'd want to be a chaperone tomorrow night. Interested?"

Travis could feel her hesitation. "Would Cassie mind?"

"I don't know. She's okay with me being there. You can make sure to avoid her all night if she does. Stay on the other side of the room."

"I guess I can do that. What do I need to wear?"

How was Travis supposed to know what the female chaperones wore? "I'm wearing a suit," he offered. "I don't think you need to be as formal as the kids." Shawn confirmed the statement with a half-shake, half-nod motion.

"I think I either have something or know where I can get something."

"Okay. We don't need to be there until about two hours after Zach is picking Cassie so you'll have time to get ready then."

"I've got to get planning. I'll talk to you later."

They hung up.

"I didn't think to ask if Kristy'll be okay with it," Shawn said with a grimace. "And everyone knows things have been colder than an ice box between you two this week."

Travis shrugged. "I don't know, but I know it'll be good for Cassie and that's the important part. Kristy and I'll work it out."

He talked to Shawn for a few more minutes about other things and then headed for his classes for the rest of the day.

Whatever else could be said about it, this weekend would sure be interesting.

Chapter Nineteen

Abi thanked that God that, somehow, Cassie had convinced her dad to let Abi help her get ready for prom. Maybe the fact Cassie would be wearing her dress had something to do with it, but more likely Kristy's apparent desertion played a bigger role.

Julie had her makeup case set out. Maile and Cassie sat on Cassie's bed, waiting for Abi to finish Maile's hair so she could start Cassie's while Julie did Maile's makeup.

Abi put one more bobby pin in the dark tresses of her daughter's best friend. "There we go. All done."

Cassie's hair was still a bit damp, by design, and Abi was just getting started on it when a knock sounded on the front door.

Cassie and Maile's wide eyes met. "That can't be the guys yet, can it?"

A female voice from the front of the house set that fear to rest. Cassie peeked out her window. "It's Kristy," she said, perplexed. "This is when she was supposed to get here, but I don't think she knew the time changed." Cassie headed for the door. "I'll talk to her and see if she wants to help us."

As much as Abi wanted Cassie to have a good relationship with the woman who was likely to be her step-mom, she kind of wanted Kristy to stay away. Jealously, Abi wanted this to be their time. A little mother-daughter thing that might, in some small way, make up for everything she'd missed over the years.

If the loud voices coming from the living room were any indication, Abi had nothing to worry about. Cassie reappeared a minute later, tears streaming down her face. Abi hung back, waiting for Julie's cues, but the slight motion Travis's mother made with her head was enough for Abi to rush to Cassie's side and pull her close. Her head rested on Abi's shoulder as she cried.

The front door slammed and was followed by heavy footsteps down the hall as an engine started in the driveway.

When Travis entered the room, the only thing Abi could do was hand Cassie off to her father, the one who'd been drying her tears long before her. Travis led her to the hallway where they talked for a few minutes before Cassie came back in. She was more composed and asked her grandma to get started on her make-up – or at least making her eyes less swollen. They had an hour. Hopefully, Julie could work some magic.

Abi followed Travis while Maile and Julie worked on Cassie.

"Do I dare ask what happened?" she asked quietly.

He shrugged. "Your car's not out front since you rode with Mom and are going with me to the hotel."

The image that immediately evoked – tuxedos, a white dress, and a long black limo on it's way to a honeymoon suite – had to be shoved to the back of her mind.

Foolish, unrealistic and completely impossible imaginings based on reading one too many romances over the last few weeks.

But still a part of Abi clung to the dream.

Even if she wasn't in love with the groom Abi saw in her mind's eye. At least not yet.

"I take it she wasn't happy I'm here."

He ran a hand repeatedly through his hair, deep furrows appearing with each pass. "She said some not nice things. Mostly about you and questioning whether or not I'm Cassie's dad." He didn't look at Abi.

"You are," she promised, trying to avoid the implications. "There was no one else." There never had been, but he didn't need to know that.

"I know. And she and I have been over it before, but just as she cast doubt on your character in rather crass terms, Cassie walked in. I asked Kristy to leave. I already told her I wouldn't tolerate the baseless accusations, especially not in front of my daughter."

"Thank you."

Travis shrugged. "It's not right. You weren't the things she was saying."

"Are you two okay?"

He shook his head. "I don't know, but unless she has a major change of heart in the next day or two, I can't imagine us working things out. I may not be happy with a lot of things you've done, but her accusations were all completely uncalled for and only hurts Cassie."

He didn't care if it hurt Abi. He only cared about their daughter. She could live with that. In fact, of the two, that was the more important.

But he looked hurt, too. She wished giving him a hug, comforting him, would be appropriate. Instead, Abi moved closer to him and rested a hand on the side of his face.

"Thank you."

"For what?"

"For defending me, even if it was only for Cassie's sake. I can't tell you how much I appreciate that."

He leaned into her hand for just a second before backing away. "There's no reason for slander. Even if was true, there was no call for her to talk that way." He took a deep, steadying breath. "I'm gonna watch the end of the game while you help the girls finish getting ready. They'll need to be ready to leave in time to go take pictures."

Abi nodded and headed back to Cassie's room to work on her hair. She wouldn't have enough time to do what they'd originally planned, but she could come up with something glamorous.

An hour later, they watched as the kids left in Zach's car. Zach had held the door for her as she slid into the front passenger seat. Maile and Jackson Dozier were in the back seat. Maile's dad, David, frowned a tad, but waved as they drove off.

Travis clapped a hand on David's back. "Wasn't it Jim Bishop who said, 'Watching your daughter drive off with a date is like handing a million dollar Stradivarius to a gorilla'?"

David chuckled his agreement. "There's some truth in that statement. Keep an eye out for my girl?"

Travis nodded. "Of course."

"Thanks. Deeanne's over at my house watching the younger kids. I need to get back so she can get to her house before they get there." From what Abi gathered, Deeanne was the neighbor of the kids Cassie babysat for a few weeks earlier. Deeanne was also Jackson's mom. She didn't understand why Deeanne and her husband both didn't just come over to Travis's house, but that's the way they decided to do it.

As soon as he left, Travis headed to his room, shutting and locking the door behind him. The water turned on in his shower. Abi'd already taken one, so she went into Cassie's bathroom to work on her hair. She had planned to pull it up on top of her head, but that would make it too similar to Cassie's now. Instead, she pulled the front up into a dozen or more bobby pins, letting the rest cascade down her back.

Once satisfied, Abi started on her make-up taking extra care to make it look the best she could. Kristy would likely be there and even if she wasn't, she'd hear about it from someone. Abi needed to look good. Not because of any relationship with Travis, but because she didn't want to be seen as the frumpy mother who ditched them.

Soft, sultry, and low key but sexy. Abi could do that. Once finished, she went back to Cassie's room, shutting the door behind her. Didn't want Travis getting an eyeful. Not to say the thought of an underhanded seduction hadn't occurred to her more than once. Maybe if he and Kristy were officially over, Abi would think about a play, but not yet. For now, subtle was the way to go. Look good. Try not to worry that Kristy was half a foot taller than her so Abi's legs, though very nice, couldn't compare. Just be there for Travis. Looking her best.

If something happened between them, eventually, Abi wouldn't say no. But she wouldn't connive her way into it.

The black dress slithered over her skin until it settled in place. Though not quite as formal as Cassie and Maile's dresses, it was probably a bit dressier than strictly necessary for a chaperone.

"Abi? Are you about ready?" Travis's voice from the hallway spurred her to action.

"Coming." Abi stepped into the heels she'd bought just for the occasion. A bit higher than she normally wore, but that helped with the height disparity. Another once over in the mirror showed her she looked good. The dress wasn't too low cut or too high cut, unless one counted the slit in the side, but even that wasn't outrageous since she'd added a few stitches to make it a bit lower.

Abi didn't want to be his date. Once he saw Kristy, she'd probably have to call a cab to get back home, but it would do her ego good if Travis would say something.

With a deep breath, she headed for the hallway and the living room beyond. Abi dug through her clutch to make sure her ID was in there along with some cash and a debit card. Just in case that cab thing happened.

And so when she walked into the living room, she wasn't paying attention to Travis.

The whistle caught her off-guard.

Abi looked up, her eyes a bit wide. "Huh?"

Travis shook his head. "You look great. That's all."

So did he. It took everything in her not to stare at him. The black suit, crisp white shirt and deep purple tie fit him just right. He'd done his hair in his usual faux-hawk rather than a more formal, normal hairstyle, but it fit him. He was the super cool drama teacher. The faux-hawk worked.

Unexpectedly, he held her door for her to climb in his car. The ride to the equestrian center was quiet, except for his explanation that the equestrian center also housed a very nice resort hotel in addition to room for 3500 horses.

That made more sense.

Travis parked a ways out to let the students park closer. Abi didn't mean to wait for him to open her door but she had something in her shoe, and it needed to come out. He didn't offer her his arm, but she didn't expect him to.

They walked into the hotel and the first person they saw was the one person Abi hoped wouldn't be there.

A very mad looking Kristy.

Chapter Twenty

Great.

Just what he didn't want to deal with and ruin his daughter's night.

More mad girlfriend.

"I'm going to talk to her," he muttered to Abi.

She just nodded as Travis walked toward Kristy.

One part of his mind noticed that Kristy looked wonderful. The other part noticed she looked furious.

"What is *she* doing here?" she hissed.

"Shawn asked if she'd be interested in chaperoning since several people canceled. Cassie was excited. End of story."

"Did she ride with you?"

Travis raised a brow. "You weren't. She doesn't know her way around. So yes. Now, if you'd given any indication you were still expecting me to pick you up, she wouldn't have. "

She let out a short bark of laughter. "My boyfriend, the one who keeps asking me to think about marriage, on a date with another woman. How romantic."

"Kristy..."

Her blonde hair didn't move as she shook her head. "Don't. It's over, Travis." She looked around to see if anyone else was looking before she undid the cross necklace he'd given her for Christmas and shoved it in his hand. As she stalked off, she called over her shoulder, "Tell Shawn I'm sick, would you?" When she brushed by Abi, purposefully making body contact, she said something he couldn't catch.

Abi's face remained stoic, but it couldn't have been nice.

Travis stared at the cross for several minutes before Abi reached his side. It didn't hurt as much as he thought it might.

"Are you okay?" she asked, her hand resting on his arm.

He nodded and stuck the necklace in the inside jacket pocket. "I'm fine." It wasn't the truth, but it was close enough. "Since I no longer have a date tonight, would you do me the honor of allowing me to escort you?" Travis offered her his elbow and she slid her hand into the crook.

"I'm sorry, Travis."

"It's not your fault." They headed for the ballroom. "In fact, I shudder to think what would have happened if we'd been married and she had the same reaction."

That thought had played itself over and over in his head many times and the answer to the question was "nothing good."

For now, Travis would focus on being a good chaperone, having fun, and making sure the kids didn't have too much.

About halfway through the dance, he wandered out to the balcony. The other chaperones had things well in hand. He leaned against the rock railing, his fingers clasped together as he looked across the fields. In the distance, a horse nickered with another replying a second later. The smell of the barns didn't drift this far, but he could see the silhouette of several of the animals in the distant field. He had the ring in his pocket again. The thought of trying to propose again had been appealing earlier in the day, though he admitted still not feeling entirely at peace with the idea. Had he just been trying to prove that he didn't have feelings for Abi? Had his feelings for Kristy *ever* been as strong as he wanted to believe?

Deep in his heart of hearts, he knew they hadn't been. Before Abi's untimely arrival, he likely could have convinced himself he loved her like a man should love his wife, but now, pulled in two directions, he knew he didn't. If he'd loved Kristy like that, he wouldn't want to spend time with Abi like he had. Not just to reminisce while avoiding any mention of the batting practice and near kiss, but to do his best to influence her toward Christ. He told himself it was strictly because of Cassie. Because her mother needed to know the Savior, but maybe there was more to it.

He'd hurt Kristy and he needed to apologize. It seemed unlikely anything would happen with Abi, but no matter. He wouldn't wallow. He'd been through much worse. This wouldn't hurt too much for too long.

He wouldn't let it.

Cassie

My first date.
Not really.
But close enough.
Me. Zach. Maile. Jackson.
Me in the front seat and Maile and Jackson holding

hands in the back seat of Zach's car. After a night of dinner and dancing.

I rolled my eyes at myself. We were going to Steak 'n Shake for dessert. We'd gone to Cee's Bakery for dinner. Not fancy, but not McDonald's. Zach and Jackson had been saving up for this but Zach only worked during the summer. His lifeguard savings from last year had to be nearly gone, especially after buying a car and putting new tires on it.

But as much as I loved Maile, I kind of wished it was just me and Zach. I wanted to talk to him about everything going on in my life. About Dad. About Abi. About actually enjoying talking with her. About wishing, maybe, just maybe, that she'd be around for good.

When we got to the restaurant, Jackson and Maile went in while Zach stopped me outside.

"I hope you don't mind..." He shifted his feet in the gravel.

I pulled Grandma's shawl a little bit tighter against the unseasonably cool May air. "Mind what?"

"Jackson and I were talking, and I told him I kind of wanted to sit just the two of us for dessert. I know this isn't a date," he rushed on. "But even though we spent the whole evening together, I still don't feel like we've really had a chance to talk."

I felt my heat rise in my cheeks. "I'm okay with that. I want to talk with you, too."

We'd chatted. We'd danced. No less than a foot or so between us at all times. Didn't help that Dad glared at Zach fairly regularly. But we hadn't *talked*.

By the time we got inside, Maile and Jackson were huddled on one side of a booth and oblivious to us. The hostess sat us in a different booth. Zach, so handsome in his tux, sat across from me. *I want to see your face when I talk to you*. His voice came back to me. He'd told me that before.

"Wanna talk about it?"

His quiet voice broke through straight to my heart.

"Kristy wasn't there tonight." I hadn't even voiced the thought to myself. "Why? Because Abi was?"

Zach shrugged. "Maybe she wasn't feeling good?"

I tore a corner off my napkin and shredded it. "You didn't hear the fighting at my house earlier. I think she thinks there's something between Dad and Abi."

"You'd know better than anyone if there is." Compassion filled his mocha eyes. "What do you think?"

The thought turned over and over in my head, and I shivered. They needed to turn the heat up in here.

Across the table, Zach stood, shrugged out of his jacket, and walked to my side, wrapping it around my shoulders. Grateful, I slipped my arms into the sleeves as he sat back down across from me, thoughts flying through my mind. "I don't know," I finally said. "He doesn't hate her anymore. I'm not sure he ever *hated* her, but from what he told me, they were never a couple." I hadn't told anyone what Dad said about where I came from, but I needed to tell someone. "I'm the result of a shared, spiked cup of coffee when Abi got buzzed at eighteen."

Emotions I couldn't really name crossed his face but mostly compassion remained. Before he could say anything, I launched into the whole story including my uncle the firefighter who died on 9/11. "And in the biggest cop out ever, Dad said he doesn't even remember the night they, you know, because of the spiked coffee." It bugged me that he didn't remember. Why? Who knows? Thinking about my parents...you know, was bad enough, but Dad raised me to believe that all human life is precious. A baby should be conceived in love between a married couple. That neither of my parents remembered my conception bothered me.

And it bothered me that it bothered me.

Zach didn't seem to know what to say. Of course not. I was talking about...that...with Zach.

Time to change the subject. "Anyway, that's where I come from. I don't think Dad wants to date her. He's nearly engaged to Kristy." Wasn't he? He and Abi had been standing awfully close earlier. I let out a slow breath. "I don't know what his deal is."

"What would you think if he and Miss Tomlinson did break up, and he got together with your mom?"

I shrugged. "I don't want to talk about it tonight. I had a lot of fun at the dance, and I know it's not really a date, but I don't want to go home cranky thinking about my dad and Abi."

The conversation turned to summer plans, including hanging out at the pool together while we worked. He could hang out with me at the front desk while he was on break. I could go to the parties afterward or get Zach, after closing, to teach me how to ride the surf machine, something I'd never mastered.

We talked for a while longer before Zach glanced at his watch and announced it was time for him to take me and Maile back to my house. Zach stood and held out a hand to help me scoot out of the booth and to my feet. His touch warmed me to my very soul. Not shocking. Zach was one of my oldest friends and the only boy to make my heart pitter pat. By the time I reached the door, Maile and Jackson were waiting for us. Zach paid for our milkshakes, and joined us so we could head home.

Travis opened Abi's car door again when they got back to his place.

"Are you sure you don't want me to take you back to my parents' house?"

She shook her head. "I promised Cassie I'd be here when she got home."

"They're going for dessert at Steak 'n Shake," he warned. "It could be a couple hours still."

"I know."

She wasn't about to let the time with her daughter go, even Travis knew that. And he didn't blame her.

Abi sank into the recliner. "I don't know how my feet can be so tired when I didn't even dance," she whined. "I can only imagine how badly they'd hurt if I'd actually gone to a real prom and danced the night away."

Travis grinned at her complaint. "You never have been to a prom, have you?"

She shook her head. "I've never even danced with a guy. Not really." Her head relaxed backward as she closed her eyes. "No one asked me once I turned sixteen because they were too scared of Mark. That's part of the reason why you were safe."

Decision made, he headed to the stereo and pulled out a CD Cassie had bought him as a joke. Hit romantic songs from the turn of the century. It and a couple of CDs filled with classics went into the CD changer. He hit random, then play.

"Abi Connealy?" Travis asked, slipping into the role.

She opened her eyes as the sound of Backstreet Boys filled the room. "Huh?"

"You're Abi Connealy, right?"

She nodded. "Yeah."

He held a hand out. "May I have this dance?"

A half-smile turned up one corner of her mouth as she took his hand. "Sure."

She stood, leaving her hand in his as Travis's other hand

came to rest on her hip. They didn't stand too close, but began to move in time to the music. He couldn't begin to count how many songs they danced to as they talked about high school, college, life since, purposefully avoiding any mention of Kristy, Mark, or the daughter they shared.

"Wonderful Tonight" came on.

"You do look amazing tonight, Abi," he told her. With one hand, he reached up to play with the curls hanging over her shoulder. Soft and silky, just like he imagined, like he remembered.

"Thank you." She smiled up at him, her eyes soft as moonlight filtered through the open blinds. "You look pretty wonderful yourself. How I'd imagined you'd look at prom. Mostly."

They continued to dance, moving closer with each song, until his arms were wrapped around her waist, and her hands rested on his biceps, with his chin leaning against the side of her head.

"Unforgettable" came on.

"I never forgot you, Travis," she whispered, looking up. Her eyes were bright with unshed tears. "Never. Not you, not..."

Travis stopped her with a finger to her lips. "Not now, Abs." With his fingertip he traced her lower lip, awed and scared by the war going on inside. "I never forgot you either and not just because..." He didn't say it. Wouldn't ruin the moment by bringing up the past.

Who moved first, Travis could never say, but a second later, she was kissing him.

Or he was kissing her.

Or they were kissing each other.

And something stirred inside him, deep inside, in a place no other woman had ever come close to reaching.

Travis framed her face with his hands, fingers tangling in

the soft wonderfulness of her hair as her arms slipped around his back, under his suit coat, setting his skin on fire even through the shirt.

Once the initial furor died down, they continued, for long minutes, exploring each other's lips with all the delicate tenderness he could imagine. Never had kissing a woman felt so right.

Except once.

Then Travis had written it off to being partially drugged, but he couldn't any longer.

The things this woman stirred in him couldn't be compared to anyone else.

When the kiss ended, they danced some more, continuing the way they had been, but closer if possible, stopping to exchange long, sweet kisses, but not ruining the moment by talking about it, by breaking the spell woven around them.

But after the most intense kiss yet, Travis knew he had to do something before he broke all sorts of promises.

"I need to take you home." His voice was husky, nearly foreign even to his own ears.

"Why?" she whispered, as breathless as he felt.

"Because if I don't, we'll both regret what could happen here tonight. I won't let that happen again, Abi. Not like this."

"Okay," she agreed. "But not before one more."

Travis lost himself in her, in him, in *them*, to the point he didn't hear the voices, or the door or anything until one voice stood out.

"Dad!"

Cold water wouldn't have doused things any more thoroughly.

Travis didn't shove Abi away but came pretty close. He started to run a hand through his hair but knew that would only make things worse as he took in his daughter's distraught face. Behind her stood Zach, Maile and Jackson.

It would be all over campus before school Monday and Cassie would, once again, be a laughingstock.

All of that went through his mind at the same time it must have gone through through hers. He could see the wheels turning before she turned and ran toward her room, slamming the door behind her.

"I'll go talk to her," Abi said, moving to go around him.

Travis shook his head. "I will." He dug his keys out of his pocket. "Why don't you take my car? I'll get it tomorrow."

She nodded and took them, the tears he'd seen in her eyes earlier, spilling over. "I'm sorry," she whispered.

"It's not your fault." Travis wrapped a curl around his finger and pulled gently. "I'll call you later."

Another nod, but this time she wouldn't look at him. She turned and headed out the garage door while he went first to talk to Cassie's friends and then to Cassie.

Travis used his best teacher look to glare at them, without scaring them. "I know this would make great gossip, but I would appreciate it if you guys wouldn't say anything. Cassie's been through enough lately, and Ms. Tomlinson doesn't need the gossip either." He didn't care too much about himself, but them...

"Uh," Zach shifted uncomfortably. "Aren't you dating Ms. Tomlinson?"

Travis shook his head. "No. We broke up. She doesn't need kids whispering behind her back any more than Cassie does. You're all Cassie's friends, so please, out of respect for her, can you keep this to yourselves?"

All three of them nodded.

"Mr. Harders?" Maile looked as uncomfortable as Zach. "I was supposed to spend the night."

Travis sighed. "Let me talk to Cassie. If she's not up for a sleepover, I'll get someone to take you home, okay?"

She nodded while he headed for the hallway

With one knuckle, he rapped on the door. "Cassie?"

"Go away!" The muffled yell left no room for interpretation.

"Come on, Cassie. Let me talk to you."

"Go away!"

Things had gone so well at prom. She'd even taken pictures with both of them all dressed up. In addition to the ones they'd taken before they left.

"I'm going to come in anyway," he threatened. "You may as well open the door."

Travis couldn't make out what the sounds on the other side of the door was, but she unlocked it and let him in, Zach's tuxedo jacket still wrapped tightly around her.

"What?"

"I want to talk to you."

Cassie through herself on the bed. "About what? Cheating on Kristy?"

"Kristy broke up with me," Travis told her. "She gave me back her necklace when she saw me walk in to the hotel with Abi."

"I thought you were going to ask her to marry you. You must have knocked her over with your proposal." Sarcasm laced her words.

"I didn't ask her. We haven't really talked since I we fought the day I worked on Abi's."

She seemed to calm down a bit and pushed herself into a seated position. "So what's happening with you and Abi then?"

He shrugged. "No idea. We came back here and she mentioned that she'd never been to prom and never even really danced with a guy because her brother intimidated all of them so I asked her to dance. Then we kissed. You guys got home. That's it." Or close enough.

"Are you going to ask her out?"

Travis reached out and brushed her hair off her face. "I don't know. How would you feel about it if I did?"

She shrugged. "I don't know her well enough to know if I want her to be my mom."

"Cassie," he warned.

"I know. She is my mom. But whenever you've dated anyone, we've talked about whether the lady would be a good step-mom. Abi's my biological mother, but I don't know if I want her to my actual live-in mom like a step-mom would be."

"Gotcha."

"So are you going to?" She fiddled with the pillow she'd pulled onto her lap.

"Maybe." He hadn't thought it through. Of course, Travis hadn't been doing much thinking at all while kissing Abi. Maybe a date was the answer. See if there was anything between them besides physical attraction and a justifiably cranky daughter.

"She's not a Christian," Cassie reminded him quietly. "You've always told me how important that is."

He sighed. "It is. And, if she was anyone else, I wouldn't even consider dating her for that reason alone. But she *is* your biological mother, so it's a bit different, you know?"

She shrugged. "I guess."

"I wouldn't marry her, though, if she didn't give her life to Christ," Travis told Cassie gently. "But there's a vested interest already, too. She's already in my life for the rest of my life, so dating her is different. Maybe. I haven't really thought it all through yet," he admitted. "I wasn't too surprised when Kristy ended things, not after the fights we had about Abi in the last week or so, but the thing with Abi has caught me completely off-guard. I guess we'll see what she says when I talk to her later." He leaned forward. "I'm not sure about it, honestly. I liked her a lot when I knew her before. I dated other girls while waiting for her to be old enough to ask out because I didn't *really* think in those terms." Not like Zach did about Cassie, but Travis brushed that thought aside. "I want to see what happens with her, but I also know things can't get too serious until she accepts Christ. I'll have to pray about it, a lot. Since you two are getting along, and you want to spend time with her, she'll always be a part of my life. But in a relationship? I just don't know how that's going to work. I'm going to ask her to go to church with us in the morning and we'll see what happens."

Cassie didn't say anything, but stood up. "I want to change. Did Maile go home?"

Travis shook his head. "No, she's in the living room waiting for you."

"Will you have her come back here?"

"We're not done talking, Cassie. We can be for now but I want to hear all about your night, okay?"

She nodded and handed over Zach's tuxedo jacket. "Not now, Dad, but okay."

Once the boys were gone and Maile and Cassie were locked in Cassie's room, Travis flopped onto his bed and stared at the phone.

"Here goes nothin'."

Chapter Twenty-One

Travis's parents were asleep when Abi walked in. She was glad of that. Looking in the mirror a few minutes later, she knew the smudged lipstick would have given her away. There was an unmistakable I-made-out-with-the-father-of-my-child look to her.

Abi didn't want to explain to anyone much less his folks.

A glance at her cell phone showed a couple missed calls from Mom, but Abi didn't want to talk to her. If something happened with Dad, there would have been voice mails or text messages, but there were none. He'd rebounded from his sudden downturn the day after Cassie's fall just as quickly as he'd slipped. So far, he'd remained stable. No news was good news and until she figured out what the night meant, Abi didn't want to talk to anyone except maybe Travis.

Flopping back onto her bed, the one Travis had slept in most of his life, Abi closed her eyes and remembered every blissful moment in his arms. Every brush of his lips against hers. Every tingle she experienced from the top of her head when he rested his chin against it to the tips of her toes where he practically lifted her off the ground while they kissed.

And now he was dealing with Cassie alone. Abi understood why. The girl wouldn't want anything to do with her long-lost mother at the moment, and Travis had been through everything with her. Part of her ached with jealousy, the rest of her threatened to turn bitter over what she'd lost, and toward her parents for forcing her hand.

She laid there, in her dress, waiting for something. She didn't know what, not until her phone buzzed.

Travis.

"How is she?" she asked, forgoing a greeting.

"Upset, confused. But she'll be fine."

Upset and confused? Sounded about like Abi herself.

"How are you?" she asked.

"Fine. Worried about Cassie, but I really do think she'll be okay once..." He didn't finish.

"Once what?" Abi prompted.

"Once we figure out what's going on with us, if anything."

If anything? From her end, everything was going on. She made herself ask the question, though the potential answer filled her with dread. "So, what is going on with us?"

He sighed. A deep, loud sigh she could almost feel through the phone. "I don't know. Kristy and I just ended things tonight. I don't want this, if there is a this, to be a rebound thing. You deserve better."

"Thank you for that." Abi didn't want to be a rebound thing. The thought had occurred to her, but she hoped it was more a resumption of what could have been a decade and a half earlier rather than a distraction from the end of a relationship.

"So." He seemed to be considering every word. "Would

you like to go out with me next weekend?"

Abi winced. "I can't. I have to go home next weekend. It's my mom's birthday."

"The weekend after?"

"Sure."

"Great. We can talk about it more later then." He seemed to hesitate. "Would you go to church with us in the morning?"

Church?

She knew they went. Julie had asked her several times before issuing a standing invitation, but to go with Travis and Cassie? That was a different story all together. But she wanted to be part of Cassie's life, of Travis's. And church was a big part of that.

"Sure," Abi answered before she could talk herself out of it. "Where and when?"

"Why don't we pick you up? About 10:30 tomorrow morning? We're not going to early service."

It was after midnight. Surely she could get a good night's sleep and be ready by then. "Okay. Don't your parents go to the same church?" Abi wanted to offer to ride with them, but at the same time, she wanted to spend time with Travis and Cassie.

"They do, but they'll probably leave by 8:10 since they teach a class during first service. I texted them already to have them drop my car off. I haven't heard back, but I'm sure they will, so if you could leave the keys on the kitchen table, that would be great."

"Um, sure." Her mind was going a mile a minute. What was a service? She had no idea, but figured she'd find out in the morning.

"Why don't I let you get some sleep?" Travis said, his voice deep and husky. "I'll see you in the morning."

"Good night," Abi whispered back. "Thank you for

tonight. It meant the world to me."

"You're welcome. Sleep well."

She repeated "good night" before hanging up.

Abi changed into pajamas, washed her face, brushed her teeth, and set the alarm on her phone for nine. Surely that would be enough time to get ready to go into the great unknown of church.

It wasn't until the alarm went off and her blurry eyes started to wake up that she realized she had no idea what to wear. Jeans and a blouse seemed not nice enough. A business suit seemed wrong. For some reason, the Queen's lemon yellow suit with matching hat from Prince William's wedding to Catherine popped into her mind. But it didn't really seem right either, not that she had one. Abi stared at the clothes in the closet for a long time before deciding on a nice pair of tan slacks and an emerald green blouse with matching heels and her regular purse.

Did she need a Bible? She didn't own a Bible. In a flash of brilliance, Abi pulled out her smartphone and a bunch of free Bible apps appeared after a quick search. Surely, she could navigate through one of them if she needed to.

A knock on the door interrupted her thoughts. Hurrying down the stairs, she whispered a prayer to the God Travis believed in. Just to help her to get through this without embarrassing herself. Sure enough, when she opened the door, he was standing there, looking amazing. And wearing tan pants and a green shirt a few shades darker than the one she wore. They matched. Sort of.

"You ready?"

Abi nodded, pulling keys out of her purse so she could lock the door. "How's Cassie this morning?"

"She hasn't said anything but Maile spent the night so they were pretty tired. Took me about six tries to get them up."

They reached the car and Travis opened the front passenger door. She thanked him as she climbed in and turned to talk to the girls in the back seat. "Good morning."

They both mumbled something that sounded like "morning" but she couldn't be sure. A few minutes later, they pulled up in front of a building that looked suspiciously like a grocery store but had a sign with Grace Community Chapel over the main doors.

"We just moved into this building a few years ago," Travis explained as they walked in. "The store that was here closed a couple years before that and it was cheaper to buy and remodel this building than to build a new one when we outgrew the old facility."

Made sense. Maybe.

The girls scurried ahead. Abi's nerves grew with every step. She had no frame of reference for this, not outside of *Little House on the Prairie* reruns and movies like *Sister Act*. She was pretty sure neither one reflected what was about to happen.

A man dressed in a nice suit opened the door and welcomed them. Travis shook his hand and said something about needing to talk to him about advertising for next year's play. The man handed her a card. She held onto it, figuring to read it later. Travis had one, too, but hadn't looked at it yet so it must not be too urgent.

The large foyer area was teeming with people, including a few she recognized.

Julie's eyes lit up when she saw her. "Abi!" She left the conversation she was having to give Abi a hug. "What are you doing here?"

Abi shrugged uncomfortably as Travis joined the conversation with his dad and a couple who looked vaguely familiar. "Travis asked me to come." Julie and Keith had both asked a couple of times, too, but she'd turned them down. Abi hoped the other woman wasn't going to ask why she'd said yes to Travis but not them.

Julie left her arm around Abi's waist and directed her to the knot of people she'd left. "Abi, this is Gavin and Bethany Parmiggiano. Cassie babysits for them sometimes."

That's where Abi knew them from.

Bethany smiled. "We met in my driveway a couple weeks ago." She held out her hand. "Good to see you again."

"You, too." Abi guessed it was.

Gavin shook her hand, too, but the men went back to discussing baseball. Bethany asked the question she'd been dreading.

"I didn't realize you were from the area. Do you live here? Or have family in the area?"

Abi shifted then, from one foot to the other, when Julie spoke up.

"Our family has known some of Abi's family for years. She's in town for business and personal reasons, so she's staying with us for the time being."

Told the truth without telling the whole truth. Abi liked it. It felt a bit dishonest to do that in church, but it also didn't seem right to tell people she was Cassie's mother.

"That's great." Bethany smiled. "So much nicer than staying in a hotel. Cheaper, too."

Abi nodded. "They've been wonderful."

The doors on the opposite side of the foyer opened, and people began streaming out. Travis moved back to her side. "Do you want to sit with my parents?"

Abi shrugged. "I'll leave it up to you." Half of her said it would be more comfortable to sit with people she knew. The other half wanted to make sure no one she knew was around when she made a fool of herself. Instead, she let him decide.

His hand rested on the small of her back directing her toward one of the side doors. Abi couldn't remember what to call the large main area with all the seating. She knew there was a term for it, but had no idea what it was.

The room had to seat several hundred and even as some people stood in the aisles talking, others walked around them to stake out seats. Once the seats had been claimed, some people sat down. Others left the room. Still more went to talk to someone else, often kneeling on the seat in front of the other person or squatting next to them.

Travis stopped at a row about a third of the way toward the front. "How's this?"

How should she know? "This is fine."

He held one hand out, indicating Abi should precede him into the row. He followed, sitting on the aisle seat. She sat next to him. As he started looking at the card he held, she did, too. An announcement about a kids' roller skating event that evening. Another mentioned Wednesday night dinner. A third, about baby dedication, was followed by the fourth about "Pastor Rick's upcoming trip to Africa." The bottom was some sort of form to fill out. She'd have to look at it more carefully later.

"Are you okay with being here?" Travis twisted in his seat until he was half-facing her.

"Sure," Abi told him with much more confidence than she felt.

"You don't have to put on a front for me," he said, one finger twirling around a curl in her hair. "When was the last time you were at church for something besides a wedding or funeral?"

Abi thought about it. "You know, I'm not sure I've ever been to a wedding at a church. I think all the weddings I've been to were at hotels or something. And I think Mark's funeral was the last one I attended. Or around then. I went to a bunch after 9/11."

"So you've never been to an actual church service?"

She shook her ahead.

"Do you want me to give you an idea of what's going to happen?" He glanced at the screen and she saw a timer counting down. "We have about eight minutes before they get started."

"Okay."

He outlined the usual order of service. The music pastor would greet everyone and there would be singing. Words would be projected onto large screens above the stage. That made her feel a bit better. Some songs would be fast, some slow, some repetitive. It seemed that annoyed Travis. He, apparently, liked the songs, but not eighty-seven times in a row. After that, announcements would run on the screen. Then, usually, Pastor Rick would move to the pulpit and preach. Sometimes, there was something else in there – a special song, or different announcements, or some other thing. After the pastor was done preaching, the musicians would come back for another song while pastor opened the altar for people to pray. Then they would pass buckets for the offering.

Abi wasn't sure what that last two things were. And she didn't think she wanted to find out.

A minute after he finished his explanation, the music started playing and the man welcomed everyone to "worship."

She stood with the rest of the crowd and muttered to herself. "Here goes nothing."

Chapter Twenty-Two

Travis drove Abi and Cassie to his parents' house for lunch. Maile went home with her parents. Jay and his family arrived at the same time.

Abi didn't say much and nothing about church. Cassie avoided both of them as much as she was able. No one mentioned Kristy. She hadn't been at church or at least not in second service. Travis truly hoped she was okay. They'd talked about her history, of her past relationships. With several bad break-ups in her past, he hated the thought that he was another one. He prayed she'd find a man who would love her like he'd thought he could, like he was already falling for the new Abi.

His mom's friend Anise had given him a cold stare. Travis thought that was odd until he remembered she was also friends with Kristy. He was going to have to talk to her. Soon. And do his best to smooth things over. He wasn't sad they'd ended things, but he really hadn't wanted to hurt her. It soothed his angst a bit to know Kris had friends like Anise to count on.

Had it really only been two weeks since he and Abi fought over Cassie's dress and a week since he planned to ask Kristy to marry him? So much had happened. Now, Travis wondered if he might steal a moment alone to kiss Abi again.

A relationship couldn't be based purely on physical attraction. Travis knew that. Abi knew that. The physical attraction wasn't a problem and wouldn't be, but there was so much more. The Christianity thing was a deal breaker if they were to try for a real relationship, but at least she'd seemed open to the idea of church and he thought she'd be willing to go back. It was a step in the right direction anyway.

"When are you leaving, Abi?" Mom asked her as everyone sat on the back deck after dinner.

"Probably Wednesday. Mom's birthday is Thursday so we can go out for dinner that night. I need to visit the office while I'm there, and we're having a small party for her on Saturday night with a few friends. I should be back Sunday or Monday, if that's okay." She glanced at both him and Mom. "I don't *have* to be here anymore, but..."

He knew she wanted to stay, to keep getting to know Cassie. And probably to see if there was anything between them.

"You're welcome to stay as long as you want, sweetie," Mom reassured. Had his mom already figured out there was something going on?

Travis could see the relief on her face. "Thank you."

"How's your dad doing?"

Abi shifted slightly in the Adirondack chair. "He's okay. He's home for the time being. I know they did that bloodwork a couple weeks ago, but I haven't heard anything about whether she's a potential match or not. And he doesn't know Cassie's one of the ones being tested. As far as I know, he thinks it's all being done through the bone marrow people."

"Does your mom know?" Dad asked her.

She nodded. "I told her the day I first talked to Travis and Cassie that I'd found her and that she'd agreed to be tested. I think Mom really wants to meet her, but she's not about to ask."

"I want to go." They all turned to see Cassie standing on the stairs that led to the backyard.

"What?" Abi asked.

"I want to go with you, if Dad'll let me skip school for a couple of days."

"Really?" Abi asked, the hope evident in her voice. Cassie nodded.

Travis wasn't sure how he felt about that idea. "Do you have any tests the end of the week?"

She shook her head. "No. I have a couple on Monday and Tuesday but not the end of the week. I've got As in all of my classes. It won't hurt me to be gone for a couple days."

"I'll think about it," he promised. "But that's it. No wheedling."

She nodded. "Okay."

Later, he would have a long discussion with Cassie about why she suddenly wanted to go meet her grandparents. He could insist on going along with them, but that was guaranteed to ruin Abi's mom's birthday.

Jay and his family left soon after, dropping Cassie at the house so she could study for her math test the next morning. His parents wandered inside to clean up the rest of the meal. He and Abi stayed in chairs just a few inches apart.

Without giving himself time to talk himself out of it, Travis reached for her hand and laced his fingers through hers. "You really want her to go?" he asked softly.

"I would love for her to go," she affirmed.

"What about your parents? It sounds like your mom would be okay with her, but your dad..."

She took a deep breath and blew it out slowly. "I don't know. Part of me thinks I should just say she's Cassie Harders, the daughter of a friend of mine who wanted to come for...some reason, and not mention that she's my daughter. Dad may not even remember your last name. He's never known, at least as far as I know, if the baby was a boy or girl. I dropped a few boy hints from time to time, just to keep him off track. If he ever...found you and realized you had a daughter, for instance, then he'd have no reason to believe she was also my daughter."

"That's an idea. Just not mention who she is to you. But if he realizes? If he starts saying the kinds of things to her he said to me that morning?"

"I'm not eighteen and scared anymore, Trav. I'm a grown woman, and she's my daughter. If he starts doing that kind of thing, I'll put a stop to it. I won't let him and I'd get Cassie out of there and bring her home if he refuses to let it go."

Deep in his heart, Travis knew it was the right thing to do even though he was scared. "Okay. She can go. But you have to stand up for her, Abi. You can't let him do to her what he tried to do to me and what he did to you."

"I won't."

Travis glanced at his watch. "I need to get home. I'll talk to you tomorrow?"

She nodded, but leaned his direction. "Do I get a kiss first?"

A genuine grin split his face. "Of course."

Travis leaned over the arm of the chair until he could cross the gap and brush her lips with his, coming back again and again for soft kisses. As much as he wanted to reach over, pull her closer and deepen the kisses the way they had the night before, he held back. The temptation that came with Abi was one Travis knew he'd need to keep tightly under control.

"I'll see you soon," he told her, his voice as soft as her eyes. "Do you want to come over for dinner tomorrow night?"

She nodded. "That sounds wonderful."

A few minutes, and a few kisses, later, Travis was headed home, whistling a happy tune.

Travis held Cassie close as he got ready to leave for work. "I'll miss you, punkin."

"I know, Dad. But I'll be fine. I'll be with Abi the whole time." She looked up at him. "And if her dad tries anything, I'll kick him."

That led to a head-tossed-back kind of laugh. "Just like when you were little." She'd gotten in trouble more than once for taking on kids who picked on her about her father the teacher or not having a mother by kicking them.

Abi's car pulled into the driveway. Cassie let go and picked up her suitcase. The one his parents had gotten her before the family trip to Disneyworld when she was nine. Abi opened the trunk and helped Cassie stow it before Cassie loaded her laptop bag into the passenger seat.

Abi came to the door where he stood watching them. "Thank you, Travis. I know my Mom is going to love this. She's asked about you and Cassie nearly every time I talked to her since she found out why I was here."

Travis nodded, still unsure it was the right decision, but knowing it was too late to change his mind now.

Ten minutes later, he gave Cassie another hug, checked for the bus, and gave Abi a quick kiss before sending them on their way. Travis wouldn't want any of the kids on the bus to see that. Kristy had avoided him and there had been a few questions, and more looks, but he still didn't want to drag it all out into the open just yet. Not when there was only a week of school left.

Once summer got here, everyone would forget about him and Kristy. By the time the next school year started, they'd be old news. Just one more week.

Travis was excited for Cassie and Abi. Just a couple of weeks earlier, he couldn't have imagined letting Cassie go with Abi to visit her parents. As excited as he was, though, Travis was also apprehensive. So many things could go wrong.

Everything from Abi's mom turning on Cassie. Abi turning on Cassie. Abi's dad going ballistic.

Or the exact opposite.

They'd all fall in love with Cassie, Abi would leave him, and sue for custody.

And since he'd never done anything to protect himself, he'd lose her.

Calling a lawyer was back on the to-do list. He hadn't because things had been going so well, but now it was time.

He had to protect himself and his daughter.

Just in case.

Chapter Twenty-Three

The knot of apprehension in Abi's stomach grew as every rotation of the tires brought them closer to Kansas.

Cassie was a quiet traveling companion, since her ear buds were tucked into her ears and plugged into her phone. Abi wasn't sure if she was asleep or not, but her eyes were closed for most of the first part of trip. They stopped in Clinton, MO to get breakfast, caffeine, and visit the bathroom. By the time they were back on the road, she'd perked up a bit, but read a book instead of dozing off.

They crossed into Kansas and headed for Olathe. Abi'd grown up not too far away from there, but when her parents left NYC to return to the area, they'd moved closer to the city. She'd moved with them, finishing college at KU and getting her own place after graduation.

About three hours after they left, she pulled into the garage of her apartment.

"This is your place?" Cassie asked as they walked through the door into the kitchen.

"Yep." Abi was oddly nervous. She'd never had someone whose opinion was so important to her actually in her place. "I don't have a guest bedroom though. You can have my room, and I'll take the couch."

Cassie shook her head. "That's okay. I won't take your bed. I'm fine on the couch."

Abi headed to the counter in the kitchen and picked through the mail while Cassie wandered around the living room.

"Is this your brother?" she asked, picking a picture up off the side table.

With a sad, half-smile Abi nodded. She'd stopped by to see him at the station one day and someone had snapped a picture of the two of them. "That was taken a couple weeks before 9/11. Mark loved being a fire fighter." He wore his navy blue T-shirt and pants and had his arm around her shoulders.

Cassie's finger traced over picture-Abi's stomach. "And that's me?"

Tears filled her eyes as Abi nodded. "I was almost six months pregnant."

"Mark was okay with it? With me?"

She nodded. "He was pretty sure he knew who your father was, though I never confirmed it. He knew Dad would flip out on Travis if he found out. He tried to get in touch with your dad, but your dad never called him back."

She set the picture down and wandered around some more. "Is your dad going to be okay with me now?"

"I hope so, but I really don't know for sure. We may not find out. I don't think we should tell him who you are."

Cassie nodded. "If that's what you think is best. But do you think he'll figure it out?" She picked up a picture of Abi from high school. "Except for my eyes, I look almost exactly like you did. It's how I knew you were my mother on the front yard the day you showed up."

Abi shrugged. "I know, but we'll cross that bridge when we get there."

And maybe if he did figure it out, Mom would be able to help calm him down.

"So when are we meeting them?" she asked.

"Mom doesn't know we're here. No one does, actually. The plan all along has been to surprise them. She's taking the day off tomorrow, so I thought we'd show up there and take her out for the day. Mani-pedis, lunch, maybe birthday shopping or a movie or both. Then take her and Dad out for dinner tomorrow night. Maybe." Abi bit her bottom lip. "That was my plan, but spending dinner just the four of us might not be such a good idea if we don't want Dad to realize who you are. In fact, spending too much time alone with him at all might not be a good idea."

Cassie nodded. "I want to meet him and your mom and since your mom's okay with me, get to know her some, but I don't want to get into a fight with your dad either."

Abi sighed. "We'll figure it out as we go, I guess."

Cassie sounded about as confident. "I guess."

CASSIE

I wandered around Abi's living room, coming back, time and again, to the picture of her and my uncle Mark. I wished I'd had a chance to know him. I hadn't told anyone but Zach and Maile that I had an uncle who died on 9/11, even if it wasn't at the Trade Center.

"I still miss him." I turned to see Abi walking down the stairs. "Every day I think about him and wonder how things would be different."

With the frame in hand, I sat in the recliner. "What do you think about?"

She settled in on the couch. "I don't think I would have felt compelled to give you to your dad."

I wasn't sure what I thought about that. As often as I'd wondered where my mom was and why she wasn't in my life, I didn't ever wish that I'd grown up with *only* my biological mother. Life without Dad? Unimaginable.

"Why not?" I finally asked.

She seemed to think about it for a minute. "I guess because I think Mark would have helped me with my dad. I never told him Travis was your father, because I didn't want him to hate Travis for something that he didn't do, not like my dad and brother thought."

"Would you have told him eventually?" Something else occurred to me. "Would you have ever told Dad he had a baby?" I didn't even want to think about a world where Dad wasn't part of my life.

Abi stretched out and stared at the ceiling. "Probably? I'm sorry, Cassie, but I don't know. I was young and scared and..."

"You were three years older than I am, and even I know unless there's something really, *really* wrong with the guy, you tell him he's going to be a dad." The silence stretched until it could be counted in minutes. I changed the subject. "Tell me about him?"

A smile crossed Abi's face. "He was three years older than me, but we were close as we could be. He didn't mind if I hung out with him and his friends, not most of the time. Your dad lived with us for a couple months, and Mark took me with them one day when they went to Chelsea Piers with some friends. Mark brought his girlfriend with him, and it turned out that all of the other people there were paired off, too. Even though we lived in the same house, I hadn't seen your dad much, but we spent a long time together that day. He never held my hand or kissed me. He moved to the city after that, but still came over all the time."

She seemed to be lost in the memories. "I think he missed his parents but didn't want to tell anyone. It would have seemed...unmanly maybe to miss his family. He dated a couple of girls during that time, and I was insanely jealous, but they were only around for a few weeks each. There was one who moved in with him at one point but that only lasted a couple of months, too."

I could see her cheeks turn red. "I probably still have the diaries with notes in them about your dad. I liked him a lot, though I never really admitted how much to anyone, not even my diary. I bet you could read it through the lines though."

When the silence stretched out, I asked another question. "Did anything ever happen between you two, before, you know, that night?" The night I was conceived.

Abi had to tell her the truth. "Not really. He did almost kiss me in the subway parking lot after that day at Chelsea Piers, but he didn't. After that, we'd sit out on the back deck while Mark and Brenda snuck off." A catch in her voice made me look at her. "She was my only friend after 9/11. She was there when you were born and just held me when I waited across the street to make sure your dad took you home."

She'd waited? Dad hadn't told me that. He probably hadn't known. "Where is she now?" I might want to meet her.

Abi shook her head, and I saw a tear slip down her cheek. "I haven't talked to her in years. She got married about four years after Mark died. They weren't engaged yet, but she probably would have been my sister-in-law in the next year. She asked me to be in the wedding, but I just couldn't. I did go, but had to sneak out not long after it started. It was still too raw. I think that hurt her feelings. I never told her why I couldn't do it or she probably would have understood."

"Why couldn't you?"

Abi sniffled. "It was your fourth birthday. I knew I wouldn't be able to be a good maid of honor that day."

That made sense. "Have you talked to her since then?"

"No." Sadness filled her voice. "I've looked her up on Facebook a few times, but I could never bring myself to click the friend request button."

A plan began to form. I didn't know much about Abi, but I did know she didn't have a lot of friends. I'd guess she didn't have any, not really. Maybe I could find Brenda.

A few minutes later, Abi said she was going to bed. I pulled out my laptop and logged into her Wi-Fi. It took a lot of searching, almost all of the coverage from 9/12 in NYC was about the Towers, not other, more trivial, stuff like a lone fire with just three fatalities, but I finally found a couple of articles about my uncle's death. One of them mentioned the street they'd lived on. Something my dad said a few weeks earlier made me think Brenda lived nearby and had known Mark for years. I Googled some more and found pictures from their senior year of high school.

There.

One of Mark.

If I hadn't been so intent on my search for his girlfriend, I would have kept looking for more pictures of him. Maybe Dad had some somewhere. Or my grandparents. Though I was here to meet them, it was an odd thought. I had grandparents other than the ones we'd lived with until I started kindergarten. Opening a new browser window, I searched for her maiden name and prayed there weren't a ton of Brenda Wardmans out there. A second later, I gave a silent fist pump. Only two as far as I could tell and only one of those was about the right age.

Brenda Wardman Parker.

"And lives in Branson?" I whispered, clicking on the Facebook page. Only forty-five minutes away. "No way."

I scrolled through the "about" section and looked at all of the publicly available pictures. She seemed to have two kids, maybe a third on the way, involved in their church, and very happy. As I scanned the profile pictures, one caught my eye.

My uncle.

In his uniform.

I clicked on it to see if there was a description. Sure enough... "'My first love and a 9/11 hero. Even though he wasn't in the Towers, he died protecting the less able that day.'" One of the comments caught my eye. From her husband. "'I still can't imagine the pain all of you went through. I am glad we found each other. I love you.'"

With a deep breath and a quick prayer thrown heavenward, I clicked on the "send message" button and began to type.

Abi knocked on the door to her parents' home as Cassie waited at the apartment. If it was Abi's birthday, she'd have slept in until noon, but not Mom. She was up with the roosters.

When Mom opened the door, dressed nicely, hair and make-up done, Abi knew she'd been right.

Her eyes lit up. "Abi! What're you doing here?"

Abi gave her a big hug. "Kidnapping you. Breakfast, mani-pedis, lunch, a movie, shopping. Whatever you want.

Plus a surprise."

Her eyebrows shot up. "A surprise? Really?"

"Yep. Think Daddy'll be okay here with you gone all day?"

"He'll be fine. Just let me tell him. Do you want to come in and say hi?"

She probably should, especially if she was hoping to avoid spending much time alone with him later. She loved her father, and except for his blind spot of fury where Travis and Cassie were concerned, he'd been a great dad growing up. Unfortunately, when she'd needed him most, he hadn't been there for her. Most of the time, she could push that part to the back of her mind. She hoped this was one of those times. Abi nodded and followed her mother in. He was in the living room, sitting in his favorite recliner and looking better than she expected.

"Hi, Daddy." Abi hoped it didn't sound too forced, but after getting to know Cassie for the last several weeks, she wasn't feeling particularly altruistic toward him.

"Hey, sweetheart. What are you doing here?" He sounded genuinely surprised and happy to see her.

Abi gave him the best hug she could and kissed his cheek. "Came to kidnap Mom for her birthday. Girls' day out."

"Have fun." He squeezed her hand, but not as hard as he would have before he got sick. "Be back for dinner?"

"Maybe. I do have some work to do while I'm in town."

"Where've you been anyway? And why are they keeping you there?"

"We have some clients near Springfield, and they asked me to represent us and do the groundwork. It's weird, but we have several new clients in the area. I can do the rest of my work remotely, so I just stayed there for a few weeks. I'm going back this weekend, actually. Kevin's been toying with the idea of opening an office down there for years. If the clients keep coming, he just may."

He grimaced. "But staying at a hotel for weeks on end? That can't be fun."

How to get around that without lying? "I ran into an old friend whose parents live in the area. I've been staying with them."

"Anyone I know?"

"I don't know that you've ever met them." Meaning Cassie, Keith, and Julie, of course. He'd met Travis.

"You ready, honey?" Mom stuck her cell phone in her purse.

"Yep." Abi gave Dad another kiss on the head. "Love you." Even if she wasn't crazy about the things he'd done all those years ago, she did love her father.

They were in the car before Mom spoke again. "So what's the surprise?"

Abi grinned. "If I told you it wouldn't be a surprise, now would it?" A few minutes later, she turned into her apartment complex. "It's in my house."

Mom entered the apartment first, with Abi right behind. Cassie stood awkwardly in the living room, not sure what to do or say.

"Mom, I want you to meet someone. This is Cassie." Throughout their conversations, Mom had avoided asking her name and Abi hadn't offered it. "Cassie Harders."

She stopped dead in her tracks and just stared at Cassie for an eternity. "Cassie Harders?" she whispered. "Travis..." Her voice trailed off.

Abi put her arm around Mom's shoulders. "Mom, Cassie is Travis's daughter." She took a deep breath. "And your granddaughter."

Mom gasped, though Abi knew she'd only been waiting for confirmation. "Cassie." Her voice was barely above a whisper.

Cassie shifted awkwardly from one foot to the other. "Happy birthday."

Tears streaked down Mom's cheeks as she walked into the living room. She put one hand on either side of Cassie's face before pulling her into a hug. Cassie's arms came around Mom's waist, and they stood there for the longest time. Tears also slipped down Cassie's cheeks as they held on to each other.

Finally, Mom moved back and framed Cassie's face with her hands again. "I couldn't have asked for a better birthday present, sweetie. I don't know why you're willing to come see me, because that implies at least some forgiveness, and I know I don't deserve it."

"None of us do, Mrs. Connealy." Cassie's voice was filled with sympathy. "But we're supposed to forgive people just like Christ forgives us. And, Lord only knows, none of us deserve His kind of forgiveness."

Abi couldn't see her mom's face but she was pretty sure Mom had no idea what to do with that. Just like Abi didn't.

"Whatever the reason, thank you." Another long hug, then Mom led Cassie to the couch while Abi sat on the chair near the fireplace. "We have all day for you to tell me about yourself, but first I want you to know how sorry I am." She reached out and brushed Cassie's hair back. "For a lot of reasons, I thought it was best if Abi wasn't a single mom at eighteen, a freshman in college, especially after we just lost Mark. Once we got back from our vacation at Christmas, I wanted to ask Abi about you, but I could never bring myself to. I figured you'd been adopted by a nice family in a closed adoption and there was no point, except to bring a lot of pain to all of us again, so I didn't say anything."

"She always remembered though," Abi told her

daughter. "She made my favorite meals and always did something special for me on your birthday."

Cassie took a deep breath and wiped the tears from her cheeks. "I've thought about it a lot over the last couple years. I've talked about it with my dad and my grandparents, and we figured the reasons were something like that and wondered if either of you regretted it. With the note from Abi, we were pretty sure she wasn't completely at peace about leaving me with Dad, but had no idea how you might have felt."

Mom brushed her hair back off her forehead again. "The reasons, I guess, aren't really that important anymore. They really weren't as important then. We just thought they were. I've never been into the church or praying thing, but I prayed you were in a happy home."

"I have been," Cassie told her with a smile. "My dad is amazing, and my grandparents are awesome. I have great friends and a great church. I love my life. As much as I've always wanted to know my mom and know why she gave me to Dad, I don't think I'd change anything because without Dad, I wouldn't be where I am, you know? I wouldn't be me. I wouldn't live where I do or have the friends that I do or have gone to prom with a great guy. So even though I've wondered, I think it's all worked out okay. I'm fine. I'm happy." She reached out and brushed Mom's tears away. "I promise."

"Your father has done a wonderful job with you." Mom pulled her close again. "Now, what do you say we fix our faces and go out for that mani-pedi and shopping and everything?" She looked up. "Unless that was all just a ruse to get me here?"

Abi shook her head. "No, we really do plan to do all that stuff, if you want to. We could stay here and have a movie day or something, but I had planned for all three of us to go out."

Mom smiled. "Then let's go." She headed for the half-bath on the main floor while Cassie headed upstairs. Ten minutes later, they headed out the door and on to the first ever Mother-Daughter-Grandmother day.

If only it would go well, and they could make it an annual thing.

With a whispered prayer to a God Abi was starting to believe in, they headed out.

Chapter Twenty-Four

Travis had managed to avoid Kristy for several days, but she finally caught up with him, quite by accident, he was sure, in one of the teachers' work rooms.

"Where's Cassie been?" she asked, not looking at him.

"She went with Abi to Kansas City for Abi's mom's birthday."

"Huh."

"What?"

"Are you sleeping with her again yet?"

Travis cocked an eyebrow at her. "Excuse me?"

"You slept with her before, you have Cassie, after all. Are you sleeping with her again?"

"You should know me better than that."

"I thought I did, but then she was at your house and at prom as your date and everything else, all while you were practically engaged to me."

He sighed. "Kristy, this isn't the time or the place to do this. But I never cheated on you. Ever. And I wasn't going to. You read more into the interactions than there was. But she is Cassie's mother. She always will be. And Cassie wants to have a relationship with her and so do my parents. Therefore, I'm going to be around her. I'm sorry it's not working out with us, really I am." He was. Or he was trying to convince himself of it anyway. "But nothing happened with Abi while we were together."

"Is there something happening now?" She crossed her arms and stared at him.

Travis shrugged. "If we're over, Kristy, then I'm free to date whomever I want, but for the record, no, we haven't gone out." Yet.

"So you let your precious daughter, who you barely let go to prom with a kid you've known most of his life, go out of state with a mother who never officially relinquished custody."

"Don't start, Kris. She's fine. I talked to Cassie last night, and she texted me a couple times this morning. She's having a great time, and Abi's showing her some of the cool places in the Bonner Springs area. Tomorrow, they're going to see marbles made."

Three other teachers walked in, interrupting the conversation. Just as well. They were going to have to agree to disagree and hope she didn't start rumors, intentionally or otherwise, about him cheating on her. *I need your help with this, God. If You can spare a second or two to help me figure out what I need to do to make it right with Kristy, I'd appreciate it. And if things could work out with Abi, that would be great, too.*

With a sigh, Travis headed for his classroom and a day of teaching kids. The prayers didn't stop, though. Throughout the day, he continued to whisper prayers for the people in his life.

The hard rubber of the basketball smacked soundly against his hand.

"Come on, Mr. H." Zach didn't even sound winded. "You can't just stand there all day."

Travis did his best not to huff and puff when he answered. "I can stand here as long as I want. Unless you're going to come do something about it."

Zach took a couple of steps his direction before Travis faked one way then went the other direction around him for an easy lay-up. "And that's game, kid."

Zach grabbed the ball on the second bounce. "Best two out of three."

Travis took a long swig of his water. "Nope. Think I'm gonna stop while I'm ahead."

With a chuckle, Zach reached for a water bottle. "I'd take a pot shot or two about you being old, but I like you, Mr. H."

Water came out Travis's nose when he snorted. "You like my daughter."

He shrugged. "Of course, I like Cassie. She's been my friend since she started kindergarten, and we sat together on the bus on the way home every day."

Travis caught the gleam he was trying to hide. "That's not what I'm talking about, and you know it."

The red crept up Zach's neck and he refused to look at Travis. "Okay. So I kind of like her a lot."

"Did you kiss her?" Part of him wanted to know. Part of him really didn't. But the rest of Travis knew he would level Zach if he took advantage of his little girl, and he knew Zach knew it, too.

He shook his head. "Peck on the cheek. That's it." He held up three fingers. "Scout's honor."

It matched what Cassie had told Travis once she was

done being mad about him making out with her mother.

Travis collapsed onto the bench Zach's mom had put along the side of the driveway for that very reason. But it was a controlled collapse. One that didn't make him look eighty-seven to Zach's seventeen.

The teen sat next to him. "Can I ask you something, Mr. H?"

"Sure."

"Can I take her out when she turns sixteen?"

Travis raised a brow at him, but he wasn't looking. "What?"

"I'd like to have permission to ask her out."

"She can't date for at least six more months. You're a bit early, aren't you?"

He shrugged. "Maybe. But I know she's the girl I want to court. So I thought I'd ask."

"And if you meet someone else in the meantime?"

"I won't." His quiet certainty was a more than a bit unnerving.

Travis didn't know what to say to that so he took another big swig of water. "I gotta get home. Papers to grade."

"I'm gonna want to court her, Mr. H. Not just a few dates." Zach looked up with a serious look on his face. "In fact, I haven't told her this yet, but I want to marry her someday."

Travis stared at him. Zach was a good kid, and he liked him a lot. But as a future son-in-law? Where he'd be kissing Travis's baby girl? And... He managed to stop his thoughts before they went any further. What was the T-shirt he'd seen on Facebook a few weeks earlier? *DADD. Dads Against Daughter's Dating. Shoot the first one and the word will spread.* That might be taking it a bit far but... He understood the sentiment all too well.

"Yeah, well, you'll have to talk to her about that."

"I will."

Great. Just what he needed.

"Thanks for the game, Zach. See ya later." End the conversation before Travis threatened the kid within an inch of his life. If he really did start dating Cassie, then would be the time to put the fear of God into him, but until then Travis would play it cool.

Or try to.

Because where his baby girl was concerned, no one was good enough.

Not even Zach.

Some days Travis wished he still drank.

This was one of those days.

A cold bottle of beer would really hit the spot.

Instead, Travis unscrewed the cap on his Dr Pepper and drank half the twenty-ounce bottle in one big swallow.

Not only had Zach told Travis he wanted to marry his daughter, his *fifteen*-year-old daughter, but that same daughter was getting ready to meet her maternal grandfather for the first time. The one who'd essentially denied her very existence.

Several texts from her throughout the day said she was having a good time so far. That she and Abi's mom were getting along well. They'd gone to get manicures and pedicures and then were headed for lunch. That was the last update he'd gotten.

He downed the last of the Dr Pepper as his phone started to vibrate, but he didn't recognize the number. "Hello?"

"May I speak with Travis Harders, please?"

"This is Travis."

"This is Tom Burnside returning your call. Rick from Grace Community Chapel gave you my name as a family attorney."

Right. The lawyer. Travis briefly explained the situation. Tom asked a few questions of his own before taking a minute to think it over.

"Well, first, *anything* can happen in family court. I've seen cases that went the way no one believed they would. That said, I don't *think* you have anything to be concerned about. I don't see how a judge would rule in favor of a biological mother who left voluntarily over fifteen years ago. Visitation, maybe, but not full custody with no rights for you. I'd have a hard time believing she'd get anything more than visitation and possibly be hit with back child support. It *can* happen, but it would be unusual."

That put Travis's fears to rest. Sort of. "Thank you, Mr. Burnside."

"Please, call me Tom. If you have any further questions or want to do a real consultation and start paperwork to protect yourself, give me a call at the office anytime."

"I will. Thanks." They exchanged a few words about the upcoming Beast Feast and said goodbye.

As Travis thought over the conversation, his phone buzzed again. This time his smile widened when he saw Cassie's picture on the screen. "Hi, honey."

"I can't do this, Daddy," she whispered.

Travis sat up, all senses on high alert. "What's wrong?"

"I can't meet him. Mrs. Connealy is fine, and she seems nice enough, but I don't want to meet him."

Where were his shoes? "Is Abi making you go with her?" They were by the door, right?

"No. I don't know. We're back at her apartment, changing clothes for dinner at her parents' house. I had fun today, but I don't think I want to do this."

"Then tell her that, sweetheart. She'll understand."

Travis could hear the tears in Cassie's voice. "I think she would, but it would make her mom so sad if I didn't. I think she has this vision of me and Abi's dad reconciling in some big made-for-TV movie moment. And I don't see it happening. I think it'll be more like the title fight in Vegas."

He slid his foot into one of his tennis shoes and wiggled his foot until it popped in place but still felt weird. The wrong foot. He toed it off and reached for the other shoe while he tried to think of what to say to her. "If you don't want to go, don't." It came out more forcefully than intended. "I understand her mom wants you to go, to meet him, but if you're not comfortable with it, don't go."

Travis heard her take a deep, shaky breath. "I'll be okay. I won't tell him who I am. And if he guesses or gets mad, then I'll leave. I can wait for Abi outside."

With his second shoe on, Travis grabbed his wallet and stuck it in his hip pocket. He snatched his keys off the hook as he headed for the garage door. The addresses were already programmed into his phone.

Travis slid into the front seat of his SUV. "Cassie, listen to me, honey. Don't go. If you don't feel completely comfortable going, stay at Abi's apartment."

Another deep shaky breath. "I know. But I think I'll be okay."

He pushed the button to open the garage door. "Are you *sure*?"

"I'm sure."

She wasn't sure. Travis could hear the fear and uncertainty in her voice. The whole idea scared the daylights out of her. It made him proud that she'd do something that scared her because she thought it was the right thing to do. But she still wasn't old enough or wise enough or mature enough to know for sure when doing the right thing was the wrong thing. It might be the right thing to do, but if it was only going to cause her pain, to cause Abi's mom to have a bad evening, to bring to the forefront issues Cassie, Abi, and the rest of them weren't ready to deal with, then it wasn't *really* the right thing to do.

He needed to be there to make sure his baby girl was okay. To make sure she had someone to defend her if needed. Dinner wasn't for another hour. It was a three-hour drive.

How much time could Travis shave off if his baby girl needed him?

Foot pressed a bit closer to the floor, he figured it was time to find out.

Chapter
Twenty-Five

This was it. Cassie and Dad in the same room. Abi hadn't known Dad had planned to have several other people over *on* Mom's birthday. All she'd known about was the party on Saturday. The more the merrier, though. Give them a chance to meet but still have buffer.

Cassie looked as apprehensive as Abi had ever seen her. Even more than the first time she'd really talked to her, that first night.

Abi reached over and put her hand on Cassie's shoulder. "Are you okay?"

She shrugged Abi's hand off. "I'm fine."

"Are you sure want to do this?"

A deep breath in and then out seemed to steady Cassie's nerves. "I'm sure."

Her phone chimed with a text message. She looked down at it and smiled.

"Your dad?" Abi asked.

She nodded. "I called him earlier and told him I was

nervous about tonight, but I'm feeling much better about it. I don't want to come between you and your dad. But Dad just texted to say he loves me."

"He does love you. Anyone can see that."

Her next question was so quiet Abi had to strain to hear it. "Does your dad love you like mine does me?"

The car glided to a stop in front of her parents' house, and Abi turned the car off before she answered. "He loves me. Very much. And he loved my brother the same way. I never, ever doubted that he loved me." She wasn't sure how to go on.

"But?"

"But there was one time in my life when I questioned his support, even if I didn't really doubt his *love*. That's when he found out about you and about your dad and all of that. Since then, it's colored our relationship. Even though we never mention it, I've never *really* felt that completely unconditional support since then, because, in the back of my mind, I wonder what would happen if I really screwed up again." Should she be telling Cassie all of this? Was it too much for a fifteen-year-old?

"I'm sorry, Abi." Her daughter reached over and squeezed her hand as Abi desperately tried to hold back the tears. "I'm sorry he's made you feel that way. That I've come between you."

Abi shook her head. "It was never you, Cassie. It was me, and the choices I made, and what happened that night. But it was never *you*. Those days after you were born, but before I gave you to Travis, were the hardest but most wonderful of my life. I knew I wouldn't get to see you grow up, so I never let you out of my arms. I changed your diaper and took a shower, but otherwise I held you nonstop, trying to soak up everything I could. I loved you enough to know I wasn't the best one to raise you." Lost in thought, Abi rested her head against the back of the seat. "How would Travis react if you had to tell him you were pregnant?"

Cassie didn't hesitate before answering. "He'd be sad and disappointed in me and my decisions, of course, but he'd never disown me for it. Not for just that. If I went off the deep end with drugs and alcohol and sex and all of that, maybe, but if something happened to me like it did to the two of you, he'd support me unconditionally. Help me finish college like his parents did. And he'd never, ever make me or my baby feel like something to regret."

Travis had given Abi no reason to doubt her words, but hoped Cassie wasn't being set up for a huge let down someday. "You sound so certain of that." Her voice took on a wistful tone.

"'Love one another as I have loved you.'"

"What?"

"It's something Jesus said in one of the gospels. John, I think. He said that He came to love us like God the Father loved Him. And He gave a command. That we should love each other the way He loves us. He loves us unconditionally, with an everlasting love. No matter what we do, He won't *not* love us. There are still consequences to our actions. If I were to get pregnant, I'd have to deal with the responsibility that goes with being a parent. No more sleep overs at Maile's. No more dreaming of going away to an acting school or trying to make it in LA. But both God and Dad would still love me unconditionally."

"I wish I had that assurance."

She took a deep breath and Abi sensed some uncertainty in her words. "You can, Abi. God loves you. He's always loved you. He was there that night when you were both drugged."

Abi snorted back a laugh. "How do you figure that?"

"A couple reasons. First, what if Dad hadn't answered the phone? What if you'd had the coffee at the party? And the guy who drugged you dragged you off to a back bedroom somewhere? What if the drugs had kicked in before you got back to the apartment while Dad was driving? Either one of those things would have been so much worse than what happened between you and my Dad. But if you hadn't been drugged, if you hadn't been at that party, without that night, I wouldn't be here."

Maybe she had a point. Abi had never looked at it in quite that way. "If I thought about it at all, I blamed God for putting me in the situation in the first place." Maybe she needed to change her thinking.

"No. You made the decision to be at a party, to drink. He chose to protect you from the worst case scenario that decision could have brought. Proverbs says children are a blessing from the Lord. And maybe, that night, what happened then, who it happened with happened was so I could save your dad's life."

Such wisdom coming from such a young girl.

"I mean, what if you had been drugged and raped by some random guy? When it came time to give me up, who would you have given me to? Left me on the doorstep at a hospital? An adoption agency? Would you have been able to find me last month? Because you knew enough about my dad to find us, you have, potentially, the means to save your dad's life. So yes, you can blame God for what happened that night, or you can choose to look at it from His long-term perspective. Decisions have consequences, or like Pastor Rick says, decisions have descendants. It's up to you how you look at it. If you look at it the way Dad and I do, you see that God was protecting both of you from the worst consequences because He loves you. And that's how my dad loves me. He lets me make my own decisions, and he'll protect me and support me when he can, but I also have to live with the consequences." She shrugged. "I know that's a bit rambly and not quite on topic, but I think it's the truth."

"Then how do you explain something like 9/11? Like my brother?"

Cassie took a deep breath. "I can't. But we have to trust He has a purpose and look for the good. It took sixteen years to find the reason why you were both drugged that night. Who knows how long it could take to find the reason for 9/11, but there's good there. What about the lifelong friends who were made after one saved the other's life? Or how few problems there were landing planes when they decided to close all the airspace? Can you imagine trying to land thousands of planes in just a couple of hours on a day when half the country is covered with thunderstorms or other weather events? The day was clear which helped with landing all of those planes, but also had to help the first responders. What if they had to do those jobs in the middle of the pouring rain? I don't think the rain wouldn't have affected the fires, but it certainly would have affected the response."

She had a point. One Abi didn't know what to do with. "You've given me a lot to think about." Abi didn't know what else to say. She knew Cassie was headed toward a conversation about the whole Christian thing, but her daughter didn't push.

Cassie spoke again as Abi reached for the door handle. "Can I pray, Abi? No pressure to pray with me, but let me pray for you, for us, for this night to go well?"

Abi didn't know what to say, so just nodded.

She closed her eyes. "Lord, be with us tonight. Be in control. Thank you for protecting Dad and Abi from the worst of the things that could have happened at that party.

I ask You that tonight turns out well, but mostly, I ask You to accomplish what You want out of this evening. If it's time for him to know who I am, then it's time. Whatever happens tonight, Lord, please show Abi your unconditional, everlasting love. Thank you. Amen."

Abi didn't know what she thought about all of that. But in her mind, she whispered two words.

Help me.

Several other people were already in the living room when Abi walked in with Cassie. Dad sat in his chair, just as she expected. Mom sidetracked Cassie so they didn't walk in together. If Abi had anything to say about it, Dad wouldn't see them next to each other any time soon.

"Who's your mom talking to?" Dad asked as Abi sat on the arm of his chair.

"Her name's Cassie." She left the last name off on purpose.

"How do you know her?"

"I met her while I've been out of town."

"She looks familiar." Since getting sick, Dad's mind hadn't been quite what it used to be. He was still himself, just a bit more sluggish, something Abi was counting on, at least for the next couple hours. "Do I know her family?"

Abi gave a noncommittal shrug.

The next thirty or forty minutes were spent mingling with some of her parents' friends who she hadn't seen in some time. Cassie spent most of it in the kitchen with Abi's mom's best friend helping do whatever it was they were doing in there.

Dinner was served buffet style. Abi filled Dad's plate and gave it to him. Cassie circulated helping in so many different ways Abi lost track.

As dinner ended, Abi saw her pull her phone out and smile slightly at what she read there. She texted someone a second before Abi felt her phone buzz. She was going outside to talk to her dad for a minute. Abi nodded as her daughter glanced over and headed out the front door.

When she hadn't returned in a few minutes, she walked to the window to check on her. Shock vibrated through Abi's body all the way down to her toes.

Travis stood on the driveway holding Cassie in his arms.

Abi hurried out the door to talk to him, demand to know what he thought he was doing showing up like this.

"What are you doing here?" she whispered as soon as the door shut.

Travis glared. "Cassie called me earlier, unsure about tonight. Something in my gut told me I needed to come, so here I am."

"Well, she doesn't need you."

If it had just been Abi and Travis talking, maybe that would have been okay to say, but Cassie instantly turned. "I always need my dad, Abi. Don't try to make this about choosing between the two of you, because that's no choice at all."

Abi sighed and pulled the pony tail out of her hair before putting it back in. "That's not what I meant. I just meant there was no reason for him to be worried. Have you even talked to my dad?"

She moved away from Travis, though his hands rested on her shoulders. "I thought you wanted me to avoid him," she said quietly.

"I just didn't want him to see us together. It would make it easier for him to put it all together."

"And you've been next to him almost all night," Cassie reminded Abi, calm beyond her years.

Abi's shoulders slumped. "Okay, you have a point."

A noise behind Abi made her jump out of her skin.

"I thought I told you to stay away from my family." Dad didn't bellow often anymore, but somehow he managed and when Abi turned, she could see him there, face florid and veins nearly popping out of his skin.

"Dad..." Abi didn't know what she was going to say, but he didn't let her.

"I told you to stay away, you sonuva..."

"Dad!"

He stopped before finishing the word, but he glared at Abi, holding onto the railing as he carefully moved down the steps. "What are you doing here? I told you to stay away! You raped my daugh..."

Before she could interject, Travis had positioned himself between Abi and her dad. And between Cassie and her grandfather. "Sir, I did no such thing and you know it. Abi never told you I did. You jumped to conclusions based on partial information."

Dad leaned around Travis and stared at Cassie behind Abi. "And that's the bastard kid, isn't it?" He snorted. "Some friend you met while working. Right. That's the kid I saved you from."

Travis moved until he was the only thing in Dad's line of sight, protecting Cassie from Dad's glare. Abi moved to Cassie's side, wrapping an arm around her daughter's shoulders in support.

She doesn't need my support, Abi realized. Cassie's shoulders were squared, and she stared straight at Travis's back as though she could see Dad through him. She had no intention of backing down or letting him intimidate her.

Neither did Travis. "Cassie is the best thing that's ever happened to me. If you want to disparage me, fine. It's not the truth, but I can handle it. But you leave my daughter, your *granddaughter,* out of this."

Dad looked Travis up and down. "Still running away, aren't you? Not taking responsibility for the mess you've created." Where Dad got that from, Abi had no idea.

"I didn't know Abi was pregnant until the day she showed up with Cassie. If I had known I would have been there for her, helped take care of her, helped pay for everything. But she didn't tell me, and neither did you that morning when you yelled at me. You may have saved my life that day because I didn't go to work after that fight, but you never ever mentioned a baby."

"My son died that day, and you lived. Lived to be a deadbeat dad until you were given no choice. And then I bet you mooched off your parents, didn't you?"

"I'm sorry about Mark, sir. I loved him like a brother."

"Don't even say his name. You wouldn't have helped Abi if you'd known. You would have run far and fast, wouldn't you?"

"No. If I'd known I would have helped her. I would have married her."

His bark of laughter interrupted whatever else Travis was going to say. "Like I would have let you."

"It wouldn't have been your choice. Abi and I were both over eighteen. I would have married her, and we would have raised Cassie together. It wouldn't have been easy but..."

"Did you love her?"

Travis shook his head. "No, but I could have learned to, for Cassie's sake."

"Do you love her now?"

"Do I plan to propose to her? No."

How could he be so polite?

"So you would have married her without loving her fifteen years ago to take care of her and the..." He waved a hand in Cassie's general direction. "But now? When no other man wants her because of her ruined past?"

Abi gasped. "Daddy! That's not..."

He held up a hand to shush her. "You would have married her without loving her then. Would you marry her now?"

Travis didn't hesitate before answering.

"Yes."

Chapter Twenty-Six

Whatever Travis had been thinking when he drove to Bonner Springs, an actual confrontation with Abi's dad hadn't been on the agenda. He just wanted to see Cassie and make sure she really was okay. Slip in, maybe take her with him if things weren't going well, and slip back out.

Her dad looked Travis up and down skeptically. "You'd marry her? No one else wants her, why would you? Oh. Right. You're the one who ruined her in the first place."

Was this guy seriously living in the Fifties? And the 1850s at that. "Abi's not ruined. She never was. I don't know why she's not married, but I've never married either. I guarantee you, neither of us was ruined because of Cassie."

"So why won't you marry her now? Why didn't you offer to marry her as soon as you found out?"

It was time to call an end to the madness this meeting had become. "Sir, I don't think this discussion can continue rationally or end well, so I'm going to leave. I'm going to take my daughter with me. If you'd ever like to continue this conversation calmly, I'd be happy to take your call. Abi knows how to contact me."

Travis turned on his heel and stood in front of Abi. "You don't have to stay either, you know. If he's going to stand there and belittle all of us, you can leave."

She nodded. "I know. But he's my dad, and I have a feeling this could send him back to the hospital. I can't leave my mom to deal with all of it by herself."

"Okay. Call me if you need anything. Bring Cassie's stuff with you when you come back?" Abi agreed and Travis walked toward Cassie, wrapping his arm around her.

Before they could walk off, Abi called to him. He turned to see her dad walking back into the house, slowly as though each step could be his last.

"Yeah?"

"Did you mean what you said? Would you have married me?"

Travis nodded. "I would have. If you'd come to me. It would have been an option on the table, anyway. There's no way to look back and know for sure what we would have decided, but it would have been one possibility."

"Even though you had a girlfriend?"

One shoulder lifted in a shrug. "Depends. I didn't have a girlfriend the whole time, but I can tell you this, I'm much happier you're the mother of my child than I would have been with Jennifer. And I knew that even then."

She stared into his eyes for a moment before nodding. "Thank you."

"You're better than that, Abi." Travis jerked his head toward her dad. "You know that? You're better than what he's saying you are."

"I know." She hesitated, thanked him again and turned to help her dad up the last of the steps.

Travis left his arm around Cassie's shoulders. "Are you okay, punkin?" He asked as they reached the car.

"I guess. It's about what I expected if he figured out who I was." Travis opened her door and she sat down, waiting for him to get into the driver's side before she spoke again. "I feel sorry for Abi and her dad."

"Why's that?" He turned the ignition on and backed out of the driveway.

"She doesn't have the unconditional love you've talked about from your parents. The kind we've talked about if I ever ended up in a jam. She doesn't have that and neither does he. Not from her anymore and definitely not from me either. He's missed out on what I have with Grammy and Grandpop. He's cheating himself out of all of it and he's cheating Abi and her mom at the same time." She gave a long sigh as Travis tried to look at the map on his phone. "We talked about God, too. About how He loves us unconditionally. There are still consequences, but it doesn't make Him love us any less."

"How'd she react?"

"Like she wanted to know more. Like she wanted to know what it was like to have someone love her like that. Maybe..." Her voice trailed off, but Travis knew what she was thinking. The same thing he was. Maybe there was some hope for Abi's salvation, and sooner rather than later.

Travis whispered a little prayer for her. Because if their relationship had a chance of surviving for the long haul, her salvation was necessary.

Staying awake was a struggle for Travis during school the next day. Cassie slept in since they'd gotten home so late, and she wasn't supposed to be at school anyway.

Travis had gotten a text from Abi saying her dad seemed to have recovered okay from the confrontation but the rest of the birthday gathering had been subdued. She had to go to work for the day but still planned to come back on Saturday night, late, or Sunday.

He'd texted his reply, mentioning that they'd love to have her at church again. She'd told him she'd think about it. That beat the outright no he'd expected.

Travis made it through the day without making any major faux pas. He spent a quiet evening at home with Cassie Friday and a quiet day Saturday together, watching movies and eating junk food. He even bought a little birthday cake since they'd left before Cassie got some of Abi's mom's cake.

Travis had convinced her to watch *Ferris Bueller's Day Off* as the last movie of the day. She pushed play just as a knock sounded on the door.

"Don't change the movie while I'm gone, got it?" Travis pointed at her as he walked toward the door. "No more of those teeny-bopper movies."

She laughed. "Fine."

The chuckles came and he didn't try to stop them. The laughs were still there when he opened the door.

Abi stood there, fidgeting with the strap of her purse. "I hope it's okay I came over."

Travis felt his face brighten and hers relaxed in response. "Of course. Come on in. We're getting ready to watch *Bueller*."

Her eyes lit up. "I love that one!"

He put his arm around her shoulders as they walked toward the living room.

When she saw who was with him, Cassie's eyes lit up just like Abi's had. "Hey! I didn't think you were coming until tomorrow or Monday."

Travis felt Abi shrug. "There was no point in staying longer. Dad won't talk to me, and Mom deserved a nice dinner without the conflict. She said to tell you she misses you, though and asked me to give you her email address."

Cassie nodded. "I'll email her this week."

His daughter moved over so they could all sit on the couch. What did it mean that she left room on one end of the couch for him and Abi? She'd seen him and Kristy sit together plenty. Did she expect him and Abi to sit together like that? Travis wasn't opposed to it, but what did Abi think?

Travis got his answer when Abi curled next to him.

An audible smirk filled Cassie's voice. "Did you kiss her yet, Dad?"

Travis coughed up his soda. "What?"

"Did you kiss her yet?"

What a long way they'd come in a week. Abi lifted her face, and he gave her a quick peck. Barely enough to register, but enough to know he wanted to give her a better kiss after the movie ended.

They laughed their way through the movie, and Cassie said good night as soon as the credits rolled. Travis's thumb rubbed up and down Abi's arm. "Are you going to church with us in the morning?"

Abi silence lasted long enough that he wondered if she might have fallen asleep. "I don't know, Trav."

Travis didn't answer, but waited for her to go on.

"Cassie and I had a talk the other night. She told me God loves me the way you love her, the way your parents love both of you. That we still have consequences of our actions, but He never stops loving us."

Nice to know the conversations he'd had with Cassie over the years were paying off.

"She pointed out some things I'd never thought about.

Sure, we were drugged that night, but how much worse could it have been? If you hadn't gotten there before it hit me. If it hit you while you were driving. Of all the potential consequences of that night, she's by far the least objectionable. And beyond that, I've already learned what a blessing she truly is. In so many ways. So, I don't think the same way anymore. That if there was a God who really loved me, He never would have let that night happen."

"I'm glad you feel that way."

"I'm still not sure if I believe in a God, but at least I don't feel like He's out to get me anymore."

"He never was."

"I'm starting to realize that."

Travis pressed his lips against her hair, breathing deeply and smelling her papaya shampoo. "So do you want to go with us in the morning?"

Another hesitation, but then she nodded. "Yeah. I'd like that. I think."

<hr />

Travis drove the three of them to church. Abi could have gone with his parents, but she drove over to his house first. Cassie took off as soon as she walked inside. Abi stayed close until they found his parents, and she chatted with Mom while he talked to Dad and some of the other guys. When first service let out, Mom and Dad headed for their usual seats near the front while Travis and Abi sat on an aisle near the back.

They both looked at the bulletin they'd been handed on the way in.

"End of year lock-in?" she asked. "What's that?"

"A thing the high school group does at the end of the year. They order pizza and have a sock hop and all sorts of other stuff. It ends at seven the next morning with drawings for a bunch of cool prizes."

"Will Cassie go?"

"Probably."

Abi rested her head on his shoulder. "So we could have the house to ourselves for the whole evening?"

There was something soft and sort of sultry in her voice. Not that they'd talked about their relationship, but there was something implied in it. They'd need to have that conversation soon. "We could go out," he said noncommittally.

The music started playing, and everyone stood. Travis lost himself in praise and worship, thanking God for the things going on in his life, the good things and the bad.

And as Travis thanked Him, he asked Him to soften Abi's heart, to bring her to Him. Because he could really see a future with her, a forever future.

It's in Your hands, God. But if You could hurry it up a bit, I'd sure appreciate it.

Chapter
Twenty-Seven

Travis sang with an abandon Abi had never seen from anyone. He stretched his hands out from his side, eyes closed, as he sang along. She did her best to follow the words on the screen, but mostly she just listened.

After a while, they sat down, listened to announcements, and then Pastor Rick pulled his notebook and Bible out from under the podium.

"Today, we're going to look at a story most of us are familiar with, the prodigal son." Travis slid his Bible over so she could read along with him rather than try to find it on the app in her phone.

Travis's Bible had obviously seen better days. The pages were dog-eared in places and notes had been scribbled on many of them. Abi read the words to herself as the pastor read them aloud, apparently from a different version because they didn't quite match up.

She listened, but flipped idly through the pages of the book. Suddenly curious, Abi pulled a pen out and scribbled on the back of the bulletin.

Where's the part about God loving Jesus and Jesus loving us so we should love each other?

She handed it to Travis who took the Bible from her and turned to another page and read for a minute before going to another page, repeating the scenario a couple of times. Finally, he handed it to her and tapped the page. She looked down and read.

"As the Father has loved me, so have I loved you. Now remain in my love.If you keep my commands, you will remain in my love, just as I have kept my Father's commands and remain in his love. I have told you this so that my joy may be in you and that your joy may be complete. My command is this: Love each other as I have loved you. Greater love has no one than this: to lay down one's life for one's friends. You are my friends if you do what I command. I no longer call you servants, because a servant does not know his master's business. Instead, I have called you friends, for everything that I learned from my Father I have made known to you.You did not choose me, but I chose you and appointed you so that you might go and bear fruit——fruit that will last—and so that whatever you ask in my name the Father will give you.This is my command: Love each other.

In the margin was a note written in blue pen. *God, help Abi to know you love her, too. And someday, let her get to know Cassie. Then she can know the love You have for her.* The date next to it was from several years earlier, on her thirtieth birthday.

Abi's finger traced the words as tears filled her eyes. Travis had been thinking about her all those years ago? Wanting her to get to know Cassie so she could understand the kind of love God has for her?

The pastor's voice cut through her thoughts. "And that's how God loves us. He loves us so much that no matter how far we've roamed, how much of His goodness we've thrown away, we can always return. He'll kill the fatted calf, rejoicing, and return us to our rightful spots as His children."

Abi used the piece of paper Travis had put in the spot where the prodigal son story was and turned back to it. This time, she turned the page to read the last couple of words in the last verse the pastor read. There were words Travis had written. *Thank you for taking back this prodigal. And show Abi.* The date on that note was 1/1/02. Just weeks after Cassie was born. Thrust into parenthood, he had every right to hate Abi, to think awful things about her, but instead he was praying for her.

"And if you've never been part of God's family, that's okay, too." Pastor caught her attention again. "He's standing there, waiting for you. And you know what?" Abi's tears began to fall, sliding down one cheek then the other. "You don't even have to go all the way home like the prodigal did. Get up, get out of the pig pen, and start walking. Turn around and head for home, toward God, His forgiveness, His grace, and He won't wait for you to be good enough, for you to *deserve* His love, because none of us do. None are righteous enough to earn God's love. All you have to do is admit, in your heart, that you're not worthy, but that you want to come home. And He'll meet you there, where you are. With arms wide open and a celebration just waiting to happen. When any one person comes home, the angels in heaven rejoice."

Angels would rejoice? Over her? Abi Connealy? Really?

"All you have to do is ask. Because when we confess our sins, He is faithful and just to forgive us our sins. He *has* to. Just like when the doctor hits your knee with the little hammer and your leg pops out. You can't help it. And He can't help but forgive you when you ask. So, now, with everyone's head bowed and eyes closed, no one's looking. It's just you and God. Do you need to turn around and start home? Or have you never been? Our prayer team is down here at the front if you want someone to pray with you. God will meet you right there in your seat, but if you'd like to come down to talk with someone, we're here for you. He loves you, and He wants to welcome you home."

He kept talking, but a force outside herself compelled her to slip past Travis and down the aisle. Abi didn't know what she was doing, but knew she had to do it. She kept her eyes glued to the floor until she neared the front. Standing there was a woman Abi recognized, though she didn't know from where. Her bright red hair and soft smile drew Abi to her.

She reached both hands out and Abi put hers in them. "Hi, honey. I'm Deeanne. How can I pray with you today?"

The tears increased until Abi couldn't see two inches in front of her face. She tried to speak, but couldn't until she cleared her throat. Then she was able to whisper, "I want to come home."

"That we can do." She took a step toward Abi, until their bent heads were next to each other. "Father, I come to you today with..."

"Abi," she whispered.

"With Abi who wants to come home."

As Deeanne prayed, Abi tried to pray along, but all she could come up with was *God, I just want You to love me.*

Deeanne continued to speak, though her words faded out as a feeling of peace began to come over Abi.

I already do.

The voice was clear as day, though she knew it was only in her mind.

I already love you, child.

"I've done some pretty awful things," Abi whispered.

Deeanne easily switched gears. "It doesn't matter. Paul wrote most of the New Testament, but do you know what he did before Jesus got a hold of him?"

Abi shook her head.

"He persecuted Christians. Killed them. But God still loved him and used him."

"I abandoned my daughter." Forcing the words around the massive lump in her throat was freeing.

"King David committed adultery and ordered a man killed," Deeanne told her. "But the Bible calls him a man after God's own heart." She squeezed Abi's hands. "Now, did you really, truly abandon her? On the side of a road where no one was likely to find her?"

Abi shook her head. "I left her with her father, though he didn't know he was a father until I showed up with her."

"When Moses was born, the Egyptians were killing all the baby boys. His mother put him in a basket and sent his sister down to the river to keep an eye on him. His sister did her best, but the princess found him floating there. Is that so different than what you did?"

Another quick shake of her head. "I guess not, but no one would have killed her."

"Did you feel like you had no other choice?"

This time Abi nodded.

"That's just how Moses's mom must have felt. You did what you thought was in your baby's best interest, didn't you?"

Another nod.

"So you didn't truly abandon her at all, did you?"

That was a freeing revelation, and Abi felt more of the heaviness drop off her heart. "No."

"Okay then."

They prayed together for a few more minutes, and Abi asked Jesus to forgive her, to live in her heart and be Lord of her life.

Abi wasn't quite sure what all of that meant, but it felt

right, and she could ask Travis to explain it.

By the time Deeanne hugged her, Abi felt better than she had in a long time, probably ever.

"Thank you," Abi whispered.

"It's what I'm here for, sweetie." She moved back. "I think someone's waiting for you. He knows how to get a hold of me if you ever want to talk."

Abi turned to see Travis sitting there, looking at her, smiling. He stood as she walked toward him. It probably went against church protocol, but Abi nearly launched herself at him, her arms wrapping around his neck as she buried her face in the hollow of his shoulder. He caught her, his arms wrapping tightly around her, until she felt secure.

And loved.

In more ways than one.

Not just this new God thing, but by Travis.

"I love you, Travis." Abi had to tell him before she changed her mind or talked herself out of it. "I think I have since I was sixteen. Seeing you with Cassie and standing up to my dad just solidified it. I can't thank you enough for taking care of her and for bringing me to church and helping me understand."

He moved back until she could see his eyes. "Aw, Abi. I love you, too." Abi could see in his eyes that he wanted to kiss her, but he didn't. Instead he hugged her tighter.

As soon as Travis set her down, Pastor Rick came over to talk to them. "Angels are rejoicing," he said. "I'm so glad you came. Travis has been praying for you for years." He clapped Travis on the shoulder. "As long as I've known him."

Abi didn't know what to make of that so she just smiled and took the Kleenex someone offered. Another person caught Rick's attention, but he said one more thing before he left. "If you have any questions, or anything you just want to talk about, Travis is a great one to talk to. So are his parents and Deeanne, the lady who prayed with you. My door is always open, too."

"Thank you."

He squeezed her shoulder and smacked Travis's again before he walked off.

Abi slipped her hand in Travis's, their fingers linking together as though they'd been doing it for years.

Cassie walked into the big room – Abi had learned it was called the sanctuary – and saw them walking up the aisle together. A grin crossed her face as their daughter eyed their hands.

"Something I need to know?"

Travis shrugged. "Nothing official." Abi felt momentary loss as he let go of her hand, but then his hand wrapped around the back of her neck. "But Abi has something to tell you."

Cassie looked between them. "What's that?"

Abi took a deep breath. "I prayed. Like we talked about in the car the other day." She didn't know how else to describe it.

Tears filled her eyes. "Are you serious?"

Abi nodded.

Cassie let out a little squeal, throwing her arms around Abi. "That's so wonderful!"

Abi held her close, feeling a bond she never had before. Maybe because she'd finally forgiven herself and started to change her thinking about abandoning Cassie. "I love you, so much, Cassie." Abi told her. "Thank you."

"I'm so happy." Cassie didn't say she loved her back, and Abi was okay with that. She'd only known Abi a few weeks. She and Travis at least had their basis from years earlier, but Cassie, even though Travis had never been one of those custodial parents who bad-mouthed the other one, still needed time.

They talked for a couple more minutes before Cassie asked to go with Maile's family for lunch. Travis said she could so Cassie gave Abi another hug and bounded out into the foyer.

Travis took her hand again. "So since we are kidless this afternoon, do you have any ideas on how you'd like to celebrate?"

Abi shrugged. "How about some place local? That I couldn't get anywhere else."

"I've got just the place." He led her toward the door. "Have you ever had your food thrown at you before?"

Chapter
Twenty-Eight

They made it back from Lambert's, Home of the Throwed Rolls, about five, but were too full from lunch to have dinner.

"I didn't believe you when you said they would throw the rolls at me." Abi shook her hand slightly. "That stung."

"Their roll throwers are good," Travis reminded her with a shrug. "They took it easier on you than me."

"Either way it was worth it."

They made it into the living room before he pulled her to him and kissed her, pouring everything he'd ever felt for her into it. She responded in kind, her hands winding into his hair. Before it got too far out of hand, he moved back.

"We need to stop."

"Why?" She kissed him again, but Travis kept a tighter hold on his desire.

He moved far enough away to take her hand and move to the couch. "Because kissing is as far as this can go until we get married."

She raised a brow at him. "Until?"

"Well, unless?" Travis shrugged. "No more unless we're married." A slow grin spread across his face. "Though, at the moment, I'm wondering how soon is too soon to ask you."

This time she was the one smiling. "Whenever you want."

In a split second, he turned serious. "Marry me."

Her smile dimmed as her eyes searched his. "What?"

"Marry me."

She leaned over, her hands framing his face. "Yes." Her voice was as soft as her lips when they touched his.

"Do you really mean that?" he asked between kisses.

"It's what I've dreamed of since I was in high school."

Travis moved away. "I'm not perfect, Abi. I hope that's not what you think based on a high school crush and the last few weeks. I make mistakes. Lots of them, especially with Cassie. I do my best, and I try, but don't put me on some kind of high school dream pedestal."

"I'm not." She sat back and leaned into his side. "I see how you are with Cassie, and I remember how much I adored you in high school. And knowing that you've been praying for me this whole time, that you never bad-mouthed me to Cassie, and everything I've seen of you since I got here... I want to spend my life with you, Travis. I always have."

Travis pressed a kiss against her hair. "Okay then. When?"

"You haven't even gotten me a ring yet." The teasing tone in her voice made him smile.

"True."

One of Abi's fingers drew random patterns on his knee as they sat there, thinking and enjoying sitting next to each other. "Travis?"

"Yeah?"

"You and Kristy *just* ended. Are you *really* sure I'm not a rebound?"

She had a point. "I know, but I never should have been so serious about her in the first place. I never should have bought that ring. It was part of denying the place I wanted you to have in my life."

"Are you really sure?"

"I am." Travis ran a thumb up and down her arm. "What's your dad going to say?"

She shrugged. "I don't care. I don't know that I even want to tell them until it's all over. Just fly off to Vegas or something."

"I don't know about Vegas, but there's no waiting period in Arkansas. I had some friends get married there not too long ago."

She twisted until she could smile up at him. "Cassie will be out of school soon. What if we drove down the day of her overnighter thing?" The sultry insinuation left nothing to his imagination.

He brushed the hair back off her face. "Don't you want Cassie there?"

"Of course. I meant we could drive down, get married, and come back in time for her thing." She ducked her head shyly. "And then spend the rest of the night together."

He tucked her back into his side. "That's a thought. What about my family? Or your mom? Do you want them there?" He'd always thought his parents would be at his wedding. Travis was okay with not having a big wedding, but he wanted his family there.

She nodded. "I'd love to have your family there."

"Will your mom be okay with it?"

"Probably not, but if I tell her, she'll tell dad, and it'll turn into a whole big thing. I'd rather just tell her later."

"If that's what you want." She tipped her head back and

up just enough for him to kiss her.

The front door opened and shut but Travis didn't stop kissing her.

"Is this what it's going to be like from now on?" Cassie whined, throwing her purse in the chair before slouching into it, as he and Abi broke the kiss off.

"It never bothered you before." Travis pulled Abi closer. "Why now?"

She waved a hand their direction. "This is different."

"Why?"

"Because." She glared then averted her gaze. "She's my mother."

"Well, you're probably going to have to get used to it," he told her.

She sighed. "Just promise you'll tell me the minute you starting talking about marriage, would ya? I'll need medication to deal with that."

Abi shifted, but Travis looked straight at Cassie. "Well..."

She jumped up. "Seriously? She left us sixteen years ago, shows up less than two months ago, you've been *practically engaged* the whole time, you had a *ring*, and now you're dating Abi a week, maybe, and you're already talking about marriage?" By the time she finished, the squeak in her voice could make dogs bark.

Travis stayed calm. He had to. "We're not just talking about it, Cassie. We're going to."

Her eyes widened. "What? You're getting married?!"

Travis nodded.

Cassie's eyes flashed. "You've known her like six weeks! You were dating Kristy a week ago! And now you're marrying *her*?" He'd never heard such venom from his daughter.

Travis voice took on that "dad tone" he'd hated from

his own dad growing up. "That's enough, Cassie."

"No."

"I've never had to ground you before, but I will. You will not speak about your mother like that." He'd never referred to Abi quite that way.

"You never cared how I talked about her before." Tears started streaking down her cheeks.

"That's not true, and you know it."

"I don't care. Dating is one thing I could maybe get on board with, but marriage? No." She glared at him. "You always told me that if I didn't like a woman who would be my step-mom, I could tell you, right?"

Travis nodded. "But she wouldn't be your step-mom. Abi is your biological mother. She always has been."

"That's not the point. You're marrying some virtual stranger and expect me to be okay with it? I don't care if she's my mother, Mother Theresa, or an alien. I. Do. Not. Like. It." She stalked off toward her room.

"This isn't over," Travis called after her. "We'll talk after you calm down."

"I won't calm down!" She slammed her bedroom door and, as a result, would lose her phone for twenty-four hours. She knew the consequences.

Abi tried not to let him see her wiping the tears from her face. He pulled her closer and kissed the top of her head. "Don't worry about her. She'll be fine. She will calm down, and I'll talk to her."

"What if she's not? What if she's not okay with us getting married?"

"She will be. She needs some time."

"So maybe not in a couple weeks?"

"We'll see. One thing I've always said, and I've always told her, is that she doesn't make my decisions about a relationship or getting married for me. But, I've also promised her I wouldn't marry someone she truly didn't like, and I wouldn't marry someone I didn't think could love her as though she were this woman's daughter. She doesn't hate you. And she *is* your daughter, so that's not an issue."

Abi stood and Travis followed. She gave him a kiss on the jaw. "I should go, but I'll call you later."

Travis walked her to the door, kissing her lightly before she left and then headed for Cassie's room. He rapped sharply on the hollow wood. "I'm coming in." After a five count like he'd promised her when she first started going through puberty, he unlocked the door.

She was face down on her bed, but turned until she could see him. Travis held his hand out flat. "Phone."

With the most exasperated exhale he'd ever heard from her, she pulled it out of her pocket and handed it over. Travis glanced at the clock on it. "You can have it back tomorrow night at six."

"Whatever."

"Do you want to talk about it now or later?"

"About what? Ruining our lives?"

Ah! Teenage melodramatics. "You think if I marry Abi, it'll ruin our lives?"

She shrugged.

"But you didn't think marrying Kristy would ruin our lives." Even if he never had proposed.

"That was different. You dated her for a long time."

Nine months wasn't a long time. Unless you counted the nine month's Abi had been pregnant with Cassie. "I've known Abi a long time, too."

"No. You knew her older brother. Then you slept together. Then you didn't see her again until weeks ago. You spent most of it dating someone else, and now you're marrying her? Sounds perfectly logical to me."

He sank to the edge of her bed. "I wasn't completely truthful with you about something."

"What? She's not my mother? You're not my father?"

"No, not that at all. Abi and I never went out on a real date..."

She mocked him as she interrupted. "I knew that. You were going to ask her out after graduation. And you almost kissed her after the day Chelsea Piers."

How did she know about that? "Yes, but more than that. We didn't date, but we did spend a lot of time together and a lot of time on the phone together. We'd talk for hours at night, the way you and Zach have a couple of times."

"And I got in trouble for it."

"So did Abi. She knew I liked her, but she was only seventeen. Her dad found out about the phone calls and saw us hanging out together. He threatened me, so we backed off until graduation. Then came the night of the party. So I knew her a lot better than maybe you thought."

All he got was a half shrug.

"You're going to have to get used to it, kiddo." Travis rested a hand on her leg. "I've loved her since before that night. That's one reason why I knew I couldn't marry Kristy. Even if she hadn't ended things with me last week, we never would have gotten married."

Cassie rolled over and looked at him through swollen eyes. "Then why'd you even think about asking her? Before Abi showed up, sure, but after?"

"Because I was in denial about how I felt about your mom..."

"She's *not* my mom. I *don't have* a mom." Her forceful words didn't really surprise him.

Now wasn't the time to pick that fight. "I was in denial about the feelings I still had for Abi. I didn't want to feel the way I did, the way I do, but things have changed. You and she are getting along well. She and I are rekindling what we could have had. And now she's a Christian. That was the only thing that could have stopped the relationship from moving forward."

"Whatever." She rolled back over, her back to him. "I'm going to bed. And I'm not going to school tomorrow."

"Yes. You are." Travis stood up but leaned over and kissed the side of her head. "I love you, punkin."

He hated it when she didn't tell him she loved him back, but deep in his heart, Travis knew this was one of those nights. He left, without pressing her and went back to the living room.

His gut said this whole thing would get worse before it got better.

Travis had been right. Cassie went to school the next morning, under protest, and not looking her best. She obviously hadn't slept well. Neither had he. Abi's text seemed to indicate she hadn't either, but she had to work. So did he. But he only had three more days. Cassie only had two more.

Of course, he ran into Kristy almost immediately. In the parking lot.

"Trouble in paradise?" she snapped his direction.

"What?" Travis didn't have the energy or desire for a confrontation.

"You look awful. Cassie's status update last night made it sound like something big was going on."

Somehow, he managed not to groan. He'd checked her text messages and email. He had access to those or she lost her Internet and phone, period. Travis hadn't thought to look at her Facebook and hadn't been on his to see what she might have said there. He'd need to get online as soon as he got inside.

"So?"

"Everything's fine and, even if it wasn't, I don't see how it's any of your business."

Travis needed to sit down with Kristy and have a talk with her, explain a bit more about why things happened and how sorry he was she'd gotten hurt in the process.

She stopped him with a hand on his arm. "Listen, Travis, just because things ended badly between us doesn't mean I want to see her hurt you or Cassie."

"I know." Before he could go on, she did.

"We weren't right for each other. Even if we thought we were, we weren't. If I'm honest with myself, I could see this coming for a long time. But I'm almost thirty-five. If I want a family, it's going to have to happen soon. That's not to say I was being calculating and thinking you were my last shot or anything, but I liked you. You liked me. We could have made it work and been happy, but we'll both be *happier* with someone else."

"You're right. And we need to talk, but not right now. Come find me after school? If I can, we can talk then?"

She nodded. "I told Anise that, too. I know she was mad at you on my behalf, and that she wanted to smack you upside the head at church the next morning."

"I noticed she wasn't happy with me. I'll talk to her and try to straighten it out." Travis's phone buzzed and he pulled it out of his pocket. "I've got to take this."

"I'll find you later."

Abi must have talked to Mom because as soon as he said "hello" she asked about Cassie.

"I think she's okay," Travis told her. "It was a fight to get her out the door, but she'll bounce back. She'll get used to the idea of me and Abi."

"But marriage, Trav? Already?"

"I know it sounds crazy, but, Mom, I loved her back then. I never told any of you that because it was safer that way, but I did."

"What about Jennifer? Or Kristy? Or all the other women you've dated since then?"

"It hasn't been *that* many, and you know it. And mostly, I think I was hoping I could love someone else the way I thought I loved Abi. Because of that night, I never knew for sure, but since she showed up... Now I know what I felt was real. This is real. I love her. She accepted Christ yesterday. What more is there?"

"Making sure she's not going to leave again?" He could almost see mom tilt an eyebrow at him. So *Mom* didn't think she was going to leave, but thought that's what scared him. Time to set that straight.

"She's not. She never wanted to the first time. She tried to find me the next week. How is that someone who wanted to leave us? And why would she again? She's been in love with me just as long as I've been in love with her, just waiting for our chance to work things out."

"I worry about all three of you."

"I know. But honestly, Mom, Abi and I love each other."

"That's not what worries me. It's Cassie. Abi said she didn't take it very well."

"She didn't, but she'll be okay. She just needs some time to get used to the idea."

"If you say so." Mom didn't sound any more sure than Travis really was.

Deep down inside, he was scared Cassie would never come to terms with it. And if she didn't, then what? Would he marry Abi anyway and Cassie would have to learn to deal with it? Or would his relationship with Abi end because Cassie couldn't accept her mom as his wife? Or couldn't accept Abi as her mom? Then what?

Travis didn't want to go there. He just wanted Cassie to accept it and to marry Abi and spend his life with her. Maybe even start talking about having another baby together.

A baby?

Where had that thought come from? They weren't too old, yet, but maybe... Maybe they could at least talk about it with Cassie.

But first they had to get through this spot, get to the point where he and Abi could actually get married.

Travis headed into the school building and for the teacher's lounge. It was going to be a long day.

CASSIE

"You look like... well, you know." Maile leaned against the lockers as I glared at her.

"Yeah. You try crying all night. Dad wouldn't let me stay home. If he didn't teach here, I'd totally skip." I pulled out my binder before hanging my backpack up. "I won't get my phone back for who knows how long."

"You shouldn't slam doors."

She got another glare. "Not only does he want to *marry* the woman, he told me this morning he wants to do it in the next few weeks. As soon as school gets out."

"I thought you liked Abi now?"

"More than I used to." I shut my locker more carefully than I did my bedroom door. It had a mirror and pictures I didn't want to fall off or break. "But not enough to want her to marry my dad next week." I leaned my back against the lockers. "I guess they were weeks away from their first date and spent all this time together before the night of that party. She was already half in love with him, and he really liked her. So sixteen years later, they just pick up where they left off and now they're getting married."

We started walking toward homeroom. "Remember when we were little, and we'd play house?" Maile asked.

"Yeah."

"You always wanted your mom and dad together. We both did."

She would have to bring that up. "That was before I knew her."

"And now you like her, so what's the problem?"

"I like her as my hang-out-sometimes person in my life, not as the woman married to my dad always around trying to be all parent-y person." I sulked into the classroom and slumped into my seat. What I really wanted was to see Zach and talk to him. I might get to at lunch. If I was lucky. And during drama but no way Dad would let us just talk.

"Give her a chance?" Maile looked like she was about to cry. "I'd give almost anything to have my mom back. Yours is here. Don't push her away."

She turned and walked to her seat on the other side of the room. My best friend had a point. Not one I wanted to hear, but one I probably needed to think about.

Didn't matter though. I didn't want Dad and Abi getting married.

Maile's words haunted me the rest of the day. I did my best to understand where she was coming from and I got that she missed her mom, but it wasn't like her mom left on purpose. Not like mine had.

The house was empty when I got home. Not unusual. But part of me was hoping Dad would be there, or maybe even Abi, though I couldn't explain why I wanted to see her. Maybe if I made dinner Dad would let me have my phone back. Slamming my door before school probably wasn't the smartest move and he'd know if I used the landline, so I couldn't call Zach either.

The question became what to make. Finally, I decided on the Mexican chicken thing Abi and I had made. Dad liked it. It would get me on his good side.

And Abi wouldn't be here to eat it with us.

I'd just finished getting it all ready when the doorbell rang. A smile crossed my face when I peeked to see who it was. Zach stood there, back to the brick, waiting for me.

He didn't say anything but just sat on the bench Grandma put on the sidewalk. I sat next to him. Close but not touching. Because if Dad drove up and saw me too close to him, he wouldn't be happy.

"Maile told me what's going on."

"Blabbermouth."

"She cares about you, and she knows I do, too." The back of his hand smacked my leg. "How are you?"

"Everyone keeps asking me that." I slumped on the hard bench.

"Because we care." He moved like he was going to give me a sideways hug but thought better of it. "We all love you and want you to be okay."

"I'd rather talk about something else. Like the pool opening next week. When do we get our schedules?" And how would he keep from flirting back when all of the girls flirted with him like they had the year before? We weren't officially anything, but I didn't like it.

"Probably at the meeting Monday. Alivia should call you."

I wanted to work a lot. Save money. Dad would sell me his car pretty cheap when I turned sixteen in December, but I'd still need money for it. And car insurance. I didn't think he'd make me work during the school year, but he might. Regardless, if I worked a lot over the summer, I'd get to spend more time with Zach. He'd work as many hours a week as they let him for basically the same reason.

Zach interrupted my thoughts. "Did you ever hear anything about your grandpa?"

"My grandpa?" Was he okay? Had Grammy called Dad?

"About the bone marrow transplant."

Oh.

Right.

That.

"No. I never heard if I was a match. Abi hasn't said how he's doing since we got back from their house."

"Do you ever wonder?"

I shook my head. "Not really. I figure if there's anything to tell, Abi'll tell me."

"What is it that bothers you so much about them getting married?"

No matter how hard I tried, I hadn't been able to put that into words, even to myself, so I just shrugged. "As long as Abi doesn't get pregnant so they *have* to get married, I don't think they actually will."

"Do you really think your dad...?"

"I don't want to think my dad anything, but here I am, aren't I?" Before I could go on, a familiar car came into view down Arizona Avenue. "Dad's home."

"I should go then." Zach stood up and took me with him. He gave me a one-armed hug. "I'll see you tomorrow."

Dad pulled into the garage, but came out onto the driveway to talk to Zach for a minute. When Zach took off, Dad walked through the front door with me.

"He didn't come inside," I told him before he could say

anything.

"I didn't figure he did." He shut the door behind him. "Smells good."

"I made that Mexican thing Abi liked."

"Good because she's coming for dinner."

I stopped. Stared at him. Ran down the hall.

And slammed the door.

He could keep the phone.

Chapter Twenty-Nine

Abi heard Cassie's bedroom door slam before Travis opened the front door. The stress written all over his face answered her questions she asked them, but she had to anyway.

"I take it things aren't going any better?"

He shook his head, but pulled her into a hug after he shut the door. "Not really, but I'm glad you're here."

Abi looked up in time for him to kiss her. Not a long, deep kiss, but tender and full of all the feelings she had for him.

"Hmm." He smiled against her lips. "I needed that."

She smiled back. "Me, too." He left his arm around her shoulder as they walked into the kitchen. "Any progress at all?"

"Not really. I told her and my mom the truth about us from before that night."

Right. That had to be why Julie had said a couple things that seemed off before Abi left the house. "What did you tell them?"

"About how we'd talk all night on the phone, mostly, but that we spent a lot of time together when I was at your house. I didn't mention Brenda, but..."

Brenda was the only friend Abi had once Cassie was born, and she loved the other woman for it, but her parents' double standard had always annoyed her. Mark could sleep with Brenda, and had, as long as he didn't do it while Abi was home. Let Travis *think* about kissing her, *once*, and they'd kicked him out of the house, though, thankfully, not out of their lives. Instead, they'd spent countless hours sitting on the back porch staring at the stars. Stars Abi looked at differently these days, wondering which one God had in mind for her.

Abi remembered those talks, had relived some of them over and over years later. "Did you ever write your play?"

He leaned against the counter, both legs stretched out in front of him and arms crossed over his chest. "Just the one we did at State. I haven't really thought about writing more in a long time. That one was hard to write because Joanna died on 9/11."

"We talked about a lot during those days, didn't we?"

He held a hand out and Abi took it, letting him reel her in. She rested her head on his shoulder. "You wanted to be a labor and delivery nurse, didn't you?"

"At one time, yes. But after everything..." After giving birth to Cassie and then giving her up a few days later, there was no way she could have helped in a delivery room without breaking down every time.

"Do you still want to?" He brushed the hair back from Abi's face. "I know you're good at your job, but is it really what you want to do?"

"Part of me would still like to be a nurse, but it's been so long since I went to school, I don't know if I could do it."

He looked into her eyes, trying to see if she really meant

that. "If you want to try, I'll support you, you know that, right?"

Looking up at him, Abi knew he meant it. If she wanted to go back to school to become a nurse, he'd do whatever it took to support her.

"You'll help me study?" she asked.

The twinkle in his eyes was all Abi needed to see. "I'll do my best not to distract you while you study. How's that?" His kiss told her how he planned to try to distract her.

It would be very effective.

"Maybe," she said when the kiss ended. "I'll think about it." Abi hopped up onto the island. "Anything else I need to think about?"

He took a deep breath and stared at a spot on the floor. "Something else occurred to me."

"What's that?"

"Kids."

Abi snorted. "We've already got one of those. She's not very happy with us right now."

"I know." He looked up at her. "I meant more kids. Another one. It's something I thought about today."

Abi didn't know what to think about that. "Wow. Another baby?"

"You guys are having another baby?" Cassie's voice cut through the room like a knife. "Seriously?"

They both turned to look at her. The look on her face nearly broke Abi's heart. Cassie's eyes were puffy, her cheeks red and the look of utter disbelief and betrayal tore at her.

"No, it's just something..." Travis didn't get to finish before she ran back down the hall.

"Keep the phone!" The door slammed as soon as she finished it.

"The phone?" Abi asked.

He explained the rule and the punishment.

"What do we do with her, Trav? I don't know her well enough yet to have any ideas. You're her dad, the one who's been everything to her. What do we do?"

Quiet desperation filled Abi, reminding her of the feeling she remembered when the test first came back positive, when she first realized she was pregnant. There wasn't going to be an easy way to fix this.

She didn't think they could.

Three days later, they stood in the kitchen. Travis's goofy grin told her something was up even before he spoke. "I have something for you."

Travis's grin was infectious, and Abi smiled back. "What's that?"

"Close your eyes and hold out your hand."

She did and held out her right hand, palm up.

"Other hand."

Confused, Abi obliged. Everything became clear when the cool metal slid around her ring finger. She couldn't wait any longer but opened her eyes, looking at the ring now on her finger. The diamonds and rubies sparkled up at her.

"Travis," Abi gasped. "It's gorgeous." Tears filled her eyes as she examined it more closely. "You remembered I love rubies."

"'A wife of noble character who can find? She is worth far more than rubies.'"

Her brow furrowed as he still knelt in front of her. "Huh?"

"It's from a Chapter in Proverbs I'll show you later about the ideal woman, I guess. Or a virtuous one anyway."

Abi nodded, nervously. She was supposed to measure

up to some biblical woman?

"But yes, I remembered you love rubies." He grinned, putting her back at ease. "So, Abigail Margaret Connealy, will you marry me?"

The words wouldn't force themselves past the lump in her throat, but she nodded.

He stood up, pulled Abi in his arms and kissed her.

"An engagement ring? Really?" Cassie's voice cut the kiss short. "And you two make out more than any high schoolers I know."

Well, she would be the expert on that one.

And she also answered Abi's unasked question. Her attitude hadn't improved in the last couple of days.

Travis said her name, a hint of reproach in his voice.

Whatever else she was going to say, she swallowed with his look.

Abi would never be able to master that look. At least not with Cassie. She had been persona non grata for way too much of Cassie's life and she'd never truly see her as her mother the same way Travis was her dad.

"Are you ready to talk yet?" Travis asked her.

Cassie just glared at him.

"Listen, tomorrow is your first day of break. I'd hate for you to spend it under house arrest with Grammy."

"You'd ground me just because I won't talk to you about why I don't want you to marry *her*."

"No. Because of your overall attitude."

"Fine. You want to talk? I don't want you to marry her." Her blue eyes flashed fire. "I liked her fine as my birth mom who wanted to hang out sometimes, but not as my step-mom-mom."

Abi rested on hand on Travis's arm. "Maybe I should go."

Cassie answered for him. "That's a great idea." She

stomped down the hall. "Just leave the ring." Her door slammed behind her.

Travis turned, a weary look on his face.

"Did she get the phone back yesterday?"

"For about thirty minutes. And I told her if it happened again, she'd lose the phone and be grounded for the next two days. I have to do end of the year stuff at work, so she'll go to Mom and Dad's."

Abi leaned up so she could kiss him. "I'll make sure to work somewhere else tomorrow."

He shook his head as his hands rubbed along her upper arms. "No. She needs to deal with it. Unless you need to be somewhere else, just go about business as usual."

With a nod, Abi kissed him again. "Okay, but I still think I should go tonight. Let you two sort things out."

With a shake of his head, he propelled her toward the kitchen. "No. She'll come out and be civil, or she can forget about the lock-in next week."

"Travis, the last thing I want to do is cause problems between you two."

"*You* didn't cause the problems. But we're going to have to work through it all somehow, so we're going to start tonight." He pulled a glass casserole dish out of the oven. "Would you mind setting the table while I go get her?"

Abi nodded and watched as he walked down the hall. Could this night get any worse?

Cassie came out of her room, sullen and refusing to talk to Abi beyond the bare minimum. Dinner was quiet though she and Travis tried to keep the conversation going.

The bloodshot, swollen eyes of her daughter tore at Abi, confirming her decision.

It was something she just had to do. Even if it broke her heart all over again.

"I'll be back," Abi promised Julie, giving her a hug.

"Do you know when?"

She shook her head. "No. Not sure how long it's going to take."

That wasn't the truth, or not the whole truth, anyway.

The truth was Abi wasn't coming back.

She'd decided to give her daughter what she wanted most. Abi out of their lives for good. Even if it meant not marrying the one man she'd loved most of her life. Josh Wilson's Serenity Landing Comedy Club open house would be held in a couple months. If Kevin made her, she'd return for the party and avoid the Harders family at all costs, then never return to Southwest Missouri. She'd tried to convince him to send someone else to oversee the final result.

God had given her a glimpse of what her life could be like, but never would she do anything to hurt her daughter again.

And so, it was time to go.

Chapter Thirty

Travis whistled as he headed up the walk to Mom and Dad's house. He was done with all his work, a day early, and he didn't have to go in on Friday after all. Maybe Abi could take the day off, and they could do something, the three of them, and Cassie would start getting used to the idea.

As much as he hated the idea of letting his teenager run things, he did need to talk to Abi about postponing for a bit, at least a month or so, to see if they could get Cassie on board.

Travis knocked on the front door as he opened it. "Hey, everyone. I'm here." Silence met him until Cassie bounded down the stairs looking happier than he'd seen her in days.

"Hi, Daddy." She gave him a big hug, immediately making him suspicious.

"What's going on?"

She shrugged. "Nothing. Just happy to see you."

Mom came up from the basement. "Hi, honey."

"Hey, Mom." Travis left one arm around Cassie's

shoulder. "What's going on?"

Mom looked from him to his daughter and her eyes narrowed. "Does this have anything to do with Abi needing to head home for a few days?"

So that's what it was. He dropped his arm from Cassie's shoulders. "That's why you're so happy to see me? Abi's gone?"

Cassie shrugged and headed for the living room without saying another word.

Mom sighed after she was gone. "I don't know what to do with that girl."

"You and me both." Travis pulled a soda out of the fridge when they made it to the kitchen. "When did Abi leave?" And why hadn't she told him?

"Early this morning, right after you dropped Cassie off. Did you not know?"

Travis shook his head. "She didn't mention anything. Something must have come up." He pulled his phone out of his pocket. No missed calls or texts. When he tried to call her, there was no answer. "Must be in a meeting or something." That's what he was telling himself. His gut was saying there was something more going on and he wouldn't like it. "Did she say when she'd be back?"

"Not specifically. A few days, I guess. Monday maybe?"

"Hm." Well, that would put their first official date on hold until at least next weekend. On what was supposed to be their wedding day.

"I did see her packing the Bible you got her into her laptop bag. That's a good sign."

"It is." She'd been reading the book of John the last few days and enjoying it. At least that was his impression from the conversations and texts about it. She'd also started reading Genesis. He wasn't sure what she thought of it. "Still it's odd she didn't email or text or anything to tell me she was going."

"I don't know, sweetie." She pulled chicken out of the fridge. "Are you two staying for dinner?"

"No. I have some stuff to do at home, and Cassie and I need to have a serious talk. Something in my gut says she had something to do with this."

"It's possible," Mom conceded, "but they didn't talk before Abi left, so it couldn't have been this morning. Cassie did give her a quick hug when she said good-bye but that's it."

He gave Mom a kiss on the cheek. "Thanks for letting Cassie hang here today. I'm done so no need for tomorrow."

"No problem."

Five minutes later, he and Cassie pulled out of the driveway and headed for their house. The drive was quiet, and Cassie went straight to her room. He went to his room to change into something more comfortable.

The next two days were fairly quiet, though Abi didn't answer any of his calls or texts. Mom seemed to think she was at some sort of conference where maybe she couldn't or didn't have cell phone reception. He waited to talk to Cassie until he felt they were both ready for the conversation, but that time didn't come.

Saturday was another quiet day spent at home. At least until the mail came. A package he'd been waiting for arrived so the mail lady rang the doorbell. It was pretty much the most excitement they'd had in days.

He flipped through the mail, putting bills in their spot, junk mail in the trash and stopping when he got to a hand addressed envelope. There was no return address on it, but the handwriting looked like Abi's. Travis leaned against the counter as he stuck his finger under the flap and tore it open, his heart beating loudly in his chest.

He stared at it for a long moment before unfolding the piece of paper.

Travis —

You have to know I love you. I've loved you since I was sixteen, and I couldn't have picked a better father for my baby if I could have chosen anyone in the world. There's nothing I want more than the life we've talked about the last couple weeks. But I can't do this if it's going to make her life so miserable. I love you, and I love Cassie — and this time, I have to put her first. I didn't fifteen years ago, but I am now. Maybe when she's grown up, married, then we can talk about us again.

I've been offered a position elsewhere in the country and by the time you get this, I'll be working there. Respect my wishes and give me some time. I'll look you up in a few years and, if you're still unattached, maybe we can try again.

The ring is in the drawer of the nightstand in your room at your Mom and Dad's house. Please thank them for me, and tell your mom how sorry I am to have misled her when I told her I was leaving.

There's never been anyone else for me, and there never will be.

I love you.

Abi

"Cassandra Julianne Connealy-Harders, get in here," Travis bellowed.

By the time her door opened, she was rolling her eyes. "What did I do this time?"

He held up the paper. "She's gone."

A hint of a smile crossed her face before she stopped it. "Who?"

"Abi isn't at a conference. She left. Said she didn't want to make your life miserable so she left."

Cassie gave a half shrug. "Are you really surprised? Leaving is what she does."

And that's when it clicked. "Is that why you've been so upset about the idea of me and Abi being together? Because you were afraid she'd leave?"

In a second, she switched from brass teenager to little girl as big tears began to fall. "She already left us once."

"Aw, Cassie. Come 'ere." He held his arms open, and she ran into them. Her body shook with sobs. Everything suddenly made sense. In trying to protect herself from her mother leaving again, she'd driven Abi away. And now her fear was coming true.

Travis didn't know much time passed, but eventually Cassie's sobs slowed. "She left because of me, didn't she?"

He sat her down on the couch next to him. "Kind of. She left because she didn't want to make you miserable. Not because of you, but because she loves you and wants the best for you. She believes that marrying me and the three of us being a family is only going to hurt you. That's why she left. Not because she doesn't love you or because you're not a great kid."

"She still left."

"I know." They sat for a few more minutes. "Do you want her to come back? Way deep down inside, do you want the three of us to be a family?"

She nodded, just barely.

"Way deep down, you want her to be your 'real mom', don't you?"

The silence stretched out. "Yeah, but I don't want her to leave again. If you guys get married, and we become that family and then she leaves..." She couldn't finish.

"The thought occurred to me, too, sweetie, but she's not a scared eighteen-year-old kid anymore. She stood up to her dad, introduced you to her mom – you don't do that kind of stuff if you're planning to leave again."

"But she did."

"Because she doesn't want to hurt you. And you've been pushing her away pretty hard the last few days, haven't you?"

"Yeah. I guess."

"Would you have wanted to stay the way you've been acting?"

She didn't move or say anything for several more minutes. "No. I guess not." She rested her head against his shoulder. "Now what?"

He kissed the side of her head. "I don't know, sweetie. I just don't know. She doesn't want to be found."

Cassie thought for a minute. "Could we call Abi's mom?"

"I don't know if she'd told them about our relationship. I don't know if her mom would tell us anything even if she did."

She turned her head into him. "I'm sorry, Dad."

He hugged her a bit tighter. "I know, punkin. I know."

They went about the rest of their day, but about six the phone rang. The voice on the other end wasn't familiar as it asked for Travis Harders.

"This is Travis."

"Mr. Harders, we're calling to inform you that a bone marrow transplant recipient is in need of a transplant from Cassandra Connealy-Harders."

"Who is it?" Had they agreed to be in the national database? He thought they'd only agreed to be tested for Abi's dad.

"I can't tell you that, sir. I can tell you that you'll need to travel to the Kansas City area in the next couple of days, and you should plan on being there for a week or so."

Travis blew out a breath. It seemed like an answer to prayer on several levels. Surely Abi would be there for her father's bone marrow transplant. He talked to the man for several more minutes confirming the details. Arrangements were being made for a hotel for them to stay in. Cassie would need to be at the hospital for a little while each day, and then would have the marrow removed from her body and transferred to his.

Cassie watched as he talked and when he hung up, asked what that was all about.

Travis didn't know how to tell her. The man who had said such horrible things about her a couple weeks ago now needed her bone marrow. "You're a match, sweetie."

The enormity of all of it crossed her face as he watched. Her spine straightened, her shoulders went back, and she nodded. "Okay."

"Are you sure?"

"Yes. I am. And maybe we'll see Abi while we're there, and I can tell her how sorry I am." She gave a weak half smile. "Maybe she'll give me another chance."

He tried to sound more positive than he felt. "Maybe she will. But we don't know if we'll even see her. I'd guess she'd be there, but there's no way to know."

"I could email her?"

Travis took her hands in his. "Thank you for offering, sweetie, but this isn't your mess to fix." He pulled her in for a hug. "You're doing a good thing."

"I know."

After a few minutes, he let her go to tell her friends she'd be out of town for the week. They were supposed to be back on Friday so she'd get to go to the lock-in if she wanted. He did his best not to focus on what else that night was to have held.

By Sunday, they were in Kansas City and Cassie received her first treatment, an injection and a bunch of other tests to measure all sorts of stuff. About an hour after they arrived, they headed back to the hotel.

"How do you feel? Are you up to doing something or do you just want to rest?"

Cassie shrugged. "I think I just want to rest tonight. I brought some books with me, including Grammy's newest one."

"Grammy lets you read hers?" Travis raised a brow. "I didn't think she let anyone see them."

Cassie shrugged. "Dunno. She just asked if I wanted to read it. Said there's a teenager in it and she wanted my opinion."

"Huh. Good for you then."

They got to their room, and Cassie curled up for a nap. The hospital staff had warned she might be sleepy or that she might have a hard time sleeping. What Travis really wanted to do was something, anything, to try to find Abi. While Cassie slept, he called the hospital to see if Abi's dad had been admitted. The lady offered to transfer the call to the room, but Travis said no. Knowing he was there was enough – for now.

He flipped through the channels and found a *Deadliest Catch* marathon. It kept him occupied enough. Mom had given him a couple books written by one of her writer friends - political thrillers, a lot more appealing to him than the romances Mom wrote.

Cassie woke up in time for a late lunch, and they headed for a sit-down restaurant across the street. They asked a couple of locals what to do while in the area, but nothing too taxing. They recommended Union Station in downtown, a place to watch a marble being made in Bonner Springs, which Cassie hadn't gotten to do with Abi, and said to go to Fritz's for lunch or dinner one day – they delivered your food by train. That sounded fun.

Instead, though, they went back to the hotel and relaxed the rest of the day. Cassie read his mom's book, and he read one Mom had given him. It took some searching, but eventually he found the St. Louis Cardinals game on one of the cable networks. Finding the Kansas City Royals had been easier, but he was a Cardinals fan all the way.

The next few days went smoothly. They did some touristy stuff around the times Cassie had to stop in the hospital. Thursday arrived, and it was time for the procedure. Both of them were grateful the procedure was similar to donating plasma rather than actual surgery to get what they needed.

The process took about eight hours. Travis sat next to her the whole time, talking and playing games on his tablet. They even watched a couple movies. By the end, Cassie was tired, but the nurses assured them that was normal.

"Do you want to go back to the hotel?" Travis asked as they discharged her. They had a reservation for another night, but she shook her head.

"I want to go home and sleep in my own bed."

Travis leaned over and kissed her forehead. "I'm so proud of you, Cassandra. After everything that's happened, you didn't have to do this, but I'm so proud of you for doing it."

"It's the right thing to do. Maybe it'll help bring Abi back."

"Do you want to go see if we can find them? He's in the hospital."

Another head shake. "No. Abi knows it was us, and I eMailed her before we left to tell her we'd be here and would like to talk to her if she wanted to. She didn't show up, but we can keep praying. And we can keep praying for her parents, too."

"We will."

An hour later they were on their way home, having never seen the one person they were both hoping would find them.

CASSIE

Dad gave me another hug.

Really.

He was starting to get overbearing.

Sure. I'd donated bone marrow the day before, but I felt okay and Pastor Justin and the rest of the group knew where we'd been and why. They'd take care of me. "I'll call you if I feel like I need to go home. Promise."

He tipped my chin up then gave me a kiss on the forehead. "I'm proud of you, kiddo. But you don't have to stay if you don't want to. You can come home and we'll watch movies and popcorn. I'll even let you pick."

A hint of desperation colored his voice. Why didn't he want to be alone? But if he was willing to let me pick the movies, it had to be pretty bad. "I'm fine, Dad. Promise." Giving him another quick squeeze, I headed for the rec hall where we'd hang out all night. Otherwise, I'd look at his puppy dog face and decide that I wanted to spend the evening with my dad instead of my friends, even though we'd just spent a whole week at a hotel together.

I glanced back to see him talking to Pastor Justin. Probably telling him to make sure I didn't over exert myself by doing something strenuous like getting my own soda.

Pastor Justin smacked Dad on the back then trotted toward me, slinging his arm around my shoulder when he caught up. "I've got something to show you." His Aussie accent always made me feel better. He held the door for me to walk through. Shouts came at me from all directions - the pool and air hockey tables, Wii and Xbox area, -

including Zach, who waved in between throwing punches on Wii boxing. Off to one side was what Pastor Justin was talking about. Out of the way but not out of the action.

"This is for you." Pastor Justin pointed to the recliner. "Your mates moved it out here because they knew you might just want to rest."

I loved my youth group, and my youth pastor. Taking good care of me. Dad wouldn't have let me come otherwise.

He put his arm back around my shoulders and squeezed. "We're glad you're here, kiddo. I'm very proud of you."

"Thanks."

"Any word from your mom?" Why didn't the term bother me anymore? Because I'd be okay with Dad marrying Abi if we could find her? Because I wanted Abi to actually be my mom? Because I wanted, for the first time in my life, to actually call her "mom"? I shook my head.

Pastor Justin made sure I was settled in the chair. I did feel pretty weak. And tired. This might the first year I didn't make it through the night without falling asleep. Usually, everyone made fun of the kids who fell asleep, good-natured fun anyway, but I didn't think they would of me given everything else. They wouldn't even make fun of me for pulling my favorite teddy bear out of my bag. The one Dad said Abi had left with me in the stroller that day. The one that held new meaning now.

Maile pulled up a chair and sat down. "How ya feelin'?"

What a loaded question. How did I feel physically? Tired and weak. Emotionally? Wrung out.

Before we left for Kansas City, I did something I'd avoided to that point.

I sent Abi a Facebook friend request.

Surely that would let her know I wanted to be in contact with her, and Dad hadn't said not to.

Over the years, I'd decided I was better off without my mother. Whoever she was. If she didn't want me, I didn't want her. I knew I'd heard Abi's named mentioned from time to time, but when Zach asked me about it a year earlier, I couldn't tell him. Just that I was pretty sure her last name was Connealy like the first part of mine.

When had all of that changed? When had I decided I wanted Abi Connealy to be a part of my life? To be my *mom*?

All of this flashed through my mind in the seconds after Maile's question.

But it all boiled down to one thing.

"I miss Abi."

Travis went home, wishing again that he still drank, because if there was ever another night to drown your sorrows in a few bottles of beer, it was your non-wedding night.

Instead, he watched baseball on cable. Read a book Mom had given him. Unable to concentrate on it, he went for a run. Miserably out of shape, the run had turned into more of a walk/jog/pant/try-not-to-pass-out thing until Doyle Dozier had picked him up and took him to his house for a soda. Something about the man lent itself to confessions it seemed, because Travis spilled it all to him that night. Doyle reminded him to keep praying, and do what he could to find Abi without being a stalker.

Returning home, he took a shower and flopped down on the other side of the bed, the dream from a few weeks earlier vivid in his mind as he tried to fall asleep on Abi's side. If he tried hard enough, Travis could pretend she was tucked in next to him, the smell of papaya from her shampoo tickling his nose. He could imagine his arms wrapped around her, holding her close as they fell asleep together.

It was a slippery slope, Travis knew, and he stopped himself before his imaginings went farther than they ever should about a woman he wasn't married to. Even if it was to have been their wedding night.

How long would it be before Abi slept at his side all the time?

Chapter Thirty-One

Abi was the smallest person alive.

She had to be.

Cassie had been somewhere, at the hospital, most likely, donating her bone marrow to help save Abi's dad's life. And she hadn't done anything to try to find them.

Cassie had e-mailed Abi, apologizing for how she acted and asking her to come back. To marry Travis. But how did Abi know for sure it was really her, and that she wasn't under duress of some kind from her dad? But surely the Facebook Friend Requests from both of them meant something? Didn't it?

Abi couldn't bring herself to risk it, not with everything going on with her dad. He'd gotten worse, and the treatments made him even weaker. If he'd known who the transplant was coming from, she wouldn't put it past him to refuse, so she didn't tell him. Mom suspected, but Abi didn't confirm it to her either.

The doctors assured them Dad was doing well, but it

would be a while before he could come home. They were told the donor had already left and was fine. Abi gave a big sigh of relief at the news.

Mom sank down onto the couch in their living room. "It was Cassie, wasn't it?"

Abi wouldn't lie to her, but it was the first time she'd asked point blank. She nodded. "I think so. She e-mailed me to tell me she would be up here donating for someone, but the donor people wouldn't confirm who it was."

"Thank her for me when you talk to her?"

Abi hadn't told Mom why she was home. She thought it was only because of Dad's transplant. Rather than telling her now, Abi just nodded. "I will tell her next time I talk to her." Who knew when that would be?

"Want to tell me the truth?" Mom's eyes were full of compassion. "Why are you here? And don't tell me just because of Dad."

Abi took a deep breath and blew it out slowly. Might as well get it over with. "Well, Travis asked me to marry him. Cassie wasn't happy about it, and that's the understatement of the year. It's like saying Dad wasn't happy about Cassie in the first place. It's always been so much more than that, you know?"

Mom nodded. "I understand what you're saying. And you don't think you guys could work it out?"

"I don't think so. Cassie was really upset. She wasn't talking to me or Travis. She was grounded from her phone and didn't care."

Mom winced. "That's pretty bad."

"I have to go back to Serenity Landing for a thing in a couple months. Julie will probably be there. I doubt I can avoid her. I'll try though."

"Julie is Travis's mom?"

Abi nodded. "She's a wonderful woman. I'm so glad

Cassie and Travis had her."

One part of Abi wanted to broach the subject of her newfound faith, but she didn't know how. It came naturally to Julie and Travis and Cassie, but Abi? She was reading her Bible, twice a day and praying as best she knew how. Travis had told her just to talk to God, so that's what she'd been doing. He'd also told her that God heard her prayers before she even knew she was praying them. Like the long lonely nights when Cassie was in her belly, and she struggled with what choice to make, knowing all along Dad would never let Abi keep her and still help with college and everything else.

God was the one who had whispered in her ear, that night in the hospital, as she held her baby girl and cried her eyes out. It was His voice who had whispered Travis's name when she debated taking advantage of New York's Safe Haven law and dropping Cassie off at Mark's fire station. It was God protecting her every year when she got drunk on the anniversary of Cassie's conception. Abi knew more than once things could have gone bad when she got smashed.

But she didn't know how to tell her mom about the new peace that settled inside her. How she knew that it would all turn out okay, even if she and Travis didn't get married until after Cassie did. Travis, Julie, and Cassie all said God had a plan for their lives. They just had to trust Him to know what's best.

Abi had even memorized a verse about it. Julie had given it to her on a 3x5 card before she left that day.

For I know the plans I have for you," Declares the LORD. "Plans to prosper you and not harm you. Plans for a hope and a future."

It was from a book named Jeremiah. Abi hadn't looked it up yet in the Bible Travis had given her, but it was on her list of things to do, and she'd repeated the verse so many times over the last week that it was permanently burned in her mind.

"What're you thinking about?" Mom's quiet voice interrupted her reverie.

"God." Abi said it without letting herself question if it was the right thing to do or not.

"God? What does God have to do with this?"

"Everything." She picked at a loose thread on the arm of the chair. "What if I'd given Cassie up for adoption? A closed adoption? Would Dad have a donor right now? What if I'd never gotten pregnant in the first place? I know Dad detests the very idea of Cassie, but she's saving his life."

"And that's all God?"

"Julie told me about a story, several months ago actually, and gave me a fictional account of it. It's the story of a queen in Babylon. The book was all about this king in ancient Babylon and his wives. The main girl was fictional, completely made up, but the other girl, Esther was real. She married King Xerxes and eventually saved the Jewish people. I read the story in the Bible the other day, just to see, and one verse stuck out to me. Someone asks Esther something like 'What if you became queen so you could find out all this stuff, so you could save your people?' The exact words were 'for such a time as this' and it struck me. What if Cassie's very existence is 'for such a time as this'? To save Dad's life?"

Mom was understandably skeptical. "You think God orchestrated everything so you'd get pregnant that night, just so Dad could have a bone marrow transplant now?"

Abi shrugged. "Why not?"

"Don't you think it's more likely God, if He exists, just sits up there in heaven or wherever it is God is, and just watches us? Making sure we get the consequences for our actions?"

Help me with the words, God. "I think there's some of that. I'm dealing with the consequences of giving Cassie to Travis all those years ago, but Cassie was the one who pointed out how much worse things could have been." She launched into the explanation Cassie had given her for all the things that could have gone wrong that night. "So if you believe there's a God, and I do, then doesn't it make more sense that He's like a parent? I had to deal with the consequences of my decisions as a kid, but you still kept me safe and loved me. You gave me boundaries. When I broke through them, bad things sometimes happened, but I always knew you loved me."

She nodded slowly. "I guess that makes sense. But I'm still not sure I buy it."

"I know. It took me a long time, too. But I'm praying for you. And I know Julie, Keith, Travis and Cassie are, too."

A quick shrug and a change of subject. "So when do you go back to work?"

Abi lay in her bed and stared at the ceiling.

Had Cassie been able to go to her lock-in after donating to Dad?

Did Travis remember this was the day they'd talked about getting married?

Was he lying in his bed, looking at the empty pillow on the other side and wishing she was there with him? Did his arms ache to hold her the same way she longed to be held?

If Abi closed her eyes and imagined, real hard, she could almost hear the sound of his heart beating as her cheek rested on his chest. She could almost feel the warmth surrounding her as he held her in his arms the first time they fell asleep together as man and wife.

And if she tried, really, really hard, she might not cry herself to sleep.

She'd tried reading her Bible. Praying. Reading a book. None of it worked.

Instead, Abi rolled to the side of the bed she rarely slept on and prayed that someday Travis would be there, loving her like she'd always dreamed of being loved.

Abi knew God had a plan, but as she cried herself to sleep, she had a real hard time imagining what it could be.

CASSIE

At least they give us good chairs. I had the easiest job in the history of the world. Or pretty close. I propped my feet up on the front desk of the Serenity Landing Aquatic Center as I tuned out the sounds of about a thousand kids splashing in the pool behind me.

"How're you feeling?"

I wouldn't tune out Zach. I turned and smiled at him. In return, he gave me the look meant for me and me alone. I loved that look.

"I'm okay."

He sat down in the chair vacated by Gwendolyn, my front desk partner, when she left sick. His legs stretched out from beneath his red guard trunks, old flip flops on his feet to protect from the effects of the insanely hot sun on the concrete. He held out one plate with a cinnamon roll. I took it, grateful. Since I was by my lonesome up here, I might not get a break of my own, though Alivia would do her best to make sure I did. Zach's plate had three times as many rolls as mine.

"Any word from your mom yet?"

"Nope. After Dad, you'll be the first one I tell." Zach had been my best friend for so many years. How could he think I'd keep that from him?

"Is your energy back yet?"

His concern was endearing. Most of the time. Sometimes he was worse than my dad. He didn't want me being a lifeguard after I turned sixteen, though he'd never said why. Maybe because he didn't want me walking around in the suits they wore? Basically a sports bra and swim bottoms, though some of the girls wore tankinis. That's what I'd wear. He said it was because he knew there was a history of skin cancer in my family, but I didn't buy that.

A family of four came by and paid for their admission to SLAC for the day, including surf machine passes for the dad and son.

"How are you doing, Cassie? Really?" he asked when it was just the two of us again.

I shrugged. "I miss her. I never thought I'd say that, but I do. I wish she was here and wanted to be my mom."

Zach had dried my tears more times than I cared to think about. Usually on Mother's Day, when everyone else had a mom but I didn't, or near my birthday when I wondered why my mother hadn't loved me enough to keep me. At least she'd given me to my dad and not up for adoption.

"She wanted to be your mom, Cassie. She and your dad were going to get married."

"And have more babies. I know." And it scared me. Still did, no matter what I told my dad. What if she left again? What if she decided after a year or two, she didn't want to be part of our lives anymore? What if they loved a new baby, one they made together on purpose, more than me? I had barely voiced that fear to myself, much less to others, even Zach. The circumstances surrounding my conception and birth were far less than ideal. Would a baby, born out of their love for each other, send me to a distant second? Or even third if they had more than one?

"I gotta get back to the Huna." Zach squeezed my shoulder as he headed for his next station after his break. "I'll see you at adult swim." I glanced at my watch and did the math in my head. By the time most of the guards took their next end of hour break, he'd be in one of the spots that got a break rather than one of the ones who kept watch. He'd come sit with me for a few more minutes. At least my job was easy. I didn't think I could stand sitting around the house any longer, even if I was "recovering." Another family walked up, this time asking a lot of questions about a summer membership, returning my attention to where it needed to be.

And off the woman who'd abandoned me.

Again.

Abi dreaded this day as much as she looked forward to it. Dad was home and doing well, and she was back in Serenity Landing, getting ready to walk into the Comedy Club to help put the final touches on everything. It turned out Julie Harders knew pretty much everyone in town, and their whole family had been invited.

No matter how hard she'd tried, Kevin wouldn't let Abi weasel out of going.

The first person she saw was Mrs. Wilson. "Hello, Abi. How are you?" Stephanie was a writer friend of Julie's.

"I'm fine, thank you."

Stephanie checked her phone. "Josh will be out in a minute. I've got to go check on something else."

"Thanks." Abi looked around to see the furniture and accessories she'd helped them pick out for the lobby. It looked good, really, really good. Relaxed and comfortable. Just what they'd wanted.

"I've recommended you to several friends, already," Josh told her as he walked her way. That took a weight off Abi's shoulders. "In fact, I have a house on my property that's going to need renovated soon. I'd like to hire you for that one, too." Another woman, this one closer to Abi's age, came into the lobby. "Have you met Anise?"

Abi held a hand out. "Yes. We met in Julie Harder's driveway a couple of months ago." And she was a friend of Kristy's. Abi had seen the glares.

"Oh, sweetie, Julie's told me so much about you I feel like we're already friends." And Anise enveloped Abi in a big hug. She whispered in Abi's ear. "I've talked to Kristy and Travis. No hard feelings."

Josh looked as awkward as Abi felt when she moved back. Anise turned to Josh. "How's Stephanie feeling? Any morning sickness?"

While they talked, Abi thought of Travis's offer to help her become a nurse, if that's what she really wanted. Deep down she did. Interior design was fine, but what she really wanted was to be there when babies were born.

Josh and Anise walked off, leaving Abi to double check on all the details. She emerged from the office area to see one of the people she'd hoped to avoid standing with Anise.

"There you are." Julie came to stand beside her in the doorway as Anise excused herself, clicking away with her camera. The call for an official photographer had surprised Abi, but she'd been happy to give Julie's friend the business. "I'm glad you're here. We've all missed you."

"I've missed you, too," Abi told her honestly. As soon as she turned, Abi found herself enveloped in a big hug. Abi wrapped her arms around Julie and held on for dear life. She'd missed Julie. She'd missed *this*. As long as she could get out of here before Travis and Cassie showed up, it would be okay.

"How's your dad?"

They talked for a few minutes before Abi moved to help Stephanie set up the hors d'oeuvres. Cee's Bakery had supplied them. Josh knew the owners of a BBQ place a few blocks away. They supplied the meat. There were Kaiser rolls, sliced cheeses, crackers and all sorts of other munchies. As Abi helped, it was all she could do not to snack a bit like Stephanie did. The other woman was pregnant, after all.

The only excuse Abi had was nerves.

Were her friends Ben and Jerry around anywhere?

Half an hour later, guests started to arrive and Abi shooed Stephanie out to greet the guests. Helping with the food wasn't really part of Abi's job. In fact, she didn't even have to stay for the whole thing, just make sure it all looked right put together. But as long as she stayed moving between the snack stand and the buffet set up counter, Abi could avoid anyone she knew.

And she saw a bunch of people she knew at least a little bit. Friends of Travis's from church. The couple Cassie babysat for. The teachers from the Sunday school class Travis normally attended.

But no Travis and Cassie.

Not yet.

It had been long enough that Abi started to breathe a sigh of relief, when she saw them walk in the front door.

Her daughter and the man she'd decided she never

wanted to see again. Even if he did make her heart skip a beat.

Time to slip out the back door.

Abi adjusted the wig with waist length black hair on her head. "I look like Cher," she muttered into the mirror. With her black maxi dress, platform lace-up boots, and dark glasses she wouldn't take off, maybe they wouldn't notice her this time. As long as Cassie didn't fall off the stage, they probably wouldn't.

Seeing them at the Comedy Club the day before had been almost too much, and she'd nearly backed out of her plan to see the summer stock program Travis was putting on at the high school with a bunch of younger kids. Cassie was in it and the only reason Abi decided to go after all.

She went in, much the same way she had all those weeks earlier. This time she was content to sit wherever she found a seat, but there were no reserved seats this time. She picked one on the side aisle, but not all the way to the side where she might attract more attention for being the outlier. The program this time was merely a piece of paper folded in half. It shouldn't have surprised Abi to see Zach as the only other teenager in the program.

It turned out Cassie was the old woman who lived in the shoe. The one with all the kids. Zach was the grocer. Presumably, he'd deliver food regularly. Muffled voices and children's squeaks came from behind the curtain until it was about five minutes after curtain time. Travis emerged from center of the stage.

Abi's heart did its pitter-pat thing as he spoke into the microphone.

"Thank you all for coming. Your kids have all worked

very hard the last couple weeks, and I'm sure you'll be quite proud of them. Thank you all for sharing them with me. I can't wait to see them in a few years when they make it to high school. Now, without any further ado, *The Old Woman, The Shoe, and the Grocer.*"

He slipped back behind the curtain as it started to open. The play wasn't long and none of the children had many lines. Cassie did a great job helping them without making them feel singled out for not remembering their lines. Zach's comedic timing kept the audience practically rolling on the floor. He reminded Abi of Dick Van Dyke. The kid would go far one of these days.

Abi planned to sneak out before the end of the play, but she couldn't bring herself to. Instead, she got caught in the crush of parents, siblings, and assorted other family members trying to get out of the theater. She breathed a sigh of relief when she made it out the doors but couldn't make it to the front door near as quickly as she would have liked.

Before she could escape, Travis and Cassie walked out of a side door ushering the kids with them. She bolted down the hallway and scooted into a recessed doorway. Breathing a sigh of relief, she leaned against the wall and waited.

As best she could tell it was about fifteen minutes later when the kids were headed backstage again to change out of their costumes. If she didn't slip out now, she probably wouldn't be able to. Time to go for it.

She hadn't made it two steps when she heard his voice.

"Abi?"

Tamping down a curse, she turned away and went down the hall, hoping to find a staircase or something else where she could duck out, and maybe find a door. Preferably one that didn't say "alarm may sound."

As lightly as she could, she made her way downstairs and looked around. Footsteps pounded down the hallway above. Abi bolted to the right and...

There!

An open door.

She winced at the creaking sound, but maybe the voice calling her name covered it.

Tears filled her eyes at the sound of her daughter's voice, but she slid inside the door and closed her eyes, whispering a prayer that they wouldn't find her.

"I think she came this way, Dad." Cassie's voice floated through where the door wasn't quite closed all the way.

Abi felt her way further into the room, not turning on the light for fear of giving away her location. Then she tripped. Let out a little cry. Landed on her hands. Felt water slosh.

And heard the door open behind her.

Chapter
Thirty-Two

Travis winced as heard the crashing down the hall. Abi must have tripped on something. What was she doing here in disguise anyway? Couldn't she have just come to the play? Or stuck around long enough to talk to them at the party? He'd even had the ring in his pocket, but she hadn't been there to give it to.

"Do you see her?" Cassie asked.

"Not yet." He pointed to a door, slightly ajar. "There?"

Cassie opened the door to the janitor's closet. "Abi?" She disappeared from his sight around the door. "Abi!"

Travis sped up the last few steps and turned around the door to see Abi sprawled on the floor in a puddle of water. He shoved the door open so he could see from the light in the hall. It ricocheted off the wall and slammed shut behind him, leaving them in the dark.

He stopped in his tracks. "Everyone okay? Abi?" He reached his hands out in front of him. "Stay still." A quick check confirmed his fear. The door had locked behind them. "Let me find you." Moving carefully, it didn't take long to find both of them. "Are you guys okay?"

"Yeah. I'm fine." That was Abi.

"Are you sure? It sounded like a nasty fall."

"I may have a few bruises, but mostly, I'm just wet." Her hand nestled in his. "Help me up?"

Travis did, wrapping an arm around her shoulder. "I'm glad you're here," he whispered.

"Can we get out of here?" Cassie asked, grasping his other arm.

He winced. "Sorry, kiddo. Door's locked."

"Don't you have the key?"

"Nope."

He felt her shoulders slump. "Okay. Let's at least turn a light on."

"These lights are key-controlled." Just what he knew she wanted to hear.

"And we're in the basement so no cell phones, right?"

"Probably not." They hardly ever worked down here. "But you're both okay?" He felt both of them nod. "Let's find a place to sit down. Over by the door maybe?" A smidge of light came through the crack underneath. With great care, they maneuvered until Cassie was sitting on his right and Abi on the left. He didn't let go of her hand, but linked his fingers with hers.

"Shouldn't we be yelling?" Cassie rested her head on his shoulder.

"No one has any reason to be down here, but Mr. Martin will double check the whole building before he locks up. We'll hear him."

Cassie sat up straight. "We should stick something out the bottom of the door so he knows something's not right."

On his other side, Abi shifted. "We can use this wig." He felt her do something with it. "Done. About half of it went under."

Could he get away with kissing her? What would Cassie think if she realized it?

Cassie spoke next. "How's your dad?"

"He's doing well." Emotion filled Abi's voice. "Thank you, Cassie. You have no idea how much it means to me that you donated after everything."

"I'm glad I could help."

Silence filled the small space. "Where've you been?" Travis finally asked.

"Home."

"You didn't move after all?"

He felt her shake her head. "No. They have me working on the Missouri side, so I am working somewhere else, but I didn't have to move."

A noncommittal, "Nice" was all he could manage.

Cassie's voice sounded small and scared. "Abi?"

"Yes?"

"I'm so sorry. For everything. I didn't really mean that stuff I said."

"I know." Silence reigned. "You were scared I would leave again, weren't you?"

"Yes."

"I didn't want to. I hated the very thought of it, but the last thing I wanted to do was hurt you by staying. I promised myself before I found you that if, at any time, I realized you'd be better off without me again, I'd leave. I really thought you would be. The only reason I did is because I was making you miserable. You know that, right? More than anything I want a relationship with you. Second even to marrying your dad. I've wanted that since I was sixteen, but if being together means an awful relationship with you, I'd sacrifice it in a minute." Travis heard her sniffle. "I know that's not what you want to hear, Trav, but

I mean it. Right now, my relationship with Cassandra is far more important than what we could have been."

It made Travis love her all the more. Sacrificing your own happiness for the sake of your child's need to be secure and loved was part and parcel of being a parent.

Cassie's voice was stronger when she spoke. "I'm not better off with you gone. I want you in my life. And my dad needs you in his. He misses you. *I* miss you."

Travis squeezed Cassie a bit tighter, before leaning toward Abi. "She's right. I do need you. And we both miss you." He let go of her hand so he could wrap an arm around her. "Will you come back to Serenity Landing?"

She hesitated before she spoke. "I don't know. I don't think so."

With that, there was nothing to say. At least not there. Not then. Once he and Abi were alone, he'd implore her. Get back down on one knee and ask her to be his wife all over again. Get Cassie to help him if he needed to.

They sat there in silence for what seemed like an eternity.

"I love you, Abi." Cassie's whispered words nearly broke his heart. "Please don't leave us. I want you to be my mom. Honest. My real mom."

Abi reached across him until she found Cassie's hand. "Are you sure?"

Travis felt Cassie nod, but she spoke, too. "I'm sure. Please?"

Still, Abi hesitated. "I don't know, Cassie. I want to, but I don't know how to prove to you I'm not going anywhere."

"You don't have to. All you have to do is not go."

"I can do that. If you're sure you still want me."

"We do." A pause. "Mom."

Abi stiffened then slumped forward. Travis felt tears

splash on his forearm. "You can't know, Cassie, how long I've prayed that someday you'd call me 'Mom.' Long before I even started believing God really existed, I prayed you would."

"Are you sure it's okay with you?" Cassie sucked in a breath and held it.

"Of course."

Somehow, the two of them maneuvered until they could hug each other. Travis left one hand resting on each back as they held each other tight. Tears were being shed, again, but hopefully, this time they were tears of healing.

Eventually, they settled back down, one on either side. Once he verified who was who, Travis leaned over until his mouth was next to Abi's ear. "I'm going to ask you again, you know." She nodded. "I won't take no for an answer and it won't be a long engagement." She shook her head.

"Are you two making out over there?" Cassie's voice, though teasing, kept him from giving Abi a kiss.

"No." But what a thought. And hot on its heels was another one. Travis let go of both of them and stood. "Hang on." He pulled out his phone and turned it on, swiping to get to the flashlight. With it, he looked around until he found what he was looking for.

Moving back to the door, Travis knelt down, setting the phone on the floor so the light shone upward. He winked at his daughter and turned to Abi. "Abs, it's been a long time since we met, since we managed to blow our first chance..."

"Travis!" A voice in the hall stopped his speech. "Are you down here?"

He dropped his head and groaned. "Yeah. We're in the janitor closet."

"I see you." A second later, blinding light hit them as a crack appeared in the wall. They all shielded their eyes against the onslaught. Once they were out and started to reorient themselves, Travis found Cassie and Abi hugging like there would be no tomorrow. He went to them, wrapped his arms around both and thanked God for bringing his family together.

Long moments passed before they finally moved away from each other. Cassie winked at him and he took that as his cue. Pulling the twist-tie out of his pocket, Travis dropped to one knee. After fashioning it into a circle, he looked up at Abi. "Abi, I don't have your ring here, but will you be the mother of my daughter? Will you marry me?"

There was no mistaking her answer.

"Yes!"

Before Travis could put the ring on her finger, she'd pulled him to his feet and kissed him. It was one of those kisses that made your toes curl. The kind you read about in *Princess Bride*. A perfect kiss he thought existed only in one of Mom's romance novels. When they finally broke apart, she shyly held up her left hand, ring finger extended.

He tugged the makeshift ring onto her finger where it belonged, kissing the knuckle above it. "We'll get yours as soon as I can get home."

"It doesn't matter." She kissed him again. "As long as you don't change your mind."

Travis grinned and held her close. "Never."

"When?" she asked.

"Is tomorrow too soon?" he responded, his grin widening.

Seriously, she shook her head. "It's not soon enough."

Cassie and Mr. Martin, who Travis had forgotten about, laughed. Travis didn't. He happened to agree whole-heartedly.

"Travis? Cassie?" His mom rounded the corner of the staircase. "We've been look... Abi!" Mom ran down the hall, with Dad close behind. The two women hugged, until Abi stepped back and held up her left hand. Mom laughed. "A twisty?"

"Just for now." Abi moved back until her arm was around his waist again.

He kissed her one more time, lightly this time, as Mr. Martin waved and continued his rounds. Glancing at Mom and Dad, Travis asked what they thought about when this should happen.

"It's too late to get to Eureka Springs to get married tonight," Mom noted.

They all gave her a look.

"What?" she shrugged. "I had to do some research for a book."

Yeah. Right.

Abi shook her head. "I'd like to get married at the church." She looked up at him. "If you think the pastor would go for it. Maybe after church next Sunday?"

Travis looked back over at Dad who knew Pastor Rick pretty well.

Dad nodded. "I bet he'd do it."

Abi looked at the ground. "I want to invite my parents. They may not come. They may not give us their blessing, but I want to give them the chance."

"I think that's a great idea." He did. He just hoped they'd take the chance given them.

Because, like it or not, in eight days, Travis was going to marry their daughter.

Chapter Thirty-Three

A bi had to do this in person.

And she had to do it by herself.

After they left school, they'd gone back to Keith and Julie's. Julie had loaned her clothes for the special church service that evening. The difference between then and the last time she'd been there amazed her. This time, Abi knew what she felt was the presence of God surrounding her, giving her the peace that passed understanding. Deep down, she believed this was all part of God's plan and that, somehow, it would all work out the way it was supposed to.

Once service ended, they waited patiently until Pastor Rick had a minute.

"Abi." His smile seemed genuine. "I'm so glad to see you again."

Travis put his arm around her waist. "Rick, we were wondering if you'd marry us after service next week."

If possible, his smile widened. "Of course. I'd be happy to."

They talked for a few more minutes about doing a counseling session during the week before the wedding and a few afterward, just to make sure they were doing okay, since it had been so long since they'd known each other, and they'd only been back together a short period. He recommended Doyle and Deeanne Dozier. That made her feel better since she already felt like she knew Deeanne.

They had a late snack with Travis's parents and Cassie, who called her "Mom" a couple of times, warming Abi's heart when she did.

"I need to go." But she didn't want to. She wanted to stay curled up next to Travis until time for the wedding.

"You want me to go with you?"

Abi shook her head. "I need to do this myself. And I need to do it in person."

After hugs all around, Travis walked Abi to her car. "Are you sure you don't want me to go with you?"

Abi kissed him, letting her lips linger on his. "I'm sure. But thank you."

"Call me after?"

"Of course." Another kiss and she got in the car. Travis closed the door and stood there, watching her drive off. It almost made Abi want to turn around and take him with her, but she couldn't.

Time to stand on her own two feet.

Even if it killed her.

Mom pulled Abi into a hug as soon as she opened the door. "How was your party?"

"Fine."

"Did you see...them?"

Abi let go of Mom and held up her left hand, where her

ring once again sat.

Mom gasped and grabbed it. "He asked you to marry him again?"

"Yes."

"And you said 'yes'?"

"Yep." Abi walked past her into the house. "And Cassie started calling me 'Mom.'" She turned in time to see tears fill Mom's eyes.

"Oh, honey. That's wonderful."

Abi told her the whole story as Mom swiped at her cheeks.

"When's the big day?"

"Sunday. After church." Abi took a deep breath. "I really want you both there."

That gave her pause. "I don't know, sweetheart. If it were up to me, sure, but your dad…" Mom shook her head sadly. "And if he doesn't want me to go, I probably shouldn't."

Abi nodded. "I understand."

"He's in a good mood, though. The Royals won today." Together, they walked into the living room where he sat in his chair.

"Hi, sweetheart."

He looked great. "Hi, Daddy." Abi bit her lip before making herself let go of him. "I need to talk to you about something."

He pressed mute on the remote and turned to her. "What is it?"

"A couple things, actually." Abi took a deep breath. "I know who your donor was."

His eyebrows pulled together. "How?"

"The person is a relative."

"We looked at all the relatives. No one matched."

"There was one you didn't check." Abi looked straight

in his eyes and willed him to realize who it was.

"The girl?" She couldn't read his expression or his tone of voice, but nodded. "After everything I said about you and him and her, she still donated?"

"Yes."

"Why?"

"Because it was the right thing to do."

He nodded then looked at her hands. The fingers of her right hand twisted the engagement ring nervously. "And what's that?"

Abi held it up. "Travis asked me to marry him."

"I take it you said yes?"

She nodded. "I love him, Daddy. I've loved him since he spent all that time with us. I know you didn't like him, but..."

Dad shook his head. "It wasn't that I didn't like him, per se, it was that he was a college kid. A couple years older. An out of work actor most of the time. Lots of girlfriends. You're my baby girl. I know it's a double standard that we weren't too concerned about Mark sleeping with Brenda, as long as they weren't at our house when you were home and were being safe about it, but there was no way I wanted Travis, or any other kid, with his hands on you. I didn't want you getting hurt or getting pregnant and him running off and leaving you." He took a deep breath and let it out. "Like my dad did."

Abi glanced at Mom who looked as confused as she felt. "What?"

He took a sip from the water sitting on the table next to him. "I've never told either of you this. My mom's date to a dance her senior year was a boy named Guy. They slept together and when she told him she was pregnant, he tried to send her to a back alley abortionist. They weren't legal back then, you know. My grandparents pressured her to give me up for adoption but she refused. Life was hard. She always worked two jobs. Never home. I knew she loved me, but deep down, sometimes, I wished she'd given me to another family."

Abi had a new appreciation for her father. He'd never said much of anything about his childhood. Now she started to understand why.

"That's why I didn't want you to see Travis. I was afraid he'd leave you high and dry, just like my father did. And that's why I didn't want you to keep the baby. I thought adoption was the best thing for everyone."

"If I'd given her up for adoption, we never would have been able to find her in time for your transplant."

"I know. And I've done a little digging since I got home and it seems like Travis has been a great dad."

"He is, Daddy." Abi knelt on the floor next to him, taking one of his hands in both of hers. "He's a great dad. He loves Cassie so much, and he loves me. He would have married me back then and he wants to marry me now." She rested one hand on his cheek. "And I want you to be there."

He reached out and brushed Abi's hair off her face. "I wouldn't miss it for the world." It wasn't much. But it was a start.

"I don't know what I'm supposed to do." Abi was whining. She knew she was whining. She didn't care.

Travis came to stand behind her. "What don't you get?"

"How to register for college. Do you know how long it's been? And I have a bachelor's degree already. Surely that counts for something."

"Do you have your transcripts?" He started to knead her

shoulders. "We can go in tomorrow and see if there's a real person we can talk to."

"That sounds good."

"And then we can all go to the Aquatic Center tomorrow night." Abi could hear the grin in his voice. "I haven't shown off on the Huna yet."

Abi leaned her head straight back so she could see him. "The what?"

"It's this surf machine thing. Gotta show off for my girl."

"He's good." Cassie walked into the room. "There's always a bunch of students there who know him, and they give him a hard time, but he's better than most of them." She flopped onto the couch next to Abi. "My tan is pathetic this year. I haven't been nearly as much as usual. At least not when I'm not just sitting in the shade working."

"You look great."

Travis pointed to her laptop. "Are you sure you want to do all this stuff this week? Isn't planning a wedding enough for you?"

"Wedding's planned. I found a nice dress. You have a suit. Cassie got a new dress last night. Flowers are taken care of. We're not having a reception. Your mom's friend Anise is taking pictures. What else is there? We can go get our license and go to the school at the same time. They're not too far from each other." She'd checked.

"Sounds like a plan."

Abi snapped her laptop shut. "I need to get back to your parents' house."

He massaged her shoulders a bit more. "Just a few more days..."

"I'm right here," Cassie interjected. "Seriously."

"Well, you're spending next week with Grammy and

Grandpop at their house."

"Since when?" Abi looked up at him.

"Since we're going out of town." He looked like the Cheshire cat.

Abi blinked twice. "We are? I thought we were staying here." Would he ever stop surprising her? She hoped not.

"Sunday night we are," he confirmed. "But we're flying out Monday morning. We'll have breakfast with my parents and Cassie and your parents if they want to, but then we're gone for a week."

That sounded like heaven. "Where?"

The grin widened. "I'm not telling."

"How will I know what to pack?"

Travis glanced toward Cassie. "We'll talk about that later."

Nice. Very nice.

Abi stood and squeezed Cassie's shoulder as she walked past. "I'll see you in the morning, sweetie."

"I'm not going with you to run all those errands."

"Then I'll see you tomorrow afternoon."

She nodded. "That's better. Love you, Mom."

Would she ever tire of hearing those words? Abi didn't think so.

Travis walked her to the door. "I love you, too."

"Back atcha." Abi could feel the twinkle in her eyes. "So what do I need to pack?"

"Your passport."

Abi raised an eyebrow at him. "My passport?"

"Your mom said you have one."

"Yes."

"Good. Pack it. Everything else is taken care of."

Abi nodded. There were a few things he didn't know about that she'd have to make sure got packed, but otherwise she'd trust him. Maybe they were going someplace warm. Like one of those huts on a private beach.

"We haven't talked finances. Not really. Can you afford that and putting me through school? I don't know if I'll be able to work much."

Another grin. "Trust me."

Abi turned serious. "Always."

CASSIE

I tapped my pen against the notepad as I tried to figure out the best way to surprise my parents. At their wedding! I'd been so dead set against it, then so disappointed, but now it was happening! It would take some getting used to, having Abi - Mom! - live with us, but we'd figure it all out.

"Any luck?" Zach flopped into the chair next to me and stirred his mom's corn and macaroni casserole in the Tupperware dish.

"No. Still trying to come up with a good present for either one of them. Or both." I leaned my head back and stared at the fan circling lazily over the desk. "I don't know where they're going on their honeymoon so I can't give them something they could use there, like a tourist guide book. Giving them money would be kind of pointless since I'd just have to ask them for more later."

"What about that lady in Branson?" He took a big bite as he looked at me over the top of his fork.

"Branson?"

"The one who knew your uncle?"

My uncle? Jay? No. Mark. "Brenda?"

"Sure. Don't know that you ever told me her name."

I turned her name over in my mind. Branson wasn't far. Maybe she could come to the wedding? "That's a great idea." Leaning up to grab my phone, I groaned as some people walked up. Tina, who had been half in love with Zach since they were in third grade and hated my guts, and her two little sisters. The younger girls walked on in, but Tina stopped to flirt with Zach. If you asked me, her cover-up didn't cover up nearly enough. Neither did her bikini.

While they talked, Zach was polite but nothing more, I looked through the computer. "Tina, does your family have a membership this year?"

She looked down her nose at me. Literally, since she was leaning on the counter. "Of course."

"I'm not seeing it in the system." I tried to sound apologetic. Honest. "Unless you've got your cards with you, I'm afraid you'll have to pay for all three of you."

Her face turned bright red. "My mother told me she'd bought our membership. I've been here at least twice a week all summer" Yes. She had. The days Zach worked. "and suddenly you look up our membership?"

With a shrug, I turned the monitor toward Zach who scrolled through it.

"I don't see you on here, Tina. Could it be under a different last name?" he asked around a mouthful of casserole.

It wasn't. I'd looked under her mom's last name first, but Zach double-checked. Not there.

Alivia chose that moment to walk out to check on us. "What's up?"

Blustering, Tina told her I was being mean, and that she wouldn't be able to go in because I was incompetent. Okay. She didn't use those words, but that was the gist. Livs looked at the membership lists and noted that Tina and her family didn't seem to be on it anywhere. Zach took off for his next station, and Aliva closed her eyes and took a deep breath.

"You're not in the system, Tina, but today, I'll let you go ahead and go in."

If looks could kill, I'd be a pile of ashes after the one Tina gave me.

Alivia sat in the chair next to me and waited for her to leave. "I know she's crushing on Zach, Cassie, and that she doesn't like you because he does. I also know you're a better actress, and she hates that, too. But you wouldn't have looked anyone else up because 99.9% of the people who walk up and say they have passes, do. Especially this late in the summer when they've been here constantly."

I closed my eyes and groaned again. "I know. It was petty but..."

"You have no idea what her family is going through right now. I don't know many details and wouldn't share them with you if I did, but cut her some slack. She needs a friend not someone picking on her."

She was right. I hated that. "Okay. I will."

Alivia poked me in the arm. "You want to spend the night at my place Sunday after the wedding?"

"Maybe." I pulled my phone out and opened the Facebook app. "I need to work on a surprise for both of my parents though. Zach gave me a great idea." The red number showed a new message. When I clicked on it and realized who it was from, and that she'd be in town over the weekend, the "whoop!" couldn't be contained.

"What?"

I didn't answer Alivia as my thumbs flew across the keyboard inviting Joanna Burgess, the woman Dad wrote the play about, and her family to the wedding. "It's not the idea Zach had but it's a good one. I wonder if I could pull both of them off." Biting my bottom lip, I wondered what Abi - Mom - would think about me inviting Joanna. Dad would be glad to see her, but I was less sure of Abi's reaction.

Alivia squeezed my shoulder. "Keep me posted and let me know about Sunday."

"I will." Before she walked off, my phone buzzed. Joanna had already responded and said she'd love to come.

Now, for phase two. Make sure Anise knew so she could get pictures and see if I could get a hold of Brenda.

"Mom?" Cassie poked her head in the ante room. She walked in and Abi felt tears fill her eyes. How would her make-up ever survive the wedding?

"You look beautiful, sweetheart." Abi held open her arms and Cassie walked into them for a big, if careful, hug. Church had let out about thirty minutes earlier. Her parents had gone with her to service. She'd stayed away from Travis on purpose and he promised not to look for her. An announcement was on the bulletin card, and Pastor Rick had made it before his sermon.

"Thanks." Cassie moved away.

Anise motioned to them, positioning them just so before snapping several pictures. Abi couldn't wait to see how they came out.

After a few pictures with Abi's parents, Cassie turned back to her. "There's someone here to see you."

Abi's mom interjected. "It's not your dad is it? Because..."

Cassie shook her head. "No. But it is someone all of you know." She went to the door and opened it, whispering to the person on the other side.

When Cassie stepped to the side, pulling the door further open with her, Abi gasped. "Brenda?"

Mark's girlfriend walked into the room, tears already

streaming down her cheeks. "Hey, Abs."

Abi gathered her skirt in one hand and ran the few steps to close the distance between them. This hug wasn't quite as careful as she clung to the one person who hadn't abandoned her as she struggled with everything all those years ago.

When they finally pulled back, Abi just shook her head. "How...?"

Brenda nodded toward someone standing just out of sight. "Cassie found me on Facebook a couple months ago. We've been emailing ever since."

She turned to see Cassie grinning from ear to ear. "When did you find her? How? Does your dad know?"

Cassie's grin took on a Cheshire cat quality. "That night we spent at your apartment. I'm a great Googler. And nope. Not yet. He's our next stop. Or maybe after the wedding." She glanced at the clock. "That's probably a better idea. I'm going to go check on Dad."

Abi gave Cassie another hug and turned back to Brenda. "I have missed you so much."

Brenda wiped her cheeks. "Cassie told me why you didn't want to be in my wedding." She reached out and took Abi's hand. "I would have understood, and I'm so sorry I didn't realize."

"I know."

The door opened again, and the pastor poked his head in. "You about ready, Abi?"

Abi gave her best smile. "I am." After giving Brenda another hug, Abi submitted to her mother's make-up brush. A few minutes later, Daddy stood next to her at the back of the sanctuary. Abi couldn't see how many people were in there, but Cassie told her it was a decent sized crowd for such short notice with no invitations.

Cassie stood in front of her, looking beautiful. She was

the maid of honor, though she couldn't actually sign the marriage license. Someone else would do that. Dad had stuck close to Abi's side, still moving more slowly than normal. He'd smiled at Cassie, who'd smiled back, but anything more would take place later.

Music started in the sanctuary and someone she didn't know opened the door just enough for Cassie to walk through.

A minute later, the music changed.

It was time to marry the man of her dreams.

Chapter Thirty-Four

M om, I can tie my own tie." Travis was whining. He didn't care.

"It's my job to make sure it's perfect." Mom tweaked it just a bit more. "There."

Travis rolled his eyes and turned to look in the mirror. It did look better than it ever did when he did it himself.

Cassie walked in the room just then and his heart slowed, so much he barely noticed his mom's friend taking pictures.

"Cassie, you look wonderful." Travis reached for her and she let him give her a hug. "When did you get so grown up?"

She shrugged. "I dunno."

"How'd you get so beautiful?"

"That's how God made me." Her childhood answer made him smile.

"And how'd you get so smart?"

"That's how God made me."

He went on. Kind. Compassionate. She gave the same

answer each time.

"God made you so special, Cassie. And I'm so grateful He let me be your dad."

"And I'm glad you're my dad."

Dad rolled his eyes. "Welcome to the mutual admiration society."

They laughed and Cassie moved to Mom's side. Mom fixed something about her hair.

"How's Abi?" he asked.

Cassie just smiled. "I'm not telling you anything."

"Nice."

"Actually, I have something..."

Pastor Rick interrupted whatever she was going to say when he poked his head into the ante-room. Or the Sunday school room. Depending on who was doing what in there. "You ready?"

"I was ready months ago."

Travis's dad and brother walked with him to the side entrance of the sanctuary. He was surprised at how many people had stuck around. Probably forty or fifty., including Kristy and some guy Travis didn't know with his arm around her shoulders. She gave him a small smile that gave him reason to believe they could still be friendly, and she wasn't going to hate him forever. But with all the people there, he hoped they'd ordered enough cake for the reception Abi's mom insisted on having despite their original plans. His brother stood with him at the front of the church and waited for the music to start. Someone else sat behind Kristy. Travis squinted. Was that...

The door opened before he could figure it out and Cassie walked slowly down the aisle. Travis couldn't take his eyes off of her. She looked so grown-up and so beautiful. As she passed Zach, he noticed the young man couldn't keep his eyes off her either. Travis would have to keep an eye on...

His thoughts were interrupted as the wedding march started. He'd avoided seeing Abi all morning, but now...

She walked through the door in a white dress. Travis couldn't tell anything else just yet, but he couldn't tear his eyes away from her. He didn't want to.

As she got closer, he could see the dress was simple. Nearly floor length and some kind of shiny material. Not glittery shiny, but shinier than anything he owned. She and her father stopped at the foot of the stairs to the stage.

"Who gives this woman to this man?"

Her dad looked at Travis and smiled. "It is my great honor, as her father, to give her to this man."

Travis knew things were going better, but that surprised him. Her dad kissed her cheek and Travis reached for her hand, tucking it into his elbow as they ascended the stairs.

It was almost surprising how quickly the ceremony went. In about ten minutes, Travis promised to love, honor, and cherish the woman standing next to him, and she promised the same. They both said "I do" and exchanged rings.

Then Pastor Rick said the words Travis had been waiting sixteen years to hear. "Travis, you may kiss your bride."

Travis's smile was so wide, his face practically split in two. He pulled Abi toward him, leaning down to kiss her. He wanted to kiss her so much deeper than he knew he could with an audience, but they could both tell the difference in the kiss.

They broke it off, both of them grinning, and turned to face the forty or so people who'd stuck around.

"Ladies and gentlemen, it is my very great privilege to introduce to you for the very first time, Travis and Abigail Harders."

They walked down the first two steps and stopped. Abi

reached for Cassie, who took her hand, and the three of them, together, walked toward the rest of their lives.

As a family.

Down in the fellowship center, a cake waited for them along with some snacks. There were no gifts. They'd wanted it that way. And they didn't do a receiving line, but one of the first people he saw was one of the last people he would have expected.

"Brenda?"

She nodded and gave him a big hug. "I'm so happy for you two, Trav. We need to sit down and talk someday about everything that happened after Mark died, and at Christmas that year, but right now, I just want you to know how insanely happy I am for both of you."

They talked for a few more minutes, with Abi joining them. Travis didn't stray far from Abi's side, one hand always touching her it seemed. Unless Anise kicked him out of the pictures. And she took a million of them, even having them go outside near the trees in the church's yard. He couldn't wait to see them.

Pastor didn't stick around long, but the rest of them stayed for a while. As much as he looked forward to getting Abi alone, she seemed to be enjoying herself talking with Brenda and Deeanne, though she did keep glancing his way and smiling.

Travis walked over and stood behind her, whispering in her ear. "Wanna dance?"

She looked up, surprised. "What?"

A new song was starting on the CD player.

"Dance with me?"

He didn't think Pastor Rick would be crazy about it,

there was no dancing at receptions in the fellowship hall, but he wasn't here, and it wasn't officially dancing. It was Travis, holding his wife in his arms and moving slowly as "Unforgettable" played in the background.

Everyone sort of stopped what they were doing to watch as he held her close, kissing her softly as they moved. There were no words, just enjoying being close to each other.

When the song ended, her dad tapped Travis's shoulder and took over. Travis winked at Cassie before twirling her around and dancing with her. His first real dance with his daughter. The ones where she stood on his feet when she was a kid didn't count.

"We're gonna dance at your wedding someday," he promised.

"I know." She glanced to her right and Travis did, too. Zach stood there.

"You like him?"

She nodded.

"You like him like him?" He felt like he was in high school all over again.

Another nod.

"He's a great kid." Travis had no intention of telling her what Zach had said about his marriage plans.

The song ended, and Cassie moved away, but not before giving him a kiss on the cheek. "There's someone I want you to meet." She led him over to a blonde woman sitting at the side. He'd seen her talking to the woman earlier, but couldn't place where he knew her from. "This is Joanna Burgess." The name seemed familiar, as did her face, but he still couldn't figure it out. "She used to live in Manhattan and worked at the Marriott World Trade Center."

Realization dawned across his mind. "Crunchy cinnamon bread on Tuesdays. Chocolate Chip Peppermint

Mocha Double Blended with Whip when available. Japanese Green Tea Mocha Frappe on Mondays. Engaged to a guy in Tower Seven, but you had family in this area?"

Joanna nodded. "That's me."

Travis stood, stunned, holding her hand in the world's longest handshake. "I thought..." He shook his head as he released her hand. "I saw your picture on the telephone poles and the storefronts." He sat in the chair next to her. "I know we didn't really know each other beyond your daily orders, but..."

"I was in the lobby of the Marriott World Trade Center when the first building fell," she told them. "A dozen or so of us were trapped there, including a friend of mine who's been on a couple of specials about the hotel. Anyway, a firefighter helped us find a way out. We weren't very far down the street when the second tower fell, but far enough away to survive. It took me two days to make it home. I got a ferry across into New Jersey, but every time I tried to call, I couldn't reach anyone because the lines were down, or they were out putting up posters. I stayed with a coworker until we could get back to Long Island a couple days later. By then, they'd already put up the posters, and they must not have taken all of them down."

"I'm so glad to hear you're okay, but what are you doing here? I mean, I'm glad, but..."

Joanna smiled at Cassie. "Your daughter found me after she saw the *Hotel Ground Zero* special and contacted my friend to see if she knew any of the other people who survived. My daughters visited my parents for a few weeks this summer, and I happened to be in town picking them up when Cassie messaged me the other day." She glanced at her watch. "I do need to get going, though. I need to help my husband, the guy from Tower Seven, get packed up and kids to bed because we fly out early tomorrow."

Travis gave her a quick hug, and Joanna promised to find him on Facebook. He turned to Cassie, whose smile split her face. "Surprised?"

"Yes." He put one arm around his daughter and hugged her to his side. "Thank you. I've always thought..."

"I know. And Zach could tell how sad it made you when you told him about it this spring. He mentioned it to me. I remembered watching the special and how they thought about forty people died at the hotel and most of them were firefighters."

"Your detective work is pretty incredible." He kissed the side of her head.

She shrugged. "I can Google."

Abi walked up at that moment, asking who the woman had been. While Travis explained, Cassie went to talk to Zach. When he finished, Abi looked up from under lowered lashes. "I don't know about you, Mr. Harders, but I think I'm about ready to get out of here."

Travis kissed her softly. "Mrs. Harders, I think that sounds just perfect."

Travis carried Abi over the threshold of the house and kicked the door closed. She surely expected him to have one thing on his mind, and he did, but first there was something else.

One arm still wrapped around her, Travis pulled an envelope out of the inside pocket of his suit coat.

"What's this?"

Travis just smiled. "Open it."

She turned her back to him, tucking herself in front of his chest. With a smooth motion, she ripped open the envelope and pulled out the piece of paper inside.

The shock in her voice didn't surprise him. "This is from my dad."

Dear Abi, they read.

I'm so sorry it took me so long to come to my senses. I know this doesn't make up for the years we all missed with Cassie — and Travis — but it's something I can do to try to make up for it just a little bit. There's a college fund waiting for Cassie. It's enough for four years wherever she wants to go. There's one for you, too. To pay your tuition for nursing school. Travis originally told me you weren't planning a trip for your honeymoon. I'm sure by now you know that's not the case. Consider it my wedding gift. There's a wedding fund for Cassie, too. I love you more than you'll ever know, and I'll regret till my dying day the way things played out.

Love,
Dad

"Wow."

Travis wrapped his arms tighter around her waist. "He loves you, honey. He's always loved Cassie. At least now we all know why he acted the way he did."

She nodded and tossed the letter on the table in the entryway. Loosening his grip enough to let her turn in his arms, he waited for the second and a half it took her to face him.

"I don't want to talk about my dad or college or anything but you and me." Her nimble fingers made quick work of his tie. "I want to be your wife."

Travis scooped her back up in his arms and kissed her. Walking toward the room they'd now share while kissing her and not tripping or hitting her head on a wall took more concentration than he had. So he stopped. Kissing her. Until they reached their room.

Then he didn't stop.

And neither did she.

Epilogue

Watching Abi sleep was his new favorite pass-time. One of them anyway.

The hut, right on the beach, was as secluded as you could get and still be near civilization. Her dad had surprised even Travis when, the morning after the wedding, he gave them the tickets. Three-and-a-half weeks in paradise instead of the week Travis thought they were getting.

And now just two days left before they had to return to the real world.

Abi rolled toward him, a smile crossing her face even before her eyes opened. "Don't get that look in your eyes just yet, mister."

"What look?"

"You know what look." Her lips barely brushed his before she sat up and headed for the bathroom.

Married for three weeks, and he still had no idea what took women so long in there first thing in the morning.

And this morning seemed worse than usual. While he waited, he pulled out his tablet and opened an email from Anise. She'd said the pictures would be waiting by morning and there they were.

Travis knew he should probably wait for Abi to look at them, but he was riveted. He loved the pictures of Abi and Cassie. So much alike. So much to be thankful for. Then there were some pictures of him and his *wife*. What a word! The first one was nice, but the second took his breath away. Did he really look at Abi like that? Was that how she looked at him? It was different seeing it on the screen. If that one made him nearly stop breathing, the next made his heart skip a beat. Anise had taken them outside and had Abi stand against the wall. Her arms were outstretched, palms flat on the bricks. His hands covered hers, tips of their fingers intertwined. He'd leaned in close, whispering sweet nothings in her ear. He couldn't see his own face, but a smile lit up Abi's. If only he could be sure she'd always smile like that when they talked.

A noise in the bathroom brought his attention back to the hut on the beach. "Are you okay?" he called.

The door opened and Abi came out holding something in her hand.

"What's that?"

"Something I've suspected for a couple days." Her grin should have told him something, but Travis didn't know what it was.

"What?"

Her smile widened. "I'm pregnant."

It took a second for that to sink in. "What?"

"We're having a baby."

Travis blinked. Twice. Then two more times. As he tried to process the information. He nearly tripped over the sheet tangled around his legs as he tried to get to her. He knelt on the floor in front staring at the satin covering her stomach. "We're having a baby?"

Her hands ran through his hair. "Yes."

Gently, he kissed her stomach, just below her belly button. "It's going to be different this time, Abs. I'll be there for you every step of the way."

"I know."

Travis stood up, his hands running up her sides until he slid them around her and pulling her to him until he could kiss her senseless.

God had answered both of their prayers. Exceedingly. Abundantly. Pressed down. Shaken together. And running over. He'd shown His unending grace in all of their lives, proving, once more, He had more than enough grace to save.

Dear Reader,

Thank you for joining Travis, Abi, and Cassie in Grace to Save! I appreciate you and hope you enjoyed it! This is the first book in the Serenity Landing Tuesdays of Grace series! There WILL be more books in the series. Anise has a story just WAITING to be told and so does Kristy, so I won't forget about them - I promise! - but as each of their stories has a 9/11 connection as well, they'll likely release around this time each year.

In just a few pages, you'll find part of chapter 1 of *Discovering Home*, the first book in the Serenity Landing Second Chances series! It's Jonathan's story! FINALLY! It's also available on Amazon and the ebook released September 15, 2016.

In just a few more pages, you'll find chapter 1 of *Finding Mr. Write*, book 1 in the CANDID Romance series - and the ebook is FREE on all retailers! Many of you have likely already read *Good Enough for a Princess*, but if not, that ebook too is FREE on all retailers!

I see a meme floating around Facebook from time to time that tells readers what they can do to help their favorite authors. Buying their next book or giving a copy away is kind of a no-brainer, but the biggest thing you can do is write a review. If you enjoyed *Grace to Save* would you consider doing just that?

I would LOVE to hear from you! My email address is carolmoncadobooks@gmail.com. To stay up-to-date on releases, you can sign up for my newsletter (there's fun stuff - like a super special novella that will be coming FREE before the beginning of my next royalty series next year!! You'll also get notices of sales, including special preorder pricing! And I won't spam!) or there's always "What's in the Works" or "What I'm Working On Now" on my website :). You can find my website and blog at www.carolmoncado.com. I blog most Sundays and about once more each month at www.InspyRomance.com. And, of course, there's Facebook and my Facebook profile, Author Carol Moncado. If you recently liked my Facebook *page* (Carol Moncado Books)...I hope you'll "follow" the profile as well. Facebook recently changed the rules again which means very few people (often 1-5% of "likes") will see anything I post there. Following the profile will show you my book updates, updates about books from authors I love, funny cat (or dog or dinosaur!) memes, inspirational quotes, and all sorts of fun stuff!! I hope to see you there soon!

Thanks again!

Until
next time,
Carol

Acknowledgments

They say writing is a solitary endeavor and it absolutely can be. Sitting in front of the computer for hours on end, talking to imaginary people.

And having them talk back ;).

But the reality is no one walks alone. Since I began this writing journey nearly six years ago, I can't begin to name all of those who've helped me along the way. My husband, Matt, who has always, *always* believed in me. All of the rest of my family and in-loves who never once looked at me like I was nuts for wanting to be a writer. Jan Christiansen (my "other mother") has always believed in me and Stacy Christiansen Spangler who has been my dearest friend for longer than I can remember.

For *Grace to Save* specifically - I can't begin to tell you the people who've loved me through this book. It was first written in 2012 and has been through so many revisions and critiquers since then, that I know I'll never be able to name them all. The fabulous Janice Thompson made it all the way through a couple years ago and made some completely invaluable notes. Laurie Tomlinson (her first book is coming!) had fantastic comments (and called Travis Harders "like your best friend's older brother - hunky with a side of redemption").

Ginger Solomon, author of *One Choice*, has been invaluable with her proofreading services.

Then there's my writer friends. My NovelSista, Jessica Keller Koschnitzky, sister of my heart. She is part of my BritCrit gals. Joanna Politano (who has talked me down off more virtual ledges than anyone), Jen Cvelvar (the best case of misidentification *ever*, not to mention best conference roomie), Kristy Cambron (who is more beautiful inside and out than any one person should be allowed to be), and Stacey Zink (who never, ever fails to have a fabulous encouraging word) are BritCritters, too. We do a lot more living than we do critting, and I wouldn't have it any other way. All five of them are beyond gifted as writers, and I thank God they're in my life. There's my MozArks ACFW peeps who laugh with me, critique, and encourage to no end. And Melanie Dickerson. What would I do without you?

Then there's the InspyRomance crew, the CIA, my Spicy peeps (you know who you are!), and all of the others who've helped me along on this journey.

And Tamela Hancock Murray - my agent extraordinaire, who despite the lack of "anything in it for her" has supported me in this crazy indie journey. This is the book she believed in as much as I did. The timing wasn't right for it to find a traditionally published home, but she very graciously supported my desire to "go indie" with it. She believed in me and this story when it seemed no one else in the "official" publishing world would - and for that I am eternally grateful.

I've said it before, but I could go on for days about beloved mentors like Janice Thompson who has poured her time and energy into this newbie, going above and beyond for me. People like one of my spiciest friends, Pepper Basham, who inspires me daily, or Julie Lessman, who has prayed me to this point. All of these and so many more are not only mentors, but *friends* - I am beyond blessed!

I said I could go on for days, and I could keep going. On and on. I know I've forgotten many people and I hate that. But you, dear reader, would quickly get bored.

So THANK YOU to all of those who have helped me along the way. I couldn't have done this without you and you have my eternal gratitude. To the HUNDREDS of you

(I'm gobsmacked!) who pre-ordered and encouraged me without knowing it as that little number continued to climb, you have my eternal gratitude. I hope you stick around for the next one!

And, of course, last but never, *ever*, least, to Jesus Christ, without whom none of this would be possible - or worth it.

Discovering Home

Ebook Available
September 15, 2016

Movement in the woods to the left of the gate caught Jonathan Langley-Cranston's eye.

Seeing a wild animal there wasn't unusual. He lived in the country. It went with the territory.

But something about this shadow was different.

He moved the gearstick out of first into neutral and set the parking brake.

Moving slowly, he tried to avoid the mud puddles. The shadow skittered to another tree, drawing him further in. He swore under his breath as his foot, in a brand new Bruno Magli shoe, slipped into a puddle just big enough to soak it all.

A few more steps, and he found the shadow huddled against a tree. Reaching down, he tried to pick up the animal, but the pile of fur seemed to shrink back even further. Jonathan used his foot to sort of trap the little thing against the tree, blocking that means of escape and finally managed to get his hands on the trembling ball of hair.

He half expected a bark or growl, but instead there was only whimpering. Caring less about his suit than his shoes, he pulled the small dog closer.

"Hey, little fella," he crooned. "It's okay. I've got you." The black fur was so shaggy, Jonathan couldn't see his eyes. "Let's get you inside. It's too wet and cold for you to be out here." July in the Missouri Ozarks was a study in contrasts. One year hot enough to be mistaken for Phoenix. The next comparatively frigid. This was a frigid year. Though nothing like it would be in a few months, the night before had been jeans and sweatshirt cool.

His mother didn't know Jonathan William Langley-Cranston IV even owned a hoodie, and he planned to keep it that way.

He wasn't nearly as careful going back to his car. His shoes were already ruined, but the suit could be cleaned. Climbing into the low-slung 2017 Ford Mustang, he gently settled the dog onto the passenger seat, but for all his fear, the animal scampered back over onto Jonathan's lap. He snuggled close even as he practically vibrated in fear.

Pressing the button on his visor, Jonathan put the car back in gear and eased through the gate as it opened. The winding drive didn't take long, and in just a couple minutes, he pulled into the garage. Holding the shaking mass of wet fur close, Jonathan went into the house and set him on the kitchen counter.

Now what?

"Is there something you need to tell me, sir?"

Jonathan turned to see George, his butler/all-around-right-hand-man, walking into the kitchen. "He was outside the gate."

"He, sir?"

The quivering mass of fur whimpered again. "I guess it could be a she. I haven't looked yet."

"Probably covered in fleas and ticks."

He hadn't thought about that, but it made sense. "Most likely." Options flooded through his mind. "Would you watch him or her for a minute while I change? Then we'll get him a bath and take a picture or two to put online in case someone's missing him."

The look on George's face told Jonathan what he thought the chances of that were. About the same Jonathan did. Someone had dumped this poor dog in the woods near Serenity Lake. Jonathan toed off his shoes and kicked them into the mud room before stripping his socks off and holding them with one finger and his thumb. "Weigh him on the kitchen scale?" Jonathan called as he headed for the stairs. "Can't imagine he'll break it."

George muttered a response, but Jonathan couldn't hear it clearly. He could figure out the gist though. There would be no weighing on the kitchen scale. It only took a couple minutes to change into an old pair of jeans and a t-shirt that had seen better days. When he made it back downstairs, a giant fluffy towel in his hand, the two hadn't moved at all, though George held his phone in his hand.

"You would do well to wash him in Dawn dish detergent, sir. Let it soak for about fifteen minutes to kill the fleas. It may or may not help with the ticks, too."

"And you decided not to do it yourself?" Jonathan kept his chuckle to himself, more or less.

"I didn't want to deprive you of the privilege."

Jonathan scooped the dog up carefully and set him in the deep sink before pulling the dish soap out from underneath. Once the water warmed up to a reasonable level, he used the wand to rinse as much of the dirt and mud off as he could. After working the dish soap into the fur, Jonathan wrapped the whole mess in the towel and held him - definitely a him - close to his chest.

"It's all right, bud. We'll get you taken care of." Jonathan wasn't up on guesstimating weights, but if he had to bet, he'd say this dog weighed maybe four pounds, five tops, and half of that was probably fur. For fifteen minutes, he tried to comfort the little thing before putting him back in the sink and rinsing him again with warm water.

Fleas and ticks both swirled down the drain, along with more dirt, mud, and suds. Jonathan washed him twice more like that before the water seemed to run mostly clear. With the dog wrapped up in a dry towel, Jonathan went into the living room to figure out his plan.

"You are *not* sitting on my couches like that, sir." George appeared out of nowhere.

Jonathan rolled his eyes and headed for the stairs. The dog was clean enough to put on the floor in his room for a few minutes while he changed again. He texted a couple of friends to see if they could recommend a vet. In just a couple minutes, he'd heard back from one of them who used one of the top vets in the area - and who happened to be open late. Armed with directions, he took off, this time in his Toyota Tundra. It could handle the dirt better than his 'Stang.

He didn't call ahead, just prayed that they would take pity on this poor dog. And him. He didn't know what else to do.

The clinic was across the street from two of the Serenity Landing elementary schools. Only two other cars were in the lot and when he walked in, he could tell they were wrapping things up.

"Can I help you, sir?"

He held the small guy a little closer. "I found this dog in

the woods a couple hours ago. I didn't know you were open, or I would have come straight here. I know I don't have an appointment, but I'd appreciate some help."

The front desk gal came around and reached for the dog. "Come here, sweetheart," she crooned. "Did someone lose you?"

"I don't think so. I've already given him like three baths with Dawn dish soap." He pulled out his phone and showed her a picture. "I know he doesn't look a ton better, but he's cleaner at least. I didn't see him until today, but I'd guess he'd been out there a while."

"Probably," she said, using an almost baby voice. "Let's get the vet to take a look at you."

Nearly an hour later, well after closing time, Jonathan left with the still-scared dog in his arms. He also had varied medicines, the knowledge that there was no microchip, and a shopping list. After deliberating on the ninety second drive to Wal-mart, he decided to look like a dork and carry a blanket in with him. No one would notice the dog inside it. Not something he'd normally do, but desperate times and all.

Once the dog and blanket were snuggled in the seat of the cart, he beelined for the back of the store and the pet area. Dry dog food. Wet dog food. A dog bed. A crate. Collar. Leash.

"Hey! I know you!"

Jonathan turned at the sound of a little girl voice. No more than four or five, the girl practically bounced on her toes. He smiled but didn't say anything.

"You danced with me!"

"Lorelai," her mother reprimanded. "Leave the nice man alone."

"But he danced with me! And let me see at Mrs. Ginger's wedding."

Jonathan glanced up at the mother and remembered. He definitely remembered her, though he'd never known her name. "That's right." He knelt down. "You sat with me for the whole wedding, didn't you? And you let me have your first dance." He winked at her. "I remember it very well."

He also remembered the dance with her mother.

The girl's attention turned to the cart, her eyes wide. "Do you have a doggy in your cart?" she whispered. "Doggies aren't supposed to be in the store."

Jonathan looked over to see the blanket wiggling. "I know. But see, I found this dog out in the woods a little while ago, and we just left the vet. He's super scared so I didn't want to leave him alone in the truck."

"Can I pet him?"

He winced. "Not right now. He's sick, and I wouldn't want you to catch it. Besides, he doesn't think he looks very handsome at the moment. He needs a haircut but can't get one until he's all better."

"I think he's handsome." Only his nose was showing.

"Lorelai, it's time to go." Her mother pushed the cart toward the food section of the store.

"Are you gonna get him clothes?"

"Should I?" He had never thought to dress a dog. That was a froo-froo girl thing to do. But he wouldn't turn this little girl down.

She reached for an outfit hanging there. "He needs this one." Camouflaged with hunter orange trim. Perfect.

"Let's find his size, then." They looked through until they found an extra-small. "He only weighs about four pounds you know."

Lorelai's eyes went wide. "That's little. I weighed six pounds when I was born."

"That's pretty little, too." Wasn't it? What did he know?

"Six and a half," her mother interjected. "And it's time

to go."

"You better listen to your mother." He pulled his wallet out and handed over one of his business cards. "If your mom will email me, I'll send you some pictures after he gets all cleaned up, okay?"

Lorelai took it and nodded eagerly. "Does he have a name yet?"

"Nope."

She cocked her head, blond hair falling over one shoulder. "Mr. Benny Hercules."

"Mr. Benny Hercules?" Not Fido? Rex? And Hercules? Really?

"Yep."

He chuckled. "All right. Mr. Benny Hercules it is."

She turned around and handed the card to her mother. "Please email him, Mommy?"

Mom sighed and nodded. "Fine."

Here was his chance. "Can I know your name so I know whose email to expect?"

"Kenzie Ann!" Lorelai practically shouted. "Unless she's in trouble with Grumpy. He uses her whole name."

Jonathan met Kenzie's eyes, gorgeous blue eyes. "A pleasure to meet you, Kenzie Ann."

"Just Kenzie is fine." She glanced at the card. "Jon."

He winced and held out a hand. "Jonathan. My mother was very insistent about that. I should probably get over it, but I haven't yet."

When she didn't take it, he let his arm drop back to his side. "I'll email you later, Jonathan." She looked down at her daughter. "We've got to get going, Lorelai."

The two walked off, but Lorelai turned back and waved. "Bye, Mr. Jonathan! I can't wait for the pictures of Mr. Benny Hercules!"

He watched them walk off, then picked up a couple

other things he thought he might need and headed home.

Jonathan William Langley-Cranston IV has come to terms with the idea that he just might remain single and childless for the rest of his life. It's not his first choice, but it seems to be what God has for him, at least for now. Until a chance encounter with a familiar face changes his outlook.

MacKenzie Davidson has been a single mom since before her daughter was born. Just once, she'd love not to worry about losing her job or what will happen if her fledgling yarn dyeing business doesn't take off. A stormy night and flooded road bring the straws that finally break the back of her independent streak.

Her knight-in-shining-SUV comes in the form of American royalty. She's read enough of the tabloids to know that's how Jonathan's family is seen and knows she can't begin to measure up.

But when he puts everything aside to help her, her daughter, and her now-floundering business, she begins to wonder. Jonathan quickly comes to believe he's found everything he's looking for. Will they find their way to each other or will they be ripped apart before discovering home?

Previews may not be in their final form and are subject to change.

Finding

Mr.

Write

Available FREE on all retailers!

ocal Woman Arrested For Stalking Favorite Author
Dorrie Miller could see the headline now. She
held the phone between her ear and shoulder as she
shoved a pair of jeans in the drawer. "Did you really buy
night vision goggles?"

"What do you think?" Sarcasm deepened the
Appalachian accent until Dorrie could barely understand
Anise.

Of course she had.

Anise had bought the night vision goggles and the ear
wig thingies, the ones that looked like hearing aids, and
heaven only knew what else.

Within two days of being at their first major national
conference for writers, they'd be cooling their heels in a jail
cell, hoping no one would use their escapades for story
fodder. CANDID stood for Christian Author's Network,

Dedicated to Inspirational Distinction, not detention.

"We're really going to stalk this woman? I know you want to meet her. I do, too. But stalking? That's a felony." Or a serious misdemeanor. Whichever. It wouldn't be good. "We'll have restraining orders and never be able to show our face at CANDID again." Dorrie checked her appearance in the mirror once more. Passable. "And how do you know MEL is going to be at conference, anyway?"

As administrator of the Mya Elizabeth Linscott Facebook page, Dorrie should know when the author had appearances scheduled. Dorrie had read all of MEL's books so many times she could quote large sections of them. Her collection would be complete with autographs, but the only way to get signed copies was to get them off MEL's website for twice the cover price. Sure, the extra money went to charity but Dorrie still didn't have that kind of cash. Instead, she had a standing order with the local Christian bookstore to get the latest book as soon as it released.

She'd even emailed with MEL a few times. Okay. MEL's assistant, but still.

How did she not know MEL would be making her first public appearance ever?

Anise hemmed and hawed for a second or two. "Well, I don't know for sure MEL's coming. But the bookstore coordinator sent me a list of authors who are going to have books and she's on it."

"One of her books is up for a CANDID Award," Dorrie pointed out. "Those are automatically stocked. She's up for an award every year. Those books are always there." Not that Dorrie had been at the other conferences, but she knew people and heard all about it.

"I know that. But she has 'five books' in parentheses next to her name. She'd only have one if it was just the book up for a CANDID Award."

Anise had a point. "Okay. She might be there."

"Let's plan how we're going to make sure we get to meet her. And bring your copies because they have a place where you can put them to be signed."

"You really think she'll sign them for free? Everyone else does, but she never has. She gives away ten free signed copies of each book when it comes out, but that's it." Dorrie had never won, no matter how hard she tried.

"You never know."

A glance at the clock showed Dorrie she had ten minutes before it was time to leave for her fourth ever local CANDID meeting. The one she was in charge of. What had she been thinking when she volunteered to be the coordinator? Dorrie half-listened to Anise prattle on as doubts assailed her once again.

Visions of George Costanza danced in her head to a Brad Paisley soundtrack as a dull ache began to seep into the edges of her brain. So much cooler in the online world. She should stay home where no one would discover she didn't belong with the cool kids.

Online, Dorrie knew she was a blast. Always fun. Always up for something. Or pretend something anyway. There weren't any real consequences to plotting with other readers to cyber-steal a flash drive with a manuscript on it from a favorite author when nothing actually changed hands. Or to resort to bribery with her peanut butter cookies. Dorrie had been known to send a box or two. Not that it had gotten her anywhere.

Another look toward the bookcase where her first edition Mya Elizabeth Linscott novels sat, unsigned, spurred her onward. She had to go. She had to follow her dream of becoming an author. No matter what anyone, especially her dad, said about it. In two and a half months, Dorrie could finally have a chance to meet her writing hero.

If she was really lucky, have two, maybe even three, minutes to pick MEL's brain about the publishing world.

"Dorrie!" Anise's voice jolted her back to the present. "Can you get the walkie talkies?"

With a sigh, Dorrie turned to the conversation at hand. "Yes, I have walkies. I fail to see why we need them if we're using earwigs."

"Back-up. You know that. Back-up your back-ups. It holds true for manuscripts and trying to meet your favorite authors."

Anise was even more obsessed with back-ups than Dorrie had ever been. The advent of "the cloud" and "cloud storage" helped, but one could never be sure it was enough. The loss of a Publisher file with hours worth of tweaks to a floor plan for her character's house proved that.

Dorrie heard something in the background. A dog barking. Dishes crashing. Followed by, "I gotta run, darlin', and I know you've got your meeting. I'll talk to you soon. Knock 'em dead."

"Ha! Love you, Licorice."

"I'm not licorice. I'm Anise."

"Pa-tay-to, pa-tah-to. Same thing." The spice, anise, had a licorice flavor to it. Dorrie rarely let an opportunity to mention it pass her by. Of course, the spice was pronounced an-iss, but her friend hailed from Appalachia and said her name uh-nese.

"Love you, too. I think. See you in a few weeks!"

They hung up. Dorrie headed from her hometown of Serenity Landing, Missouri to Springfield and her first CANDID meeting with a for-real published author as the guest.

She just prayed she wouldn't make a fool of herself.

Dorrie sat at a table in Panera Bread wiping her hands on her dress slacks. The nice ones. The ones that made her feel a little more professional than jeans or her usual scrubs. It was only the fourth meeting but who was she to think she should be the one running a group like this? At twenty-three, Dorrie felt woefully unprepared to run the local meeting of the country's premiere group for Christian writers. Unpublished. Unagented. Uneverything. And inadequate.

And with a line-up of such prestigious guest speakers coming? Why her? Right. No one else volunteered to do it.

And just one guest speaker for now, .but Dorrie had to introduce her to everyone.

So what if "everyone" meant seven people?

Kathleen Watson really was very nice. Dorrie knew because they'd been talking on Facebook for months.

Dorrie took a deep breath and jumped in. "Okay, everyone!" Her voice echoed in the almost empty room as her nerves took a beating. "I think everybody's got their food, so it's time for the Springfield Area Christian Authors' Network, Dedicated to Inspiration Distinction group to welcome best-selling, award winning author, Kathleen Watson." What a mouthful! It made her even more grateful everyone just called the organization CANDID.

The half dozen or so writers gave a polite smattering of applause as Kathleen moved to sit on the table at the front of the meeting room. "Thanks so much for having me today. I was thinking I'd tell you a bit about me, my journey to publication, and life since then. Afterwards, we'll open it up for questions."

The door opened and in walked Prince Caspian – fresh off his voyage through the Seven Seas on the Dawn

Treader. Dorrie's logical side knew it couldn't be the Narnian king, but had to be his doppelganger. Her romantic side didn't care. He was, after all, about six feet tall with longish chestnut colored hair that looked silky enough for every girl in the room to be jealous, and eyes the color of Hershey's chocolate.

"Is this the CANDID meeting?" His voice, smooth as velvet, melted Dorrie's insides.

"Um, yes," she managed to stammer. "Have a seat. We're just getting started."

He smiled, though Dorrie had the impression his full grin was much more drool-worthy.

Before she realized what he was doing, he slid into the chair next to her. If he got any closer Dorrie would be wearing his cologne. Very nice smelling cologne, too. Not at all like she expected from someone who spent most of his time on a boat with a giant talking mouse.

How was she supposed to concentrate? Ask insightful questions? Keep everyone on task during the Q and A if she spent the next two hours wondering if he'd take her back to Narnia with him?

Somehow, Dorrie managed to focus on Kathleen. She talked about what the industry had been like twenty years earlier when she first broke into publishing and how it differed now.

After about thirty minutes, Kathleen looked at Dorrie. "You know what? Why don't we skip straight to questions? You guys ask me what you want to know about life as an author. I don't know all of you so why don't we do introductions, then questions?" The look she gave left it up to Dorrie.

Dorrie moved to the front of the room to direct the conversation and told them a bit about herself when one of the other gals interrupted.

"Did I see your name on the New Beginnings list?"

Heat rose in Dorrie's cheeks. "I had two manuscripts final in different categories."

"New Beginnings is the CANDID contest for unpublished authors, right?" The question came from the other new member. Dorrie didn't think she'd heard the lady's name yet.

With a nod, Dorrie confirmed the statement but turned to the next person. All but two of the other seven people she'd met several times and halfway tuned them out. The newbie who'd asked about the contest introduced herself as Julie Harders. And then they got to Prince Caspian.

"I'm Jeremiah Jacobs. I've been writing for years, but decided to switch genres to political thrillers."

"What did you write before?" Kathleen asked.

He shrugged and looked uncomfortable. "A bit of everything trying to find the elusive voice. I think I've found it writing political thrillers."

"Good." Kathleen turned to Dorrie. "Do you want to handle the Q and A?"

Dorrie gave a half-shrug. "Up to you."

They spent the next hour asking Kathleen questions about how she came up with new ideas year after year, about what life was like on deadline, how to avoid the deadline crunch, and on and on. Two hours after the meeting began, they wrapped up, chatting a bit in little groups until an employee stuck her head in and said another group was coming in a few minutes.

Grabbing her laptop bag, Dorrie thanked Julie for coming and asked her to come again. She needed to do the same with Jeremiah. If only she'd out-grown the high school "stammer-when-I-talk-to-cute-boys" phase.

"Jeremiah?" Here went nothing.

He looked up from where he was gathering his trash.

Don't look him in the eyes. You'll drown in pools of chocolate that would make Willy Wonka jealous. The glimpse or two she'd gotten had been more than enough to realize drowning would be a marvelous way to go.

His voice jolted her back to Panera. And there were those eyes. Could he be smiling at her? "Thank you for letting me join you today."

"Of course. Are you new to CANDID?" She'd been told someone would send her an email telling her when a new member from the area joined, but she hadn't gotten one yet.

He shook his head. "No. I'm here for a few months trying to decide if this is where I want to move." At her puzzled look, he went on. "I work from home so it doesn't matter where I am and I'm tired of Chicago. I thought I'd try out a few other places before making a decision."

"That's smart. How do you like the Ozarks so far?"

"I've only been here ten days, but one of the things I looked at when deciding where to go was a CANDID group. It's not a requirement for wherever I settle, but it would be nice."

"Well, we're glad to have you for as long as you're here." Dorrie told him when the next meeting would be and got his email address so she could put him on the mailing list.

Dorrie went to take a sip of her soda, but the condensation on the plastic made it more slippery than she realized.

Like one of those slow motion scenes from the Matrix movies, every drop became individually visible from every other as the dark liquid first flew upward then plummeted down to Jeremiah's laptop bag. Dorrie could see his eyes widen as they both followed the trajectory of the cup downward. He grabbed for his bag, but it was too late. The sloshing brought everything back to real speed. At least it seemed to be in the non-laptop portion of the bag.

"I'm so sorry." Dorrie reached for the napkins sitting on the table next to her, frantically blotting at the papers inside.

Jeremiah pulled them out, spreading them on the table as he muttered something that sounded a lot like, "No, no, no, no, no."

Dorrie continued to blot at the papers. When she moved one of the file folders, papers and photos fell out – a sticky, wet mess.

Dropping to the floor to pick them up, tears filled her eyes. Just what she needed to make a good first impression on this guy. Not that she really thought he'd be interested in her of all people, but this ensured he would not. Especially if she ruined his photos.

She flipped one over and gaped.

He reached for it, but Dorrie sat back on her heels and stared. "Why do you have this?" The words escaped before she could stop them.

"Give it to me."

"This is the cover for the new Mya Elizabeth Linscott Cambridge Family Saga book. Not the one coming out in a couple months but the one that comes out in January. The title hasn't even been announced yet." Of course, after seeing the picture Dorrie knew, but the official announcement wouldn't come until the day before MEL's August book released. MEL would send out a newsletter with information on upcoming promotions, like when her eBooks would be discounted, and at the end, she'd announce the title and preview the cover of her next book.

Dorrie looked up at him. His face was an unreadable mask.

She had to know. "How'd you get this?"

Ebook FREE on all retailers

Jeremiah Jacobs moved to the Ozarks for a fresh start. He knows no one and has no plans to get romantically involved with anyone. Ever. He's already had his heart ripped out once and once is enough. Besides he has contractual obligations that prevent him from talking about work - and what woman would want to be involved with a man who has to keep his job a secret? When he attends his first local writers' group meeting, he finds the leader so intriguing, his instant attraction to her threatens to complicate his currently uncomplicated life.

Dorrie Miller has never been good enough. Not for her father or any of the guys she's dated in the past. She's pushed beyond her father's disapproval to have a good career while pursuing her dream of becoming a published novelist. The Christian Authors Network – Dedicated to Inspirational Distinction, or CANDID, is hosting their annual conference in Indianapolis and who's rumored to be in attendance? The super reclusive, super-star author, Mya Elizabeth Linscott.

The hunky new member of her local CANDID group, Jeremiah, wants to carpool to Indy. Dorrie can handle not making a fool of herself for eight hours each way. Right? But she never imagined doing a favor for someone during the conference would leave her accidentally married to the gorgeous guy she barely knows. How will she get out of this mess, married to a near stranger? Does she want to? Will her insecurities and Jeremiah's secrets tear them apart? Or can she trust that, all along, God's been helping her with Finding Mr. Write?

Finding Mr. Writeis a mega-romantic story with amazing chemistry between the two characters, and Jeremiah is one of the most memorable and loveable heroes I've read in a long time. Carol Moncado's writing reeled me in and hooked me, and I was eager to see how Dorrie and Jeremiah would overcome their secrets and unusual circumstances to find true love. I loved this story! ~ **Melanie Dickerson, award winning author ofThe Healer's Apprentice**

Previews may not be in their final form and are subject to change.

When she's not writing about her imaginary friends, USA Today Bestselling Author Carol Moncado prefers binge watching pretty much anything to working out. She believes peanut butter M&Ms are the perfect food and Dr. Pepper should come in an IV. When not hanging out with her hubby, four kids, and two dogs who weigh less than most hard cover books, she's probably reading in her Southwest Missouri home.

Summers find her at the local aquatic center with her four fish, er, kids. Fall finds her doing the band mom thing. Winters find her snuggled into a blanket in front of a fire with the dogs. Spring finds her sneezing and recovering from the rest of the year.

She used to teach American Government at a community college, but her indie career, with nearly two dozen titles released in the first 2.5 years, has allowed her to write full time. She's a founding member and former President of MozArks ACFW, blogger at InspyRomance, and is represented by Tamela Hancock Murray of the Steve Laube Agency.

CANDID Romance

Finding Mr. Write
Finally Mr. Write
Falling for Mr. Write

Montevaro Monarchy

Good Enough for a Princess
Along Came a Prince
More than a Princess

Brides of Belles Montagnes

Hand-Me-Down Princess
Winning the Queen's Heart
Protecting the Prince (Novella)
Prince from her Past

Serenity Landing Lifeguards

The Lifeguard, the New Guy, & Frozen Custard
(previously titled: The Lifeguards, the Swim Team, & Frozen Custard)
The Lifeguard, the Abandoned Heiress, & Frozen Custard
(previously in the *Whispers of Love* collection)

Other Novellas

Gifts of Love
(also available as part of the *Snowflakes & Mistletoe* collection)
Manuscripts & Mistletoe
Ballots, Bargains, & the Bakery (also in the *Table for Two* collection)

Made in United States
Orlando, FL
15 June 2022

18827917R10225